THE
ARCHITECTS
ARE
HERE

Also by Michael Winter

Creaking in Their Skins

One Last Good Look

This All Happened

The Big Why

THE
ARCHITECTS
ARE
HERE

MICHAEL WINTER

VIKING
CANADA

VIKING CANADA

Published by the Penguin Group

Penguin Group (Canada), 90 Eglinton Avenue East, Suite 700, Toronto, Ontario, Canada M4P 2Y3
(a division of Pearson Canada Inc.)

Penguin Group (USA) Inc., 375 Hudson Street, New York, New York 10014, U.S.A.
Penguin Books Ltd, 80 Strand, London WC2R 0RL, England
Penguin Ireland, 25 St Stephen's Green, Dublin 2, Ireland (a division of Penguin Books Ltd)
Penguin Group (Australia), 250 Camberwell Road, Camberwell, Victoria 3124, Australia
(a division of Pearson Australia Group Pty Ltd)
Penguin Books India Pvt Ltd, 11 Community Centre, Panchsheel Park, New Delhi – 110 017, India
Penguin Group (NZ), 67 Apollo Drive, Rosedale, North Shore 0632, Auckland, New Zealand
(a division of Pearson New Zealand Ltd)
Penguin Books (South Africa) (Pty) Ltd, 24 Sturdee Avenue, Rosebank, Johannesburg 2196, South Africa

Penguin Books Ltd, Registered Offices: 80 Strand, London WC2R 0RL, England

First published 2007

1 2 3 4 5 6 7 8 9 10 (RRD)

Manufactured in the U.S.A.

LIBRARY AND ARCHIVES CANADA CATALOGUING IN PUBLICATION

Winter, Michael, 1965–
The architects are here / Michael Winter.

ISBN 978-0-670-06627-8

I. Title.

PS8595.I624A73 2007   C813'.54   C2007-902646-X

ISBN-13: 978-0-670-06627-8
ISBN-10: 0-670-06627-3

Visit the Penguin Group (Canada) website at **www.penguin.ca**

Special and corporate bulk purchase rates available; please see
www.penguin.ca/corporatesales or call 1-800-810-3104, ext. 477 or 474

for CLP

ONE

ONE

THIS IS A STORY about my friend David Twombly and about the nature of our friendship. David is gone now, and there's a temptation to eulogize him in some time-honoured way that would implicitly deny the intensity and texture of what we shared. I intend to avoid that. I want the immediacy of the quotidian, its take-no-prisoners feel and sharp whiff. And I want to tell as much of the truth as is important. To do that, I must tell you something about a third person, a woman named Nell Tarkington, who years ago entered our lives, Dave's and mine, and stayed there, changing each of us in complex and idiosyncratic ways. So the beginning of this tale is also hers.

I met David Twombly one winter when we were building igloos out of snow ploughed from driveways behind the drug store. I knew him because we both played peewee hockey and carried our duffel bags full of gear down to the rink before school. He was good, and I was picked last for things. But the igloo-building made him like me. His parents were American and mine were English and so we recognized in each other the outsider in this Newfoundland milltown. We had carved out the USS *Enterprise* with connecting tunnels, the whole starship, with lit candles in alcoves. It possessed the muted intimacy of the womb. And one night, while we sat at the control deck, the igloo began to vibrate. Then one entire side of the igloo was sheered off and the loud orange blade of a snowplough ran past us. And there, out in the shining dark, was the city we lived in.

My father taught industrial arts, and I feared that I'd be tortured about it. But boys respected him—he was, in their eyes, a cool guy. Strict but cool. He let them build useful things, slingshots and gun racks and box kites, even a totem pole. The main plus for my father was that industrial arts was a two-hour class and he allowed the boys to smoke out by the double doors between periods. That showed real understanding.

Dave and I spent our teen years hanging out in each other's basement. I preferred his basement because the cement floor was painted with a grey marine enamel that you could slide across in your sock feet. His brother, Zac, had a race car set and a cardboard rocket that blasted six hundred feet in the air and landed with a parachute. His father was the first person to offer me a cup of coffee made in a bodum. We shot hoops above the Twombly garage door and we drove our banana bikes down to the river and constructed dams on tributaries and in winter we made our mittens into puppets and the mittens, puddies we called them, smoked cigarette butts that were still lit. They were cigarettes we picked up after people had tossed them. We were privately childish and publicly strong. We both boxed and were in the same weight division, although I was tall and jabbed while Dave worked inside and hooked to the kidneys. Once, while sparring, Dave sent a hook to the temple. I was down. I felt the buzzle and lightness of my body. I woke up on the canvas and a dullness in my skin. I had been out. I was out for about ten seconds. It made me realize this is what death is like. There is no life after death. There is no duration in the dark of waiting.

As teenagers we grew our hair long and feathered it and we bench-pressed with Zac's friends with a barbell and weights made of cement in gold plastic casings. We played handheld electronic sports games and stole valve caps from the wheels of fancy cars that we screwed onto the chrome rims of our ten-speeds. We grew soft moustaches.

We were the last of the Grade Elevens—they were phasing in Grade Twelve to keep us up with Canada—and so we graduated high school at the early age of seventeen. Because we were so young we decided to stay in Corner Brook for our first year of university. There was an offshoot campus where you could do two years of a degree, and they would not accept you at any mainland university with only a Grade Eleven. So we signed up for English and physics and geography and I chose an elective offered by Dave's father. Professor Twombly taught communications. And this is where I met Nell Tarkington. She was in the class. I noticed her because she was new—Nell was one of the only students on campus who was not from the province, and so a curiosity attached itself to her. She was tall and wore shiny dark hair and when she answered a question she leaned forward in her seat and curled her shoulders a little. I realized there were other shapes and physiques to both men and women. Because I was English I did not look much like a typical Newfoundlander. Anthropologists and linguists parachuted into our island with six-week projects that analyzed an isolated gene pool and accents that have withstood the North American persuasion for twelve generations. This was something we learned in Professor Twombly's class. He brought in music and documentaries, and one film was about the premier visiting Cuba with Geoff Stirling, a Newfoundland millionaire who was involved in radio and television. I remember Mr Stirling standing on his head on the Cuban beach. Joey Smallwood composed questions aloud for Castro. Between Stirling and Smallwood, on the screen pulled down over the green chalkboard, was the silhouette of Nell's shoulders and head.

Nell was someone who, if I had to be slightly perverse, looked and acted a bit like me. But I was shy back then and sat at the rear, whereas she favoured a desk up front. She was, I guess, a keener.

I paid my tuition that year with summer jobs. The only thing I knew to put on an application was manual labour. I used a drawbar and ripped thousands of linear feet of clapboard from old houses. David worked with his brother on tech assignments that involved video equipment and digital software—Dave was the first person I knew who owned a CD player. That fall I lived at home and worked four-hour shifts at McDonald's up on the highway. I was there when they changed the sign over from 999 MILLION SERVED to 1 BILLION SERVED. I worked with Joe Hurley and I'd meet him down in the valley and we'd ride up together on our bikes until the snow hit in November. We grilled burgers and toasted buns and drained the grease troughs into plastic cartons full of ice, and walked around the lot emptying the castle bin liners. I liked working close with Joe because we got to take down the flag, and the maple leaf fluttered over the highest point of land over Corner Brook. We felt like explorers.

That first year was pretty much like high school, though some of the harder cases were not around any longer, and both Zac and my own brother were about to leave home for work elsewhere on the planet. Zac was twenty and had been studying in Michigan, where his parents were from, and he was being headhunted by firms in Seattle and also Palo Alto, a place I had never heard of before but was the cradle of the new age about to befall us, Zac said. That of the microprocessor. Zac had started a small company that David now helped run and, before Zac left for the West Coast, he wanted, of all things, to go moose hunting with his brother. How many chances will I get to do this, he said to Dave. And we both imagined him, in hot California, driving his blue Matador into town with a set of moose antlers cinched to the roof rack.

The Twomblys have a cabin on Grand Lake and they hunted from there. Zac had applied for the hunter's safety course and bought a rifle with his father at an RCMP auction at the Rod and Gun Club. I operated the trap shoot there on Wednesday nights through the summer, and Zac would drive up in his blue Matador and step in line as the clay pigeons exploded into the spruce brush. Zac seemed the type to smoke, but he did not smoke. Once, when I was twelve, he had told me, privately, how to masturbate in the shower. They had shot the moose up near Glover Island. They were using a seven-horsepower open boat and they'd gutted the moose and packed it in quarters into the boat. They were sitting low in the water, motoring back down the lake to their family cabin at Boot Brook. The wind was a northeasterly and the chain of lakes is a diagonal scar that follows a geological fault that cuts off the Great Northern Peninsula, sinks into White Bay, then travels five thousand miles under the Atlantic and ends up dividing the Scottish Hebrides. They came up into the wind and pulled into the lee of Glover Island to wait it out. They knew the wind dies down at suppertime. It began to slash rain, the flanks of moose wet. They were proud of the moose and did not want it to spoil. There was a pond on Glover Island and on that pond an island. It's the only island on a pond in an island on a lake in an island in the whole world. They shouted through the storm about how one day they'd camp on that island in the very centre of what they called the planet. They were excited by the plans and they pretended everything was okay.

Dave was sitting in the bow, keeping it down in the waves, and they crouched there in the growing storm. The shore was sheer cliffs and the light was leaving the sky. If they got far enough out on the lake they'd see the Hurley lights on at the cabin next door, the one out by the point, for they had seen Loyola Hurley and they could guide themselves back by his lights. They made a tack for the sheltered side of the lake and when a swell rose Zac nosed into it and they were getting near the far shore, the points of land were breaking away to form coves. They were called the jaws of the land. They had to turn into the wind and then bring the bow back around, and as Zac wheeled her the chop grew serious and the boat tilted high and slammed down and shook Dave, then the bow rose again and he grabbed ahold of both gunwales. Dave twisted around and saw that his brother was frightened. Zac was looking at something in front of them. A second wash of wave from the starboard side caught the bottom of the boat and turned it into a sail and it swivelled the boat forty degrees and a rogue wave swamped them. There was a sizzle of foam and the shock of cold water on his face and Dave was in the water and could not breathe. Then he went deaf and weightless. He found the noise again and the propeller blade of the overturned outboard motor dripping in the air. Then a wave pushed him against the propeller. He looked around for his brother. He dove for him and felt around for him and tasted gasoline and then under the boat which had an air pocket. He found a hairy body inside the boat but it was not his brother, it was a quarter of moose with the hoof hooked under the middle seat. Then something swollen and nylon and it was the hunting kit. He let that go. The yellow anchor rope, taut and heavy. He followed it up and found his brother, hanging on to the side of the boat. His mouth in and out of the water. They were going to be all right.

The anchor rope, Zac said, it's looped around me.

The weight of the anchor was pulling him off the gunwale. The side of the boat dipped and Zac went under and came up again. The yellow rope wrapped tight around his shoulder and chest. You needed a knife to cut it. Zac's grip slipped and he went under and Dave grabbed his shoulder and pulled him back up.

Can you unwind yourself.

Dave had a go at unravelling his brother's arm, the arm felt dead.

Zac was calm. The gutting knife, it's in the hunting kit.

I saw the kit, Dave said.

He dove under for the hunting kit. It had been in the bow above the moose. He'd had it in his hands and then had pushed it away. The vulgar carpet of moose, like a piece of bog. He felt around the ribs of the hull. He searched for the texture of nylon which he'd felt before. He knew he'd find it because the gutting knife would solve it and he had to solve it. So it panicked him that the hunting kit wasnt where it was any more. And then he remembered when he had ahold of it he sort of let it go again and maybe it had drifted off or sunk.

It's only an eight-pound anchor, Dave said.

Zac: I can't seem to move.

Dave searched around the boat. He tried for the bottom but there was no bottom. He was looking for anything sharp now. Something that wasnt technically a knife but could cut. The little can opener where was that. Then he remembered he had a pocket knife. He put his hand down under his jacket and tried to wriggle his fingers into his jeans pocket, but the jeans were wet and his hands were numb and he could not get into the pocket.

Zac, he said. I've got a pocket knife but I'm all numb.

He sidled over to his brother and Zac said which pocket and Dave put his brother's hand on his right jeans pocket. Zac shoved his hand in and he had the knife and he pulled it out but he did this too quickly. They both saw the knife. Then the knife slipped out of Zac's hand. It glinted and fell through the water and Dave grabbed for it then swam down to find it but he could not see it, he pulled himself down through the dark water and batted for it in the water until his lungs were screaming and when he came up again he realized they were drifting. They were drifting into the open water of the lake. He remembered the contour lines on the topo map and the bottom must be two hundred feet deep.

I'm going to bring up the anchor, he said to Zac.

The anchor rope was threaded through itself in a bowline. Dave tried to carry up the anchor. He had to hold his breath and cradle it. It was an eight-pound navy anchor which doesnt sound like much but there was no way to get ahold of it, his hands were so numb. He carried it in his arms like a baby and kicked and counted seconds. He was giving his brother a rest. He could see his brother's legs above him and he knew that Zac was going to be okay. Then he had to let go of the anchor. It was like giving up a child. He looked for his brother but his brother's face was under water again. He tried to hoist him up but Zac was frantic and he thrashed. So he dove again and followed the rope past his brother and lifted the anchor and held it once again in a cradle at his waist and prayed to God it would be all right. He hated having to let go of the anchor. He followed the top of his head to the surface. The black rain and wind. Dave was chilled to the bone and his hands were dead. He was going to die of hypothermia. He could not hold the gunwale now and had to hook his elbow through the very yellow anchor rope that was tying down Zac. They had lost the hunting kit and the pocket knife and even the lighters and the small can opener. He dove back down but there was nothing in his brother now. He pounded his brother's chest. He opened Zac's mouth and put his own mouth to him and blew in air on his cold lips, but the air bubbled back onto his face. He thought one last try to bring up the anchor but he could not even get down to the anchor now.

LOYOLA HURLEY found them on the shore with the overturned boat. Loyola was my father's age. As kids we called him Cake Hurley because he worked in bathroom maintenance and the little deodorant cakes that were put in urinals had his name, Hurley, stamped on them and we delighted in pissing on the Hurley name. We did not, of course, call him Cake to his face. Loyola Hurley had the cabin next to the Twomblys and he'd seen the boys go up the lake and knew, when the storm hit, that they would not get back. He had to wait for first light to get his own boat out and drive up the lake after them. He knew where they must have gone for shelter, a place where you can beach a small boat on a shore full of steep hills. He saw the white side of the boat drawn up and there was David Twombly hysterically waving—he must be shouting though Loyola could not hear him over the sound of the outboard, or the way the wind was. Just his mouth and hands wide open.

DAVE WAS ONLY SEVENTEEN, and to witness the death of your brother, to feel the guilt of your own part in it, will affect your character for life. People who met Dave Twombly could not guess he suffered such a mishap. But in times of stress, or in moments when he was pushed forward to be talented in the world, the death hampered him, and he became diminished and stepped away from what could have been a big life. I saw it when he arrived back to school—he drove up to campus in Zac's car. I saw how he sheltered himself, as though people might turn into a storm at any moment.

Not that he lived a small life. He was living large, but those close to him, or those who had known him in his youth, as I did, could see the potential in him. We went to campus until Christmas and then Dave said how about St John's. He couldnt take the grief in his house. The looks from his mother.

Randy Jacobs poured a rink out of a green garden hose and we skated, all of us, for one last Christmas together, while a band of poplar trees watched. Dave held his nose with the thumb and finger of a hockey glove and hawked. We were all friends back then, Gerard and Joe Hurley, Randy Jacobs, and the young black kid, Lennox Pony. We hung around the S-turn with the older boys, men almost now, who worked the maintenance shift at McDonald's, who were planning to drive the school bus or replace their fathers at the pulp mill. Others were slipping into dope dealing, like Gerard Hurley. I had gone to school with Gerard. In Grade One we got gold stars. We were the top boys. One day we were spelling words. Gerard had to spell *England*. He thought it began with an "I" because there were so many words that ended in -ing, and a country like Ingland would be responsible. English is my last name so I was a little dumbfounded at his error. A gold star for me while Gerard Hurley got a red stamp. It was his first red stamp and I saw his face collapse. Gerard Hurley realized he was working at his limits. He could not understand the new work, he was about to fall away. He had been applying himself full-on while I was coasting. Gerard's predicament I wouldnt understand until university physics: this realization that people around you know how to do something with ease, while youve squeezed your eyes shut forcing a connection, and knowing deep in your chest it is beyond you.

The S-turn was a strip of road on the west side near the Lemon Yard, a salvage operation run by Lennox Pony's father. The S-turn was where, at night, you could smoke under a single street light and drink a beer while sitting on the galvanized guardrail. If it wasnt for Dave I wouldnt have been allowed to play hockey or baseball with them. Even Lennox, who was three years younger, got to go in net, or catch. But Dave said, If Gabe doesnt play then I won't play. I guess I'll always be grateful to him for that, and I'll back him no matter how bad it gets.

Dave wanted to leave because his mother, he said, had closed in on herself and his father had become artificially chatty. He couldnt walk around the house with Zac gone. His sister was still in high school and he felt bad abandoning her, but he was the one who was guilty for Zac's death. He was dealing with the recriminations. But Dave did not want to go alone. Could we both move to St John's and do our studies there. So we enrolled, but we were too late to get into residency during the middle of the year. Let's share an apartment, Dave said. On New Year's Day we drove across the island in Zac's Matador and found a two-bedroom apartment near the university and we studied. We had hours of study each night. And David bought a piranha. He fed it goldfish. He bought the goldfish in a clear plastic bag. He opened the bag and tipped the goldfish into the aquarium. The piranha, like a rock on its side, lunged and the orange fish was gone. It was startling and yet unsatisfying to watch. So Dave took to just tossing the entire knotted bag in. The piranha was puzzled by this, but learned to punch through the bag. It often took him three or four attacks to tear open the plastic. I think the goldfish often died of a heart attack. It missed the severe final twenty seconds of its own body.

Back then Dave had a saying: The architects are here. It was a phrase that summed up his experience with his brother, that bad times were lurking, and even though Dave is one of the luckiest men I've known, he is possessed with a fatalism that one day he will be walking around home- less and broke, or unloved. The expression comes from a book by Suetonius, perhaps the only book Dave read thoroughly. There is a plot against Caesar. And when the assassins are in place, a guard issues the word: The architects are here. Dave would say it to the goldfish, as he cradled it in its baggie of water and slowly lowered it into the aquarium.

WE DROVE HOME in June, and it was our last summer together in Corner Brook. Dave was involved in a technology fair at the Glynmill Inn and asked if I'd man the booth with him. I let Dave talk about his soft- ware products and the computer languages he and Zac had worked on. Then a man came in we both recognized. It was Geoff Stirling, the millionaire who had gone to Cuba with Joey Smallwood. He was about sixty now but still wore a bomber jacket and tinted glasses. He looked over Dave's software. That's what this province needs more of, he said, is this entrepreneurial spirit. Who are you son? You need a job this summer?

This meeting greatly impressed us both. Geoff Stirling had given Dave the number to the news room in St John's. You boys can work in news, he said. So Dave called. But the man he spoke to made Dave realize that there was no work in a news station for an eighteen-year-old. I'm headed for the mainland anyway, Dave said to me, but by the fall he'd heard back from the schools he'd tried to get into and his grade point average did not meet the standards. So we ended up living together for another full year in St John's. He studied harder. We listened to late-night radio and Dave fell in love with the host of a show from Montreal and he wrote her letters. I helped with the letters. He cracked up at the little stories I made. We shoved the letters into homemade envelopes and invented names and sent them to Allegra Campinghorst, care of the CBC, in Montreal. In this small endeavour Dave could see the artist in me.

I remember his father coming to visit. He arrived at the apartment on Elizabeth Avenue. He was in town for a conference, he said. Mr Twombly remembered me from the class I'd taken, but he did not know my family that well. When Zac died, I had gone to the funeral. I'd asked my own father what should I say. We were laying a bed of pink insulation in the attic. My father thought for a moment, crouched with the blade of a carpet-cutter in his hand, poised. He was thinking about what he'd want someone to say to him, and in that space I realized he was imagining me in a box. I'm sorry for your loss, he said. If there's anything I can do.

But when I approached Mr Twombly at the funeral I could not say those words. They were too adult and Dave and Sasha and their mother were in line. I felt the corners of my mouth move up and I thought, My mouth shouldnt be doing this. And Mr Twombly shook my hand warmly. He knew it had taken guts just to offer my hand.

He knocked on the door and I answered it. He had a pair of green tickets in his hand, for a senior hockey game at Memorial Stadium. Mr Twombly came in and did not take off his shoes. He opened the fridge and helped himself to a glass of orange juice and glanced around at his son's living conditions. He looked like he hadnt formed an opinion before on how his son would live independently, and so wasnt disappointed. He was observing. He asked if I'd like to come, it would be easy enough to scalp a single, and while I knew it was a family occasion, I didnt know how to refuse. So I went with them and we found a ticket and, in the stands, Mr Twombly asked a man if he would shift over so we could all sit together. The way he said it was polished, you couldnt deny him. And yet there was a contrast to this public know-how and the inability he had to talk to his son. Mr Twombly had played hockey at the University of Michigan, and he fitted both his sons out to play as well.

Landscape makes character, he said. Newfoundland would be like Michigan if it warmed up ten degrees.

After the game Arthur drove us downtown. To the restaurant in the Battery Hotel. We had a view of the city from there, the harbour flaring from lights at the shipyard. Dave and I had not known the downtown existed. Neither of us had drifted below Military Road. So youre doing well. Dave's hands tightened. His father often opened up with a question about quality, or hoping things were fine, or telling you that life was good. Dave wished his father would just tell him a story, rather than rating the experience of his life as it was happening. They had never had a direct relationship, their experiences had run through Zac or Sasha or their mother. I'm fine, Dad, he said. And I wished with all my heart I hadnt gone with them, it was an awful dinner.

TWO

THERE WAS THE SWIRL of rumour about an affair, that Dave's father had come to St John's during our second year not for a conference but so a girl could have an abortion. And this is where Nell Tarkington comes in. Nell had moved to Corner Brook when she was eighteen. She was so young back then she took snapshots out her airplane window as they ascended from Pearson. Three hours then the wing banking over Deer Lake, how wet the province looked. She lived in residence in Corner Brook. Nell shared a cinder-block apartment with Lori Durdle and a woman from India. She had this communications professor, Arthur Twombly. She felt threads of her body pulling away from her when he lectured. He was American, about forty. He gave a tough assignment due just before the drop date, and that whittled the class down to seventeen. I was one of the seventeen. I knew how she felt, that we had managed a hurdle and something interesting might happen. By November Nell had learned how to write a paper that made Arthur Twombly want to see her in his office. His office did not have a window, but he tacked up a print of an impressionist painting of a window in France. What about your parents? he said. She did not want to tell him they were dead. She said they were neither proud nor disappointed. You get a BSc, great. You get a masters, fine. Does that mean we have to show up at your grad? Excellent.

We were a quiet bunch, I remember that, and Arthur Twombly enjoyed discussion. So Nell and I kept the talk going, though it was through the bridging of Professor Twombly's associative leaps. He was a man who walked around with his hands in his pockets, his shoulders back, ready to enjoy himself. And during his period we learned how forces interpret an event rather than learn about the event itself. He engaged us in a world larger than the one of Corner Brook. And for Nell he confirmed her innate hunch that the modern world was the most interesting one to be living in.

But then Arthur Twombly was not present for the fifth class. Nell hadnt heard, as I had heard from David, what had happened with Zac.

Nell's mother was a Newfoundlander but had left when she was very young. Nell's parents had died the year before in a plane crash in northern British Columbia. That was why she had come to Corner Brook, to get away from her past life. She had taken a course from Arthur Twombly because she'd seen him in the gym on registration day and liked his demeanour. A son, Lori Durdle told her, had died in a hunting accident. Nell thought about the son and it made her feel a kinship. Zac Twombly. She herself was newly orphaned. And she wondered if children have much to say in how they get adopted. She had spent the summer in Burlington with her uncle. They'd gone for a trip to Connecticut and her uncle and aunt have a son, Howard, who is her age. Howard was spoiled, but Nell had enjoyed herself. It had been three numb months since her parents had fallen in a float plane and this had been meant as a distraction. I like Connecticut, Nell said, to be polite. It's too much travel for Howard, her aunt said. And Nell realized that because of cousin Howard they would never go to Connecticut again and that any love she received from them would be conditional love.

She was involved, she realized, in monastic improvement. At the campus in Corner Brook she found a Buddha decal and stuck it to the back of a bronze bust of Wilfred Grenfell that stood in the foyer. She left notes inside the bust hoping someone would find them and write back. The college was named after Grenfell. Grenfell once ate his dogs and used their pelts to make a flag to attract attention. He was lost. Grenfell has a wonderful hospital in Labrador with thick banisters and ochre paint and glossy skirting boards. If you ever go there.

The next week Arthur Twombly was back and he mentioned the son and he hesitated and looked out the window as if Zac might be there, but then he stared hard at us. His son was in his students. You could see his arms galvanized to this realization and it made him touch his neck around the collarbones and breathe deeply.

Once, when she was about twelve, Nell was looking for Christmas gifts in her parents' closet. She found a dozen bags of white sugar. They were stiff and stacked like bricks. There was trouble with Cuba. She realized her mother was preparing for a siege. There was something in how Arthur Twombly now arranged himself that made her think he was under siege. Some internal force had him cornered.

Arthur put his feet up on his desk. He wore shoes that were leather on the bottom and his socks had a pattern to them. They were expensive socks. He was vain. What do you want to do with your life?

She stared at his impressionist painting. I want to be a famous artist.

Do you know you just said famous.

She found it hard to talk to him. It strained her eyes. She wasnt used to concentrating on a person's face. Or engaging. Concentration was something you did alone. You did it with a book.

I was kidding, she said. But she hadnt been. She knew she wouldnt paint or write or sing, but she had ambition and she wanted to be noticed. That's where the Buddha came in, to shed these desires.

I want you to really see things, he said. Even dangerous things.

That Christmas she went to visit her aunt and uncle in Burlington. Burlington is about forty miles southwest of Toronto. It is named after a British parliamentarian who spent some time advocating land reform in the colonies (marshland from the Humber River should be drained and turned into port facilities). Those days are gone, the naming days. Now things are named with no connection between the place and the name. Anyway, my forlorn sadness at the state of things in Nell's early adulthood. There was a carton of apple juice cans under her bed. She watched her uncle climb into his car, the way he closed his eyes as he ducked in. How he shut the door and pressed his brake lights on and pulled the choke. If only he could believe in me the way he believes in that car.

She switched her ticket and returned to Corner Brook before New Year's. She took a pair of orange cross-country skis from the rafters in her uncle's basement. They were Howard's skis. She found matching lacquered bamboo poles tangled in a bunch in a corner. Her old cracked boots in a top closet and a bag of ski waxes in lead containers.

Nell skied up to Crow Hill at midnight and watched the cold, lonely fireworks spiral in a grey disappointment over the paper mill. In a way, Corner Brook was a Burlington, but at least it had geography. She realized, standing there in her brass bindings, she had chosen this town to be a new Burlington, and what did that mean about her ability to think wide. She looked around at the deep clefts filled with snow, the chain-link fence, the mill pummelling out steam. Suicides came up here, and couples in compacts to make out. Sometimes a car had two couples in it. If Nell had peered into the frosted windows of a blue Matador, she'd have seen Arthur's son stretched out in the back seat with Gwen Hurley and myself badly drunk in the front with Maggie Pettipaw. Gwen and Maggie were not our girlfriends, just girls we'd known in high school who were now studying nursing and occupational health and safety and were more than happy to enjoy us before we left Corner Brook for good. For we had decided to leave on New Year's Day. The white tongue of the bay, frozen over. The large peninsula of bark and waste that marched out over the frozen inlet. And the mill humming along, the cement almost green, alive in the way mould is alive.

Nell skied down the unploughed roads. She broke through the herring-bone pattern she'd made on the way up.

In Margaret Bowater Park there was a guy sitting on a freshly sawed stump. He was looking at a parked car. The car had a flat. It looked like he had just cut down the tree so he could sit there and watch the tire lose air. He was drinking a beer.

There was a second course with Professor Twombly after Christmas. She decided to risk it. Nell had come to study communications, but was veering into physics and sociology. She tried narrowing her eyes, but in that focus nothing meaningful materialized. It was like the surprise she had in movies when someone searched with binoculars, and then that sideways-8 framing of the screen occurred as the thing in the distance was found. She had never found anything with binoculars. She had to discover it first with the naked eye and then use binoculars. So her narrowing eyes had nothing to focus on. She did a course in cartography until she woke up one night with a map multiplying in her head, it was like cell growth. It made her think her brain was pregnant. She had taken communications for an easy credit, but it was her hardest course. Who knew reading *King Lear* was the study of a society transforming from roles to jobs? She turned nineteen in that cinder-block apartment with no friends and felt like she had to try and get close to him. She wanted to be alluring.

She skied every day, doing a loop in behind the Curling Club. She loved the quiet of it, just the sizzle of the skis. One afternoon she noticed off in the woods a spruce tree with a blaze mark. She peeled off to look at it. The snow was wet and her skis stuck, she was using orange klister but the snow temperature had dropped. The scoring on the trunk had been done with an axe. Then she saw another one about a hundred paces in. She skied to that. She was on a blazed trail that was full of new snow. The snow was deep but mainly downhill and it was nice to get off the main run. Then she saw a moving white on white. A dark blinking, the ears set back. It was an arctic hare. The fur around the neck was wet and matted and a raw red ring lifted like a gill, the dull noose of wire. Its alert eye. The snare had cut through the fur but the rabbit was sitting and breathing. She was alarmed and stopped but then skied up to it and the rabbit flung itself away from the snare and the snare tugged it back. She stood quiet again and then she knelt near it, her knee down on one ski. She was frightened by something so wild and alive. But it wasnt alive it was pretty much strangling there. She released her bindings and took off her skis. She tried to walk around behind the rabbit. Its ears followed her. She fell on her knees and made a grab for the panicked back. Thin. Its strong legs plumed up snow. She closed her eyes and pushed the wire through itself and slipped the head out of the noose, but she felt the neck and it was rubbed down to white bone. The noose was picture frame wire. The rabbit hopped off and did a comic swoon and tumbled over. A stain of blood along its white coat.

She stood over the rabbit. Then she dug a hole in the snow and laid the rabbit in the white hole and buried it in snow. She felt very down about it all.

Nell skied along the blaze. She felt blood pumping in her head and took off her hat and stowed it in a pocket. She unbuttoned her coat. The next small cut was on a fir tree. Another grey snare just in a ways. Empty. She unwound it from its stump. She knew what they looked like now and collected twenty-two snares. When she got back to campus she put the snares down through the white lid of a garbage can.

They dont die from the snare, Arthur Twombly said. They perish of hypothermia. She stood very close to his shoulder as he suggested they walk down the hall for a coffee from the machine. They have to keep moving, he said, or they freeze. He handed her a coffee. There was a poster of graduates from the program, their faces in ovals. From a distance it looked like honeycomb, with portraits of all the worker bees.

In her bedroom that night she imagined Arthur Twombly bending his knees. She could hear typing and the AM radio station Lori Durdle liked with the commercials that were louder than the songs. The way the rabbit had kicked up snow, it had scratched her wrist. The excitement. It made her think of how Proust sometimes needed two starving rats in the room to get aroused. Professor Twombly had told them that and she didnt believe it until he provided the letter to André Gide. The deep throb of the small city. But it was not the city, it was the refrigerator.

Nell knew she was focusing on him because she had shut herself down. She felt deprived of stimulus and here the erotic side was leaking in. She nodded to herself, she could see how unhealthy it was. She watched the fantasy life reel out and she let herself dream the entire way.

In her mail slot at the laundry room there was a note from Arthur Twombly written with a fountain pen. A man who had developed a loose writing style. That last paper you handed in, the idea of men dying on the battlefield, and the death sounds, when recorded, were indistinguishable from the sounds of orgasm. That's a beautiful thought, Nell.

She looked at the word *indistinguishable*. No one had ever written her a note with the word *indistinguishable* in it. Something in it rhymed with *inextinguishable*. She felt definitely that the note was code.

He stood by his desk, slightly leaning as he had his fingers touching the desk. It was the new year, he said, and he was starving for students like her. Why on earth had she ever come to Corner Brook? She was the only student he had who wasnt from the island. She should think about communications but she should not stay in Corner Brook. There were better programs at McMaster and U of T. I'll recommend you, he said, and there are bursaries you can apply for. Wasnt she an Ontario resident? There was a tax credit for parents in Ontario, her father or mother should receive the forms.

His face was turned to her and she closed the door. She had stopped smoking because he didnt smoke. My mother was from here, she said. My father had come to do a locum and met her and then they were married and moved away. They had me. We lived in Burlington, but they often spent a season of the year in a small place.

They were on their way to northern BC in a little plane. Her father was doing a locum there and her mother wanted to ski. The last thing she saw her father do was collect a handful of AA batteries. He was picking them up out of a drawer in the kitchen to put in something portable. That's the last I knew of my parents, she said, and then I had to handle their mail and transfer monies and decipher how my father had balanced the bills. There were a lot of numbers to go through and I was only eighteen.

She had just finished high school and had been applying to universities on both coasts. Her uncle—her father's brother—arrived and he loved his brother and was useless.

Uncle Charles lived in a hotel for three weeks and expensed all his costs to the deceased. I had to encourage him to go back to Burlington, that I'd handle it. Which I couldnt do. I was an only child and I felt angry that no one was around to help me.

There was insurance and a pension, but then there was a mortgage and there were ordinary debts. If she sold the house she'd have three hundred thousand dollars. It felt like a lot of money and then at other times it felt like no money at all.

He put a hand across her shoulder, the soft fabric of his good shirt, a youthful shirt. He kissed her in his office and she accepted his open face.

She pushed his hand up under her breast. Then his mouth moved away and he opened the door. Arthur, being this close to her mouth. But now nothing had happened and she noticed his teeth were bad.

He and his wife had a friend visiting from New Mexico, Arthur said. A guest lecturer that she should go hear. Youre good with numbers and if you like him we'll bring you over for dinner. She went to Room 112-A to hear him. Perhaps it was about computers, or essays on computing. It was prose but it was short and the talk was about what had been generated on a computer. She realized students around her knew who he was, that Richard Text had a book with a modest cover and this book was on several of the study desks. Published by a small university press in the States.

She saw Richard the next day on West Street in a barbershop. He was sitting by the window and across his shoulders was the shadow of letters: FOR ME. And she thought, He's for me. She looked at the window: HAIRSTYLING FOR MEN. He was reading a book. No one reads books in public.

She went over to the house to meet him because she wanted to see what the inside of Arthur Twombly's home looked like. And how he got along with his wife. Nell was devoting a good chunk of energy to becoming a different person from the one she'd been in Ontario. She'd learned a repertoire of behaviour that made people enjoy her, but she knew the repertoire wasnt really her. The repertoire had gotten out of hand. Kissing Arthur Twombly was something she'd done unintentionally and yet, when she saw the opportunity, recognized it might be considered a new development and progress rather than repetition.

Still, she wanted to live and to listen to interesting people and she decided on a course of action which was to be kind and open and veer on the side of boring people rather than rely on the repertoire.

THREE

THE TWOMBLY HOUSE is a rich dark brown with red trim. It looks like a piece of raw liver, it's the only house in town that's painted that way. The wife, Helen, was a business lawyer who worked for the pulp mill. Different last name, Helen Crofter. I'm not sure if back then she went by Crofter or had Twombly as a last name, but she's a Crofter now. All the lights on both floors were on. In one window a chandelier. It was full of cut-glass pendants laced around a green copper base and below this was where the four of them would eat their salad. Nell would be partnered with Richard Text and she was encouraged by the generosity in this length of light-bearing windows. Nell opened the front door and was surprised to see other students. It was a big party. Of course it wouldnt be just the four of them. She was depressed when Helen met her with a polite face. She felt ashamed of her coat, of the wear line where she'd dropped the cuffs, when Helen took it up the stairs to lay on a bed. Youre nineteen yes? Arthur made her a vodka martini and a flurry of delight rushed through her skin. Arthur Twombly was attending her. She concentrated on the surfaces of things so she could make it all a dramatic event in her diary. Richard Text came over. He was eating an apple. Then he held it away from his mouth the way truck drivers hold the ham radio to listen.

I like shorter books, Richard said.

Arthur: For instance.

I dont want *Middlemarch*.

You just want a couple of days in March.

A bath of good feeling swamped them and Nell was surprised. Arthur Twombly, she could see, dusted off the goals a man had let sit in the back of a closet since second-year university. He converted people with his scrutiny that was barely judgmental, or at least the judging was generous and without doubt. He did not possess an attitude that made one self-conscious or stutter, and it was only after leaving Arthur Twombly that this impression would be noted. It was true that, under focus, when the diaries were trying to note the precise nature of his performance, the performance could not be crumbled into sentences. You had to be there, more than one person has said. If you only knew him, and a wondrous marvel came over the face.

I first understood Richard at a bullfight, Arthur said.

Youve never truly understood me, Richard said.

Then a young man came over, and Nell knew him.

I saw you, she said, sitting on a tree stump.

The young man thought about that. What was I doing, he said.

It was New Year's Eve, she said, and you were trying to come up with an equation that would measure air pressure in a deflating tire.

Joe Hurley, he said, and he touched his forehead with his thumb. And that's exactly what I was doing.

Which got Richard's attention. But then Nell saw that Richard knew Joe Hurley, and of course Arthur Twombly had invited him. Joe had received a bursary to attend a summer program of study with Richard and Arthur in Madrid. They had been to the Sunday bullfights, drunk sherry in a bar with a wall of oak barrels. They had sat on aluminum kegs of beer, you remember that Arthur? Joe called him Arthur. They had stayed up all night on a train to Pamplona and visited the shining tips of white horns behind a fence before the running of the bulls, and they all jumped aboard another train departing for San Sebastian and arrived with drinks in their hands to stumble down the cold sand to the surf and plunge in, still holding their mix of cola and red wine aloft. There was no real difference between student and teacher in Madrid, it appeared. They were comrades.

There were five students and the three adults at dinner and Nell Tarkington clicked in and did her party pieces and at one point got up from the table to do a dance. She did the dance with Joe Hurley staring at her. They had no idea who she was. A lot of the food at dinner as well as the clothes that Helen and Arthur wore were not things you could purchase in Corner Brook. They took trips to Montreal and New York and filled their carry-on bags with clear vacuum packages of deli items and jars of pesto and Italian shirts and boxed sets of chamber music. There was no work in Montreal and they couldnt live in Toronto because it was too ugly. You had to sign a form at the liquor store, Helen said, marking what alcohol you wanted and the reason why you wanted it. The *reason*.

As she was finding her winter boots Richard was on the third stair and suggested she go up with him. He was in the room with the coats. He had a record player and he played the son's records. The son he was talking about was David, and David was, at that moment, in St John's sharing an apartment with me. I get a kick, Richard said, out of living like a teenager. Even though youre thirty, she said. Even though I'm thirty-one. He lives in Santa Fe, working for the US military. His office is on a road named after Robert Oppenheimer. He seemed very right wing. Yet he was bohemian.

She walked home pretending she had Joe Hurley in her head, sort of standing in her hair, and she was cloaked in the thought of getting his attention. The snow falling. There was a hum from the paper mill. In fact it felt as if the mill was a power generator and the city drew its life from its conversion of fossil fuels to light and in the dark the light was turned to snow.

She figured Richard wanted to sleep with her, so she stayed separate and then he ruined it. She was inscrutable, her hair pulled tight from her face, a slick product, a green hairband. As if she's doing a lot of work with her face and has to roll up her sleeves, which is her hair. Yes, her face looks like it's working, even when she's quietly sitting. It's her thoughts. Her face is obviously chewing over many thoughts.

Richard: What are you thinking?

Nell: Nothing.

But you are, he thought.

He said Arthur had shown him the paper she'd done on the dying men and loved the image and wanted to say that he was meeting students one on one. There was something analytical in her, something that he could adapt to the computer lab. It was as if he had brought her to the door of his bedroom to tell her this. It made her realize what she wanted, which was Joe Hurley. Joe was a student of his too. Joe, he said, was going places. He was going to hire Joe Hurley.

THERE WAS DISTANCE between Arthur and his wife. They tended not to look at each other, and Nell knew her own trouble at facing someone you are raging at. But it was also true that you cannot quickly sever a bond when youve stood in private rooms and kissed like polite animals smelling scent in the woods. They had gone through a death. It was the death of something to which they'd given birth. Nell didnt feel like a shit disturber, that her own feelings were so new that they must be prized more highly than the jaded and experienced feelings that coursed through this well-educated middle-aged Twombly couple stationed in the hinterland, coming through mourning. She was young, her parents were dead, and she was not wise.

She took the ski trail and slipped into the track left by an earlier skier. At the bend she stepped off into the blazed trail and looked to see if any more snares were set. Even the thought of the snares made her anxious. She stopped by the first old blaze mark and looked for a snare and there was one. A new one, it wasnt one she had missed.

Missus you should stay on trails youre welcome on.

She wheeled around. A man in a checkered woods shirt. Smoking a cigarette. On snowshoes. He had an axe and he was not wearing gloves. She was about a hundred yards off the orienteering loop.

You come down here youre liable to get caught in a snare yourself, he said.

Just the hint of a threat. The ski loop was not well used but there had been another set of skis on it before her. If she yelled someone could hear. The road to the university was just up there. But she wasnt ready yet to be alarmed enough to yell.

I was upset by a rabbit, she said.

I know I lost one. Saw the mess. Thought at first a lynk got him. But then I never known a lynk to go taking up snares.

He looked like he was seesawing towards anger.

Maybe if you didnt hunt so close to the university, she said.

Maybe if the government didnt go building universities on my rabbit line.

He sat himself down on an overhanging bough. He smoked his cigarette and looked away from her.

Then he got up. Come over here, he said. He was walking into the bushes.

She skied up above him and saw him pause near two trees. She could easily outgun him on skis. He was waving her down. She skied down to be ten feet from him.

See this ring here, he said.

He pulled a rusting wire hoop out of the snow with the hilt of his axe. It was like a band saw blade that he snagged up out of the snow.

That's my moose snare. You dont want to be falling into that. This'll take your leg off.

He finished his cigarette and threw it in the snow. It sank in the snow.

There's a big bull, he said, bawling away in there all fall.

He pointed with his chin deeper into the woods behind Margaret Bowater Park.

WHAT DID HE LOOK LIKE.

Nell described him.

Sounds like Loyola Hurley, Arthur said.

Hurley. She thought of Joe Hurley. I went to your office, she said.

Youre a little shaken.

I didnt know I'd want to talk to you.

You probably need to talk to someone who knows the place.

She popped her ski bindings and knocked the skis together and leaned them against the side of Arthur's house. It was three in the afternoon. His wife wouldnt be home until after five. She saw the stairs and at the top in a room the foot of Richard's bed where Helen Crofter had put Nell's coat. There wasnt enough time to weigh the effort it would take to haul herself out of not following him up there if he'd said I'll be waiting for you in the bedroom.

Let's go for a walk, he said.

She walked in the ski boots, which made her feel like she was walking on another planet. Nell caught him looking over her head at the neighbours' house. Or out on the street, though it was a quiet street. He had put on his boots and a puff vest.

Loyola, he said, was the one to find my son. They have a cabin next to mine, that's how I know Joe Hurley. Joe was a smart kid, he came over to play chess. He knows how to wire a house. No one in his family has ever gone to university, but I talked to Loyola and I got Joe a bursary. Now his brother, Gerard. When it comes to that kind of power, it can go either way.

Richard had taken Joe to Santa Fe for a month. They were setting up a computer lab. This was in the days when computers were as big as rooms and the chess champion could still beat a machine. Richard had explained to Arthur that Joe had it, a kind of manner for machines and numbers. He wanted Joe to work for him, though Joe was considering the reserves. That was the new work now, the work of moving information and storing it in vast boxes, and the army was a good place for a paid education. The reason Joe Hurley was in this kind of study was because of Arthur Twombly. My wife is at work, Arthur said. She's searching for a legal title.

Nell followed him as they walked down his road and through a trail that ran between two houses. A dog joined them, a neighbourhood dog. Arthur began telling her how Tolstoy, in *Anna Karenina,* made a dog think. How much in Tolstoy was said in a reproachful or mocking manner. People think, he said, that I sleep with students. I've never made a pass at a student. I had an affair with a married woman, and my wife knows about it. I'm just coming out of that, he said. You know about our son's death.

The one in the picture in the bathroom.

It's been five months, he said. You dont really know what I used to be like.

But she knew. She knew the heart of him. She knew too the difference in herself since her parents' death. The difference between her new self and the old one was parallel to Arthur Twombly's own drift. I was in your class, she said, when you announced it.

I have, he said, several times, been very, what's the word. Smitten. By a student.

You can give off, she said, alluring eye behaviour.

When his son died Arthur had gone crazy. The love Arthur had for Zac was what had made David move to St John's. Sasha was having to live with it. It was difficult for Sasha, he knew that. It's been hard and my wife and I we're both understanding. So this affair with a married woman. That's what got around. And once you have one then of course youre capable of sleeping with everybody. That's called gossip and for some reason I want you to know this about me.

That he was smitten, she guessed.

FOUR

ARTHUR DID NOT SEE HER for eight days. He wondered why she did not come to class or knock on his office door. He was not fully aware of the power he had, and could not see her predicament. He inhaled and kept inhaling until the balloon of his lungs hurt his back. Arthur was not confident that he was worth being loved, and since the death of Zac he didnt care. He was forty-five. He had another son but he was angry at him. It wasnt that he thought Dave should have done more to save Zac. It was that Zac was him, whereas Dave, Dave did not remind Arthur of himself. He'd said that once to him, when they had a fight. I dont know how I had a son like you. Arthur didnt worry any more what people thought of him, though he did respect what people thought of his wife. The truth is, he realized, he missed Nell's face.

One day he walked down the orienteering trail where he'd seen her zipping through on skis, but the snow would not hold his weight. Then his wife was away in Chicago dealing with the North American head offices of Bowater and so he approached Nell with a note in the residence laundry room. He missed her. Then he was in the lounge pouring coffee and the window exploded. A snowball. He looked down. Nell was bending to make another one. The second snowball landed on the white patch left from the first. Good aim.

He pulled her skis through the length of the Audi. He drove her back to his house and they went inside and she peeled off a Nepalese sweater then a turtleneck and a pale blue top and collected all her things on the seat of a kitchen chair. Young style. She flipped the back of her hair up and stared inside herself. What was he doing with this situation.

He made two tomato sandwiches. The tomatoes cost a dollar each.

They sat in the living room and listened to a taped radio program of a man describing Frost's poem about stopping in woods on a snowy evening. They drank a glass of white wine with the sandwiches. Nell touched his knee and then he put his hand on her hand. They sat there holding hands like old people.

When she left he looked at his watch. She'd been in the house forty-five minutes. She skied away from the house along the trail they'd walked that one afternoon. He knew the neighbours had clocked that.

THE NEXT DAY the doorbell rang and it was Nell holding her skis. He pulled her in by the bottom of her coat. Let's go upstairs, he said. And Nell unlaced her ski boots and went up first and waited at the top of the stairs and said hello in her head to the room that had held the coats. Arthur walked into the bedroom that Richard was using. Nell's waist was narrow and she was hot from skiing. Arthur pushed her away and she walked back to where she had stood and he pushed her away again. She ran back and shoved him and he fell into a shelving unit. Then she was on him and held the buckle of his belt and she turned the belt buckle over with her cold fingers and knelt and kissed him where the mark of the belt was on his bare stomach. He stood her up and pushed her away again and then walked towards her and cornered her and forced her to sit on the floor. He knelt down to her. He watched his hands land and judge the middle of her. It was as if he was alone in the corner of his son's room, his forehead pushed against the wallpaper. Though it was Richard's room now. He had been both jealous and proud of his son, how strong he'd been and his girlfriends and how Zac Twombly wouldnt have settled as quickly as he had. If I could have it all back, he thought, I would not have married Helen so early. Zac was him on a different path. My god they were only what, twenty-two. He thought about that time and he pulled the top of Nell's head towards himself. The scent they were sending around the rooms. How long would his wife be away. How did smell dissipate. Was this using, was this a breach in goodness. He stopped Nell and helped her up and collapsed his hand in her hair. He kissed her and on her mouth he knew himself and he was alarmed at what he'd allowed. He ran his hands down her body and then pushed her away again and she fell on the bed and she bounced up and laughed and grabbed him and pulled him down. Okay, she said, and opened her legs. He fell into her. They were fully clothed but he discovered himself inside Nell Tarkington. It was one of his other selves that he decided he could keep at a distance from himself and his wife. The root down there and the nerve endings behind his eyes were separate channels of evidence.

Then watching her ski away from the house. If he saw that it would be an affair. How quickly an object recedes.

A week went by. He caught himself thinking of Nell's skin. The course it followed. He realized she was not nothing, it was not just himself he was wrestling with. There was a personal part leaking through. He sat back and thought of her and thought about her as deeply as he could. Yes, there was no twinge. He worshipped her body.

Look. I am not going to leave my wife.

Nell was too young for this kind of reasoning. She was tenacious and wasnt easily winded. She had no discretion. But the trickle of gossip was not of a new variety—he had been judged already and so no new word headed his wife's way.

That spring and summer, at least twice a week, Nell met Arthur down by the orienteering trail that doubled in winter as a cross-country ski loop. She got in his car and they drove to Grand Lake. He drove an Audi. It was diesel and he had purchased it out of a dealership magazine and had it shipped from Bremen. It had come aboard a long blue freighter that steamed in the five calm miles of the Bay of Islands, docked near the Humber River and then unloaded the Audi in a yellow box made of Hungarian lumber, the crane swinging it over to the harbour apron where three stevedores touched it on the corners to nudge it a little and make it land flat. He was impressed with how little was needed to alter the course of a three-thousand-pound box. The infrastructure for Corner Brook was huge. It was all built in a time when the prospects for Corner Brook blew off the charts.

She was tall and had long dark hair and she wore the same clothes over and over. He had chosen her because she was the only student he had not from here. You could get into trouble with families. Her mother was from here but her mother was dead. He loved Nell's body and yet she was too young for him, or he was embarrassed to think of himself with a girl that young. If they were alone on their own planet, but he laughed at himself. There was no future in it. Arthur held her by the shoulder and she felt the peculiar angle of her shoulder blade. Once, when she was nine, she woke up in hospital after a small surgery. Her father had noticed a lump and it was benign. But she thought they had taken the shoulder blade out of her arm. She saw her hands and arms but knew in her back there was no shoulder. She realized she enjoyed this thought, though she immediately worried if women would pity her. She knew that men did not care. It was women who were the problem. Her mother, for instance, an assumption that a weak arm would limit her. As a child she had been scared to death by the war amps commercials. How they pitted children losing an arm in accidents against old veterans with limbs blown off in war. There was something bizarre in the connection of these groups, and with the idea that funding came from depositing lost keys in red mailboxes. She knew an arm without a shoulder blade placed her close to this collection of misfits and she decided in that hospital bed to avoid the stigma. And then the anaesthetic wore off and she realized her arm was normal.

They drove out along the Humber River and parked this time out by Boom Siding and the salmon run was on. Men up to the tails of their coats in the river—I could have been one of them. They watched the anglers arcing rods over their shoulders, a white wet dripping off the corners of their waterproof clothing. Then they carried on to Arthur's cabin on Grand Lake. There was a lusty carelessness that almost wanted him to get in trouble. He thought she must have other men. The man inside him was lazy. He laughed at himself one day in his office while holding the phone receiver to his forehead. He could hear the student through his skull. I am the other men, he thought.

Arthur Twombly was busy that summer. David was home from St John's and the family was flying to Detroit to spend the summer in Saginaw Bay. Arthur liked to complicate things. If he were rain he'd fall on the land and flow into a stream and enter the ocean by a river. Some people would just as soon evaporate and rain on the ocean direct—his son David. There's a lot of rain that falls on water.

Nell didnt see Arthur for two months. She took Richard's computer lab with Joe Hurley and learned how to send green messages to other students who were sitting in labs like this back in Richard's hometown of Santa Fe.

She walked through Margaret Bowater Park and enjoyed her choice of aloneness. She did five hours of weekly volunteer work at the hospital, reading to elderly patients. She felt like if she worked hard, then good things would happen to her. There was a man who combed his hair in the polished mirror of the floor. Once she walked along the green orienteering trail and found the old rabbit line. The snares were up and the band saw blade was gone too. She climbed up through the trees to Jubilee Field and down the quiet street to Arthur Twombly's cul-de-sac. The town had been planned, the workers up on the hills, the managers of the mill here in the valley. The town was also divided on education— Catholics to Regina, and the Protestants to Herdman. She walked past the Twombly house and looked back to catch an angle of its dark brown siding. Sleeping with a man she could not have, something about it still felt like an ascetic life. She had to be careful with her money because she had decided to give the insurance money to Oxfam in her parents' names. She knew her father would like that. They had not spoiled her and three hundred thousand dollars might be the wrong thing for her when she's nineteen. It wasnt easy to give the money away. Oxfam did not want the money. They were suspicious. They suspected she might be acting in a bereaved manner. They forced her to tell her uncle, and Charles was not supporting the donation. Charles sneered at organizations like Oxfam. What about Howard, was his thinking. Howard working at StresCrete. It took six months for the paperwork to make the money go away. Charles thought that was throwing money into the sea.

Her Indian roommate Rasha Vangela. She made curry and the one meal Nell loved was when Rasha had her girlfriends over and they cooked a head of cauliflower. The saris in the cement walls, the intense humid boiling and frying in garam masala. Rasha had a jar of coconut pomade in the bathroom. A strand of hair caught in the twist of the lid. Thick black hair, you could almost see the texture of it, as if the hair were strings of Indian DNA.

September, when she knew Arthur had returned and the son had gone. She waited. She walked down Main Street. There were boys on the hill above the movie cinema breathing gasoline from grocery bags. And beyond them the solid, permanent pulp mill. She liked Corner Brook for the eddy it provided. It was a milltown, and she found the pulp mill comforting. Whenever she told someone that they laughed at her. No, she said, it's like a hearth. And she meant it. The soft unravelling steam that rose and carried itself downwind over the mouth of the Humber River where the salmon were returning to the sea. Sometimes you woke up and the cars in the university parking lot were covered with ash.

They met three times in the fall, to talk. Arthur had missed her through the summer. Nell had been like a pharmaceutical prescription for depression. They had not sailed on Saginaw Bay. They had stayed on land and his son David was aloof. David had seen a speedboat in a scrap-yard and that felt like the family that summer, he told me. But the sunlight and Michigan had revived his parents. The waitresses wore minis and orange plastic hoop earrings and even that felt like a reason for living. Arthur understood they'd both pushed back from the brink. Arthur and Helen had sort of fallen in love again.

Nell listened to this and heard the spiral of thought that meant it was over and now they were to be friends. It complicated her feelings and she pushed them down like plunging at water. Arthur Twombly was the first man she had let carry her heart on a plate. That's how she felt, as if her heart were being lifted on a plate out of water. Now she felt the hoses of her heart held her down. She realized she had moved to Corner Brook as the start of a wilful life. She had been passive, afraid of crowds, worried about her own talent. And here she had moved around the powerful Arthur Twombly and had fallen for him and now they were just talking.

It affected her gait. It was walking through cement. She felt like she was wading. It is hard to turn a corner when there is no wall.

Then, in early November, a note in the laundry room. See me at 4.

THEY WALKED to Arthur's car and he drove her out to the highway, but they turned south rather than out towards Steady Brook. Open the glove box, he said. The light inside came on and there was a red scarf. Arthur slowed down and pulled over. He took the scarf and wrapped it around her eyes. They drove for ten miles with the blindfold on and then he stopped and helped her take it off. There was a man with a truck. This is Gary Tilley, he said.

She thought they were going to rape her. Then Gary's face opened up. He operated a Cessna off of Pinchgut Lake. They climbed in, Nell in front. The lake was choppy. The dashboard was very old. Dials. Arthur was in the back with a heavy seatbelt buckle across his waist. Gary flicking on the silver tabs and gauges lighting up with real bulbs. They skimmed along and the pontoons clipped the chop and they teetered up and banked to the right. The coastline of the island yawed across the windshield and she thought of her parents. What they must have felt as they knew they were not going to make it. It was a clear evening, you could see a hundred miles. And all along the coast were these little flickers of orange. Bonfires. It was Guy Fawkes night.

They circled back to Pinchgut and landed and said goodbye to Gary and they drove around the very coast that they had seen from above. There was a bonfire through the trees and they took a road down to the beach. Boys were throwing tires on the fire, the exhausted coils of steel-belted radials. A dog was jumping over the fire, until he hurt his paw. Someone gave the dog a beer. Then he took off down the beach. He goes over those rocks, Arthur said, like he's doing forty miles per hour.

Owner: It's a wonder he dont break his fucking leg off.

It was Gerard Hurley. Nell could see Arthur was stiffened. Then Joe Hurley came up from the shore and smoothed it over between his brother and Arthur. They had lost land when the pulp mill had raised the level of the dam, and so Gerard was blaming Arthur's wife. Nell had slightly forgotten about Joe Hurley. Then the whole side of the power of Joe whammed her in the face. She could hardly stand. She needed to sit down. She felt her heart and had not felt anything like it. They got back in the car and took a run at the dirt road up to the highway, but it was loose gravel and Arthur slid the Audi into the grass and then found the right front wheel was spinning. He sat there, his headlights painting the tall grass white and the dark sky above the grass. Then a knock on the window and Arthur rolled it down.

We'll try lurching the car, Joe said.

There was an insurance refusal box that Arthur had checked and he saw it now, sitting in the glove box under the blindfold, and he read these words: FULL VALUE. Three kids came up from the beach. A girl of nine looked at them. That's not a good place to get stuck, she said. Then her grandfather drove up on a red quad. It was Loyola Hurley. He looked at the front of the car. She's brought up, Loyola said. I'll get the young feller in his four-by-four.

Gerard Hurley was in the pickup. And they winched the Audi up. They are careful with bumpers and brake lines and they shout at the fact they make cars now with nothing to hook onto.

Even the nine-year-old girl is disdainful of the new automobiles.

They are wearing white shirts and with the rocking and the winching, Arthur has them covered in mud. But theyre out of the ditch.

Now park that, Loyola Hurley said, up by mother.

We should be getting on, Arthur said.

They took a run and made the hill. And there, at the top, with her arms crossed standing by a place where trucks and ATVs are parked, was Loyola's mother. Four generations of the Hurleys.

SMOKE DRIFTED ALONG the tablelands. They drove on and Arthur calmed down. He said he'd had a piece of land down there that he bought off the Hurleys. He wanted to build a summer cabin there. He'd poured a foundation and a man from the church came down, asked him what he was doing. That it was church land. I bought this off Loyola Hurley, Arthur said. And the man said the Hurleys had owned all of this land a hundred years ago but had sold it to Parks Canada and to Bowater or it had been expropriated to widen the highway, or they had willed it to the church, such as what had happened with this piece here. Yes Loyola Hurley may not agree the church owns it, but does he have a deed to the land. The church has the deed.

And so that was the beginning of the bad blood between Arthur Twombly and the Hurleys. When Helen had described to Arthur how the mill was to raise the level of the lake, he took out a topographical map and made a line on it. He saw that his cabin was safe, but the Hurleys would have water at their front door. They had built too close to the shore.

They drove back into Rocky Harbour over the oldest rock on earth, rock made at the beginning of the earth's cooling period. And Nell felt it. Like they'd left an ancient time and were heading for civilization. They ate in a straitlaced diner in Rocky Harbour. Doilies on the tables and chowder with edges still to the potatoes. Then they doubled back and stayed in the cabin on Grand Lake. Arthur took her down to the beach and showed her the Hurley land, how the water came up now around the cabin. They used to have a hundred feet of land jutting into the lake, he said. That's where Loyola was when my boys drove up the lake. That's how he knew they were lost, when the wind picked up.

They made love and Nell felt something happening to her. Something deep in her pelvic bone was being massaged. It was an inner thrumming, was it vibration or was it sound. She was moved in a way gravity moves things. In a way that is impossible to reverse.

FIVE

SHE WAS NOT AVAILABLE to see Arthur. It had stretched to nine days. She was counting. He wanted to see her but she could not explain the thrumming feeling. Then she was in the post office and could smell the scotch tape. She felt as if she had outgrown him. At first it was Arthur who had been mulling over a cease in their relationship. She hadnt been able to muster the big heart needed to see that he had been in grief and was pushing through at least that first white gulf and had regained character and an attention to his family. Since then he's regressed. Arthur was complicating grief-retirement with turning middle aged and the resentment a man has of ploughing his carnal will into one woman for twenty years. Something about that resentment built into a knot and turned her. Nell had noticed his backside, that he was old. But it was also that she had received a feeling from Joe Hurley, a boy her age, and a recognition filled her body that it was someone like Joe Hurley she should be with. Well, her feeling was open on both ends. What Nell felt was that until she saw Joe Hurley that night she was falling in love with Arthur, and now she understood she did not want to waste her life on a man she could not have. He wouldnt want kids. He had David and Sasha and the memory of

Zac. You only have one life, she told herself. It was something you had to remind yourself all the time.

She saw Richard Text one day sitting in the dark windows of the Holiday Inn bar, reading a book. She walked in and he looked up and was happy to see her. You, he said, now there's a reason to live. She was surprised at how warm he was.

Youre the only person in this town who reads a book in public, Nell said.

It's an excuse to drink, he said.

Sometimes she did not like herself, and it was so lovely to have a man say youre worth it. He had grown a beard and wore a new light jacket that someone must have bought for him. He looked good in the neat beard.

Richard.

Nell.

He bought her a drink but she did not drink it. Her body wouldnt allow her. The smell repulsed her. He was writing down strings of numbers. He was writing with a pencil in one of those blue essay book-lets. He was a chewer of pencils. There was something well-contained in the pencil, the notebook and the little glass of whisky. His notes on computer algorithms. What the hell, she thought. And he took her back to Arthur's house. There was no Audi in the driveway, but she felt the betrayal to Arthur with each step. Or the right foot was betrayal and the left foot defiance.

Nell: I didnt know you were still in town.

I wasnt, he said.

I knew Joe was back so I guess I should have known.

There was something in the light in the room. There was a cheeriness that might have to do with paint or windows or the way the stairs opened more light from below. Richard had gone back to Santa Fe with Joe, but

Arthur had more work for him this term. The Santa Fe work—overseeing a thesis, marking papers, he could do all that on computer.

Richard: Joe just went back to Santa Fe.

I think I'm pregnant, she said.

All this time she knew Richard had brought her back to make love to her and she did not know she was going to say this. They lay on the bed and listened to a record. She knew, and relied on the knowledge that she was confident. Richard's momentum halted. The room smelled of the son who had spent the summer here. There was a mixture of Richard and David in the room.

It just occurred to me, Nell said. She had never been pregnant before. There was a trickle inside her like one of those false drinking glasses with liquid embedded in the glass. You didnt have to worry about drinking it. In retrospect she pinpointed the evening of the bonfires and the sudden weight she felt as they left the bed and cleaned up. Sunset. She had been thinking of Joe Hurley when they made love. It had been the first time she had made love thinking about another person.

She lay on the bed with Richard. They just looked at each other with a warmth between them. He was understanding her. Then he warned her. You know the one about not being able to step into the same river twice, he said. Well that's true with emotions as well. Arthur won't fall in love with you the way he fell in love with Helen. The only thing that happens twice is, you can recognize an old feeling you had bloom in another person. And Arthur's probably seeing it, that old feeling. Seeing it in you.

It moved her, this caring. Did this man love her. In the end, he didnt want to have sex with her, and she realized she had misjudged him. Richard wanted to be a friend. He looked like he wanted to say more but was deciding it was against his best interests. He was deciding to give her advice, a warning about men, even though he was a man.

She bought a test at the pharmacy and used the public restrooms. But when she was in the stall she felt it was wrong to find out there. She took a city bus back to the apartment. Lori Durdle from Stephenville was watching a soap opera in the living room. Nell sat on the toilet and unwrapped the wand and held the wand between her legs. It was often hard for her to urinate when someone else was nearby. She could hear the actors on the soap. She could imagine Lori Durdle, fat and unloved, living through the hyperbole of these soap lives. She waited for the see-through window to change colour. Then she forgot what it meant if it changed colour. She'd left the box in her room. The yellow stick in the window was turning pink but she did not know if this meant she was pregnant or if pink meant status normal or even if the pregnancy kit could detect the sex of the baby and that she was having a girl.

She crossed to her room. Lori Durdle said hello. She was very nice, Lori Durdle. She was good-hearted and was so right to her marrow. So what if she'd never eaten a red pepper before moving into residence. Lori Durdle didnt have to act at being good.

The box said yellow was not-pregnant and pink, if it crossed into the A half of the window, meant pregnant. She looked at the window. It was all pink.

ARTHUR SAT NELL DOWN. No children, he said. She was eating dark cake from a piece of kleenex. They were in Arthur's office in the arts building. She thought about what Richard had said. She thought how often on the dance floor she's danced with everyone, including women twice her age. She often led. Okay, Arthur said, there's no one here to take care of you.

I already know that, she said.

But youre okay with what I'm suggesting.

I'm nineteen.

But she was not okay with it. She had never thought about having children, not since she was fifteen, which felt like a long time ago. She'd thought about them, but it was a bit like thinking about heaven. It would happen way down the road. She had never been pregnant so she said okay to Arthur because he had opened with that position.

I've checked again, he said, and there's no safe place here.

You mean word would get out.

It's that it's legal in St John's.

She had seventy-one dollars in her savings account. At one time she had three hundred thousand dollars and she'd given it to help a continent. Now she was thinking that might have been rash. She remembered the man at Oxfam she had spoken with, how Roger Edgecombe had listened to her and let a silence occur to see if she'd blurt out anything else after she had told him her idea. Roger said a reserve of money could come in handy. There were eventualities. The people who work for the third world are the most aware and conservative when it comes to personal well-being. She had been reckless, but no one could persuade her out of the recklessness.

She agreed to Arthur's driving her. They would make separate plans to be absent for four days. The drive across took eight hours and Arthur hardly spoke to her. They drove through five hundred miles of woods. Arthur had a lot of music to play on the car stereo. He liked a sort of jazz, she realized. He had arranged an appointment. They stayed in the Newfoundland Hotel. She had never been in a large hotel. She had once left Burlington and hitchhiked to Montreal to see a Picasso exhibit, and had slept outside of a hotel that had been sandblasted. She finally found John Mennie, the man she'd lost her virginity to, and he let her sleep at his apartment but she had to sleep with him. She didnt even take a bath, and had grains of cement in her hair from having slept under the canvas-wrapped scaffolding.

There was a narrow window near the coffee maker. The window had a slice of the harbour and the ocean. So this was the wide-open ocean. That night Arthur cradled her and she could feel his tears while lying in the vise of his elbows.

She wasnt that worried about moving towards what Arthur wanted because it wasnt like he could reach over and snatch it from her arms.

Arthur parked on LeMarchant Road and they looked out upon the orderly fences and the overhanging trees that were not changing colour as they did in Corner Brook. It was more like the wind was tearing the leaves off. Arthur tilted his wrist and compared the time to the turquoise digital counter on the dash. The hospital, the Grace, was across the street from the clinic. He did a mental check of the road, as if he was on duty. That's where babies were born, whereas the clinic, that's where the white suction hose is slid into you. There were seven people carrying signs outside the clinic. The signs had all been made by the same hand. They were all women except for one man, Arthur realized, a young man of about twenty. The people needed someone to wind them up. The man looked like the plumber he'd had in last week to fix the bathroom sink. At first he hadnt looked at the plumber, it was just one of the young men Chester Dawe had recommended. The plumber wanted to use sealant and then was vexed as he had to cut the pipe and take the throat of the drain to a hardware store. When he came back Arthur asked if he wanted a coffee. Not if youre making it special. He had coffee on. Do you take milk or sugar. With both, the young man said. Arthur hadnt poured sugar into a coffee mug in a long time. He stirred it and he remembered stirring coffee as a boy with his father in the woods of Michigan. He'd given up sugar when he was twenty. He'd had a roommate in college who asked him why he put sugar in coffee. Dont you drink coffee to taste coffee.

He'd made the plumber the coffee and brought it up to the bathroom, where bits of sink were on an old newspaper and the tub had streaks of oil and dirt. Then he knew who the young man was, Gerard Hurley. He remembered him from that bonfire night. He knew from the eyes. He'd seen Gerard as a kid on the beach at the cabins they had at Grand Lake. His brother Joe and his father, Loyola. Plumbing and bathroom supplies. Gerard's hands were busy, so Arthur put the coffee on the floor. This is the original pipe, Gerard Hurley said, from when the house was built. So what he had in his hand was a piece of plumbing his father had installed. That happened, Gerard said. He often came across his father's work. He noticed the coffee on the floor and said, Thank you for the coffee. There was something wrong in the thank-you and in Gerard Hurley's face, and Arthur had wondered if he shouldnt have put the cup on the floor.

It was the same look in the face of the young man holding the placard. A rough look. He was not strident, just noting a breach in etiquette. He wasnt from town either, he was from around the bay. And he was the only man. One of the women laughed and another was looking at her watch, just the way Arthur did. I won't have it, she said. And Arthur slowly realized what Nell was saying. Arthur Twombly lit a cigarette and waited behind the wheel of the car he loved. He had given up smoking when his second son was born. Almost twenty years. He was going to see his son tonight. He felt the chill you get when you leave a public swimming pool. It may not be yours anyway, she said. And he knew what she meant and had hoped with eighty percent of his heart that she would say that. Other men. He would be generous though, he would not cave into anger, because part of him knew she was giving him the easy out. He was alarmed at the sudden new creation and how a corner of his brain thought it was Zac coming back.

Okay, he said, whose might it be if you dont mind me asking.

A boy, she said.

Okay, a boy. And they returned to the hotel and did not talk until he was changing his shirt and said he was having dinner with his son, which meant she was on her own for the night.

HE ARRIVED at the apartment on Elizabeth Avenue, the one I was
sharing with David Twombly. And that was the night we went to the
hockey game and had an uncomfortable dinner at the Battery Hotel.
There was a moment when the visiting goalie asked for an ice repair, and
Mr Twombly pointed this out. That the referee shaved some ice with his
own skate and tamped the fresh ice in the gully with the hockey puck and
sprayed the shaved ice with the goalie's water bottle. He liked that the
referee had used everything at his disposal, and nothing new specifically
meant for ice repair.

SIX

HELEN CROFTER DISCOVERED the green envelope of photographs Arthur had sent in to get developed on Caribou Road. They were lying in his study the weekend he went to St John's. She'd picked them up to look at them again. There was one of herself that she wanted to destroy. She felt she wasnt photogenic, and that was too bad as we were going to be photographed more and more. She'd seen the pictures, or some of them, the ones he'd said were good of her but were not, some of the dinner party and a few of their son just before he'd left for university. She'd asked Arthur to give David the one of her and him, to remind her son that his mother loved him, for there was love in both of their faces. But Arthur had forgotten it, it was still there in the pack. Though it did not feel like a full pack of film and she counted them and there were fifteen photos in the package. She withdrew the negatives to see which ones he'd brought. There were four hinged panels of six. She lifted a strip of negatives to the light and saw faces that were not faces she knew. She focused to turn the black face white and the white hair black. They looked like someone else's photos, entirely foreign, and she was prepared to return them until she saw the one face, they were all the one face now. Photos of a student who had been to dinner. But it wasnt the dinner. There was utter delight and abandon and shyness and entitlement in the negatives, a linked sheet of them, an inappropriate gesture in every goddamn picture of this girl. And the things in the background were not of this house. It was another time and place these pictures, there was no dinner party going on in these pictures at all.

She had thought, like Arthur, that they had turned a corner. But what if it had only been before the summer. Could she forgive it if this was last year. But he wasnt here for her to confront him. She had to wait.

Helen waited the three days. She forgot about the photographs for twenty minutes and then remembered them for an hour or two. It wore on for the three days that Arthur was away. Then she heard the car door. She ran to the porch. She couldnt believe she was running.

The pictures, Arthur.

Oh you found them.

I found the negatives.

He collapsed in the hallway. He was carrying his soft carrier bag and it was this shoulder that slid down the wall and he was sitting on the bag, one leg bent beneath him. He could not think of a thing to say. Nothing seemed plausible. He was surprised to see that he was crying.

We had a little thing, he said. I've barely kissed her.

But he knew that Nell's predicament would be discovered. There wasnt much inventiveness happening in the factory of his brain. His brain knew he was done for. He had collapsed partly for the shock value but the crying was unexpected. Then he thought of something.

Richard, he said, has been sleeping with her. Those are Richard's pictures.

Are you all right down there. Youre not having a heart attack.

I'm exhausted, he said. It was exhausting.

So you had a little thing you were saying.

There was a tone in his wife's voice he had heard before, but usually when Helen was discussing with him her father who hurt her emotionally when she was a teenager. Arthur opened his mouth. I kissed her once, he said. It's Richard. She's actually pregnant.

You dont know a thing about your friends, she said. Not one thing.

He wasnt afraid of his wife. He wasnt afraid of anger and being the cause of upset, but he was unnerved by this tone of voice. He had partly forgotten that he had slept with Nell Tarkington. Nell's admission that it was not his baby had made him think of Richard, and that solution overwrote all that had happened before.

I think theyre seeing each other.

It hasnt occurred to you, Helen said, that Richard is gay.

What was she saying, and could it be true. And of course it was. What kind of mind did he have, that he could not see what Richard really was. His wife knew, his wife knew everything. She was the smartest woman ever. Did she know that the weekend he shared with Nell in St John's they did not make love. Would she know that. Would she give him some points for that. They hardly touched each other. When a man decides to stop seeing someone, it's as if they have never slept together. An unclear window remains, which he shares with the woman he's slept with. But the majority of him feels loyal.

It was a relief to him, especially after the fiasco of the St John's trip. It irritated him that so much had been planned and, in the end, nothing done. But then he realized a lot of work had been done. Sometimes saying one sentence is a lot of work. It couldnt be Richard's child. He had been trying to figure out a way to tell Helen and now he could say it. But it was worse than she'd thought.

Pregnant, great.

It was a boy, he said. That one, Joe Hurley. She said it was someone else's.

That was not the information that would exonerate him, he now knew that. Helen had been upset when he'd had an affair with Debra Logan. Debra was Helen's age, there was the utter loss of reason after Zac had gone. It was the idea of a student and that he'd invite her to their house. That she'd see her things. She'd compare. Perhaps he thought a student was not a threat. A student can propel large folds of life into the sexual act. Helen had been a student, she remembers crushes. Debra Logan was married and thirty-nine. It was more like a form of yoga to Debra Logan, sleeping with Arthur Twombly. But a student. That reflected on her, on Helen getting old. It had been over a year since Zac's death. She wouldnt be judged that way. It was mean of Arthur to have hidden it. Was it cold, it was an insult. And worse than unthinking. It suggested nothing that she could improve on except a time machine. She did not for one second believe he had only kissed her. You slept with her here, she said, in David's bedroom.

When she met Arthur, in graduate school in Ann Arbor, she took him boating in Saginaw Bay (her parents have a cottage at Worth Corners). They skied and hiked in White Cloud—Arthur's neck of the woods. His father took blind people downhill skiing. She'd watch him assist amputees climb in a bucket with outriggers. The blind he skied in front of and told them what they were hearing. That's a gondola, those are trees to your left. It was deeply moving and it made her want to have a piece of him, the son. They both got summer jobs as interpreters at the Henry Ford Museum in Detroit. The Vietnam War made them marry early, but Helen was never in doubt. It wasnt cavalier and, even though she'd been a wild teenager with liberal parents who encouraged her to go to university and not entertain marriage, Helen could think of nothing more correct than marrying Arthur Twombly. She was immediately pregnant and that made them think about raising children in the States. What about Canada. Helen saw everyone as both insecure and entitled. But Arthur Twombly was the opposite: confident and humble.

They felt Canadian already, in that Canadians surrounded them. Michigan is very Canadian. They applied for work all over Canada and she had Zac in Ann Arbor. It was easy then to emigrate, and they received bright pamphlets about small towns in Ontario and British Columbia and Newfoundland. The Newfoundland one was hilarious. The ambition of the government and a colour photograph of the premier holding the five hundred thousandth Newfoundlander in his arms. In front of a new hospital. As if hospitals were factories. The hospital was in Grand Falls.

They went for an interview and landed at the military base of Gander. There was a college in Grand Falls where Arthur could teach classes in English and history. The concierge at the hotel said that Fidel Castro had just spent the weekend. Fidel likes to go rabbit hunting, the man said, handing them their room key. At the interview Arthur asked about that. When Fidel's missing for a few days in Havana, the college administrator said, you can be guaranteed he's here in Grand Falls.

But they had seen nothing as bleak as Grand Falls. It wasnt on the ocean. The trees were spruce and fir, grown for the pulp mills. Perhaps Fidel likes to snowmobile and set snares, but the biblical phrase of seed thrown on arid ground came to mind.

In their hotel room, Helen found an ad in the *Gander Beacon* for a legal position at the air base in Stephenville. She called, made an appointment for Monday afternoon, they rented a car and drove there. That's when they first saw Corner Brook. A fjord, my god the city is built on a fjord. And a mountain range. There were birch trees and hills and the sun shone well even though the city was facing north. Hector Martin at the interview agreed with Helen and said the Appalachians fell into the ocean off Maine and then pulled up again to form the west coast of Newfoundland.

Now she felt like the mountains had fallen into the gulf. Her knees were sinking. She wanted to be the one to collapse, but if they were both on the floor they'd laugh and she wasnt about to let Arthur laugh. She shouted at him for five days. She beat on his neck and a hardness, like a fold of aluminum, rose over her shoulders. Then he'd see her soft and sorry for herself. Once she let him hold her and Arthur knew it would be okay. But then the aluminum rose again and cut through his hands. One day she tore the plug heads out of the power bar, as if the connections made him do it. A chair was thrown and a leg went clean through the drywall. Arthur was afraid to turn his back on her, he saw her coming at him from out of the dark and felt the plunge of a carving knife in his kidneys. Then she recovered, or at least returned to a calm pool, and in that calmness she announced in a dead tone that she was leaving him. I will debit whatever it costs, she said. You'll keep the joint accounts open and filled. The voice was the same instructional tone she used when reminding him to get a haircut. But the new plan was to construct a fork in the river. She was through with the vast promise she had trusted was there. Helen Crofter fell into a hatred for her own amateur romanticism.

Arthur had woken up in his son's bed. Helen was in the doorway. At first it looked like she was forgiving him. But then it was a stare of desperation.

We have beautiful things, she said.

Youre the strongest woman, Arthur Twombly said, I'm ever likely to meet.

She sat on the edge of the bed and stroked her own shoulders. She was trying to encourage herself. Big lives, she said, depend on finding those sorts of women.

Arthur looked beyond rescue. He looked drowned. But what if you ruin them, he said.

You believe too much in the self, Helen said. And governing one's emotions.

And he knew that was true. I tend, he said, to cut losses even when it means severing love.

Neither of them knew if splitting up would help them get over Zac. They both thought probably not.

HELEN WORKED LATE at the office on Main Street. There was much wrangling over jurisdiction of inland coastline and she lost herself in the wrangling. The mill had dams through a chain of lakes, and Helen had secured ninety-nine-year leases on a quarter of the timberlands of the entire island. She needed access to power from the Deer Lake hydro station, and Bowater required laws that were already on the books be observed by cabin owners. Now she was having to visit dams and take photos of the water-level meters for court hearings, to supply evidence of the pulp mill's solid management of the water supply. Building codes were being ignored, she argued, and properties flooded and lawsuits filed when the mill raised or lowered the level of water for its tugs and pulp-log booms.

When she went home she had to turn on the lights just for herself. Sasha wasnt home much these days. She was staying a lot at her boyfriend's. They had agreed that Sasha could do what she wanted. But now Helen wanted her daughter here to make it less lonely. She was in the house where her husband had been sleeping with a student in their dead son's room. She ate a cold leg of chicken with salt. She liked the idea of eating one thing at a time. Richard Text would be back soon. Could she live in the house with Richard. Could she tell him to live somewhere else. Did she need the money for the mortgage. Why was she so unhappy and would moving away help. Her parents in Michigan, what to say. David was coming home for Christmas. My god Christmas, they'd have to tell him.

She went up to Zac's old bedroom and looked at the bed. She saw them there, her husband and Nell, and it bothered her. She was hot to it. She refused to become her husband. That men can do that. She was not impressed with the callous behaviour of men.

She stripped her own bed and looked at the mattress. She decided he at least hadnt been with her here. She tried turning the mattress and the next day she felt a pain in her lower back. She felt like that girl was jumping on her tailbone.

For three weeks Helen worked and grew less happy. She lost nine pounds. A colleague, Lisa Tremblay from Trois-Rivières, was looking for a roommate. If you know of anybody.

Arthur came by to pick up more things.

I dont want to stay in this house, she said.

He hadnt known she was unhappy about the house. She told him about Lisa Tremblay. She could share a house in townsite with Lisa. You can have the house.

Arthur: What about Sasha. What about when David is here.

I can't look at things in the house, she said, it makes my heart too heavy.

How do things spiral into mad behaviour. Arthur called his son to warn him of the separation. Should he come home or just stay in St John's. No, come home. Your mother. We both love you.

David hated the fact that his Christmas was ruined. Sasha was going to her boyfriend's for Christmas, so it would be just him and them. He swam laps at the university pool, and while he was underwater and in the rhythm of the crawl, he understood that he was a little scared of the new situation. He loved going home to the peace of his room for ten days and relaxing out of schoolwork and driving his father's Audi in the snow and seeing his friends who had returned to Corner Brook for the holidays. He realized he was not comfortable in the house alone with his father. They needed his mother as a buffer. They were not used to direct communica-tion. They were both good at talking, but somehow the presence of the other made them feel self-conscious, as if they each knew the tricks the other generated to be convivial. David's mother, they both realized, helped shape themselves around each other, the way Zac used to. They sat at meals and ground out conversation. They were too much like each other.

My parents have split up, he told me. And my father's been having a fling.

David and I had been taking a philosophy course, a course I found very difficult for the dense reading. He said, Youre *reading* the books?

Everything except the introduction, I said. He looked astonished. That's all I read, he said, is prefaces and introductions. And I realized he read short philosophical books like the maxims of Rousseau, Pascal's *Pensées* and the aphorisms of Nietzsche. When he had an argument it was usually coloured by the sayings of whatever philosopher was open on his night table. But he was also good at knowing who had written what, even country songs. Once he heard a singer say he loved "The Gambler" by Kenny Rogers. And David said, quietly, That's not a Kenny Rogers song. Don Schlitz wrote that. Don Schlitz was twenty-four when he wrote it. And then he'd leave the room. There was something anxious in David to succeed early.

David woke me up at three in the morning and we pulled the plugs on several appliances and drove home for Christmas. It was Zac's old blue Matador. David liked to start well before dawn and have the sun come up in your rear-view mirror and arrive in Corner Brook by noon. His calf-skin leather gloves left on the dash to dry. He liked saying to coffee vendors that he was in St John's that morning. The air vents in the dash sprayed out frost.

We fell into a lull, the hypnotic lush of snowflakes in the dark speed-ing past us like we're some spaceship drifting through the spackle of a solar system. The ground we drove over, I now understood its geologic makeup. One of my professors had published the first tectonic map ever made in the world. It was of Newfoundland. The land we were driving over was a mix of North American rock and African rock and the first ocean this world ever had, a precursor to the Atlantic: the Iapetus Ocean. That's what we were driving over now, the world's first ocean. This sense of the past made me conscious of who we were. We were living our brothers' lives. We were in Zac's car. We had grown up in a time when we missed the major cultural events. We had the second-best of things or the sequels to the classics. We watched *Rocky II* and *Grease,* whereas our brothers had seen the original *Rocky* and *Saturday Night Fever*. This sounds trivial but it can affect the level of importance one gives the world. Ali was past his prime so Dave and I settled for other boxers to champion, in the lighter divisions. We followed Salvador Sánchez and Alexis Arguello. We loved the sound of their names, but also the intensity of having to make weight. It was like reading the minor poets, even preferring them to Shakespeare and Donne. David said if he ever had a son he was going to call him Salvador and suddenly this thought of a child hurtled us into the future. This was a time when our future was up for grabs. We still believed in the childhood truth of comic books. We read comics. I had British comics and David had the richer American comics. My grandfather sent the English comics overseas, rolled up, with the hollow of the roll filled with a bunch of red-and-white ballpoint pens. The pens were from Ladbrokes the Bookmakers. And I thought Ladbrokes made books, that my grandfather knew people who produced books. I read of Captain Hurricane who flew into a raging fury, and bullets bounced off his chest. David's DC Comics showcased Sergeant Rock. Rock was lugubrious and ambivalent. He was in colour. David looked at my black-and-white English comics and touched the illustrated panels. As if the whole point of comics was colour. But then a realization struck him, that black-and-white was the best that England could do.

The sun came up just outside of Whitbourne and the world was now coming into colour. David had been forcing the car, pushing it past the range of its headlights. Then a set of legs crossed the highway. The headlights rammed into the legs, a flare of moose, and a body rolled heavily onto the hood and smashed in the windshield and bent the door posts and landed in our laps. It was like someone had thrown a bunch of heavy luggage on us. We had seatbelts on. The impact knocked the light out of me, I couldnt breathe, and I woke up with a policeman shining a flashlight in my face through the passenger window. It was about six in the morning. The back of the moose was across my chest. The policeman was Randy Jacobs. Boys, he said. Boys youre some lucky. David's hands pinned to the steering wheel. He could not get them out from under the moose. It took a winch and a jaws of life to open up the door posts. David's hands all cut up from the windshield glass. That was the end of Zac's car. We got home on the bus.

It was eight oclock at night and my father was standing at the stove, pouring dried milk into his second cup of tea. How'd you get home. And I told him about the accident and the bus. My father looking for David. He was shaken and he stared at me and saw the small cuts in my jacket from the nubs of windshield glass. Then he leaned towards me and hugged me. He said, Son, that boy is trouble.

The dog remembered me, and I stayed in the room that I'd grown up in, in the bunk bed below my brother's. The texture of the masonite panelling and the slats of wood under the mattress above me. There is a prison which is the view from a bed, and this view slung me back into the confines of childhood, and I could handle that for about three days.

SEVEN

IN THOSE DAYS of Christmas I walked around my hometown, amazed that I had grown up here. I was all of eighteen. David borrowed his father's car and we picked up Gwen Hurley and Maggie Pettipaw and walked through the Millbrook Mall. That's where I saw Nell working at the photography shop, and she took my picture. She was getting off shift, and I saw her borrow a snowsuit from a waitress. She must have been pregnant then, though I didnt know it. Nell was taking a ride at night across the bay ice on the back of a snowmobile driven by Joe Hurley, I heard Maggie Pettipaw say this. So Joe was back in town and had called her. The snowmobile was a big purple Arctic Cat with a reverse gear and a heater in the windjammer and a stereo by Joe Hurley's left knee. Even if this is what I am, must I defend it. Even if, does it mean I must dislike it. These are Nell's thoughts. Even if I think it's for the best, perhaps it's not. For instance, Ayn Rand. Perhaps I'm not gutsy enough to know what's best.

Joe Hurley was from St Judes. The Hurleys had built an extension onto their house. And now they were knocking down the house and building an extension onto the extension. Nell was having dinner with Joe in the house wrapped in vapour barrier. His brother, Gerard—who

I went to school with—and the father, the one she'd met in the woods, Loyola.

Back at residence Lori Durdle said to her youre not going home, and couldnt understand it. Youre not staying here by yourself, she said, over the holidays. And she invited Nell to her home in Stephenville. It was flat, an air base, and Lori's father had worked as ground crew for aircraft before he lost his hands in a sheet-metal machine. Mr Durdle played the accordion with his stumps and Nell was given a soft drink with a bottle of rum waved over it and on Christmas morning there was a pair of knit socks and trigger mitts and a toque and they were for her cross-country skiing, Mr Durdle said. They were made with Phentex wool which is not wool at all. A man with no hands had given her mittens. Lori's mother wore a long white cardigan and she made apple pie and those chocolate cookies with mini marshmallows, cookies you kept in the freezer. Mr Durdle played cribbage and in the afternoon his brother came over with his family and they had a turkey for fourteen. In the living room an entire wall was a wallpaper mural of a riverbank in fall with a road beside it. The windows had white sheers and every house around had white vinyl siding. On Boxing Day the air base had a meet-and-greet and they rolled up the hangar door to seven American fighter jets and the pilots let the land crew sit on the wings and they served them cans of Milwaukee beer. These men were being trained to service the space shuttle, for Stephenville was one of three bases in the world on alert for an emergency shuttle landing. They had photos of the shuttle taped above red shelves of tools and, while they fixed and flew jetfighters, they sometimes talked about an afternoon when they might welcome the heavy fuselage gliding in for a quiet landing.

SPRING, THEN SUMMER. In July, just three weeks before her due date, Nell made an appointment with social services. She signed the papers and she did it alone. She had a coldness, or perhaps it was distance. She saw the writing hand and it was not the hand that belonged to her eyes. I will live on no matter what happens to the people around me. A nurse nudged her while she was sitting there signing the paper. The nurse needed a sink to wipe grease off her hand. They were not being respectful. She met the doctor who would deliver the baby, Dr Manamperi. He sat down to talk to her, and as they spoke he took a mango out of his pocket and cut it in half with a scalpel. Then he peeled the mango and he offered some to her. My brother was visiting, he said. He brought these from Chicago.

She ate the mango. Youre not from here, are you, he said. And then he laughed.

This was my way into Canada, he said. Two years in this hospital. And now I've been here five years.

He had been written about in the paper. He had survived a skiing mishap. Dr Manamperi and two colleagues were to spend five days in the woods. His friends were on snowmobile and he was to meet them on skis. He was flown in by a bush plane. They had the frozen pond marked where the plane was to land, and Dr Manamperi would ski all day and meet his friends on another pond thirty miles to the west. They had his supplies. It was a cold bright December morning. He skied all day. He had a topo map in a clear plastic bag strung around his neck. He had an apple and a chunk of cheese and a mango. He was aiming for a knoll on the horizon. And when the sun touched the knoll he stopped skiing and checked his map and looked at the hills around him and the path he'd taken all morning. By four oclock he knew something was wrong. He had been forcing the landscape to agree with his map, but now he knew that he wasnt where he was supposed to be. The men on snowmobiles should be on that knoll, and there were no tracks or any sign of anyone. It was getting dark. He had no matches and no tent. He checked his compass and he skied on until midnight. And now he understood the mistake. The bush plane had dropped him on the wrong pond, though he did not know which one. He did not know where exactly he was. The men could be twenty miles away, but in what direction.

He built a snow wall and slept out of the wind. The stars were bright and very cold but he took the cold. He preferred the cold to the wet. If it warmed up he would be in trouble.

He studied his map. There was a grey line that dropped south of the highway and crossed the lakes. If he made for that line he would intersect it at some point, and then he might find help. He would have to ski for three days to meet the grey line.

He peeled and ate the mango. He pushed snow into his water bottle and melted it in his chest pocket. But it did not melt fast enough so he had to find brooks that were running into the ponds. He skied night and day, resting for an hour every four hours. He was afraid to fall asleep and he hoped it would not get mild and rain on him. He skied towards the grey line, and on the night of the third day he was worried. He had not crossed it. He built his wall and knelt behind it and drank the brook water and ate half of the apple.

Then a light snapped on. A prick of light in front of him. And, in the dying sun, he saw the faint silhouette of transmission lines.

He skied towards the light. It was dark when he got to the hut. He skied up to the door with half an apple in his pocket. He knocked. Then tried the door but it was locked. Then a latch shunted across and the door opened. It was a woman. Hello, he said. My god, she said, come in.

What Helen Crofter saw was a brown face burnt with frost. I'm with the paper mill, she said. And youre lucky I'm here.

There is no luck, he said.

ON A THURSDAY in early August Nell was admitted to Western Memorial Hospital. She gave birth and Dr Manamperi let her hold the baby for a minute. It was a boy. A nurse came back with the sheets she had signed a few weeks before. You havent put down the child's father, the nurse said.

Does it matter, Nell said.

The father's name has to appear on the forms.

So she wrote down a name. She knew that Arthur would be mad at her, so she did not put his name in. She wrote down Joseph Hurley.

Then Dr Manamperi had to check the baby's heart rate and that was all she saw of the child. She lay in bed for three more hours but felt strangely kept. Like someone had used her to have a baby. Yes, she felt used. But they would not let her go. Was it much meconium, I mean we had meconium. Her breathing was elevated. Could be pneumonia. So they left her in the room while two other women had their children and were let go. There were children all over the place and she felt like maybe they were making a point, could she just see her baby once more.

Arthur had been there. He'd been in and out. He suggested a hotel. I didnt want to say anything, he said, but I could hear the doppler going down. The baby's heart rate had been a hundred and forty beats per minute before he was born, now it was dropping below a hundred.

Youve seen the baby.

They told me not to touch him too much, because he was breathing rapidly, more than a breath a second.

Youve got such a warm and cold heart, she said.

She got out of her gown and a nurse helped her dress and the nurses, she realized, were both sympathetic and judgmental. Then Arthur booked her in at the Holiday Inn on West Street. It was the last thing she was expecting to do after she gave birth, was stay in a hotel.

THE HOTEL BECAME WRONG. The same emotion that she'd had at the hospital was visiting her here. She had to be self-reliant. She was packing her bag when there was a knock on the door and she said come in but she had the door on the chain. She went to the open door and it was Joe. There was someone with him further in the hall. She opened the door.

Youre doing okay are you, Joe said. You remember my dad.

It was Loyola with his arms full of shopping bags. He had baby blankets and diapers and bottles and some clothes that still had their price tags on them. He was looking around for the baby. Hello, he said. How's the youngster.

She brought them over to the hospital. This is your family? said the nurse. This is the father, Nell said. They've come to take the baby home.

SHE TOOK THE CITY BUS back to residence and knocked on Lori Durdle's bedroom door but Lori wasnt there, it was August and Lori was back in Stephenville working at the mall. She phoned and Lori's mother said for her to come and visit and she did, she took the bus into Stephenville and she curled up in Lori's narrow bed until she came home from work. Lori made her tea and buttered toast cut into triangles. My god you got more guts than I got, Lori said. The next afternoon Nell heard the soaps on the television and dragged herself out with the blanket and pillow and Lori made her a can of condensed soup and they watched three hours of soaps, eating soup and crackers.

Then Mrs Durdle had the Hurleys on the phone. She was talking to Loyola. It was Joe's baby, that's what the nurses at the hospital were after saying. Mrs Durdle thought Loyola should know about that but Loyola said he already knew and that it was all taken care of and the baby was sitting right there beside him in the bassinet.

Joe Hurley came to visit. He said, Why didnt you tell me. I'm set to go now. I'm all signed up I got no way out.

He was flying to Petawawa for training. My dad and mom, he said, theyre going to take care of Anthony. I mean I had no idea, right? I had a job with Richard and I turned that down. I couldnt see myself in the middle of a continent like in Santa Fe. I want to go overseas. Is that all right with you?

Anthony, she said. You named him Anthony.

ONCE THE BABY WAS GONE she found she couldnt live in Corner Brook. She'd been sending messages to Richard. First it was about Joe Hurley and the baby and then their messages accumulated in emotion and commitment. It was easy to promise things in these computer messages. It felt like souls were talking without the bodies interfering. The good soul. Nell had a good soul, she had just veered into bad behaviour. Richard said she could come down and work for him in Los Alamos. She could have Joe Hurley's job. And while she was independent and free, part of freedom's cliché is being blown by the wind and wind comes from some deliberate force. That's when I saw her again, in this window of being pushed around by many impulses. I was home for the summer working with my father on building houses up on Bliss Street. It was a Sunday morning and I was coming home from a party at Dave's. It must have been about six in the morning, I was cutting past the green side of the Anglican church on West Street. And she was sitting on a park bench with Joe Hurley. They had the baby with them. I noticed Joe because he had a new haircut, he had joined the reservists and his ears were bare and white. They had obviously been arguing but now they were exhausted. Joe Hurley with a little bit of the woods on him, like he might have sawdust in the cuffs of his jeans. And so they made an incongruous pair to be having a baby but at the same time, as soon as you see a couple like that, you make allowances and they both warp into other characters capable of new behaviour and being parents.

That summer I was playing squash with Dave and Dave was using his father's office. We played at the Grenfell gym and I went by to get Dave at the office when I saw Nell again. Her dark shiny hair pulled back tight. She was surprised by us.

I'm the son, Dave said. For he knew who she was, and who she was expecting to see in the office.

It's like expecting someone, Nell said, and then seeing them as they were twenty years before.

I'm borrowing the office, Dave said, to be close to the library. My father is in a card shop. He likes to read cards.

It had never occurred to her. But the son was her age. He was studying in St John's.

Dave knew who she was but he did not know that Nell would affect him. Then he became cool with himself and then the coolness was displaced by activity in his eyes. Dave was a charmer and he found himself overtly flirting and was outraged at his flaunting of taboo. I am defiant, he said to me once. But I'm drawn and there is something in her that is drawn to me, too.

He felt her attraction to his father was something they shared, and that perhaps Arthur Twombly was the bridge to their meeting. After she left he said to me, She's only interesting because of the relationship with my father.

She had looked preoccupied. A woman talking to Dave in his father's office. Nell had gone through something serious and hard. She was alert with anxiety and doubt. And she turned to walk away and saw me. I was part of a plan to trap her in the hallway and kill her in that room. It was a thought she pressed into me by the look she gave me. An animal look of fear. I didnt know Nell would affect me either.

THAT SUMMER was my last with Dave. He moved to Montreal and began a degree at McGill and I continued on with my studies in St John's and, for a while, forgot about Dave Twombly and Nell Tarkington. There is no will, there is reaction and a column of choices that men, usually, have listed down for you. Nell wasnt creating her own list out of the blue. Richard asked her to come down. That's how she ended up accepting a registered letter with a one-way airline ticket in it. All the men she'd been with understood and forgave her. Is this a disturbed past.

TWO

ONE

DAVE LEFT NEWFOUNDLAND and moved to Montreal. He was working part-time on his tech business, and then McGill received him. I did not lay eyes on him again for fifteen years. During those years I lived in St John's and finished a degree in economic geography. That's the study of what gets built where, and why. I worked as a city planner. I worked on horizontal infrastructure: cloverleaf highway junctions, sewer systems. I saw plans for road design and, in one instance, we were brought in as consultants on the new bypass for Corner Brook. It cost ninety-four million dollars and when it was completed transport trucks could not make the turn and angle of ascent. They had to tear it all out and redo it and eventually they ruined the view from the highway of the entire bay.

City planning. I was following the practical road of making a living, but even here there was a man who wrote plays. A city planner, Arvo McMillan, wrote about a gorilla in Argentina. I went to see it at the LSPU Hall and realized St John's had a downtown. It was artistic. There were people I liked and I took a few courses in creative writing and began, at night, to write stories.

St John's was my kind of town. Dave, I understood, did not quite fit
in. He was oriented to money and that looked aggressive. He was looked
upon as a typical Corner Brooker. Not the raw poor of the outports but
the new money offered by Canada. The western shore of Newfoundland
was seen, by those in the east, to be dipped in the national blood. David
represented the Canadianization of Newfoundland.

But I enjoyed myself with my artistic friends. This is how that slow
conversion began. I was researching a paper on road salt. I looked up,
in the card catalogues at the QEII Library, the usage of salt on roads.
I flipped for a SALT header in the alphabetical drawers of the card cata-
logue and came across "Saltus, Edgar *A Transient Guest* a novel." Then I
searched through the TRANS drawer for Transportation Canada's role
in road salt management. And this card appeared: "*A Transient Guest,* a
novel by Edgar Saltus."

I took down the call number and went up into the stacks. The book
was small. I sat on the carpet in the stacks and read the first page:

Since the *Koenig Wilhelm,* of the Dutch East India Service, left
Batavia, the sky had been torpidly blue, that suffocating indigo which
seems so neighbourly that the traveller fancies were he a trifle taller
he could touch it with the ferule of his stick. When night came, the
stars would issue from their ambush and stab it through and through,
but the glittering cicatrices which they made left it bluer even, more
persistent than before. And now, as the ship entered the harbour,
there was a cruelty about it that exulted and defied.

Because of this book I gave up economic geography. I remember my
last day at city planning. A man arrived. He said he heard there was a
photocopier. I showed him to it. He looked at it. I left him alone, but
I did not hear it working. He was staring at the top of the machine. How
do you use it, he said. I lifted the lid and put his original down on the

glass and pressed the button and the green light tracked across our eyes. The copy peeled out and he was astonished. He was one of those old-time Newfoundlanders. He had never seen a copy before. He thought there was printing involved, some kind of pressure. He knew nothing of the new age.

I took some time off and went travelling. I was finding myself. That winter, about two hundred Bulgarians had sought refugee status at Gander. Their plane was refuelling on their way to Cuba. So I thought I'd go to Bulgaria. Then I headed south to Greece and ended up on Crete. I like islands. I visited Nikos Kazantzakis's grave in Heraklion and read *Report to Greco* out loud. I stayed in a youth hostel in Mirthios and traded *Report to Greco* for one on the table by the woodstove. It was a book called *House of Hate*. It was a Canadian novel, I could tell from the cover, and then I was surprised to see that it was set in Corner Brook. The first line: Hate is the child of fear, and Saul Stone had been afraid of one thing or another all his life.

No one had told me about this book. I was stunned by it. It was a Corner Brook from a generation before my own, but I understood the sense of it. And what's more, it made me realize I could write about my life. I did not have to be fanciful like Edgar Saltus.

I wrote short stories and then two novels. During this, because of my degree, I was hired by the federal government to track natural gas inventories in underground storage facilities across the country. It was mind-numbing work, but I'm dogged and I was afraid to live without money and I was frugal and saved, and I managed, during periods of downtime, to write sneakily. I met other young writers and we encouraged each other to publish. I dont think it would have occurred to me to publish without these people—St John's is like that. If you feel alternative at all, you'll end up writing a book or making a small film.

Although I barely saw Dave during those fifteen years, we wrote letters. They were handwritten letters and then they were typed and finally, during the past few years, we went to email. They were like the letters we had sent to Allegra Campinghorst in Montreal. He was delighted that I wrote books. He said that was the reason he'd been friendly to me as kids—he knew I had the artistic temperament. He also insisted that any money I had I should sink into the stock market and he advised me on many high-tech companies and then told me, during the crucial spring of the early nineties, to sell it all quickly at market price and I did and, while I missed the final crest of new highs, I was one of the few to avoid the east slope of the Nasdaq bubble.

When a relationship broke down I left the province and moved to Toronto. Most people are hemmed in by the country they live in. In Canada, if youre through with a mid-sized city, then the only options are to go rural and raise animals or move to Toronto. Montreal, perhaps, is the exception. Montreal was where Dave had gone. But for me, I wanted Toronto. I was thirty-five and I thought to change my life. On the plane, as I recall, I thought of the word *suddenly*. If you looked at the coat of my skin you'd see it slightly shirred. I was ruffled and drove with the wind and I lived hard and light at the same time. I did damage to myself but I also opened up and became less narrow-minded and as long as I did not break down too badly the wildness was for the good. I often thought of what Dave would do, the Dave I knew before his brother was killed. But it wasnt all pretending to be Dave. Part of it can be chalked up to being in your thirties and needing to widen out.

I had bought a one-way air ticket to Toronto and vowed to act the opposite of the way I had acted back home. I had a month to find a place but apartments were tight. I was lining up with seventeen other candidates in hot, cramped bachelors and filling in forms with too much financial information, then bicycling home on a French bicycle I'd bought for fifty dollars, coasting behind propane-fuelled taxis and waiting for a landlord to call. I had a buffer of money and I was not interested in writing or in doing anything to make money. I had enough to live for a year like this, but I had no work, which appeared desperate, and both my references were in Newfoundland. Natural gas, and all liquids, had turned into a steady bearish stream for a decade now and there was no work in the oil patch or in commodities generally. But I was not worried about money, though I did not want to throw a lot of money at rent. It looked like I was going to share a house with three other men who were attending Ryerson, and I was imagining that, how we would move around the house, when the phone call came from Dave Twombly.

Dave, I said.

So when were you going to call me.

And I wondered about that. If I'd ever call Dave. Why hadnt I. And I guess I was embarrassed with myself. I didnt want him to see me in the state I was in. I was broken-hearted and, while I'd written fiction, I thought I wouldnt write again. I was beside myself and I mean that literally: I was sitting next to the shell of the person who walked around and lived. For one thing, I'd written about people close to me and, in small, unforeseeable ways, at least unforeseeable to me, I had hurt them. My brother, for instance, had written me a letter. He said if I wrote about him again, he would deliver a punch to my head from which I may not recover.

Dave gave a light high chuckle when he heard that. And then he grew earnest. Call me David, he said, and I knew that was a clue to his new life. In Toronto he wasnt Dave any more, he was David, and this cheered me. Hurrah to the new life. He'd heard I was in Toronto through people in Corner Brook. You need an apartment, he said. I can get you that.

And sure enough, in three days I had a place. It was from a friend of his who was in Italy downsizing a billing company that was merging with twenty-one other billing companies throughout the new Europe. This man, who I still havent met, was overseeing the transition. That's all I knew of him. And the books he'd left behind, which were on Vietnam and the history of the machine gun.

That was how David Twombly came back into my life, from his act of generosity in helping an old friend. It had been fifteen years. His face had widened and his shirts had lavish collars. He had shaved his head.

Youre the only man I know now, I said, from Corner Brook.

And I called him David. In the end, why should we be troubled by a man's attempt to be an adult. I liked people who called me Gabriel rather than Gabe. Though I enjoyed collecting both sets of people. My father calls me Gabe, my mother, Gabriel.

The truth of it is, I saw that David could live with or without me. If I was close by he knew he could enjoy himself with me and there was something alluring about reclaiming a piece of the past, brushing it off and seeing it trot around the infield of the game youre trying to set up.

We got together at his house and I met his wife, Sok Hoon, and their new baby, Owen. David called him the Oven, because he was so hot and he ate a lot. He said, Are you still in treasury bills and bonds.

I told him about my hiatus and the buffer and yes, the buffer was in cash accounts. He did not look like a man who needed money, and I must have said this using my face.

He said his company was going public and I should get in. His company was called Itinerant Knowledge Workers.

I had spent years choosing options that were anti–Corner Brook, so the thought of returning to some material that was laden with Corner Brook appealed to me, especially a revitalized spinoff of Corner Brook that seemed complicated and international. For instance, David's shaved head was a new unfolding of the possibilities of a Corner Brook childhood. That his wife was Chinese-Canadian seemed an event that could only have happened in the twenty-first century. This all was now part of the Corner Brook experience, for we had grown past the notion that place is confined to geography. David had met Sok Hoon at McGill and it was during McGill that the hockey players had begun shaving their receding hairlines, and so he did too. These, the simple answers to almost everyone's complex scenario. And now they had a baby boy, Owen the Oven, and were living in Little Italy.

Sok Hoon I liked—she was a fashion designer who made eco-friendly textiles, fabrics of the future, she called them. She used a lot of high-end cloth, premium fabrics that felt like the pelts of extinct animals. And Sok Hoon knew how to handle her husband's friend with the wounded heart. But there was more to it than that, no mere one-sided empathy: for I was from the small milltown where her husband grew up, and there is something about Newfoundland that perplexes foreigners to that heritage. There are a handful of places like Newfoundland on this continent, I suppose—the American South, the Arctic, Quebec, and the Appalachians. She turned to me often, after David had remarked on something, as though I might provide a bilingual service. Even though what David had said was a result, not of any Newfoundland upbringing—for his parents were American—but more to do with his own character and bias, a position that far exceeded any influence Newfoundland could weigh upon him.

During these early Toronto years is when I went a little crazy. A new city and a broken heart and a nest egg will do this to you. My father, from a distance, grew worried. I got a call one day from Lars Pony, the father of Lennox, the black kid who had hung around with us in Corner Brook. Mr Pony, who was living in Toronto, was asking if I needed a job. He worked for a magazine that sold second-hand cars. He said I heard you can write. This made me laugh. How's Lennox? I said. Lennox is in Alberta, Mr Pony said. And he did not sound happy with his son that far from him. So they had sold the Lemon Yard and moved to Toronto.

I went and had a coffee with him. I told him that I didnt need a job at the moment, but thank you. Lars Pony is a tall man, and he had been the only black man I'd known in Corner Brook. Not that I knew him, just his son Lennox. Lars told me his father had been in the navy. His father was stationed out of Boston. During the war the black enlisted men were segregated. They ate and slept in separate quarters. Their cruiser was torpedoed one night in the Atlantic. They were seventeen nautical miles off the south coast of Newfoundland. They sent out a beacon and steamed for land. They threw over green lifeboats and his father found a vest. He hit the water and that's all he can remember of what happened that night.

My father woke up, Lars said, and he heard a woman saying, I can't get it off his skin—no matter how hard I scrub it won't come out. He was in a big room with nurses, these white nurses bathing the men. He was naked. This white woman cleaning his arms and legs. He said, It won't come off. That's my skin.

He spent three weeks in Newfoundland convalescing. He had never experienced such care from white people. No one seemed to mind that he was black.

My father, Lars said, told me that story often when I was young. To let me know that whites arent all bad. So when I got to leave home, one of the places I wanted to go was Newfoundland. I ended up on a paper boat that docked in Corner Brook. And I swam ashore. I worked in a meal plant in Benoit's Cove. Then I met Lennox's mother.

They live now in Regent Park, in Toronto. Lars and his Newfoundland wife. Did she ever think she'd live away from home.

DAVID HELPED PUSH ME through my crazy days, for it was a phase, anyone could see that, though phases can last decades. He arranged dates with women. He took me to extravagant parties. This, too, is how

Newfoundlanders take care of one another in the larger world, which they claim to be pan-Newfoundland, or at least their minority interest in a stock they cannot fully control but which listens to them intently during the annual shareholders meeting. David had found me an apartment, then invested my money wisely. Now he was grooming me for a woman he thought would be good for me.

I thought, let it roll. I invested the socked-away money in David's company. I kept telling women, using mainly body language and tone of voice, about how my heart was played out, how I wasnt suitable for commitment. I thought that would be the state of things, and it wasnt all bad. Though I was turning into someone who enjoys being alone. It takes all kinds, but I wasnt sure I wanted to be that kind. David was vexed. Over long dinners in his red leather dining room chairs, eating pears and hard cheese and British chocolates, I told him I couldnt commit, and he lectured me on the merits of a long-term relationship and having children. Owen, he said. Reason for being. But I wasnt ready for monogamy and neither did I think I'd find anyone. Monogamy, he said. Who's talking monogamy? And then, in a voice piped in from a third lung: You have a lover on the side, he said. This, on the occasions when Sok Hoon was in Malaysia or in the next room with music dampening our voices. I looked at his big hands and then his shaved head. He had a life on the seat beside him.

Me: The same woman?

It's marvellous, he said.

But he would not get into it.

David began introducing me to single women he thought I could have kids with. These were different women from the ones he'd chosen for my cavalier days. It was superior of him—he had shucked the moroseness of his brother's death, even though his father had not forgiven him, and now he wanted everyone to be living his life. His intentions were generous: He loved his life. He wore short-sleeved shirts and he looked good in them. His forearms. He had good healthy forearms and a platinum watch that sat nicely on the hair at his wrist. There was a confidence there. I could never pull that off. If I was meeting someone for a deal I'd wear a long-sleeved shirt. A short one would be like wearing sandals. Too vulnerable. But I saw David cut a lot of deals in sandals.

Youve developed a small pocket of acting that isnt entirely untrue, David said, diagnosing me. You can get away for thirty-six months, he said, with a line about an exhausted heart. But that's it, youve run out your line of credit.

I bought a used car that my brother had chosen long-distance over the phone, and I drove it home to Newfoundland. I lived in St John's during the summer, subletting a house on Signal Hill that has a garden and the earliest postal code in Canada: A1A 1A1. You can taste the salt water in the arugula leaves and at night the lighthouse strobe from Cape Spear flares over the Atlantic. I hung out with my old friends and their growing families and I hunted big game. At the end of summer I drove the car to my brother's and I flew back to Toronto with two styrofoam boxes full of frozen caribou. My brother sold the car and we split the profit. I did this, with little variation, for three revolutions of the sun.

TWO

THEN THE SHARE PRICE in David's company doubled. I sold half and
the remaining half tripled. I was trying to figure out what to do with the
money, but it was hard for me to be frivolous and so I banked the money
in the general coffers. Then I thought it was wrong, somehow, to be
paying the rent and buying food with windfalls. I decided to write again,
but this time it wouldnt be fiction. I did not want to be cutting edge.
I wanted something old fashioned, and it was not out of a desire to
resuscitate a dying art. In ways I've always been drawn to the arts that
are extinct rather than the methods that are avant-garde. I thought about
what my ideal job would be and it came to me that copywriting was the
most humble of writing jobs. I would love to write for a TV guide,
someone who writes out the synopses for television programs. I did
not own a television, which made the enterprise all the more beguiling.
So I walked down to the local cable network and asked for a position. But
that sort of go-between job doesnt exist any more, they just format what
the stations feed to them, a receptionist told me, which meant working
for a television network in Buffalo, and I have my limits. Then, when I left
their studios on Queen Street, I passed the newspaper vending boxes

and looked at them and noticed the free weekly guide called *Auto Trader*.
I flicked through one and realized, under the masthead, that it was the
magazine that Lars Pony worked for. People's cars. Why did people sell
cars, why did people buy them. I looked around at the busy network of
commerce and gridlock. There was something in this, something that
reflected the changing fortunes of a populace. I took the magazine home
and looked at it again at my desk. I stared at it intently, as though it were
a work of art. I looked at the column of names of who worked at *Auto
Trader*. Tessa Walcott web design. Lars Pony photographs. You dont see a
name like Lars Pony very often, not in print, and there he was, Mr Pony
of Corner Brook, whose father had learned the magnanimity of the
innocent. Lars had operated a salvage yard, his son managed the severe
torment we all gave him, though Lennox was a good goalie. My father
knew Lars and liked the Ponys. So I contacted *Auto Trader*. I talked to
the woman named Tessa Walcott. I told her my skills and I explained
that I knew Lars Pony from when I was a kid. That Lars had called me
some months before. I went in and met them. How is Lennox, I said
again. And this time Mr Pony looked prouder. His son was in the oil
patch. He was one of those Newfoundlanders who had gone west to
Fort McMurray. There were more Newfoundlanders there than in
Corner Brook. You want a job, he said, you got a job.

   And so I wrote captions that accompanied the vehicles. I was good at
it. They liked the adjectives I employed and the narrative voice. I turned
every car into a little story. It was like an orphanage, this magazine, and
it advertised the love you could receive from a loyal vehicle. I felt it was
a creative output that was humble and I enjoyed being sneaky with
language and wondered if anyone would notice.

   Lars worked at the magazine during the day and picked up an extra
two hundred a night teaching a photography course. And during the fall
he persuaded me to take the course. Again, photography, in the age of the

internet, seemed like a practice from a previous century, like copywriting, so I took to it. And Lars liked me, he humoured my penchant for old-fashioned things. Sometimes we walked home together. Then I saw him at the Y bench-pressing fifty kilos. I used to work weights with David back in high school. So I spotted him. He asked if I was any good at basketball. They had a pick-up game. I told him how Lennox, much younger than me, was picked before I was for sports. Lars was now in his late fifties and played guard. Once, about thirty-five years ago, he'd had a ten-day contract with the Indiana Pacers. This was before he'd ended up in Corner Brook. It was his last attempt to live an American life. Did we know this story about Lennox's father? So I played with him—I was the only white man on four teams of five. We played ten-minute games and Lars took me on as a project. What if you came with me, he said. I take the pictures and you do the interview.

I was spotting him and he strained with the weights and popped open his eyes as his elbows straightened out. And in this way a column was born in *Auto Trader*. A sort of day-in-the-life of a vehicle owner. Lars snapped pictures of light trucks, classic cars, boats, bikes and RVs. It's a good way to get to know a new city. I told David Twombly about Lars and he remembered Lennox and I suggested he should have Mr Pony over. That never happened. Somehow Lars Pony was not the person David wanted over. I realized there was a limit to David. That I represented some kind of artistic talent that he wanted to foster, but Lars Pony was a dead end, literally the scrap heap of civilization. I took it as a failing in David, but not something to argue about. I felt lucky that I could be happy with both ends of modern western living. I felt it vaguely important to know a black man. But David had this desire as well, he had gone to school at McGill partly so he could study French. For him, diversity in information was important for personal growth.

Lars lived in a block apartment in Regent Park. His wife was a
Guinchard from Frenchman's Cove, she wore a trucker's cap with a
pompom on it. I realized I'd never met her in Corner Brook. And then,
one day last spring, Lars said he was leaving soon, moving to Montreal
where his wife wanted to live. He told me this as we sat in a cafeteria
eating German sausages. His legs bent so deeply that his knees almost
touched the floor. You should come on board, he said, as a shadow. And
take the pictures.

Under Lars Pony's tutelage I've shot cottages and all-terrain vehicles,
sleds and heavy equipment, using a digital camera, of course. I felt I had
begun a new segment of life and it's true that since I'd turned thirty-five
I had begun to note that a life can be captured in seven-year intervals. But
the past kept hauling into view.

For instance, David Twombly.

The rise in our relationship reached a crest and then continued on in
a flat line, not increasing or decreasing in volume or activity. Perhaps
there was only so much we had in common. We got together to drink.
I was his legacy of artistic promise, but for how long could a connection
be maintained based on a legacy? Especially since I'd surrendered to the
fiction censor. I'd come to that convergence of talent and critical eye
that stymies creation, that tells you most work is mediocre and so is
your own, and why bother foisting it on a public when wiser, funnier
and more dramatic examples of contemporary realism exist.

David invited me to house parties, grand affairs full of guests carrying
passports. There were caterers in his kitchen and then stacks of white
Italian plates that were handed around the circle and bright large cutlery
rolled in powder blue napkins. We were to eat sitting where we could sit,
with a shiny grilled scallop the size of a baseball sliced in half. And then
a platter of carved beef that looked like chocolate, a chocolate filled with
pink rhubarb. So it was like camp although I was alarmed to see that I was

the only one wearing jeans. I sat between a woman who could not explain the work she did and a man who made synthesizers involved in speech recognition. His wife, he said, was at home. She was an artist. She made chocolate using a bicycle.

That's where I saw her—at a catered party celebrating Sok Hoon's birthday, where it was hard to count your drinks. Waiters kept filling your glass. There was dancing and through the dancing I noticed the movements of her body. You should trust how you react to a woman's body. A bit of her jocularly cut dark hair and her sleeveless arm, her arm that kept darting in the air and then she pushed back to laugh. Watching her was like peering through a fence. A moving fence, or I was moving.

David barrelled into me. He was all hugs and leaning on my shoulder. Who is that, I said.

You dont remember Nell.

His voice was both grave and delicious.

I know her?

A long long time ago, he said in a songish voice.

And I knew he wasnt going to tell me. So I said, You got rid of the furniture.

David: Sold it. Every last stick.

Me: Times are tough.

Sok Hoon is leaving me.

I took a cracker and dipped it into olive paste and as I ate the cracker I thought of David without Sok Hoon. I realized I'd held a hunch that she was going to leave him, or at least should leave him. I'm not a diehard stay-together type of person. And Sok Hoon was smothered by David. Even her birthday was more about David's lavishness at presenting her with organized love. She wasnt rash, either—her wisdom was perhaps superior to both mine and David's. I also felt that David was strong enough to get through this, that in fact he might enjoy her departure. I wasnt upset or thinking I should help him. In fact I was looking at the dancers. I thought of Owen. And I knew that this might be David's last house party. It was early summer, there were crocuses.

Nell's the one, he said, who had the affair with my father.

Nell, I said. Nell Tarkington.

David was saying that this woman who had caught my eye, this Nell, who had seemed to be someone who might be from a country with a name like Formosa, had come to Corner Brook to study and ended up breaking his parents apart. It seemed improbable and yet not unlikely either that lives you know a little about, or have affected friends in the past, might flare over one's own life in the future. I knew in my bones that this was the type of woman I could enjoy—in a sense it was like revisiting that old printout of my face, a face I once knew. I wasnt happy with strangers or people who did not know me when I was young. It was the appeal, I realized, of Lars Pony. And part of the reason I wasted talented women in Toronto was I needed a woman who knew something of my past from her own experience. What an odd realization. Nell Tarkington. She was just there, dancing with a handsome man who was too well dressed to be attractive. Nell, if I spoke to her, would know of the things I speak. A fantasy thought, yes, but real nonetheless. And I felt I was in one of those moments where the tectonic plates of life's deci- sions move over each other like platters of cake in a revolving glass cabinet. I could get together with this woman, I thought. If I tried very hard. Why not be wilful? She was dancing with a man who looked like he wanted to enjoy her.

Me: Is she with that one?

That one, David said, works for United Architects.

United Architects, I said, in a tone that meant nothing to me.

They were the ones, David explained, with those fabulous towers for New York.

Me: The ones that were never built.

We all liked that design.

It had bent knees, I said. It looked like five people needing to pee.

I would have to break the bond of the hands of that man. He had big hands for a man who worked on a keyboard. As I considered his genetic gift I felt my mouth crack in half, as if my skull had split open and I reeled back with the shock and my tongue collected a tooth, I spat out a tooth and it was black, the nub of a black tooth and of course I had a mouth cancer, I was doomed. My life was over and it was a good life. I'm an easy man to give up the spirit.

David held up my black tooth. An olive pit, he said.

I wanted to drive someone in the liver, but thank god. Then David said, They are wearing bras that turn tits into tennis balls.

His voice altered the focus in my eyes. No, it was the tears from the pain of cracking my tooth on an olive pit. She was gone now. A woman was disappearing and my head was full of a blurry David Twombly. He added more information: Sok Hoon was taking their son, Owen, and going to live in Montreal.

I'm sorry Dave I'm dying here. I just broke a tooth.

Which did not seem to Dave like I was helping him. I guess he noticed me wiping my eyes and rubbing my jaw. Can I be myself with you, he said.

I assured him he could.

He said, They are shaving. The young ones are shaving everything off.

He was ignoring me and so I left him to feel sorry for himself. I searched for a mirror to check out my injury. I needed to spit in a sink and then find Nell. In this way I was not there for David Twombly. I did not notice, really, that Sok Hoon and David were at opposite ends of a photograph of a road disappearing to the horizon. David was in the deep background, chained into the landscape, whereas Sok Hoon had every choice available to her. She was busting out of the frame.

I ventured upstairs to find an available bathroom. I passed the two framed maps David loved, one of Manhattan and the other of Glover Island. They were the same size, these islands, twenty miles long and two miles broad. One with the most densely populated real estate on the continent, the other where not a soul lived.

In the mirror I checked my mouth and all seemed sturdy. I swivelled a flank of mirror to light up my molars. A prescription bottle on the shelf behind and I picked it up and read that it was an antidepressant. Sok Hoon, I thought, but then saw the name. Which was another surprise and yet it is hard to remain forever surprised. Once a shock is received we get used to it.

I scanned about for Nell again. For her mirthful hair. And I realized then that I had created a fanciful projection, using my Wyoming, which is a little game I play with myself. The inner self unspools and I catch that self taking over my body.

My mouth was ginger, the tooth felt both nervous and solid. I returned with drinks. And there was Nell, bending her knee at the side of David's leg, a leg I now realized was artificially exuberant, staving off a desire to lie down and be depressed.

She's looking for a place to live, David said. I was thinking you.

Yes, Nell said. You were the squash buddy.

Me: You walked up to me in the cafeteria once and sat with me and said why do you look like youve just gotten out of bed.

Yes, she said, that was my way of flirting.

Isnt it strange, David said, the way the world touches back on itself.

Nell's eyes narrowed as she tried to see me, almost eighteen years ago, walking through Corner Brook. Eighteen years—it was part of a larger realization we'd all been having that we were now of an age where peers were grand enough to have huge backstories. There was something enjoyable in our wonky connection, and we live in a time when all sorts of coincidences are celebrated. The past is pushed into our eyes.

She was working for IKW and needed someplace to stay. A sublet for the summer would be ideal. We went out to the dark garden and a joint was passed around, rolled in a paper that had a wire in it, so you could bend down the wire as a roach clip. Her mouth had these little folds on either side of it that indicated she was a happy person. Nell liked to laugh. The light from the party seemed to make the green shoots of perennials glow, and there were many of them, like an audience in a dark theatre. Then I was left alone with Nell. Something moved in behind a dark shrub—David's old dog, Wolf, was arranging foliage with his nose. I might have done the same. It was a warm night.

I looked at Nell's face as she watched Wolf and I remembered the few times I'd seen her from such a long time ago. I realized she had the same face, she hadnt changed. She had made an impression and yet I had not thought of her in all the years since. Behind us the buzz of the party, a kitchen chair pulled out as if clearing its throat, the intense recessed lighting, a slice of another room down the yellow hall, the bend of a woman's elbow in the front porch, collecting a light jacket. If you blasted through that elbow, you'd see the open door, guests rummaging for keys, the quarter panel of David Twombly's hearty Land Rover—the car Sok Hoon would load up and buckle Owen into and drive to Montreal leaving David with the dog, a dog that will have to be put down in six months, and then a deep funnel of night (David's Toronto house is on a corner), and far away, perhaps a thousand feet down, a red and silver Dundas streetcar slips across an intersection, so sly and distant you could believe it was an inner gear of clockwork shifting, some packed-in-grease mechanism to allow the course of events to be manipulated, if you were prone to believing the world was a contrived stage propped up to make you think all stimuli were natural. I was, of course, slightly stoned.

You had a job, I said, at the mall in Corner Brook at a photo developing shop.

That was my first real job.

I passed by and you reeled me in with your finger. Stand there, you
said. Just there. And you took a picture of me with a machine on a table.

That was the second method I had for flirting.

The machine had hummed and out of a dot matrix printer unpeeled a
sheet with my picture, a pixelated image in black and white, it was as if
someone had made my face on a typewriter. I still have it.

I could feel the heat off her face. We stared out into the harder night
and I knew now that no one was left inside except for the caterers and
David and Sok Hoon. Sok Hoon was probably in bed. Someone had
turned up the music, it was religious music. Nell was in Toronto after
leaving Richard Text, she said, her husband in Santa Fe. I was going home
to St John's for the summer and I was wondering about that. I could
sense the profile of Nell's face in the periphery. Very quickly, a few clouds
converged and caused a short, tremendous thunder that made the dog
afraid.

Do you want to change anything, Nell said.

I turned and faced her. I think, every day, about Leonard Woolf's
caveat about his wife's journals—that Virginia was happy and fun loving,
but only wrote in her diary when she was depressed.

Youre a loving person, she said.

She was filling me up. She was pouring fuel into me. Do you want to
see a sublet, I said.

And we walked out of David's, which was empty now except for the
three caterers stacking their stainless steel tureens in crates and collecting wine glasses upside down between their fingers. David was in the
front room, alone, with the stereo cranked to nine. He was listening
to Mahalia Jackson. David was the least religious person I knew, but in

the dark hours he was devoted to Mahalia Jackson, a woman who refused to sing anything but gospel. We left him to Mahalia, he was in good hands, and we took a cab over to my apartment. We could still hear the music when I closed the cab door and the massive chassis jerked away from the curb.

THREE

Thanks for having me over.

Youre welcome.

That was nice.

I like doing nice things.

It's a nice apartment.

We stared at the dark ceiling and Nell held me with an affection I knew belonged to couples who have been together a long time.

Nell: You lead a sort of retro life.

I believe, I said, the past is coming back.

This is your fault, Nell said, and tomorrow morning it's still going to be your fault.

The dimple in the nails of her thumbs, something she said only women get. I was holding both of her hands like they were a pair of leather gloves.

So are you happy enough, I said. Just to bump into each other like this.

She thought about that. I was glad to know she could think about it. It was giving my question the correct amount of consideration. Nell Tarkington was honest and could not be criticized.

Me: Because I'll be coming back in a few months.

I dont think, Nell said, I'm capable of anything more.

Yeah.

She nudged her nose into my neck. Because.

Yeah I know. I'm just gonna lie here a bit more and pretend we love each other.

For some reason the immense loneliness of the world had descended upon us, and we were little animals that had found shelter, but a shelter neither of us thought could last. We lay there and she looked at her watch. I should be going, she said.

If you want there's a couch. I mean, I could sleep on the couch.

She thought about that and said she wouldnt put me out, that she would sleep on the couch. I thought of her asleep there. In the morning light. When youre in your thirties you get to say things like this. Cavalier, risky, betting on the final loves possible, or loves that might have enough long haul in them for you to be old and witness opinions melt and grow with time. Nell was a good woman. She was sexy and funny and smart. She knew two and a half languages.

I got up and rinsed out the percolator and let the water run and brushed my teeth. I made coffee.

I'm going to make like a dog, I said, and fetch the paper.

Okay, she said.

She said okay into my pillow on the couch. My god she is so comfortable there. She is no trouble.

I almost fell down the stairs. It would have killed me. The paper and eggs and some bread. I did this purchase with the film of the night before stretched over my skin. I was veneered in the debauch and the tension of seeing Nell Tarkington, a woman who had been David's father's lover. I shunted back to the apartment with the resignation of a hangover. It was not a good life, but all other lives were worse.

The percolator wheezed and Nell would not eat a poached egg, just some jam on the toast. We shared the paper and she didnt like doing things like this, sharing the paper over toast, because she felt so many people in big cities—she couldnt do it without feeling the cliché. It was the notion of an aftermath. What one is left with. The action of the night before was marvellous, it was muscular and eventful and she loved being witnessed and interesting. But this is what it got her. A morning with a man she could not love, winding up the ritual with coffee and the paper. But I was no cliché. I refused it as well. I was in the same boat and had as much experience of these moments as she did. So that was interesting. I put no pressure on her. It wasnt my acquiescing to her unspoken wish, I wanted her to go.

Nell was putting on her top. She whipped her head forward to bare her neck and tie the top behind her neck, with a shoelace bow. Thick black hair, that she ties back. Neither of us says I love you, but we both see it heavy in our eyes, though a flexing in the eyebrow says this is ridiculous. I mean, one night.

I didnt even say I'll call you. She put on her wool coat, the kind of wool they wear in warm countries, and kissed me. She was mature and knew all about me. She was through in her life with wasting years on reluctant men.

I ATE SOME LEFTOVER MEAT and then the phone rang. It was Nell, and so I said Hey! as if I hadnt heard from her in a hundred years. She had gone to work and then located my crumpled number in her pocket. Yes the apartment, I sublet it while I'm in Newfoundland. Okay, she said, I'll come and look at it.

Havent you seen it.

I wasnt paying that much attention to the apartment. And what I'm saying is, you should invite me to lunch.

And in twenty minutes she was inside my apartment again.

She said, You moved the table.

What are you a detective?

I have forensic training.

I like to shift things around. I showed her the leather chair and how, if you sit in it and then get up, it talks to you. See, I said, what did it say.

Nell: It said, How about a tuna sandwich.

We ate and I told her how I had come to Toronto after having my heart broken.

Sometimes, Nell said, I like to throw myself against the fridge in false tears. When a man is watching. For instance that man I was with last night.

The man from United Architects.

But if I'm on my own, she said, I'll sit there, my knees touching, and stare at the edge of a chair.

That is when she told me about her walk home that morning. She had strolled along the inside routes to back-yard garages, thinking about her husband, Richard Text, and her new date from United Architects. Brainy men, she said. She followed the interior small streets until they spilled onto Queen Street and hailed a cab. She found the hotel IKW was paying for and took the stairs to cry unabashedly, almost joyously, on her made bed.

Youre working with David, I said.

Toronto feels like a lonely city, she said.

She told me about her last goodbye to her husband. She was a woman who had a box of tissues in every room. Then she realized I might know Richard Text. For she had met him in Corner Brook.

Nell: He was the computer instructor.

Yes, I said. I might have met him. Or seen him in the halls. I was only there for the one term.

They had married, she said, to help each other out. It was profession-
ally important for him to be married, and it was her way into the States.

She had not spoken to Richard Text in three weeks. Would it hurt him
to see her with someone.

We werent that kind of couple, she said. As I've tried to point out, it
was a marriage of convenience.

Which meant a lot of things in my mind, but it did not seem appro-
priate to press her to be exact.

You didnt fight over having a child.

I have a child, she said. I had a child when I was eighteen.

And I remembered, then, the entire old history of Nell Tarkington and
David's father. I had forgotten that the affair had resulted in a child. But
then I remembered and it felt a bit like remembering that Antarctica is
one of the continents.

I saw you once, I said. On a park bench. You were with Joe Hurley and
you had your baby.

You saw my baby?

You were with a baby. When you were working at that photography
shop. You served me and took my picture.

Do you remember me in Arthur Twombly's class.

You asked good questions, I said.

NELL TOOK MY APARTMENT and I bought a second-hand Toyota and
drove through Quebec and the Maritimes for a summer in St John's. I felt
like a carbonated litre of drink left open on a table overnight. I woke
myself up. I exercised my mouth. I reverted to a plane of concentration,
it's a sort of looking under one's brow at the world. I refused to be
polite, yet I wasnt selfish. I opened doors but did not open myself to
a compliment. I took up smoking cigarettes during the trip home and
enjoyed winding down the window and leaving my hand with the

cigarette on the rubber flange of the window. I wore the same jeans until I hit St John's. I had a good ninety days in that city. I used every bit of it up. I fished in rivers and drank in the little side bars that connect Duckworth with Water Street and I grew salad greens. I visited my parents in Corner Brook and I used the rifle that I keep in my father's locked cabinet and shot a caribou with my buddy Randy Jacobs. Randy was with the Royal Newfoundland Constabulary, so we had to hunt super legally, though I knew Randy had a darker side. Randy had connections with men who swallowed condoms full of heroin and brought them into this country. But that was a complicated, discreet and lucrative activity, whereas poaching was a blunt exercise not worth ruining an honest reputation for.

IT WAS A SATISFYING RURAL SUMMER, and I appreciated the place as a visitor, a bit like Nell must have enjoyed it when she first arrived eighteen years ago. She described to me, through phone calls and emails, her early life and her affair with David's father.

I drove the car over every last mile of dirt road in Newfoundland. It was a little mission. I spent five weeks doing it. I grew filthy and enjoyed the greasiness of my hair. I boiled coffee in the morning or drove to a gas station, and was pleased that not once had I unpacked the Coleman stove (I used its grate over the fire). The fire kept me company, the coals of a fire are more absorbing than television. In a convenience store in Colinet a woman warmed formula in a take-away cup of hot water, and I imagined I was her husband in a Japanese car, and that I was taking care of her child. I realized I wanted a child.

When I visited my parents I noted how Corner Brook was changing. There was an art college now and there were youngsters who had something going on other than the pulp mill. There was an air of frivolity rather than pure drive to make money or merely replace the aging mill workers and Vachon cake truck drivers. I doubt if any of the eighteen-year-olds now graduating high school thought to work the night shift as cleaners for the fast-food restaurants up on the highway, which I had considered for a while, purely out of lack of vision.

I drove up the hill past the RCMP detachment and the junior high school and the high school and finally the university campus. All of my early education had been on this hill. I looked into the windows of the classroom where I'd met Nell, where I'd seen David's father tell us about his son. Then I drove past David's house, now occupied by his mother, Helen Crofter, and Dr Manamperi, and knew Nell had gone in there many years before to conduct her affair with Arthur Twombly.

My mother wanted a closet cleaned out and in it I found an alumni book from the year Nell was at Grenfell. I was shocked by her face. Her face wasnt the same. She was a girl then. There was nothing in the face that made her an adult or gave any hint that she would become older. I thought she was the same but this photo made me realize how young she had been. Then I found that printout Nell had taken of my face. We were all very young. We had the faces of children because we were children.

I sold the car and took a flight back to Toronto. My seasonal peregrinations had the odd result of making my body think of Newfoundland as a warm place and Toronto a cold one. I had chewed over the wilderness of Newfoundland, and was prepared now to enjoy the company of a curious woman. Nell Tarkington. And she too was at the corner of the twelfth floor to her own soul, trying to attack the world in as honest a light as she could. We had flirted through a summer inside the tiny packages of email and long-distance phone calls. I liked the shape of her and the words that came out of her mouth and she was devoted to a kind of work I found interesting. There didnt seem to be anything about her that annoyed me. I had arrived at a brave shoal, and I toyed with my emails and held Nell's emails in my mouth, sucking the taste out of them. Was she coming on to me? Was I?

I stared at Nell Tarkington with the fresh autumnal buds of anything. She had found an apartment close to mine. We went on dates. I watched her eat a pomegranate over the sink, with her forehead pressed to a cupboard door. We did not kiss. I kissed her once goodnight. There was not a fear of losing momentum. Her name was Nell Tarkington, a name like a ptarmigan ringing a bell, a name full of innocence and foreboding. Death knells, and it also harkens. Her great-grandfather, I discovered, had written *The Magnificent Ambersons*. Which meant nothing to her, what was a twelve percent resemblance in the genetic code?

But that's vulnerability for you. We had both opened up that compartment under the arm, a window into a new lung that made it hard to stay heavy about anything. The first kiss was in the shelter of someone's stoop after a party at David Twombly's.

Nell was still working with David at IKW. She was focused on a thin wrapper that concentrated binary equations, which are long strings of ones and zeros. It's a good thought, that any number can be made of counting a series of numbers that are always doubling: one, two, four, eight, sixteen. It reminded me of my one nightmare, of a box that grows and I have to push the box back into the distance, only to have it expand again. Push, expand, until I awake, my head crammed with a universe.

I could not follow her for a sentence, but I was happy to live next to it, to see her success and somehow be a part of the new world without having to stretch my brain around the very world she was helping create. Having said that, I'd abandoned to some degree the old world. I used to write about it, the world of my family and friends, but now I was in a stage of dormancy. There's a fallow period in the soul and I'm content to let the good times roll and witness it without too much hassle.

One night, after coming home from work, she looked worried. I asked what was wrong. David's in trouble, she said. He took the company public and there's a missing level of funding.

He'll be all right, I said. David's resourceful.

We ate pears sliced in half and took the ferry across to Ward's Island and watched the city turn dark. It was the only place in Toronto where you had a skyline. I was looking for rural things within the city, romantic things. We loved public, free things.

But Nell was wary. I'm seeing someone, she said at last, though it isnt a full commitment. I took the small deflation. I remembered the big hands of the man from United Architects. I ate it and the world I had imagined imploded. I did not even realize I had projected a world onto the future. I'm usually a man of the moment. But I'd felt then that I wanted to get Nell pregnant.

I saw an emotion tracking her forehead, an impulse—Nell had a beautiful intent. She was struggling to be as honest as she felt it was necessary to be. We went to movies and I bent my possibilities into a trickling vein of enjoyment. She was seeing someone.

Through the fall we took streetcars to art galleries and ate in Chinatown and Little India. Have I mentioned her hair? It was smooth and black and she spent money to thin it fashionably. She pushed at the knuckles of her fingers, as though pushing on rings. I saw no evidence of the architect.

FOUR

A MONTH WENT BY under the normal rules of conduct and then Nell
came by and told me that David had cleared his desk. I called him and he
said I'll pick you up and we'll go for a drive. He liked speeding out to
Ajax, a city named for a battleship, and as we sped out there in a silver
convertible we imagined Ajax was moored on Lake Ontario, waiting
for its papers to tell it what to destroy. Since Sok Hoon had taken the
family car David leased vehicles. He kept them for three months and
traded them in. He picked up hitchhikers and talked to them about
their families and then let them out when he got bored. The economy
had turned during the year, he said. Now all the tech money was flowing
back into materials, trains and steel distribution and the shipping of
potash to China. David was the IKW field worker. While the partners
created information, David was the one on the ground that talked to
sources, and when projects ran aground, he was the heavy who tried
to smooth things over, and if that failed, he resorted to power and
manipulation. IKW had gone public six months ago, he said, but had
then been kicked down and to save it from collapse there'd been a stock
buyback. But the buyback was less than the initial public offering.

There was a criminal investigation, David said, and I was charged with assaulting this soybean grower in Saskatchewan.

Soybeans, did I know IKW was involved in soybeans. He was not convicted but in the deep company investigation of itself it was noted that David Twombly had taken a forward strip out on IKW. He'd put a target of twenty-five dollars on the stock, but the price of IKW was sinking two percent a day and Massimo Sythe and the board were forced to ask him to leave the company.

They were trying to put lipstick on a pig, David said. There's been no mention of a leak to friends so your money is safe.

This alarmed me—the idea that I might have done something wrong, and also that my money might be in jeopardy. David's position sounds extreme, but it had all happened over a year, in increments, and I guess I hadnt noticed the buildup of trouble that David had created and now was having to abdicate. IKW was to go private again and the partners, David said, will make a paper fortune. I went from shame, David said, to feeling I was fucked around.

He had shifted his money into real estate. Information was overrated, he said. In the long run you can't beat land. He'd bought a chalet in western Newfoundland. He'd sold virtual condos to people who have property in South Africa and New Zealand and Mexico. People who needed safe havens and Canadian passports. He was at home now, with software from the company. He was trading in soft commodities— orange juice, cotton and hot rolled steel. Futures are better than gambling on stocks, he said. All you have to do is predict the weather. He had taken a few software projects with him, and was developing them into handheld devices.

As we hit Ajax I realized you could trace the downturn in the David Twombly economy a little further back. It had begun when Sok Hoon left him. At first she threw a portable radiator at him. He was in bed.

She'd come home and he could tell Sok Hoon thought he wasnt a friend. She decided, David said, that I was against her. She threw the radiator but it was plugged in and didnt travel far. Then she hoisted a lamp and it too was plugged in so she unplugged it and threw the wire at him also. How cold and heartless I am, Dave said to me. How in the final six weeks she had lost all her confidence, she cried when David wasnt around.

As he drove me home I thought of David's phrase from university: The architects are here. I think of it because we all wonder if we're at the end of the good times. Our generation will be the last, we think. And if not the last generation, then the last of the old generations. A head and shoulders has formed and now there is nothing but, at best, a slow decline in the natural world while the man-made world has accelerated and we will be the last ones able to separate the two. These were the last days before people began sending a hologram of themselves to conferences, before we strapped on sensory devices and experienced other places without leaving our bedrooms, before the West sent robots to war instead of real American soldiers. It was a complicated time, a transition period that made many of us skip having children because we couldnt muster the hope needed to pass the new world off onto youngsters. The architects are here, we said to ourselves, and to the future.

He turned off the Gardiner at Jameson and found an off-ramp to Spadina and, now that he had to gear down to second, he retracted the top and we drove up through my neighbourhood, in the dark, feeling like kings.

That's only half the truth, what I've said about children. Another crowd went out doggedly to have children. You defied that feeling, and rammed it in the teeth. Take that, you said. David Twombly was like that, and I had decided that was my position as well.

The seeds have grown and are bearing fruit. A crop of goodness next to a lake of repercussions. We have all been good and we have all dished out our share of asshole behaviour. You can get away with that for fifteen years, but then assholism too bears fruit.

I WAS FORCED to sell the rest of my IKW shares and I had fifty thousand dollars in the bank. What to do with it. It felt wrong to leave it as a number printed in a book. I like money to be converted into things, and yet the paper world we were now in did not reassure me. All of the information that was now considered valuable could vanish. I preferred something solid. And I remembered meeting Geoff Stirling as a kid. How he'd encouraged David at that employment fair. Not enough people have the entrepreneurial spirit, he'd said. But my father had told me how he'd made his money. Geoff Stirling had bought gold. He bought bullion just before the world left behind the gold standard. At the time gold was thirty dollars an ounce, and most analysts thought it would sink further—there was no need for banks to keep it and so the world was awash in gold. But instead gold went up. It reached a hundred and fifty dollars, hovered, and then it burst through eight hundred dollars an ounce, where it's never been since. But in the past couple of years gold was ascending again. It was making a comeback. Stirling had made a fortune out of gold and so could I.

I went online and looked at gold. I had enough for a hundred-ounce bar. They're pretty, these Engelhard bars. They look like something out of a pirate movie. The shipping was only thirty dollars. But when I clicked to purchase a bar I received an email. What if you need to cash some of it out. You can't very well cut ten ounces off your bar and sell it for five grand.

I spent three days emailing this woman, trying to convince her to part with a bar. But she directed me to the coins. I could get one hundred one-ounce maple leaf coins. And so that's what I bought. It cost thirty dollars to ship almost seven pounds of gold.

It came on a Tuesday. The doorbell. A security man in sunglasses. Another standing outside of a grey Securicor truck. I had to sign for it, and the man opened a canvas bag and lifted out this small green box trimmed in silver. Very heavy. Thank you, I said.

The gold was not in coins, they were wafers. They had sent me little squares of gold. It was like a precious box of chocolates. I showed them to Nell. We lifted them out of their stacked column and they made a scraping sound I had not heard before. I guess a metal has to have a certain density for that sound. The light shone over their pocked surface. They possessed a rough inner glow. I feel, Nell said, like putting one in my mouth.

Where should I keep them, I said.

Nell: That's what banks are for.

For a few days I left them in my desk drawer. I carried a wafer in my pocket and pulled it out to look at it. Five hundred dollars. But Nell was upset with this. I'll pay, she said, for a safety deposit box.

But I like them close at hand, I said.

Stash them someplace, she said. They make me nervous. Put them in the freezer. Your freezer locks. Put them in that.

I slipped the wafer of gold back in its slot in the box and put the box in a waterproof pouch meant for whitewater rafting. I shifted a few ziplocked packages of caribou and stuck the pouch of gold in between roasts and pounds of ground meat. I locked the freezer. I had a hundred ounces of gold in my freezer.

THAT CHRISTMAS Nell took me to visit her aunt and uncle in Burlington. On the pelmet above her guest room window, the track trophies and the one medal. How can anyone live in Burlington, I thought. But Nell had lived here. Even in the time since she'd grown up here, the city had changed. There was nothing geographic to anchor the city. You drove past a steel mill and an auto parts factory that supplied the Big Three in Detroit and you knew you had left Toronto and were on your way to Burlington. Her uncle worked for StresCrete, a company that makes utility poles. Cousin Howard was working there too. All over Burlington, light fixtures and power lines and the new receivers for cellular transmission. They were involved in that and it was Uncle Charles really who made her do a communications degree.

One night in a movie theatre we saw the guy she'd lost her virginity to, John Mennie. When she was fifteen she had been home sick from school and he'd phoned her up. He was twenty, Nell said, and I knew his brother Carl. This is John Mennie, he said on the phone. I was wondering if you'd like to come over and play cards.

She had walked over to the Mennie house. It was the only house she knew of with aluminum siding. She was fifteen though she looked older. You could tell she was fifteen by the size of her head. John had a motorbike that he drove in the snow, long blond hair and tinted glasses. John Mennie smoked and she took a cigarette from him and they played crazy eights on the kitchen table. There was music coming from upstairs and then it stopped. The side of a record. I'll show you my room, he said. He worked maintenance at the auto parts factory, he worked the night shift and he had just gotten up. His brother, he said, had a crush on her.

His bedroom was in the attic of the bungalow, there were posters on the angled wall of models hauling themselves out of the surf. The posters leaned down on them as though the models aimed to pull up on the beach which was John's bed. He had *Playboy* magazines and cars made of plastic that ran on batteries. He was bored, he said, and needed someone to talk to.

They lay on his bed and listened to a band from Vancouver, a band he was fond of, and they watched the snow fall over the white bungalows.

FIVE

On the weekends through that first winter we bought live carp wriggling in wet styrofoam boxes and barbecued them on the cold roof. Small lines of snow fell from the wires. We walked into High Park to visit the cold llamas and the indifferent American bison. A few nights she stayed over and we fooled around without taking our clothes off. I felt like the side of my head had been blown off. But Nell needed convincing. Duration is the great convincer. We cooked meals together and listened to the radio and browsed through Korean grocery stores and, in spring, rented a car and shook the city off our backs and drove through the Bruce Peninsula. It was rural but it did not remind either of us of Newfoundland. We fished in the Credit River. I caught her staring at me hard while I was singing a song on my guitar. It was one of those heartfelt songs. The heart can sneak up behind you and bowl you over. She came to me one day with her hair cut off. It was dark short hair, a little long at the back but shorn around the ears. I held her ears and talked to her and she couldnt hear me because I was ruffling her ears.

Okay, she said, I'm willing to try this.

A heat travelled through my body, a heat of responsibility. She was saying yes to me. That meant that the future was locked down. I had willed something into being. I couldnt believe it. I blinked and touched the little lines around the corners of her mouth. They were delicate, like the folds around the eyelid. It was as if her mouth could see.

We abandoned my apartment and moved in together near High Park and lived as a couple. We pranced down the hall like fan-tailed deer. She got up early and jogged then went to work and on the weekends she wore different, older clothes and became a homemaker. She made broth from bones. She had plastic containers of broth in the freezer. But there was a surfboard quality to Nell's soul that she clung to. A softness leaked out and then hardened over again to the spine of a surfboard that is confident and durable and entertaining to be around, if not deep and vulnerable. This can happen to anyone in their thirties.

One night she did not come home. And then I got a phone call—I had to collect her from a bad party. It levelled me. She was drunk in a penthouse condo off Bloor. She hardly remembers this night and I grappled hard with my Wyoming, which allowed her to be depraved and hungry. She went to work promptly at eight and came home that night with a stuffed fox. Meet Toby, she said. What's that, Toby? Toby whispered in her ear and then Nell made his head go wonky with sorrow, with mea culpa.

Toby was her promise to me that she was going to be good, she was to have no cold heart and no wildness without my knowing it.

In the mornings I felt Nell get out of bed and I knew it was six-thirty. Nell wears a watch for the deaf, so the alarm does not wake me. But I can sense the motion of the bed. I heard her making her quiet breakfast sounds, little packets of tinkering like the frozen plastic lid of the espresso coffee unpuckering, and the scour of an egg in a hot pan with fat. She likes one fried egg and one cup of coffee and no toast. She left the dishes, the small zip of her purse, I have told her to leave them. The satisfying slip of the deadbolt as she inserts a key behind her. In case anyone should attack me in bed. I tell you I live for things like that, the sound of her brass security key protecting my back.

An hour later I would get up and make coffee and take a coffee up the ladder to the roof. There is a billboard sign up here, with an advertisement for Cuba. I liked to drink the coffee under Cuba and stare out at the city and the planes taking off from Pearson, some of them, I guess, on their way to Cuba.

Sometimes Nell had trouble sleeping. Her legs kept her awake. Nell had caffeine or glucose in her legs. But it was her mind sending chemicals to her legs as a by-product of all her thoughts, that was my opinion. We're hiring subjects, Nell said, around the world to wear sensory devices hooked by satellite to computer terminals so you can stand at a kiosk and feel like youre in the other place.

She was staring at the ceiling in the dark, her legs slowly rotating at the knee or a swimming motion with a foot. You can't be there, but you can sense it. Fly on the wall.

Two of the projects my wife was working on.

Her little aluminum laptop has no keyboard—another IKW prototype. She works on a black table, and the screen illuminates a keypad on the table. She types on this keypad of light. It reminded me of the brilliant cluster of white stars that forms the cat above the jewellery store where I was contemplating a ring to make Nell my wife, the cat's curled tail breaking the face of the sign. Arrogant, sexy and rich.

Her fingers curled up and she tilted her head down and spoke aloud to a corner of the room and then occasionally looked up at me, as though the space between the corner and me was what separated humanity from the man-made world. Last year, according to the quarterly reports, they sold data to make accountability features on a Taser. Though not in one of the reports or request sheets handed to her did she ever see the word *Taser*. Disgust, but there is an awe attached as well, like some ascending submarine and we are breaking open the hatch to the conning tower, to be baked in the direct sun.

SIX

ONE MORNING, Nell came up to my side. I could feel her by the bed, the texture of beige and turquoise stay-ups. She was dressed for work and she wears very sexy things. But this last-minute visit wasnt something she normally did. I'm quick to wake up. I can be up and out the door in under a minute. But I took it calm and stroked the inside of her thigh. What is it, I said.

I've heard about my son.

I stretched the face around my eyebrows.

He's in Corner Brook. As you know the Hurleys adopted him. He's eighteen and his name is Anthony. They think, or his brother thinks, that Arthur Twombly isnt doing right by him.

I hauled up the file on Nell's Corner Brook life, the one that I've presented to you. And did I already know this little wrinkle, some form of extortion. Youve heard trouble, I said. Youve heard of your son because of trouble.

Gerard Hurley called me.

I know Gerard.

I went out a few times with his brother.

Yes I'm aware of Joe Hurley.

Gerard says Anthony needs money and Arthur Twombly is not being as generous as he could.

I blinked some more. Was he asking you for money.

I think that's what he was asking.

Was he asking on your son's behalf or his own.

Could you just listen, Nell said. And not treat it as if you can solve it.

She became tight and impenetrable and anything I said was going to be used against me. So I closed up and, in a selfish gesture, thought how inconsiderate of her it was to blurt this out when I wasnt even awake. I had no fuel and then, instead of getting up for a slight pause, she actually left the apartment and went to work. I called in the afternoon and left a message but she didnt return it, and when she came home she said it was nothing, that in the morning she'd thought it was large but now it was just information and a light bubble of joy was back in her chest. Nell knew where her son was and her son knew her. But even though she had the bubble she didnt look me in the eye, she was staring low at a corner of the room.

That talk happened maybe six months ago. It was as if the talk never happened and we resumed the life that we were meant to be living. Nell. When she's alone, she goofs around the apartment. She daydreams, making up stories of helicopters and gangs and the searchlights of police. I caught her once peering around an invisible wall. Sometimes, in mock frustration, she will run away from me and jump on the bed with Toby in the jaw of her elbow. And wait for me to come. She'd murmur into the pillow. And then we'd hold each other and mutter the names from the news we loved to say, Hosni Mubarak, Boutros Boutros-Ghali, the mujahadeen. We spoke as though we were on television.

Murmur, I learned, used to mean rebellion.

I was in love and happy although the modern world did perplex me. I wasnt sure if I could keep up. Nell tried to keep me up-to-date. I wanted to know her things. She was good at it, she was never condescending. A timestamp, Nell said, is a shared secret. We're in bed when she tells me this. I find it soothing, for her to smooth out her calf muscles with that rotating massage, and recite the new information that fills her business head. A salt is a private comment known only to the server. If a timestamp is modified, the hash will be corrupted. If an attacker tries to recompute the hash, he will need the salt, and he can get that by bruteforcing.

It's about here that my feet begin to float away and my head bumps lightly into a corner of the room. My head is full of helium and I can only think of emotional things. There was the time on the subway last winter, when a young woman got up to let Nell sit down. Nell thanked her. Then we both saw it: Nell looked pregnant. She had pushed her big gloves into the pockets of her coat, she had a bulge. And suddenly I wanted her to be pregnant. But she wasnt going to have a child with me. She had a child. She felt ruined, she has told me, to that kind of domestic living.

But now that I look back on those months I remember that Nell was going through something. I wasnt alert to it, but she was more willing to talk to me about her Corner Brook life. Sometimes I had a strange desire to back away from her, thinking, as I had thought of her, that she's only with me because of this connection to our youth.

SEVEN

THE GOOD WEATHER made us walk home from the movies and sometimes after the sushi we cut down to College Street and had a drink at
Ted's Collision. It was warming now and I admired the first cluster of
drinkers who pushed a table out onto the street and preferred to drink
in the cold open air full of exhaust fumes from the traffic, and while the
music was smaller here you had to contend with the streetcars and the
pedestrians who might brush your shoulder accidentally and not say they
were sorry.

We ordered the local microbrewery beers and occasionally just a plain
old-fashioned beer our fathers drank and we always drank from bottles
rather than the pints that were poured from hoses. I was convinced draft
beers were home to mould in the tubes and also the mixing agents were
not as clean as a bottled beer, especially during the warm months. In
winter I'd give in and order a pint of Guinness.

From Ted's we often met up with David Twombly. In the past year,
David and Sok Hoon had separated and then David had lost the company
and Nell had heard about her son. It made Nell and me think how lucky
we were not to let the world cleave us, that we understood and were both

in our thirties and had survived early relationships when jealousy, ambition and your own boredom crept in and destroyed the apple orchards.

We clinked bottles and waited and David Twombly arrived. His house
was around the corner on Grace and he often popped in to look around
to see if anyone was there he could talk to. He was happy to see us. David
didnt do that Toronto thing where people kissed, he was too affectionate
for that, so you had to settle for his big happy face and how silly he could
be at seeing you. He hadnt wanted Nell and me to get together but then
resolved himself to it, and I had that feeling you get with confidence that
made Nell a filter to my own emotional landscape. I preferred a man to
be intimate with me through the agency of a girlfriend. They had known
each other a long time. They had worked together. That's an entire world
to share and sometimes I found them commiserating. They liked to hold
hands. They did not, actually, have much to do with each other these
days, but David understood the assholes and tension and elevator Nell
was working with every day.

David ordered a red wine, a bottle of it. He put his communication
box in front of him, it was called a pebble, and I touched its soft chrome
surface. It was one of his new projects since leaving IKW. It felt like
rubber, like a sex toy. It was a device that connected him to anything
man-made that he owned, he just had to think of it. I'm field-testing it,
he said.

Me: It's not as small as I'd imagine.

They can make them smaller, but what's the point.

Theyre making them to fit the hand again, Nell said.

David was on wine because he didnt want to get fat. I was the
opposite. David had always been fat but now was working out and there
was a pinched quality to his face. I was broadening. When youre skinny
all your life you enjoy the thickening that happens, and I was giving in
to my slowing metabolism.

He drank the wine carefully and Nell switched over to the wine. He was the only man at Ted's Collision to be drinking wine. I think we talked about potatoes, and how you boil red potatoes and fry yellow ones. Or is it the other way around.

In the mornings David swam and then came home to work on his laptop. He traded call and put options. He invested in thirteen junior mining stocks, juniors that he had visited while working for IKW, or he'd met management at the Spoke Club or flown over property in a helicopter and knew that one of the thirteen would strike it big. Those arent bad odds. Only one junior in three thousand ever turns into a mine, he explained. If you have success with the drill bit, David said, there was the factor of ten thousand. But David wasnt looking for an operable mine. What he cared about was a mine with sizable opportunity. Where there was tremendous upside only in the ability to attract capital. Then you had to time the rise of share price and tabulate volume and get out before the price faltered. David realized he had a facility for stacking plates into piles and recognizing when those plates teetered too wildly and selling before that moment and buying back later at the very instant that other traders were shitting their pants and reeling in the panic of a throat-slashing, bottomless, no-buyers vacuum, and as soon as they had sold to you out of tremendous relief for your foolhardy risk, that's when plates were again being stacked and faith restored in markets, in the idea that objects and raw materials and services could actually be looked at as money. You traded on consumer confidence and trader sentiment. Sometimes though all the plates were smashed and someone went into the warehouse and took a sledgehammer to the crates of stock still in their boxes and then someone lit the corner of the warehouse and the side of the town the warehouse was in was blown off the earth. David learned to read the signs of men lifting their sledgehammers or a warehouse prone to fire and shorted everything. He borrowed stock from anyone who was holding long and returned the stock seventeen minutes later. He worked in financials and housing and then when the flavour was sucked out of those equities he'd trade over in technology and commodity futures, in wool and cotton and precious metals.

That's where he was at now, in the soft commodities. When the volatility in that market felt played out he'd move into consumer discretionary. He watched the plates stack and teeter and the number of bids outnumber the asks and he withdrew his support and watched the plates crash again. Or it was like fire, the embers flaring up and down and wood being consumed or withdrawn. Sometimes there was no air and other times no fuel and then in spots there was tremendous fuel and oxygen and you had to be fully in then and let the entire position roar into life and get out again before the fire understood that it was hovering over water and had no right to be over the surface it thought it owned.

WE LEFT David at Ted's and walked home. Nell and I had just come back from a weekend trip north. It wasnt a good trip. Nell was tense and had something on her mind. We had been with David and friends from IKW. Massimo Sythe had been loyal to David, had backed him up. Massimo had a cottage on an island. A pale blue kevlar speedboat picked us up. We were asked to bring cold wine and food and ice. It's wonderful to feel a jet boat plough through water. They had piled wood on the beach, a broken chair on top. And Massimo was operating a chainsaw after wine and a toke. He was a little jubilant on it, carving off lengths of an old fallen tree. At one point he passed the saw to me. He was afraid of nipping the blade and he knew that I was used to chainsaws.

We left the pile like that, the chair sitting on the heap of beach wood. The chair wasnt something you sat on, it was sitting itself. It had leapt out of chairness and become its own master.

We ate and then changed into our swimsuits and Massimo brought down a two-gallon container of gasoline. It's windy, he said, and hard to light the fire. He handed the gasoline to David, and I realized in that gesture that Massimo was risky, but he wasnt about to take foolish chances. The gasoline chugged out of the yellow nozzle over David's hands. And then a flame licked his wrist and leapt to the wood and a plume of boiling fire spewed like something out of a forge. David Twombly sucked in his chest to stop himself from being savaged.

We stripped off and swam, baked ourselves against the hot fire, dipped again. But Nell is not close to me and it makes my brain bang open and shut and I drink my face off.

When we came home thieves had ransacked our apartment. Pictures were off the walls, some ornaments above the fireplace were broken. Books were strewn on the floor. Toby the stuffed fox had been lifted and thrown. Then there was shit on the couch and on the floor. Small smears of grey shit. Just to rub it in.

A bird, Nell said.

Thieves brought a bird in.

Nell had gone through the books before we left. She wanted some-thing to read. She had left the mess. And we had left the front window open.

A pigeon was in the apartment. We found birdshit in the bathroom and birdshit in my study. The pigeon had gone to every window, frantic with an energy to be outside.

This seemed to exhaust us. We filled buckets of sudsy water and cleaned up. And then Nell checked the messages and we went to bed without talking. But then I felt a nudging and Nell was in tears. She said the bonfire had reminded her of that night with Arthur Twombly. The little plane flight and the time she was pregnant. She missed her parents, she said. Could I hold her. Could I bring Toby over and give her a hug.

EIGHT

A YEAR WENT BY and Nell and I were both excited now to know what the weather would bring and how we could plan to grow tomatoes on the roof and put away the winter slippers for the lighter Chinese slippers Nell had found on Spadina Avenue. We marvelled at how much food we cooked, how little we used the restaurants except for the favourite two. There was a Vietnamese one and a sushi bar which we lined up to eat at after watching a movie at the repertory cinema that no longer had many old films at all but simply showed the new films that had come out six months before. We loved the movies and the simple food and the walk home along Bloor Street to our apartment on Roncesvalles Avenue, which is a Polish area of Toronto. I was sometimes surprised that we could walk the mile home without feeling bored or unloved and I took that as a sign that she loved me and was happy. It was true that I'd find her sometimes crying or the evidence of crying appeared on her face and when I asked if anything was wrong she cheered up and said it was allergies.

I thought the story of Nell's history and how I came to be living with her would have been enough for a novel, one with enough drama and tension and happiness for a version of these aforementioned incidents to form a satisfying narrative, but more was to happen that turned this short history into a preliminary hearing for the more important events, events that, in retrospect, take on the whiff of the inevitable, of fate, though I heartily disagree with people who are satisfied with fate.

Nell and David were both involved in the transformations that were under way to move us from a society based on moving objects to one relying on the transportation of ideas. I was happy with the old ratio of these two qualities. It's not that I thought the old balance was better, I was comfortable with it and thought younger people should adopt the newer ratio, not us. But besides this, I had no doubt and yet I guess in a relationship there is someone who will doubt. But when you are content you dont look under rocks for trouble, at least I dont. I'm like a dog when I'm happy, I just eat my food and sleep and run after the ball. Then last night, when Nell came home from work, I could tell she was vulnerable and I wanted to reassure her. I knew she didnt have the being-a-dog talent that I had. She was wide open and then I could sense something soft and unformed fall out of her. She said I havent told you this and I should have told you. I didnt want to tell you because I didnt want it to affect your relationship with David.

What, I said.

I've been seeing David.

She'd been seeing David.

I just told him. I said this has to stop now.

Now. It has to stop now?

I've been seeing him, she said, every year perhaps twice a year. For the last. For the last forever.

Seen him.

And I felt like I'd dropped a novel I'd been reading into the bathtub. The shock of a world you believed, solid, flat and dry, was turning wet, dissolving to pulp. It hadnt been the man from United Architects.

Whenever we're away someplace, she said. It's never been here, just some other part of the world. That was the arrangement. It was supposed to be our other selves.

And it all clicked like tumblers in a lock. How David had tried to settle me down, and reassure me that you can have a woman on the side. Youre his French affair, I said.

She was trembling and I tried to say the right thing but perhaps the right thing would have been to hold her and the hell with it I couldnt hold her. I'd been wanting to have a kid with her. What a joke. They had been to a conference three months ago, I remembered that. I guess that constitutes another country. We were standing around the sink, a lot of work for us gets done around the sink.

Me: So youve seen him since we've been together.

When we got together, she said, a year ago, I decided it was the last time.

When you cut your hair.

But I've seen him twice. So this last time I thought I had to tell you.

I had an eerie feeling, like looking at words written in a mix of capitals and lowercase letters, and then the words exploded.

So are you telling me you slept with David Twombly.

Yes.

And since we've been together.

Yes.

Just the once?

No.

Twice?

She explained the reasonableness of the affair and that's when I pounded the wall. The wall needed fixing. When David said *affair* I had imagined a woman half his age plus seven years. But Nell was our age. She was actually a year older than me. Then I realized David had never used the term *French affair* and neither had Nell. I was imagining the phrase, I had come up with it the night David had urged me to have kids. Something on the side, he said. But this was a mistress. This was about as European as you could get in Canada. Such are my inaccurate leaps. I wanted to approach Nell but all I felt was a rage the size of a bag of oranges that ebbed after ten minutes. I wanted to know the details but Nell said, I guess that must be a man thing.

And she kept walking around, bending over surfaces to tidy them. She wasnt giving me her full attention. She was folding laundry. Why David, I said, why be so unimaginative and what about Sok Hoon.

She stopped the folding and sat on our bed and Nell confessed her affair using words that were honest and careful. It's true that it was a moment that widened my heart to her, or at least some part of my heart, perhaps the left ventricle. She said she did not think about Sok Hoon, that it had nothing to do with her. That her arrangement with David predated his relationship with Sok Hoon, and that she was like a farm in another country that a man visits to keep the infrastructure going and to reassure the farm that he loves and understands her. But when I started seeing you, she said, I realized how awful it was. How it would be good to distance myself from Dave. I thought he loved me. But it began because David wanted to piss his father off. Perhaps we both wanted to piss him off. And then it became something underground, a visit to the underground that feels like a double life, some life that the rest of your world doesnt have to know about. But now I see how terrible it was of David not to tell Sok Hoon.

Me: So does he know I do that act where I pretend I'm on television.

I might have mentioned that.

So he knows the private stuff.

He knows everything.

Does he know about Toby.

I told him about Toby.

I asked her to be quiet and I walked around the apartment finishing glasses of water that Nell had half drunk and left. My mouth was dry. It seemed like that was the only good thing I could chalk up for her now, that she was a leaver of fresh glasses of water.

Too good to be true, I thought.

I couldnt help looking at her as if she was someone else. As if it was not honest and I'd been made a fool. But I tried to pull back the actor that wanted to voice betrayal. I wanted to be myself and perform in a unique way for this original moment. All of her life now seemed coloured from what I thought it was and I decided to be mean.

Youre used goods.

She closed her eyes and fixed her mouth in a disappointed firmness and I left her in the living room under the little painting she did of her ex-husband that I thought would be cute to have up on the wall. Now I looked at Richard Text and felt an affinity. I felt I knew what he must feel about Nell right now.

You'll always be used goods, I said. To any man living or dead.

Whatever that meant. I had a fury in my head and I put on my shoes and remembered when I was young and my parents fought, and how my father would leave the porch and I'd hear the car start up and the side of the house all red from his parking lights, my father driving someplace.

That's what I did. I walked around the neighbourhood. I walked past the mosque on Boustead where the line of taxis idles, their vacant lights on. The taxis are not waiting for customers, it's the drivers who are in the mosque. A little white dog made for me and then stood and barked, his pink nose. And the dog represented the ridiculousness of domestic strife. It made me turn around. I was about to go back to the apartment and apologize and do some work on the ground to instill a sense of love, but then a streetcar slid down Roncesvalles and stopped and so I got on it and let it carry me towards the lake and then twist east along King Street and I watched the benignly crazy people get on and off as if there was a movie happening, and I made up a story that happened in a room much like this room on a streetcar. You could see the dome of City Hall and I remembered the afternoon I ambled in there, to take in a council meeting, and was surprised how much the place looked like a spaceship. The streetcar took me a long way east, out past the old racetrack. I was on it for an hour and it only cost a token. I got off at the last stop and found some yellow store lights. A man had his mouth inside a shopping bag full of gasoline. I walked into an orange diner. I ordered a pint of beer and a small order of fish and chips and it was okay and my spirits rose. I heard the fat cry out as it doused the fish. I knew I'd be all right. I could withdraw three hundred dollars from the bank machine and keep going. I was hard in ways, though I had opened up to Nell. It was better to be alone and I could do that. I laughed at the position. I'm happy with looking at little things, these people in this diner. I'm very good at feeling sorry for myself and then laughing at my small complaint. I've got enough money and I can enjoy looking at a tree. In the end I'll be one of those men dying in a hospital bed laughing at a memory of a tree. I'll be okay. What I need is to evacuate, but then I remembered I'd evacuated Newfoundland and perhaps part of living the human life is learning from past experience.

I WALKED PAST all the churches I could think of and stared at the stone and brick, trying to soak in some of the solidity of those faiths. There's a new Baptist church and an older, Catholic one that took confession fifteen minutes before mass. There is a Buddhist temple that was built when we first moved into the neighbourhood, so I felt a kinship with the Nepalese. It was wintertime when we moved and we watched the Buddha arrive, a gold figure on the end of a crane hook, being lowered through the roof. And he sat in there all night with snow on his shoulders.

I looked up at the apartment and the lights were still on. But there was no activity, no shadows moving on the wall, no flicker of a computer monitor. It was about four in the morning and I was cold and tired but full of the fried food I'd eaten on the east side of town. The bed was big enough and I knew I could just slip in without touching Nell. If, in the morning, I felt the same way then I could gather some things together. I walked up our stairs, past the second-floor apartment where Irene Loudermilk was asleep. The top door was locked. Nell wasnt in the apartment. Which was worse. It made me worried. I slept a few hours until the recycling trucks came by and I got up to look at the men vigorously emptying blue and grey containers.

I went back to bed without Nell Tarkington in sight. I took up her great-grandfather's book, the novel *The Magnificent Ambersons,* which we kept by the bed and often, as a form of horoscope, opened to a page and read out a line. I did it this time for myself: An ideal wife is any woman who has an ideal husband.

I sank ninety feet into the mattress and thought of Las Vegas, the dryness, the wet lights. Nell had gone to Las Vegas. That was where she had begun the affair with David. They had attended a conference at the Bellagio on police security and the new software. There were men operating Tasers and CCT cameras for both private use and for distribution through airport terminals and casinos. I remember her saying she wanted to go to Vegas, whereas I had wanted to go to Cuba. She was a betting woman. She was betting on the proper future for herself. Perhaps she was having the same impulse that drove her to leave home all those years ago.

I SLEPT THEN WOKE and it was still early but I had to go out for a walk. Grief is smaller when you make yourself small. Streetlife is big. A take-out booth with seven lit chickens rotating on a spit—who eats chicken at six in the morning? A variety store with thirteen varieties of phone cards. There was an argument outside of a nail, wax and toe joint. It was the butcher who specializes in halal meat. A car pulled out and jerked into early traffic and the butcher ran after it with a wooden chair. He threw the chair and it caromed off the rear window and clattered onto the road. The butcher walked into the traffic, yelling at the car, and picked up the chair. He dragged it by its two rear legs. He brought the chair inside his shop and sat down on it and he seemed now to be looking at me. These were the businesses with adjacent property taxes on a mixed-use parking lot.

I went back home but I didnt sleep and then at about nine in the morning the telephone rang and I heard, in the receiver, a big room, a noisy atmosphere. It was David Twombly. Can you speak up, I said. He was using his pebble. His father was in an accident. I'm flying home, he said. David was in Terminal 1, punching his way through the express check-in, that faraway boarding call. His voice was rattled.

What kind of accident.

The Hurleys, they T-boned him.

The what. They what.

David, patient: He was hit by a van with a moose bar.

Then I remembered what Nell had said six months before, that precipitated all of this. About her son. I did a moment of heavy concentrating.

He was driving the Audi, David said.

Where is your father.

He's in Western Memorial. He's in hard shape, Gabe.

He meant the hospital in Corner Brook. I pictured the Audi, the safety features and the reinforced cabin. An Audi, I said, it gives you a lot of protection.

David wanted Nell to know that he was flying there now. She'd want to know.

My hand gripped the receiver hard. Nell isnt here. You fucker, I thought. You red-arsed fucker.

If you see her.

I NOTICED NELL had left her newest diary in her green purse hooked on the doorknob to her study. If she doesnt show up, I said to myself, I'm going to have to look through it. For her own good. But here I am, ordering the notes this way to give them some cohesion and I've injected a narrative where no narrative exists, but I've imagined no emotion or detail. I've knitted them together using my Wyoming, which is the dream life that cannot be mentioned in the born world. It is a world of the head, a land of web and light, imagined things. Occasionally I'd sort the chaos of life out loud, as I'm doing here, until Nell told me to shut up with my Wyoming. That's how it got called Wyoming—because I often began with a question, Why, and then an answer, Oh.

Nell: You and your Wyoming.

I could not sleep on that final morning, waiting to hear Nell return. I'd shut my eyes and then realize I was forcing them shut. My ears were perked. Then I heard an asthmatic sound and I tensed my ears to locate the sound and it was coming from the living room. I'd heard it all night but was too tired to move. Nell. And then, during that morning's small hours, I tried to turn it into a radio or a telephone line or the little bubbles underneath a glass drying on the counter, and it sounded right until I knew it was too loud. I walked out to the living room and he was sitting there on the back of the couch, in profile. Mr Pigeon. I leaned over him and he batted his wings. I opened the window wide and he knew his way out. I thought, if a pigeon can creep through a one-inch gap, what sorts of animals can creep through us. There's no

logic to this thought, just the wild associative leaps one makes when
one is in Wyoming.

I waited for ten oclock and then I phoned IKW. She wasnt at work,
Massimo said. At least he hadnt seen her. I thanked him for that weekend.
He said, You guys. You guys should have a kid.

I MADE COFFEE and then walked down to the library. I spend one
morning a week on the second floor of the public library. I associate
green carpet with study, that's why golf courses seem like a good place
to read a book. I link to the internet and discover all sorts of world activity. I choose a monitor that faces the wall, so I can discreetly look up sites
like a Japanese artist who, naked except for a pair of white sandals,
slowly climbs onto a plexiglas cabinet. Under the cabinet a naked man is
stretched out as if waiting for an operation. There is a trap door at his
face and this is open. She crouches and defecates on his face. You can see
her sphincter muscles contract and the blat of urine and feces. He looks
like he's in a coma.

Then I searched for the Corner Brook paper online. I used to deliver
this paper and now you could read it, if you wanted, anywhere in the
world. I found a photo of Arthur Twombly's accident. It was a plain white
Audi sedan, demolished on the driver's side, not a bad shot. A policeman
stood in the foreground and I knew him, it was Randy Jacobs. I thought of
David, on his way back there now, an executive first-class seat reclined,
orange earplugs in, his own personal DVD player scrolling through graphs
of force, williams percentages and Wilders DMI. A glass of champagne on
a blue tablecloth. A pulse of anger at his temple. Getting to the bottom of
the Hurleys. The newspaper said Arthur Twombly was in critical condition.

An old superstition kicked in and I waited for the third bad thing.

I realized the truth as I walked back home, a truth about the Japanese
artist: I dont know which person is the artist. I also know that the world

that I visit at the library will soon become the dominant world, it is the world David and Nell participate in, and it's a world I wish would only exist for half the year, or maybe a season, or on three of the seven continents, but it will come and supplant all other worlds.

I CALLED THE POLICE and felt that I'd done all one man could do. And in that I relinquished some of the burden of worry. Or it was more like putting my concerns aside for a time. I knew worry was there, panting in the corner. I went across the street to the coffee shop and had a coffee in the window. I took in the building I lived in and the CUBA SÍ billboard that stands on the roof. I say "took" because I like to think of it as a degree, this looking, that I've earned it with my study. The only degree I have is in economic geography, which has allowed me to paint crosswalks and inspect natural-gas storage facilities. Cuba sí. We were scouting flights to Cuba, because of this billboard. Someone had secured our roof rental, the permit for air rights, followed the approved building standards and stress tests, hoisted up lengths of steel, erected a billboard tower (we saw them and heard them, it took three days) and then pasted this aqua-dune advertisement. It must cover eighty square feet (the scale is hard to gauge, even from the roof). Now it was dictating what we do with seven days of our winter. Such influence!

I took the stairs and checked for messages, then climbed the ladder to the roof. I ducked under the Cuba billboard and put one foot on the lip of my building and stared deep into the city, at the top of the building that houses the offices of IKW. It's just beside the Canada Life building, the one with the lights that ascend and descend depending on the temperature. I began my Wyoming. How I'm easy to like and Nell both admires and resents that. Her self-worth rests mainly on the respect of her incredible head. But Wyoming is halted by the shape and sturdiness of the IKW building. It looks made of soapstone. The power of strong buildings like that makes you realize how a place like London England will never lose it. Teach durability and thoroughness, and might will maintain itself, especially in a world where all the best talent is devoted to making arms and entertainment.

FOR THE REST OF THE DAY I stared at the phone. First it was an hour and then three hours and then I left a note and went to a movie but even during the movie I was worried and could not escape into the white face of the film. I called from the cinema and there was no answer.

I tried David in Corner Brook, even though I knew why she had left. I knew she wasnt hurt in a hospital, for I had called the hospitals. But David wasnt in Corner Brook. He was still in Toronto.

Me: What happened to flying.

I wouldnt give up my pebble, he said. They said the pebble was unusual and could not be brought aboard. I was at the departures gate, you know where the last thing you read is a sign that dares you not to say anything that could be construed as violent.

You lost your temper.

I probably said something sarcastic about blowing up the plane and now I'm grounded.

What do you mean youre grounded.

I've got a no-fly caution in my profile.

Youre banned from airports.

I've been with security all day. I'm allowed in airports I just can't get through departures. It's like I'm allowed to read the preface to a book on airports.

You fly forty times a year.

I flew. I'm unemployed now, Gabe.

So what now.

He wanted to see me in the morning. So I tried to summon up the good side of me, the unhurt side that could help him now that his father was dying. I felt like perhaps I should have known about David and Nell, and that he was doing his best under the circumstances. He was greedy but then men can be greedy. I didnt want to let David Twombly know what Nell had told me. I wasnt ready yet to receive the emotions I was bound to go through with him. And I was anxious that night and in the morning too until I heard him come through the door. He was beside himself with anger. I could see he had a right to talk to me about it, about the injustice being done to him. I had my own fierce feelings about his role in Nell's life and yet I wasnt mad at Nell, I was worried for her. I wanted her to be alive. I had called the hospitals and begun a file with the police. This was the start of the changing of my life, where I no longer felt in control—that big machinery was grinding around me and I had looked up to see myself in the bottom of an elevated cone erected at dawn, with wet cement peering over the lip of the cone, churning like ice cream, a threatening ice cream.

He wanted some breakfast. I melted a chunk of butter and stirred up six eggs while he looked through the books on the kitchen table. I like to leave books in every room. David doesnt have books. He reads things from his pebble. He was proud that he had a friend who had written books, was perplexed about why I never tried to write something popular. How Canadian books are so literary and, in his mind, boring.

I made the eggs loose and scrambled, the way my father would make them on mornings when we were up early to hunt or fish. I shrugged off the animosity and decided to postpone the anger I had towards David. I would get him through this rough spot with his father. I hunted for my slippers then realized they'd be where I left them. Nell had this thing. She'd wear my slippers in the morning and then sling them off, perhaps violently, when she left for work. I've found them behind books on a bookshelf, and I enjoyed the little hunt I had to do to find them. But here they were in their little compartment in the shoe rack. That made me sad, that she hadnt even worn my slippers.

I served up the eggs and tore the bread in half. We would eat like Europeans. David was drumming his thumbs on the table, waiting.

Why not write a good old-fashioned mystery, David said. He wasnt the only one. Everyone who loves you will get a narrowing of the eyes and a pursing of the lips. They are trying their best not to tell you what to do. They want to see you on American talk shows. To shut him up I said okay I'll write a mystery. I'll write about a Canadian who tries to become the president of the United States—for that was David's private wish. He was, by birth, an American. He was born on a US army base.

He was hauling the scrambled eggs into his mouth now, dousing them with hot sauce. He didnt know I was in the room any more, he was eating privately, like a rich man. Maybe they were all rich. Both he and Nell had made, for a time, a shitload of money. David ate his eggs and asked for more coffee and then we took the ladder up to the roof where we stood straight and saluted the Cuban beach above us and then just stared out over the top of the city.

Hey you can see IKW from here, he said. And he looked further, as though he might discover the rim of Newfoundland sitting out there two thousand miles away.

There's trouble, he said, in Corner Brook. It has to do with Nell's son. With his adopted family. There was a threat.

So youve talked to Nell, I said.

She called me a few days ago, he said.

Okay, I said. I understood this. Nell called you.

I've got to see my father, he said.

Me: They hit him really hard.

They nailed him in a van. A moose bar, Gabe, it had a moose bar. And he's strung up to all these machines.

It looks like they might have been over the limit.

They were given breathalyzers.

I mean the speed limit, from the damage to his car.

Do you remember Maggie Pettipaw? She's a nurse now. I was talking to her at the hospital, she's on that ward.

Maggie Pettipaw, I said. She was very kind to me in biology.

She's on the ward and she was almost married to Gerard Hurley.

It's a small town.

She said Gerard is capable of that. She wouldnt put it past him.

And with that he looked over the vast new city of Toronto, the roofs of all the buildings. He looked like a conqueror. Or someone about to conquer.

Have you ever met him, I said.

Who.

Your half-brother.

I didnt know for years. It was never talked about. I heard the rumours but what Dad had told me was the boy was Joe Hurley's.

So when Nell left Santa Fe and came here.

I was curious.

Your dad told you and you felt kind towards her.

Well and she's sexy.

He was toying with me. He did not know what I knew. That's a real twisted—

Men are beasts, Gabe.

Me: Nell's disappeared.

This was my way to get David to mention the affair. I'd meant to talk about his father, but it was hard to separate it from his situation with Nell. I looked straight at him and his eyes were honest and clear. What an asshole. He was dealing with me in the same manner as he dealt with troubles in business: He was just a heavy in an environment that needed charming, physical men to act as their receivers and their protectors.

I told him we'd had a fight. That she had mentioned her son. I did not explain that she had confessed her affair.

He reached into his pocket and tossed me his pebble.

Call the police, he said. Ask them for an update on Nell.

What do I do to start this thing.

Oh yeah, he said. Pass it back.

The warmth of his hand turned it on. It was powered by solar and thermal heat. He thought of the police and handed it back. A staff sergeant from 44 Division on Dovercourt. You could see that building too from the roof. There was no update on Nell.

David: Have you called the hospitals.

I've spoken to every hospital in Toronto. It seemed like, in the background of every conversation I had, there were men restraining patients.

Hospitals are full of police officers.

I didnt know what to ask. I said, Hello. And this woman said: Emerge. She said, Name please. I said, My name? The patient's name, sir. So I gave her Nell Tarkington. And she said, There's no one under that name, sir.

David: Was she implying that Nell could be using a pseudonym.

That never occurred to me.

Did you try Toronto General.

I called every Emerg, Dave. And every one had a background struggle of calm prevailing. No one had a Nell Tarkington.

Nell grew up straight, David said. The coffee and eggs had made him arrive at a thought confirmed.

She's allowed me to be wild, I said. I'm her little acre of wild pollinate-the-wind garden.

Youre wild because your parents were restrained.

We were deciding on children, I said.

So she told me.

I listened to this.

We're colleagues, David said. We yabber.

Is Nell aware that you know about your half-brother.

We've talked about it.

DAVID SAW HIMSELF OUT and I watched him, from the roof, walk down my street looking determined, hunched a little, big and yet not that threatening. Maybe threat was a power that had to be consciously turned on.

NINE

THE DOORBELL WOKE ME EARLY. I bent over to discover the clothes
that I'd shrugged off onto the floor. They were clothes that had done me
well the day before, so why abandon them. I took the stairs down and
there was a man in a thick grey shirt with a military patch sewn on the
arm. We've had a report of a gas leak, he said.

I dont smell gas.

Our instruments indicate missing gas.

The man was absorbed by a handheld chip device with a probe
antenna. A bead was pulsing. I could sense a bank of propane, feel the
nuzzle of it. The smell registered as a softness.

It's nothing much theyre just switching off the gas and they'd prefer
the building—he looked at the corners of the ceiling—empty for the
morning. We'll relight your pilot lights. I mean absence isnt something,
you know what I mean?

Could this happen on another day. My wife has left me.

He checked his chip device and said, We have to empty the building.

MY JAW ACHED so I sprayed my back teeth with medicinal cannabis. It was the tooth I'd cracked at David Twombly's party, and so I associate the pain with meeting Nell—I'm realizing that now.

I grabbed my coat and my *Auto Trader* camera and a lozenge for my throat. I made sure the freezer was locked and I put Toby on the shelf above the books. I patted his head, as if I may never see him again. I didnt even brush my teeth. Outside the light felt different. It was warm. They were digging a hole and laughing. There was a big white truck and hired police. A man with a cement cutter   a white metal box the size of an ice-cream vending machine with a revolving thirty-inch blade at the front and wheelbarrow handles. I tried to look greatly inconvenienced. There was a hose to wet the blade as it zipped through the sidewalk. It was just him and the machine with a hose connected to a generator and a water pump in the back of a green cube van. The man with the probe rang the next doorbell.

Youre just cutting through the cement here.

I'm a cutter.

The blade zipped at the cement in a brittle, angry way. There were splinters of concrete and sparks and I noticed the unconcern at the twist of unpainted pipes that led to the natural gas. A leak and my god but hey theyre pros.

It was early and I had three cars to photograph. I had a life and then I had voluntary employment. It'll take your mind off Nell, of course it will. So I walked to the first client. I do not show up in a car. Long ago I realized this can give off the wrong odour—you never know the reason for the car sale until you arrive. It would be like inviting someone to your home in order for them to sign over their mortgage, realizing they are doing it to finance the medical bills of an ill child. So I arrived on foot, after taking the subway. I like this, and I enjoy mapping the city, discovering how it is bulking out at varying edges.

That degree I did in economic geography. We know that the spilling lip of a city is governed by many trickling advances and interests that affect votes on re-zoning. They are extending the Toronto subway system to the northeast.

My advice to you? If you have money for real estate get a list of the ravines and a chart of the subway stops and overlay them on a map of the city. Find a neighbourhood near to these and when mortgage rates dip near prime, you will make money.

A client to *Auto Trader* can supply their own photo, but often people who want to unload a used car fast dont have the means. And who has a recent picture of their car? I approach the photo-taking as an artist, as a trapping of the car. The man I learned from was that way, Lars Pony, and I do it partly in homage to the retiring Mr Pony's taste. Everything can be done with taste. I like to place a vehicle so the hood is acknowledging the sun. If a car has to go down, let it be sold facing the sun, like a bull. I bank the light off the front window, I catch a ten percent angle on the flank of the car facing the camera. I crouch sometimes, other times I'm on tiptoe. I try to work for the client, to eke out some enticing quality from the car and when they see this effort they are more inclined to open up and tell me a small story from their lives. This I use in the column. I shoot in colour, I shoot digital, I frame it so there is space for Tessa to drag in a yellow price window and overlay a startling zigzag frame. The frame is meant to make the vehicle look like it's alive, that it's gone to bed early after doing its homework and is ready for a long day in the field.

I can send the work to the shop, but half the time, if I'm riding by Auto Trader, I'll make the detour and deliver the pictures straight to Tessa Walcott—she enjoys my walking into the shop. They are not the first unit in the plaza, but in Unit 15 between Pro Choice and JK Parts. Tessa believes car honkers should be lined up and shot with a blank.

I shot a Mazda pickup north of Eglinton and then a snazzy coupe just at Kipling station. My last stop for the day was Alice Stebbins. I took the bus to Jane and Finch. It had been three months but I remembered the lane into the back of an apartment tower. I angled the light off the windscreen to avoid glare. I'd been by once before to take pictures for Alice, but the car hadnt sold and she wanted to blame it on the photo. I knew the car because it was a Matador, the same kind of car Zac Twombly had driven, the one David and I hit a moose with. It was nice to visit the car, I sat in it and remembered my youth. The car had been Alice's father's, he was on the force in Los Angeles. When he retired he bought his own cruiser from the LAPD, and they moved to Canada with it. It was an unmarked ghost car. He died one night six years ago when he volunteered to break up a gang fight near here in the Jane and Finch corridor. In the will Alice got the car. What I like about it is the paint. It's the original deep blue paint, and there's something satisfying about factory car paint that's thirty years old. I tapped the fender with my fingernails, it was a hard enamel, like teeth. Alice Stebbins works at a swimming pool and has had no luck selling the car because she's asking too much. She blames it on the photo I took but the trouble is she's in love with the car. She formed a bond last winter when the snow was bad and the cruiser pulled her through some slippery roads on her way to the Royal Yacht Club. Developing a bond with a car is a severe condition. And since the spring she's put a third of her income into the steering and pinion mounts. The shocks, she said, are shot.

What did you love about this car, I said.

Alice didnt mind this question. It was as if it was customary. I know I'm being unusual, I said.

And we both admired this service vehicle, a police cruiser that was in retirement, loyal and game. It was a car from that era when people bought vehicles by the pound.

I loved this car, she said, for the triangle on the dash by the fuel gauge.

That's a good feature.

A lot of cars dont have it.

Indicating the side of the car with the gas tank.

Were things truly built better in the past, with more care, or do we just build things differently. And we mistake difference for care, because to make that difference now, intentionally, we'd have to be careful.

That's a dangerous gas tank, I said. There were recalls.

She said, I dont trust cars with LCD readouts.

They'll last longer than anything else on the car. LCDs are good and accurate for forty years.

I dont trust things that I can't pick up and turn over.

Alice Stebbins walked down the back alley while I took the pictures. She'd dyed her hair since I last saw her. She has great posture, I noticed. Then I concentrated on the camera. I could hear Alice singing. The alley was the cement backsides of houses and stores. Then as she came back she quieted to a hum.

You won't be offended if I ask you if you sing?

She looked at me as though I'd said something about her face.

Because you have a real singing voice.

Alice Stebbins: Youre being sarcastic.

No, youre good.

You dont interrupt someone who is singing to ask them if they sing, especially couching it with the words "you won't be offended."

Me: That puts them on the side of suspicion.

Youre better than me with words.

What I'm better at, I said, is unmasking intention.

I clicked through the pictures but she didnt care.

Did you know, she said, theyre building cars in modules now? If you dent a quarter panel they'll just stick on a whole new chunk of car.

Her brother, who made jute-back carpet in Mississauga, had told her that.

A car like this, she said, it begs to be driven.

And with that she fell onto the hood and hugged the car. She was, of course, hugging her father.

I collected the pictures and showed her the window on the back of the camera. This one, she said. And this one.

I TOOK THE STREETCAR back to the shop. I gave myself time to think about the term *pathetic fallacy*. Nell had used it the night before she left. It was what she loved about me, but often it repulsed her too. That I would have a talking chair, and that I'd animate Toby and speak to her in a Toby voice. It is hard not to think the world and its contents are full of human thought. I guess, in a way, rather than reducing the world to the numbers one and zero, I prefer to ramp up the material of the world and infuse it with love and intellect. And yet, I also knew that everything in the apartment I tended to animate, and I realized that if we had a child, I would probably give up that tendency, I would devote the impulse to understanding another human being.

Auto Trader. I pulled the cable and jumped out at Parliament and King. I dont use the garage door, but instead what Tessa calls the man door.

Me: Time for a drink?

Tessa: I've got eighteen pages left to set up.

I can't go home yet theyre discovering a natural gas field and selling shares in a private offering.

She asked after Nell and I said she's left me.

I've had drinks with Tessa and she's told me her story. I have it here in the notes. Her husband told her once, joking, that theyre incompatible. They dont live together—two houses. They dress the same way but

Raoul's place is a fussy Victorian because, as Tessa puts it, he's interested in a lot of things.

She swivelled in her chair and took my knee. She made my knee bend. I'm sorry, she said.

For a second I had forgotten I'd confessed that Nell had left me.

Tessa tapped in another line of text with her lively fingers and then stared at the screen as though it were about to tell her something. There are over two thousand listings in each issue of *Auto Trader*.

I'm monogamous, Tessa had said once, by default.

She also said (but I'm not sure if my notes are correct) that lesbians have it figured out.

THEN I WALKED HOME in the disappointed sun. I realize I have a warm relationship with Tessa, a warmth that began at a weekend ATV and Motocross race school out in Havelock. That was two years ago. I had arrived late and Lars was already there, photographing the moving parts of machines. Tessa's husband was introducing her to people, and she was kissing them in greeting. When she saw me she was excited and leaned in for a fondness kiss. She put her arm around my neck to kiss me. The heat from her neck and the opening of her shirt, she was wearing one of those western shirts with the pearly clasp buttons. And instead of kissing on the side of the cheek, we kissed on the mouth. It was an alarming kiss, or a feeling ambushed me. It reminded me of my first good kiss, from the girl I'd had a crush on in high school. Maggie Pettipaw. She had lived in the Bean, a series of multicoloured apartments on the hill above where I grew up. Maggie is probably part Micmac. But one New Year's Eve at midnight, in a party at David Twombly's house, Maggie Pettipaw, who was someone else's girlfriend, walked over from the stereo and gave me a kiss on the lips. Wonderful.

Since meeting Nell I've reserved lip kisses for her. If I met you and wanted to welcome you I'd give you a hug or shake your hand. No kisses. And thinking of Nell, of the shape of her happy mouth, it broke me up a little. Then in a store window I saw the little tops Nell favours. Tan, flared pants. In winter she wears a fake fur hat—white—that makes her look like she's ice-skating. She puts a product in her long black hair that creates a shine, like an animal's pelt, and the edges feather up like eyelashes. She's confident, and can walk into a restaurant and eat by herself, or have a drink in a bar and be left alone. I noticed these things during the first few months when we played around, before we moved in together.

It took an hour to get home and I let the streetcar trams and taxis overtake me as I walked. Everyone should have a thinking place. Here in Toronto I dont yearn for parks or nature. I like visiting the wastelands of ill-advised city planners. There's something amusing about disaster and neglect. That this city will never be right because they buried the subway line under University rather than Spadina or Bathurst. The crink of polit- ical indecision is on every map of the underground. There is no centre to Toronto, you can't concentrate a rally if your blood runs to protest. All the buildings near the perimeter sit lightly as if to say we are not here long, especially if anything tax-wise happens to piss us off.

They were tearing down Regent Park, which is the area of town where Auto Trader is located. It was where Lars had lived. The excava- tions made me think of the wreck of a car David's father had been in. I'd known that car from youth, he'd had it for twenty years. A smart, white European vehicle. Indicating off the arterial road while a bunch of the Hurleys had reeled over a rise in a van. It was five oclock, the sun setting behind Arthur Twombly. Happy, he made the turn into Corner Brook. Arthur was leaning towards the driver side window when his skull cracked through his ears. He felt the movement of the trunk of his body as if it was being stacked into a filing cabinet. His arms elongated. His sternum shifted back twelve feet and the crack roared like a jet plane through his eyes. And then the shell of his body whipped back to follow his chest. Now the whump of the cage of the car and he had become a part of the car. He understood composite materials. It struck him that all this time he had never known he was the car. This division was like a Matisse painting, lines around things, but instead it was Cézanne. Cézanne was right, he thought, and then he climbed into a soft air mattress and sank deep into it face-first and became part of the mattress too. That was something. Airbag powder in his nostrils. He had looked himself up at ratemyprofessor.com and there were a lot of postings, most of them rated him hot and an excellent communicator. Arthur Twombly had changed lives.

I GOT BACK to Roncesvalles but the police had cordoned off the sidewalk around the apartment building. I sat in the coffee shop across the street and stared at the CUBA sí billboard. Then a flash and shower of orange from a welder's torch.

This kind of life has been going on now for three years, since I moved to Toronto and chose this photography work. You dont need me to tell you that when you leave an environment, it changes in ways that you dont change. And so, the similarity I had with both David and my wife was beginning to alter. I had spoken to Nell about this a total of three times. I have the notes.

Time one: Oh dont be silly we're the same, Gabe, we're immutable we do not change not in any intrinsic way.

Time two: I love what you are. (Pause) What are you?

Time three Nell brought it up. She said, Do you think we're different? Her feet moving in the sheets, as if she's running. Are we getting any different?

TEN

THERE WAS A CONCUSSION of air. It powdered itself through the gaps between the buttons of my shirt. Then the three tall windows of the café crinkled and shone and collapsed in a shower of wet ice. A wall of boom forced its way in, a buckling gulf of heat and wind. It was a bank of startled atmosphere in the city that made the glass tinkle, but then I saw it wasnt glass at all making the sound, but the pressure had blown jars of coffee beans from their shelves, coffee beans were alive on the floor. The hot buttons pressed into my chest and then the pelting of hard, dry coffee beans. I exhaled with the force of it. Then the light, the brightest light that sheered off my body, it burned away the bridge of my nose and the orbital cavity and I touched my face and was surprised to feel that I was whole. I was made of cold light. I thrust my hands out to shield my eyes but my hands vanished in the intensity.

The stripped building across the street, the top half shuddering with mad flame that peeled up the brick and then a white ball leapt into the low clouds and was gone, as there was nothing to eat but the tar on the pebbled roof and the roof was consumed. There was a sound, too, that felt like it was living in the top of my ears. A torn roof was on fire, the windows, my windows, busted out and a dance of delighted light on all the bald ceilings.

Here then, Nell, was the third bad thing.

THEY GAVE ME A HOTEL at the Days Inn. I lay on the bed and then felt bad being inactive so I stared out the window at a billboard on the Queensway advertising an eye-gaze system. Arthur Twombly, if he ever hauled himself out of his coma, would have this system. IKW had sponsored the billboard, their initials in the corner.

The police suggested I return to the apartment at four the next afternoon. But the foundations kept breaking into fire and three trucks doused the embers. You'll have to wait another day. They dumped seventeen hundred gallons of water on the building, they have a meter on the hoses. I got to talking to one of the firemen. He had a black eye. The temperature had reached a peak of two thousand degrees, he said, I dont know in what scale. I dont know what kelvin is, but maybe it was in kelvin. It was like the eyelid of a waking volcano. We werent allowed to search through the charred debris. When I say we I mean myself and Irene Loudermilk. Irene rents the apartment below Nell and me. Rented.

So the following day I walked up Roncesvalles to a stain of brown on the sidewalk. This, a good two blocks from the apartment. Like tracking sign from a wounded animal. Then firemen in their tan coats and trousers, green reflector tape, their names on the tails of their coats, as if their mothers had sewed them on. One man, with the visor on his red helmet pulled up, was applying torque to a large silver wrench on top of a hydrant, like something giants use to open preserves. Six fire trucks, then five more further up the street. They are waiting to see if the building will crack open again. The hull of the building, all three storeys, a scorched shipwreck pulled out of the sea and left to drip. The landlord was talking to the firemen, it was the first time I'd seen him since Nell and I moved in and signed the lease. He had become old. Or maybe it was the shock of his expired real estate. He was alarmed at the thought of loss of life, which I found touching. They were talking next to one little white fire truck, an older model. They'd sent that too. In fact it looked like the brains behind the brawnier fire trucks. Six firemen were at the door next to ours, breaking in delicately. Rummaging a hackapick through the glass door, trying to release a hapse. The slow movement of firemen. It's as if they know they couldnt possibly keep up with the friskiness of fire. We were to have ten minutes to search for personal articles, said a policeman in a flak jacket and black shirt. He was rerouting pedestrian traffic. He was one of two officers at the Bloor and Dundas intersection, senior men, called in to perform an old task, of directing traffic. The flourish of their white hands, movement at their elbows. They enjoy this, like riding a horse.

It was safe, engineers had walked through it. We were asked to wear forensic garbage bags on our feet. Myself and Irene Loudermilk. We had a laugh at the bags. Then I walked up behind her and I felt the heat still in the walls. I peered into the monochrome darkness of her flat. It felt like a Russian submarine. I watched her in there with her hands behind her head, tallying, like she was surrendering to the blank charring forces around her. She did not notice me. Then I took the stairs up to the sky. Our apartment was no longer an apartment. There was a lot of light from above. The fire had turned our apartment into a convertible.

Cadaver dogs had found a dry skull in the back room. A child's skull.

Me: There were no children in the apartment.

It was in your apartment, an investigator said. As if he hadnt heard me. Tone too. I can't imagine accusing a stranger of anything.

But even as I said it I doubted it. Perhaps we had children, or perhaps one stowed away. It's true that I'm often surprised to realize that ten

years have gone by, and I'm no longer twenty-five. I knew that I wanted
a child and that Nell had been stout in saying she'd had one child and she
was not interested in going through that again. Secretly, or in my own
secret manner, I knew I was trying to make her pregnant. Perhaps this
was proof, this skull.

My ordinary unconnected laptop. A plate of melted circuit board. The
books on the bookshelf torched. Toby's face singed off. I picked him up,
savaged. Something had melted in his eye, it gave him a mad look. I stood
at my desk and stroked the charcoal laminate, the roofless study where
I took my notes and read my books. I liked this room and now it all had
been reduced to carbonized shells of a blind and deaf material. I opened
a drawer for a pair of scissors. And there was Nell's green diary. Every
page blackened. The scissor handles had melted but they still worked and
I shanked off Toby's burnt fur. I cut him down to the nub and stuck him
under my arm like a shorn poodle and waded through the shale of the
hallway. It sounded like loose china. It felt like I was walking through a
midden at a rich archaeological dig.

A large flat section of the roof had fallen on our bed and flattened the
melted foam of our queen mattress. The blackened ridges of heavy
burning. Imagine if we were under that. The roof had metal brackets.
Then I saw a faint trace of beach and that patented blue sea.

It was the CUBA sí billboard.

Cuba had crushed us in bed.

There was a Canada goose in the bathroom, drinking fire retardant
from the tub. It looked huge. I shook Toby at the goose, for its own safety,
and it waddled down the hall into the kitchen, slipped, and then got
scared and hopped on the stove and one-footed it up to the fridge where
he opened his wings and lurched his shoulders and dove into the blue
air. He fell like a stone then crested and gathered himself and rose
again, banking over my head to give a long-necked rather joyous honk

through the vacant space where Cuba used to be. I made Toby watch him. Then I remembered the definition of a pathetic fallacy. Why did she have to use the word *pathetic*.

The kitchen cupboards sagging from the wall like a sad black accordion.

I stood at the metal sink where so many of our conversations had occurred. I tried the tap and clean water blurted out. It rinsed off a bright patch of stainless steel that looked like a leaf made of pewter. It offered a leaf of hope, as though all this massive damage was minor repair.

The melted handles of screwdrivers. A burnt hammer. My father's wrench, the only tool in the sunroom not damaged. Men with a machine out back.

Our chest freezer, hanging in the crotch of a scared fruit tree. Must have blown out the roof. My gold. The fire department was lowering it on a cable encased in yellow plastic, a winch from the front of a short fire truck. Hey, I said. The freezer was smouldering, like an airplane engine, or a bank vault from an airplane. Something heavy that had flown a distance. Three men guiding a hose to hose it down.

The lid and hinges fused shut.

There's things in it, I said.

Youre not going to want to eat anything that's in this.

It's not a perishable, I said.

We waited until they could handle it. Then they cut through it with a chainsaw for metal. They ripped open the lid vigorously. They enjoyed the destruction, but then a waft of what was inside. A sticky coating of blue plastic and then chunks of cooked meat. Caribou. Men were walking away from the stink.

I got a thing stored in there, I said.

I hoisted out the chunks of caribou. They were desiccated and warm. Then in the bottom I saw the gold. It was one bright turd of gold, but it looked hot. The gold had melted together and formed a bar. A nubbly bar like a dumbbell. An eight-pound dumbbell.

Can you tell if it's hot, I said.

A fireman reached in and picked it out. They hosed it down. Water against the gold, like a panhandler. Then the adjuster came around to the back and caught what I was doing. Nothing surprised him.

It was the arc welder, I said to the adjuster.

No, apparently a woman was out here burning a love letter.

Forensics had tested the skull. Probably raccoon. This from a guy in a blue police jacket. There had been a raccoon living in a false wall, he said.

ELEVEN

NELL'S JOURNAL was not dated but I could tell from the scenes described that it covered large swathes of life. You could read the print on the charred pages. Some of it. Some of it you had to guess at. I went to the post office and asked what I should do about our mail. That was you, he said. As if I'd torched the building. He rerouted our mail to a general delivery address. Then I thought about our phone, and that I'd have to do the same thing because the phones were destroyed. But then I realized the telephone message system still worked. In some ways your life can be utterly ruined but all the systems for that life stream on. There is, in selective corridors of tragedy, a brute force that persists.

I crossed Roncesvalles and went online at the library. Roncesvalles was named by a man from the area who had fought a war in Spain. I emailed Nell. I told her about the apartment. I tried to be composed. I said, gently, Where are you. I left off the question mark, that's what made it gentle. I told her about the freezer and her journal and that if I didnt hear from her I'd have to read it, though it was an idle threat as the journal was hardly readable. Then I went online to check Nell's stocks. She was involved in numbers and something in my head thought that, with an unreadable journal, perhaps I could understand something of her disappearance through the rise and fall of stocks. They were stocks chosen by David Twombly. Since IKW had gone private I hadnt had the guts to get back into the markets. I had made a windfall through David and put it into this bar of gold. But I keep a fantasy list, and thankfully I'm way down. What I had been doing was following my hunches. But to think one has independent hunches, as David told me, is to be fooled into believing there is no machinery in the world devoted to persuading us we have original thought. So what I had decided to do was to drum up my hunch and then act on its opposite. This too had failed. For often we are drawn to the dark side (David's advice again). We prefer the bad. And in finding my hunch and then bidding on its opposite, I had done what I have done with friendships and occupations my whole life: chosen the thing I thought would be bad for me—or good for me—both in an attempt to open up a bright wing of Gabriel English. But this never leads to a new appendage, or at least the new work is no alteration of your essence. We're creatures of routine, and the only way to jar ourselves from the repetitive nature of our actions and thoughts is to find new people in new places and live there with them. This was a revelation, this sense that fate was not ordained, but that our lives pan out in what can be called fate with hindsight, only because we are not awake enough to derail the replicating mechanism's role of keeping us safe for a very long time.

I WOKE UP at the hotel and not in our apartment and I made coffee with one of those coffee satchels that looks like a diaper. On the table I had lined up Toby with my father's wrench, Nell's diary and the nubbly bar of gold. It was all I had left in the world. I called the front desk for messages but there were no messages. Then I remembered my home phone. Anyone calling would not know that the phone had died. There was a message from David.

David had spent the last two days glued to his pebble, working all his connections to get his no-fly status revoked. At times the appeal worked, but then, each time he arrived at his terminal, the airport computers refused him. The tone of his voice was patient rage. He had to see me, he said. So I called him back and said meet me at the Inter Steer.

I ate a bison burger at the all-day breakfast and talked to two Caribbean vendors I often saw in there. They were eating veal parmigiana sandwiches and playing backgammon and drinking coffee from a big aluminum thermos they had brought in themselves. They asked me how much their cars could fetch. They spoke a lot about money, how much they made, who paid well and where paid well. Getting paid bores me, so I thought of Nell and where she might be. But a bit about being paid filtered into the Wyoming, and I remembered that Nell had said she was paid the most when she worked at the pueblo casinos in New Mexico. I'd shouted at her and she didnt need to be shouted at. She needed to think about what to do and she needed help. She'd called a cab to the airport and asked the cab driver what airlines flew into the States. She would have got out at Terminal 1 and wheeled her carry-on to the American Airlines desk. They had an early flight into O'Hare and from there a connector to Las Vegas. Not that she knew anyone there. But she had been destroyed in the heart. She had worked for these American casinos, she knew the security systems. She would have gone there as a neutral site to think about things, about what to do. The plane passing over the Nevada desert, stippled with coarse bushes. She had no checked baggage. She just stepped into a cab and told him to take her to the Desert Fox casino. She had breakfast of black beans with one sunny-side egg and a tortilla shell with chilies. It reminded her of Santa Fe. This breakfast summoned up Santa Fe and her life with Richard Text. Then she walked into town as the sun built up a little nest to the east, past the Bellagio fountains but the fountains werent on. She wondered what time they began. A concierge explained that they were broken. Just a pool of still water. Lights shone on the water, and there was something quiet about the fountain, you knew it should be churning. All that money was for the water to dance. It made her uneasy and she went back to the Desert Fox and realized she was still hungry so she ordered room service. She did not turn on the television, and she kept the curtains open. She had asked for a floor high up. She was standing there, looking north, at the rim of the Canadian border, wondering why she was choosing such a small thing to do with her life.

I hooked up with David Twombly at the Inter Steer, a romantic place. He was used to private clubs, but was willing to slum it. The Polish car thieves were flipping through the mechanical jukebox pages. They were nocturnal men, who worked in pairs in the wealthy neighbourhoods, scouting out luxury cars and breaking into houses for car keys and driving the cars down to Lake Ontario where they rolled them onto shipping containers destined for Dubai.

We ordered the big Polish beers with the red and blue labels, Zywiec. The back of David was lit up by the cheery pockets of light from the jukebox. It was like someone had shook him out of a box of wine gums.

Driving into the sun at the speed limit. It got David riled up for some kind of action and yet here he was, stymied. The thought of the Hurleys made him slap his shaved head. He rose from his seat slapping his skull. He was going to have to drive his convertible there. How long a trip is that, he said.

A good three days, I said.

Youve done it, he said.

The last three summers.

Then I told him my place had burnt down. I told him the whole story and he enjoyed it, the place exploding like that fascinated him. He forgot it was my place, it was just an entertaining story. I said I was staying at the Days Inn.

You can stay with me, he said.

The hotel's fine. Theyre paying for it.

Then he asked about Nell, if she'd shown up, what the last thing we'd done together was. He seemed to think there might be evidence in finishing touches.

I sense my wife will return, I said, without saying where she's been.

Nell is not your wife.

Me: She'll return as if no time has elapsed, and that might stick if she keeps a calendar and smudges off seven days.

David: If she folds time to the week and returns at least on the proper night.

Me: As though that window of time was something only I experienced while she continued on in the chronological world.

That's the type of mindfuck, David said, women are capable of.

Now that's bad. I touched the table with the tips of all five fingers. What youre saying.

David was echoing some deep resentment towards his ex-wife.

Hang on, he said, we're at the Inter Steer, yes?

I agreed we were. I agreed that the Poles were going through a hard time. They had lost both a Pope and a heavyweight champion.

And how bad are you, David said. If you had to name a percentage.

One of the car thieves was making a slit-throat gesture to a song choice.

I'm half bad, I said.

We're all half bad. It's a seesaw battle like most elections. I like to let my badness reign in a place like the Inter Steer.

I said, Anyone can rationalize a lapsed week.

He ordered a plate of kolbasa sausage and it came with two slabs of dry rye bread. You know the Hurleys.

It's been twenty years, I said.

You know what happened twenty years ago?

I stared at him.

Nell Tarkington came to town.

David said it like the start of a western. Then I noticed he was wearing a pair of blue pants with a yellow stripe. Cavalry pants. To Corner Brook, I said.

And met my father. Twenty years.

He did it as a newspaper headline, and I nodded to that.

You know the full extent of Nell and my dad.

The words *full extent* made my muscles below my ears prickly. I knew the full extent, pal.

What can be fuller, I said, than having a child.

I'm just making sure you know everything.

I'm the type of guy to forget facts like that.

But the image of Nell with a child bloomed in my head. Mother Nell. Keep talking, I said.

You know this.

I hate it when you pause over delicious facts.

He went back to chewing his sausage. Did I want to strangle him. To press his big bald head in the vise of an arm. There was a lot of work in his cheeks as he chewed. A burnished indent, fleshy. Rough and soft and a variety of colour, plum, ash, pink. A crevice and those fangs of flesh, as though he'd gone through some aboriginal ceremony of cutting, a slice with a surgical blade, seasoned and weathered.

I grabbed the hand that was holding the fork. Youve got the kind of cheeks, I said, a gay man might have.

And David was surprised. Then he opened his mouth and laughed. You could see the chewed sausage in his mouth. He was like that god who eats his children, an articulate thug.

She was eighteen, David said. He wrenched free his hand. My father's child, Gabe, you think about that the next time I talk about women and mindfucks.

Were these reasonable points of cause and effect.

The Hurleys, David said, adopted him.

Me: The Hurleys.

Old man Hurley.

I used to meet him, I said, on the Humber River, fishing. Loyola Hurley. The Hurley boys in a van with a moose bar. The plumbing company, we called him Cake.

Cake thought the kid was Joe's. He loved kids.

And so I told him that Nell had mentioned this. That Nell's son, with Dave's father, had grown up with the Hurleys.

The very ones that nailed my father in a van with a moose bar.

You say moose bar with a certain vitriol.

There's got to be a premeditation.

You mean a cause and an effect. Between your dad in hospital and Nell disappearing.

A connection. They rammed him intentionally.

But David had told me, on the phone, that it was his father's fault. Randy Jacobs had told him that. I guess now David wasnt so sure. Gerard Hurley. We both knew him, we'd gone to school with him. Gerard had sold hash and was the first to use the metric system. The reason he used it was he could make more profit from cutting kilos into grams than pounds into ounces.

Me: And you think Nell would know.

Why disappear.

And I said I'd been thinking the same thing, only in my Wyoming state. It felt strange, I said, to be speaking it out loud to someone else. It made it more like an episode of a science fiction series.

Your Wyoming state. You want to elaborate on that.

I told him about Wyoming and then how death came in waves. When we were eighteen some of us were killed. Then recently friends were being killed again, cancer, the army, accidents. It felt like if you could get through the eighteen-year barrier you'd be okay for another eighteen years. The assassins come to the door in eighteen-year cycles.

Her Twombly son raised by Hurleys, David said. My half-brother. Anthony's eighteen now. Stick that in your Wyoming.

I can do the math.

He's a mixer for North Star Cement out by the Humber River.

You probably know his entire work history, I said.

And he did. He'd asked Massimo Sythe if he could use the IKW toolbox. From the toolbox he knew that Anthony assisted Loyola last winter stringing new wire through old outlets and that he's used a pneumatic staple gun and he's torched on roofs on Cobb Lane. What else. Anthony's operated a backhoe when the men were on a lunch break. He's taken apart the electric components to stoves and decoupled the coolant in freezers.

You know this, I said, because my youth was the same. You witnessed my youth.

Information, Gabe. Sales receipts, surveillance cameras, CPP contributions, vacation pay. Anthony is in the construction business.

I had applied for manual labour jobs because that is what my brother put down on the applications at manpower. I've mowed lawns and painted creosote fences and mixed plaster and combined gelcoat with hardener for fibreglass countertops. David did none of this. He's never cut cords of birch and sharpened the chainsaw's teeth or french-polished rocking chairs and sold wooden figurines at the craft shop up on the highway. When I was thirteen I took over my brother's paper route with a hundred and seventy-four customers and I operated the trap shoot and sold a salmon I'd caught at six in the morning for twenty dollars to a man who saw me trying to fit it in the pannier of my bicycle. I've collected rifle cartridges and sold them as scrap metal just as I've sorted through my mother's cash register at the Bank of Nova Scotia and replaced the pre-1967 quarters and dimes that have a high silver content. Dave made money by supplying code to machines.

This work has made us the people we are, and now the new work has created Anthony Hurley, a presence in the world that was causing David's world to warp and revolve around his. Though one could argue it was not the work but the domestic background of Anthony Hurley that was offering a form of blowback.

One of the Polish men came over and it broke the narrow focus David had. The man was carrying a travel chess set in both hands. We will play, he said, for those shoes.

He was pointing with his chin to David's shoes. He was standing too close and I had to get up and breathe something that didnt have David's breath in it. I'm going to drive down, he said. You could come with me.

Me: Why would I do that.

For the drive. Your apartment's burnt down, Nell is gone. It'll clear your mind, he said.

I left him in his cavalry pants with the kolbasa on his fork, to play chess and keep his shoes.

But as I walked home I knew that I needed to get away. I hadnt gone to Cuba, in fact Cuba had come to me. Cuba had tried its best to crush me in bed. I needed a breath of air and one island was as good as another. And true, there is something masochistic in me that desired to be close to the man who had deceived me. Who had pretended to be my friend. No, that's not right. He was a friend. He was wrestling with the facts. Or perhaps, as I've suggested, David Twombly was oblivious. Perhaps the affair with Nell meant nothing to him now, and he addressed me without any feelings of superiority. This all fascinated me, and I had no sense of pride or manly indignation. Those were old-fashioned positions to be jostled with in twentieth-century books. No, the truth is I did feel like ramming the barrel of a shotgun down his throat and pulling heavily on the trigger, but I also enjoyed resisting that urge, and coddling a restraint. This is not a book my father will enjoy.

TWELVE

DAVID TWOMBLY WAS, technically, an American. He had an American passport and he voted during American elections. His parents had moved to Newfoundland in the sixties. It was that great pulse of immigration to Canada, which had brought my family over. For Arthur Twombly, it was sympathy to those younger than himself in the States who were avoiding the draft. David's mother found work at the US army base in Stephenville, she was a civilian lawyer for the army, and Arthur got established with the newly built college. They returned to the States for the summers and sabbaticals. They had Zac in Michigan and David was born in Stephenville, on the army base. This army base birth gives David, occasionally, the ambitious comfort that he could one day be president of the United States. He believed in a free market, he did not criticize, as his parents certainly did, American culture and expansionism. He was more like his grandfather, an internationalist who believed in trickle-down economics but had a good heart. The idea of Canada he found, in the end, to be one of a fifty-first state. While he was at McGill he did not think about Quebec separatism except in how it might facilitate the American absorption of Canada and Mexico. He took French. He was excited by developments, that he was living in an era of change. His peers were men and women about to be handed the reins of Canadian power, but he saw Canadian power as a diminished position. He was agreeable to the notion of insidious takeover. That Canada could retain its name, the way that an airline turned private can keep a country's name, as long as it never raised an army against US trade law or foreign policy. He predicted a Canadian wing in the US military. His work encouraged software and special forces that Canada could provide for any American occupying force. And yet he donated ten percent of his salary to causes, as long as the causes were tax-deductible.

THEY FOLLOWED HIM HOME. They cased him. They slid a back door open and took the keys. They were in David's house. That's the worst part, he said. Like I'd invite any of those guys back to my house.

But he was awake and aware. He'd called the police. He gave the police a good profile.

The convertible, I said, is not a good cross-country vehicle.

It's a rental, he said. And what are you saying about my taste in automobiles.

I told him about buying a car that we could sell. Why be stuck in Newfoundland having to drive back. By that time, I said, your no-fly status will be cleared up and you can take air travel again.

Some hybrid, he said.

Me: Theyre expensive.

Hang the expense. No perhaps we should worry about expenses. I might have to go bankrupt, I was just meeting with my lawyer. What about one of those cars from India. One of those two-thousand-dollar cars where they use strong adhesives rather than welds.

Me: You want to drive around in a bamboo crate.

Theyre made with lightweight composites, Gabe. Theyre made with the same adhesives as airplanes.

Dave youre not going to find one of those cars around here.

There was a pause on the phone which meant I did not realize the world was a neighbourhood now. And perhaps with David's connections he could order and import and license one of those Indian cars in three days. If he was going to go cheap, he wanted to go futuristic.

I'll find a deal at *Auto Trader*. Let's make a trip of it, I said.

He thought about that. What I want to drive, he said, is something state of the art.

BUT THEN A DAY WENT BY and he was against the whole thing. He'd rather spend his energy fighting the no-fly caution on his airport ID. That's the other thing about David, an enthusiasm for any adventure that quickly burns off and an underlying force takes over.

But I felt trapped now in Toronto, without an apartment, with no Nell, and no reason to be here. So why not begin my summer early and purchase a car and drive. I was thinking about an Audi, like the one David's dad had been creamed in. A boxy, foreign car good on gas and they depreciate slowly. But then I remembered the converted police cruiser, Zac's car. Now that would have some hustle. A pursuit vehicle. What would it fetch in Newfoundland. Three grand. I walked to the library and looked it up online at the *Auto Trader* auction. Twice in the last three months Alice Stebbins has called Tessa Walcott and trimmed a hundred dollars off the asking price. She's down to twenty-four hundred dollars. Tessa finds it odd when a client doesnt want to run the old photo. Though Alice has not asked for another photographer.

I went over to look at it. As a buyer.

The engine leaks oil, Alice Stebbins said.

Worn valves, I said.

Alice: Too many car chases.

She popped the hood and I lifted it and found the metal wand.

Or a tapered cylinder wall, I said.

We both stared hard at the engine.

That allows oil to enter the combustion chamber, I said. That's what causes the oil burning.

I would take a loss on it if you factored in the miles per gallon. But she was desperate and had removed her reserve. A minimum bid. I could key in fifteen hundred dollars. I liked the idea of bringing something from Jane and Finch to Newfoundland. But I also wanted to make it a personal transaction, to hand Alice Stebbins cash on the spot, the old-fashioned way.

I TRIED TO PUT ON HOLD my new life in Toronto. I sent Nell another email, in case she was alive in that form. I warned her the apartment was gone, and that I had put in a claim to the landlord's insurance company. I said I was going to make a trip with David. That we would talk about what happened and do the male thing and come out the end stronger for it. Bonding. That would make her terrified. She'd want to warn him.

I made a fist and touched the screen, which was her solar plexus. I brushed it with my knuckles. Youre not to do that Nell, I said quietly. I was pretending she stood before me.

NEXT DOOR TO ME at the Days Inn I saw Irene Loudermilk inserting her key card.

Hey, I said.

Neighbour.

Some fire.

Some love letter.

It had been Irene burning the love letter. It was a man who had made her move to Toronto in the first place, a man named Arnold Cream from Calgary who worked in oil and whose head offices relocated to Toronto during the Conservative years when Ontario's provincial government loosened corporate tax regulations.

I'd never spent much time thinking about Irene Loudermilk. She was polite and sorted our mail on the stairs without its ever feeling snoopy. She was quiet and smoked a lot of pot and played guitar in a country-and-western band. She was older than Nell and me but she was still beautiful in a forty-five-year-old way. We sat at the hotel bar and had a drink and I realized beauty from the past can still visit in pulses and in fact could be a more vivid beauty for its gathering and diminishing returns. It made the present more urgent and vital. We knew nothing of each other, though she said she could hear a lot through the bathroom, that Nell and I argued a lot in the bathroom, or it could have been elsewhere but came to her through the bathroom.

I didnt know we argued.

You yelled at her a lot.

I yelled?

Irene rested her chin on the rim of her scotch. I hadnt seen a woman do that on a first drink. Did we argue or were we passionate? Was it about David Twombly or was it Nell assuming more of my inner life. You can be territorial when the country of your own thoughts is devoured by the one you love.

Irene Loudermilk had a whiteness around her eyelids and her nostrils were flared from drug use or just a lot of colds. I realized I hadnt looked at her before and she was interesting. She did interesting things with her fingers when she spoke and she wore a topaz belt buckle that flashed as she leaned in and out from the bar with her elbows. It was as if she held a map on the bar and was pointing things out, a map of emotional terrain. She'd had a child when she was sixteen, she said, and then met Arnold and he urged her to give the baby up so that they could start anew. I was astonished at how close her story was to Nell's. It was a terrible mistake, Irene said. They lived Arnold's life for twenty years. He forgot completely about her early sacrifice and did not understand how the friction between them resulted from his wrong-headed starting gate. But even so Irene stuck by him and moved out east when his office relocated (to Irene, Toronto was the East Coast). But then Arnold's mandate at work was revised and he was more often in Alberta than he'd been when they lived in Calgary. He visited junior oil companies outside Red Deer, there were drilling services and regulatory bodies he had to negotiate with inside the shale till zone of small pocket reserves. They were living in Richmond Hill and, even during the ten years they lived there, the place became unrecognizable to them.

There were photos of us and it looked, she said, like we'd kept moving house.

Fields of maple turned into malls, schools imploded for automotive showrooms. So Irene sold the house one winter while Arnold was in Red Deer and moved down into our retro neighbourhood, Roncesvalles, where she could at least see some history and attach herself to a big park. She stripped the house of all its furnishings and sold them in the paper and had the Salvation Army pick up the rest. Arnold had given her a vibrator. You can't really give it to the Goodwill like the sheets. So she left it in the house.

Her mother was Ukrainian and the Polish area felt like her mother, but Arnold never liked it and when he came home he stayed in a hotel and she went to visit him.

For a moment we both realized we were in Arnold's hotel, and I half expected him to appear perhaps to freshen our drinks.

Then she got a letter.

She caught the attention of the bartender and I realized this was a big deal coming now and she needed a stepping stone into the depth of it.

How excited he was, Irene said. Arnold had fallen in love with a woman at work, a woman they'd once had over, her and her husband. The letter didnt literally say Arnold was excited, in fact he wrote about how sorry he was, but Irene could tell in the enthusiasm and urgency that he was excited, if a little guilty. It was an admission that avoided both deceit and distrust.

So that was it. Irene was burning a letter on her back step when a corner floated away and slipped through a crack in the siding. She felt the whip of light flow into the apartment and a murmur of hoses expanding and she had her bare shoulder against the brick footing of the basement and that's what protected her, well all the effort went north, went out of the top, went through our apartment.

We drank and the light outside became darker than the bar. I was drinking with Irene Loudermilk, homeless and abandoned and we both had the sense to laugh at that. I'm not that attracted to you, she said, but I wouldnt say no if you wanted to come to my room and compare it to yours.

I must have told her about Nell. Though I didnt recall telling her, and then I remembered Irene saying we argued.

We lay on her bed and it was the exact set-up as my room, in reverse. So our headboards were adjacent. We were both old enough to take pleasure in an embrace without being nervous. We lay on her bed and she opened the mini bar and poured us some mini drinks and we lay there and I closed my eyes and listened to the traffic flow down King Street. Then we made another assault on the mini bar and we drank standing up, sort of pointing at each other with our shoulders and listening to the street. The streetcars were having a hard time making the tight turn into their depot, it required a lot of friction on the track. One could hardly believe steel to be so resilient. We didnt think to open the cupboard doors to watch television, at least it never occurred to me. I could hear Irene's drink doing work around her lips, the clink of teeth. When I heard that I turned and kissed a part of her body, then I fell asleep with my clothes on. Though I did not know I had fallen asleep. I was thinking about Nell and where she was gone. I thought about Vegas. That was where she had met David again. I turned into a bird that watched Nell at thirty feet. I was in a desert with Nell walking along Highway 93, a dirt road just east of the Nevada Test Site. This is a story she had told me about how she had met David. A truck from the Moapa Indian Reservation had slowed past her and heaved over.

Where you headed.

Nell: Vegas.

He was trucking gauges, oxygen tanks and flippers.

Youve got scuba gear, she said. In the desert.

You never know, he said.

They drove into Las Vegas. He had grown up admiring Jacques Cousteau, or perhaps he was a grandson, a descendant who had come out of the oceans to live on dry land but still carried the apparatus of his origins. Nell had wanted to see how far she could get away from Vegas just thumbing but then had grown tired of it and thumbed back. She had a conference to attend. The man didnt think that was unusual. He looked like he'd seen a lot of things, and that's why he was prepared for all eventualities, dry or wet.

They drove into the Bellagio and he parked up on a concrete ramp beside a thick palm tree. He parked with the windshield in the shade. The fountains were silent. They were not working. They got out and he stripped to his shorts. He dragged out a tub which had his regulator and buoyancy compensator vest and flippers. Can you help me with this tank, he said. She tilted the tank on the open tailgate and he crouched and slipped it on. Turn that nozzle a half turn, he said. And he leaned on her shoulder for support as he slipped his feet into the flippers. These are dainty manoeuvres. He walked backwards to the edge of the pool and then bent his knees and fell over into the water and twisted himself down with a little shrug of his hips. He was going deep, a pulse of bubbles distorted the surface and when they calmed he was gone. Nell waited but he did not come back.

She had gone into the conference, the cool wave of air conditioning, and received her name tag and album of papers. The name tags were spread alphabetically over two desks and she saw David Twombly's name below hers. There was a plenary session that lasted two hours. They heard of the new police security, Taser technology and CCT monitors. The world, it seemed, was out to get you and you had to be diligent. Three hours later she found him. He had been looking for her. He had seen her name in the schedule. They went outside and quickly put on sunglasses. Out here in Vegas, why not give in to a little thing. Men dressed as gorillas pitched dinner coupons at them, there were at least three heavyweight champions of the world. Bullfighters and pigmies. It seemed everyone was dressed up as someone outrageous, asking you to come to dinner for ten percent off. They leaned over the railing in the bright four oclock sun and stared at the malfunctioning fountain. Then an object, blurred, rising in the pool. He lifted a wrench over his head. Hey, David said. And the frogman gave him the okay. He was negotiating the cement stairs. His tank clanked against the side. Hey you, David said. And made for him. Nell had to run after David, and explain.

I WOKE UP and Irene Loudermilk was under the covers. She had undressed and was trying to pull more over herself except my weight was stopping it all. So I got up and this made my jaw thump, and I thought of the word *thrombosis*. I looked at Irene and her eyes were open. Her eyes had no expectation. She was taking care of herself.

If the insurance company hears about this, I said, we'll lose one of the rooms.

You better go in and ruffle your sheets.

I went in and messed up my bed. What a strange thing to do.

Then I went back to Irene's room. I had to knock as the door had sprung shut. Irene came up to the shut door and said, Look I have to shave a sweater.

Okay, I said. I realized she was reasonable, what the hell was I thinking. And I felt awful for the things I had done with Irene and the lack of fear I had in wrecking things. But then I remembered that I was wronged, that I had every right to be bad if I wanted, though in fact I'd behaved well. My gum was inflamed and I looked for the cannabis spray but that was gone now in the fire and I had to make do with headache pills.

I had a shower and I grated an aspirin over my back teeth. I chucked Toby under the chin and did some arm curls with the gold. I spend perhaps three nights a year in a hotel, so I'm up for enjoying the experience. This one had a mirror on an expandable arm that magnified your face. My face looked horrendous and my jaw was puffy. So I flattened the mirror and draped a hand towel over it.

I checked the rate for local calls and it was a dollar twenty-five, so I went down to the lobby and used a payphone. There was a woman there with a boy watching a cop show on TV. The boy looked like he'd never seen TV before. He was talking excitedly about it and she said to him, Use your indoor voice.

David, I said, I'm all for getting out of here today.

My friend let us drive our troubles away.

I hung up and the boy had turned from the TV to ask his mother a question.

Mother: Throw them in jail is an expression, honey. They dont really throw them in jail.

I TOOK A TAXI to David's and he was waiting there in the road, checking his stocks on his pebble. He jumped in. We kept going up to Jane and Finch and I saw him wince. He was not used to these areas of Toronto. The wide roads with narrow sidewalks and no trees. Noisy and dusty. What kind of car, he said. I didnt want to tell him. I wanted to see his face. He had this look now. Like he was being patient, but also that he was game. It was the same look when he flipped through my English comic books. How did anyone find black and white entertaining. But he did flick through the comics. He was willing to look at the world my way. For ten minutes.

We walked over to the Matador. He was walking like he was out on a day pass. Then he put up his arms in mock surrender.

I'm not driving across Canada in that, officer.

We're only driving across half of Canada.

There's a van for sale in the Loblaws parking lot, David said. A silver van with a handicapped licence. We could sleep in it.

David this baby can move.

Dont I know it, he said.

And then he thought about it. We both knelt at the grille and were impressed. You want to return to something in the past, he said.

It's not Zac's car, I said. It's a genuine LAPD ghost car.

It's Zac's car. With an oil leak.

I knew the oil leak wasnt from worn piston rings. I was keeping that from Alice Stebbins. Usually I'm a very honest person, but when car sales are involved, I chisel. It was just a clogged crankcase ventilation system. The PCV valve. It would cost thirty-two dollars to fix.

Alice Stebbins came out and so too did her mother.

My husband, the mother said, he loved this car. He took such care of it. He made sure of all the inspections and he changed the oil regularly and he waxed it every Saturday afternoon before the ballgame.

Alice was jangling the keys. She was carrying a portable radio with a cigarette lighter adaptor cable. She said, You have to kiss me. You have to hug me and give me a nice kiss.

You got it, David said. And kissed her. She looked like she had a sweet mouth.

She's all yours, she said.

Mrs Stebbins: Honor rotated the tires and he never drove it hard and he was careful even when he shut the doors.

Honor? Men are named Honor?

David got in and slammed shut the door. He rolled down the window and then started it up, the powerful low rumble of a V8. The mother leaned in through the open window and told David her husband treated the car like a member of the family.

Well all that, David said, is about to change.

WE TOOK IT for a test drive along Dupont and under the railroad overpass. It had one of those stock-car rear-view mirrors where you can see everything coming behind you. My god the suspension was rock-hard. But the power was strong, and in a parking lot David tried some sharp cornering and the steering was fine.

This car grew up in Los Angeles, David said.

Toronto is a lot like Los Angeles.

This car is the opposite of a time machine, he said. It's a wayback machine.

David had once spent a month driving through Byelorussia in a Belaz truck. That's what we want, he said, a Belaz truck. You could fix it with a hammer and a wrench.

We drove back to Alice Stebbins and signed the paperwork and I handed her a cheque for fifteen hundred dollars. I know people in garages and so Dave went home while I got Carl Thoms in Unit 6 to sign the emissions certificate. Carl stared at the Matador from fifty feet, whistled, and handed me my cleared inspection. I flipped the registration for sixty dollars and filled the tank until the pump clicked off the trigger on the nozzle. I took her in for an oil change and filter. I serviced the charcoal fuel vapour canister myself. I know what to spend on a car to get your money's worth. I checked the tire pressure and was astonished to see the gauge pop up to eighty pounds. We were riding on four bombs. I let out, in total, a hundred and eighty pounds of air. And I drove away on suspension smooth as cream.

I PACKED UP Toby and my father's wrench and the gold. I wedged Toby onto the shelf below the rear windshield. He looked insane. The gold I kept between my thighs. I couldnt think of a better place. I dropped off my last disc to Tessa. I said I was heading home for a little vacation. I told her about the fire.

That was your place. My god Gabe my god youre all right.

The whole apartment, Tessa. The works. A raccoon family was burnt due to a leak and a love letter. The CUBA sí billboard fell on our bed.

Tessa stood up and hugged me. For the second time in as many visits, Tessa Walcott had reached out to be affectionate. It was erratic and quick and she felt nice. It was good to be held and to bury my nose in her ear.

You need a place to crash.

I found a goose in the bathtub.

A live goose.

I mean it was in the bathroom.

That's not a good omen.

What isnt.

A bird in the home. It's supposed to be bad luck.

It's the second bird that's been in the house. There was a pigeon.

You are probably asking yourself if I have ever thought of Tessa Walcott. Guyanese by birth, raised in England, living here in Toronto. She's twenty-eight, a narrow frame and she wears coffee-coloured pants with an overcoat and rubber boots, her hair clipped short, gold earrings. Married, no children. Here are the reasons I have not:

(1) She has flirted with me in only very small pulses.
(2) In three years, I have spent more than an hour with her on only two occasions.
(3) Her husband. I like him.
(4) Her husband. He big and strong.
(5) In Wyoming, I do not like to fantasize about women I know well.

I told Tessa I was at the Days Inn. I told her I couldnt do the work any longer. I said that it was a lark and now that my life was being shifted on me I had to stand my ground and solve the things that were within my range. I couldnt just be taking photographs of vehicles. Youre leaving us, she said. And she gave me a look that said she loved me. Those are the best looks, when people you know slightly give themselves over to you with a look. We're all in it together, that look said.

Tessa: Nothing is going to happen between us.

I thought she meant us, but she meant her and Raoul, her husband.

We went for one last afternoon beer. That is the big difference between cities and the wild, I said. You have to make your own happenings in the wild, Tessa. You have to act if you want one moment to stand out from another.

My husband, Tessa said. Raoul doesnt want to do anything that will keep the peace. He wants to be who he is unbudging.

You want to feel good, I said.

Then choose to leave him, Tessa said. Leave when I've done no wrong and leave not when I'm feeling jealous. Have a good footing.

But you have felt jealous.

We were at his friends, Tessa said. Playing charades, and I saw Raoul carrying this woman, his friend's wife. Put me down, she said. Then I heard her say, Put me down because Tessa won't like it.

I knew what that meant. I used to be in a relationship like that. It's hard on the valves in the heart.

He started serenading her, Tessa said. Two inches from her face. So I said to Raoul, Do you want to sleep with her? He looked at this thought and said to me: Tessa, pay attention.

I closed my eyes and tried to become Tessa. I said, So you walked away.

Tessa: I was upset.

I understand.

We were playing charades, she said, and Raoul crept around a doorway and pointed at me. Who is that, he said. Meaning Tessa. His fat cruel finger. No one says anything. He's drunk. She's jealous, he says. And they all share a look. He's right, she is jealous, and there's no recourse. But it made her feel small and frail.

Between you and me, I said, what you said is kind of sexy.

Tessa: I'm not up to being big enough. I had a bath last night, she said. And as I thought about it all two strands of hair floated together and made a Q. I thought, questions.

Me: The guy you dont officially trust.

It's as if Raoul leaves it all out there but when you stare hard you realize there's nothing of himself there at all.

The devil, I said, is a lived life.

Is there anyone out there who, if she called tonight and said come meet me, I'm in love with you, would you go?

I was ambushed with the face of Nell. And then I pushed her away to
see if there was room for another soul, as Nell had abandoned me. When
Tessa was that close, she reminded me of Maggie Pettipaw.

Come on, Tessa said. I have to pick my husband up at his ballgame.

I'll drive you.

We stepped outside of ourselves, Tessa and I, and looked at each other
out on the street. There was a long mirror in a framing store and we saw
that we werent right for each other. It was hilarious to see we cared for
each other and that was as far as it could go. We were both in a plight,
different ones, and we saw each other's humanity, though neither could
fully save the other.

We drove the Matador along Parliament. The night was bright and
warm. Then I parked on a side street and we walked to a green ball field
lit with powerful tall lights. There was a soccer match at halftime. Raoul
was playing. Tessa was supposed to walk over and stick her finger in his
ribs. Instead we watched the players resting. Her husband was sitting on
the sidelines, his diabetic kit out. Raoul was pricking the tip of a finger.

He has a photo of me, Tessa said, in his wallet. When I was seven. He
gets in trouble when he tells people that's my wife.

I touched Tessa's shoulder once at that Havelock motor race and when
she leaned over to listen she saw it was me. She'd forgotten and thought
it was Raoul. Thing is, I would not touch her where I had if I was Raoul,
but she accepted it as normal for Raoul.

THIRTEEN

DAVID'S HOUSE was on Grace. In the window a fan, he waved his hand at the screen. I walked in and looked up the white staircase, the plaster walls a little bashed, from the corners of moved furniture.

The car looks good from above, he said.

When Sok Hoon left he repainted and he did the painting himself, the walls a pastry colour, with cream trim. The walls were edible. No doors, just arced openings, Spanish. No books, he'd packed and sold his books after Sok Hoon left him. The one bookcase I saw was used for objects. David still read, he just read off the screen on his little pebble, he bought books online and read them on the pebble. I walked into the kitchen and admired his open cupboard with the little tins of condiments he liked to collect from various parts of the world. When he travelled he came home with something preserved or a jar of small fish that had an ornate label, a bear made of treacle or olives wrapped in a red painted ribbon in the claws of a golden eagle. David came downstairs with his luggage, sat it down, then opened the silver fridge and offered me a peach on a saucer. He had washed the peach. He said, what's that.

I was handling the bar of gold. I told him the story.

Pass that here, he said.

He weighed it while I ate the peach. He looked like a man who had heard about gold but never seen it. I guess, beyond wedding rings, most of us have never seen it.

Do you know Gabe, if they put all the gold ever dug out of the earth together in one big square, it would fill a tennis court. That's all there is.

He was wearing those cavalry pants again. I sat in the only chair in the kitchen and David decided to sit a few feet away from me on a plush cushion. He kept the gold. The furnishings were new and expensive, but poorly made. The couch, with winged angles, stained to mahogany, was broken in the centre, the back held up by a stack of technology magazines. There was something Savannah Georgia about it all.

Well, he said. Are we ready to hit the road?

What's that, I said.

There was a small case in his luggage.

That, he said, is for hunting Hurley.

I finished the peach and I put the stone in David's hand because I couldnt find the garbage. Then I looked at the case. It looked like it could hold a rabbit. Taped to the case was a photo of Sok Hoon wearing a wig that made her look like a transsexual. She was reading a paper and you could almost read the column. It was like an intimate kidnapper's portrait.

I opened the case. A futuristic pistol.

Dave, I said.

That's registered, he said. It's all legal. Well legal if we were in the States.

I lifted it up and it was heavy. I used to box and when the trainer taped your hands for a fight, this is how the gun felt. Like you wanted to hit something. I suddenly understood the term *pistol-whipped*.

Dave I'm not driving with this in the car.

Forget it's in the car.

I'm not into murdering anything.

Stun, Gabe. It's a stun gun.

This thing can scramble brains.

I'll show you the papers.

Dave this is staying home.

He brightened. Compromise, he said. I like you. Youve got a big-game rifle. Maybe we'll see a moose.

My rifle's in Corner Brook.

Well that's when I'll need it.

SO HE LEFT THE TASER on the promise that we could ride around Corner Brook with my rifle, a promise I had no intention of keeping. We drove back over to my place because David wanted to see the damage. He noticed Toby right off, how ugly he was. He'll guard the car, I said and David said what he'll do is guard your gold.

The sidewalk was still cordoned off around the building. Dave whistled and shoved his hands in his back pockets. He was not into physical gestures, or mannerisms. He found hand movements a sign of male weakness. His father used them and he did not want to replicate his father.

He said, Is that your computer?

He was pointing at my melted laptop sitting on the wet sidewalk along with all the furniture from the two apartments. It had been tagged, photographed and listed for insurance purposes and was now set for removal to Michigan in a convoy of twenty-one yellow trucks that motored down there every day with Ontario waste. The melted computer was standing there like it was a normal place to conduct business, but the stacks of burnt pre-cargo were a line of homeless people maintaining their dignity when no dignity was present.

It's slightly damaged, I said.

They ship these to China, he said. You drive up to a farmhouse in Hunan province and you'll smell the reek of burning plastic. There's a man standing over a wok frying up the chip board, melting the lead off the chips. There's a woman hoisting a hammer to blow out the monitor glass on a television to get at that nest of copper wire. Down by the river is a hill of copper wire on fire.

Since his conversion from stocks to soft commodities David had become ethical to the third world. He looked like he was going to slip the laptop into the trunk of the Matador, but then he let it slide back onto its tower of garbage. His outrage had turned to resignation.

David: What kind of eat would you like to bite?

Let's go to Franco's.

David asked if I'd detour down Churchill Street off Ossington.

It reminds me of home, he said.

It's the only street in downtown Toronto that has a hill. And so we drove down it and he was right, for ten seconds it was just like being back in Newfoundland.

The boy in Franco's said no they have no roast chicken, but you can get some good chicken at Rabedairas at Dundas. They speak English too, I know because theyre my uncles.

The boy tapped the end of a ballpoint pen on the counter.

David: There's more than his chicken in this town.

And his family's chickens.

Chickens of his entire race.

The Portuguese didnt invent chicken.

David: What's the difference, something invented something discovered.

Me: It's a processing thing.

No, it's not.

Can you say something positive, Dave? Can you say, Interesting point?

I thought that was obvious. Did I say it was stupid?

Me: It's part of the response. Interesting point, you say, a process.

That's condescending. You want me—

I want you to be nice, if we're driving three thousand miles let the miles be nice.

I can be nice. Nice as roses.

Good Italian chicken, the boy said.

DAVID BOUGHT THE CHICKEN at the Pacific Mall up at Kennedy and Steeles. I'd been up here to photograph cars, but never in the mall. It's all Chinese and wealthy. David said Sok Hoon used to come here. They'd have dates. It's a good place to buy computers and chicken. In the chicken store he stared at all the varieties of milk and it reminded me of the year we lived together and went grocery shopping once a week, how he bought a fifty-pound bag of potatoes and it lasted us twelve days. Dave took three different milk products out of the fridge and started reading the ingredients. While he did this, a fan in the cooling system caught a blade against something metal, just touching as it whined and it made all the milk seem possessed by a fast and threatening thing. Automobiles and accidents and high insurance.

He bought chicken, milk and a travel pack of thread and needles. This is for your gold, he said. And he meant to be mysterious. As we walked back to the car we both admired a jet streak in the sky. It was such a straight white line. David had proposed to Sok Hoon in the Concorde as it hit Mach 2. Elton John was on the plane, just eight seats up. David decided to tell Elton John that he'd proposed, and Elton said, Congratulations.

Hand me over Toby, he said.

What are you going to do with him.

I'm going to open him like a chicken.

Get him yourself.

He put the chicken and milk on the back seat and tugged Toby by his burnt tail. He flipped him over. Then pulled at a seam. He tore away at the belly.

Hand me the gold, he said.

I took the gold out of my pocket. The gold bar was about six inches long. He pushed the gold into Toby's belly. Open up that packet and thread me a needle.

It was a good idea. I chose a thread that was the colour of Toby's skin. And David had him sewed up and propped back in the rear window. He looked unlikely to be of any value.

Then we drove out to Highway 404 and David tore into the chicken and drank the milk from the spout.

Me: Youre deep into breast meat.

It came off with the wing.

Some good hey.

I couldnt have imagined you'd get this. A whole chicken for seven dollars. How much effort went into making it.

Or discovering or inventing it.

David: How many chickens do you think get demolished in Toronto in a day.

There's a Lorca poem about that.

You know what's really good? Is that we can be so silly in the midst of this major tragedy.

And his face fell, the colours of plum and ash and the folds of skin around his nose. It was a waxy profile and the sides of his seat cushioned his temples. Even though his eyes were open they felt dead. David Twombly was looking straight ahead, the way a corpse stares out of a coffin.

THREE

ONE

We were driving through the short, clogged collector lanes that fed into the big bend of the 401. Concrete sound barriers and the muted roofs of subdivisions. There were green highway signs alerting us to forthcoming cities, their population tallied in neat round numbers. Being numbered makes you feel like you belong, but also that youre part of a penal colony.

Places like Whitby and Kingston, I said. Who knew they were the same size as St John's.

I slept with a married woman once, David said. She was from Kingston. The husband was big. One time he took my skull in his hand. He pressed it and said: What are you doing to my wife?

David gripped his hand around a skull of air.

Me: What were you doing.

I was thinking about how much you'd disapprove of that comment.

I'm lonely and I'm thinking about Nell.

I'll tell you your problem, Gabe. You think everything can be told. You think you know everything, every thought Nell has. The secret life and it's not always devious. Sometimes you get caught in things that are impossible to find words for.

She's caught up in an impossible thing.

That's what she's doing.

I wanted to take a ceramic insulator and bash him in the temple. Then I breathed deep and tried to forget about it. I adjusted the stock-car rear-view mirror to get correct and very wide angles. It was encouraging me to enjoy myself and so I rolled down my own window and let the empty heat of the early summer pummel us. But now I had to think of Nell caught up in an impossible thing. I sank the gas pedal and we throttled our way out of the bottleneck of the Lake Ontario basin and zipped along the grey fields of tarmac past the very modern power lines on towers that looked like columns of newsprint. We overtook transport trucks. How invigorating, David said, staring up, like we're involved in a greater economy, a taller scale.

There was that night when she did not come home. A phone call from a man I did not know. Your girlfriend has to get out, the voice said.

Girlfriend, I said. And then thought of Nell. And then the realization Nell was my girlfriend. It was the same realization I had one night hearing David talk about Sok Hoon. And understanding she was leaving him, that she wasnt his wife any longer.

I took a cab over to Bloor and Bedford and the cab driver did not know the address. It is hard to think in a taxi, or the thoughts are more mean-spirited than the thoughts you have on a streetcar. I said wait and realized I had never asked a taxi to wait before. The numbers were erratic, as though the city planners panicked when they came to this neck of town and just threw the jumbled numbers from a passing loader. It was a penthouse off Bloor Street. The disarray quickly turned neat and gentrified. A doorman, a fountain in the foyer. I took an elevator up to the top floor and did not knock but stepped in. There were plush white carpets and two grand pianos. One entire wall just glass overlooking the city. There were photographs of Castro and Churchill. In a green library three men were playing cards. They were in dinner jackets, but there was a staleness of cigarettes in their clothes, a wilted boutonniere. I've come for Nell, I said. But the men were exhausted, they looked like they'd been playing straight through several nights. They ignored me. In a deeper room, a long white couch and Nell's bare legs. She was passed out. It looked like the couch had come with Nell. She was barefoot and I did not want to look for her shoes. They were where the couch used to live. Which one of you called, I said. But the men couldnt hear me. I felt like I was entering a stranger's dream and could not communicate. There was a chunk of parmesan the size of a cinder block. A knife. A birthday cake with one piece removed. Then a man of about fifty came out of a bedroom wearing a tuxedo shirt. He had his thumb in a health prevention book. He said directly to me, Youre a lucky man. I was prepared to swing at his face but he looked slightly familiar and not at all mean. The fact came to me, some kind of verdict, that Nell had been on a bender and had pushed these men past what they were capable of or cared about. They just wanted to play cards now and eat cheese and read about how apricot pits can prevent cancer. I had been lucky to get a phone call. It was a call meant to get rid of a difficulty. The night had been complicated and intense but now, at eight in the morning, they all wanted to calm down and revert to the simple gear. I took Nell by an arm and bent her over my shoulder. I'll get the door, the man with the book said. I did a fireman's carry down the elevator and into the cab. She slept for five hours. When she came round she said Richard Text had been in town. I described the men and the one who was fifty sounded like Richard Text. I asked if he liked cheese and she said just about as much as an average person. She said she felt okay, that nothing bad had happened, it just looked bad. But it shook me.

Remembering that made me exhale and I waggled my head. I'm not good at waggling, there's a hard ball in my head that rattles, like when you shake a can of spray paint. It hurts. It made me want to lead a simple life. Those men. The simple gear. I'd had enough. You should have kids in your twenties. When youre older you can't withstand the same torment. God had I ever gambled in life? And too late now. David was leaning against the door post, he was feeling the vibration of the car, cutting out the middleman of the ear. The weather had turned hot and then there was a short gallop of rain that pelted the window so hard it was like looking through grease. Some music is like that, like trying to read vaseline. Then the sun again. An hour later the radio began to weaken. Battery dying on us. I slowed down. Just check under the hood, I said.

Dave looked and called me out. I dont know what to look for, he said.

I saw it. The alternator had cracked through the casing. I am my father's son and I know about the integrity of structure.

We veered into Whitby and followed signs for Nick's Salvage. I parked where we wouldnt put a hole in a tire, and we walked into the busy yard of flattened, rusted wrecks and men peering for parts. David found a blasted Chevy with a newish alternator. I stood behind him, just breathing deep and slow.

David: You got a wrench.

We made a paper copy of where the mounts were and I walked back to the Matador with the paper to compare it to ours. Our car shone with objects—it looked like a piñata. The alternator matched, so I fetched the adjustable wrench my father had given me. It was made in West Germany. It has my father's initials stamped on it, from when he worked in the Hawthorn Leslie shipyard of Newcastle.

Seeing David in the distance, in this field of ruined commerce.

David went at it. He hammered at the crankcase like you bang a lid on a jar of new pickles. When we get to Montreal, he said, I need to get glasses.

You require glasses.

I keep trying to look around something.

You need an optometrist.

What I need is an ophthalmologist. But a new pair of glasses would help.

He joggled off the alternator and we walked up to the salvage yard office swinging it.

David: You got something like this but in better condition?

What we got is what we got.

Better than what we're bringing you here?

Put that thing on the waste paper if you dont mind.

David had landed it right on the wood counter. He picked it up and held it like a shot putter.

Go take a look, the man said.

What if I just chucked our old one at you.

The man gave Dave a cold stare.

Well then we won't bother you.

And we walked out with the alternator.

Me: So what is it about not paying.

David: The guy just pissed me off. Now you know how to slot one of these in?

Not without a belt winch.

We drove into Whitby and received directions to a back-yard mechanic named Tyrone Gill. His shop had a sign that read My Autobody Experience. Tyrone Gill was training a black puppy to retrieve a goose wing. He had the wing tied onto forty feet of twine. He had nothing to do. He stared at the car. That's about the ugliest car I've seen come in here. Which made me want to drive it over his face. But when in Whitby, do as the English do. We let him look under the hood. It'll take an hour, Tyrone said.

David: You mean it'll take an hour or youre charging an hour.

It's a unit of work, he said.

We ate in a three-star place Tyrone recommended out of spite in a mall across the road. Dave opened his pebble and retrieved the restaurant review that hung in the ether outside the restaurant. He said the review was not good. Well I'm hungry, I said.

There was a sign below the regular menu that advertised three different sizes of gravy. A man dressed in new leather and boots of bright yellow. He too had detoured off the main route. Biker gear, ribbed leather that had a bubble of air at his lower back. Like he's wearing a scuba suit that doesnt fit him. David was tapping his black card nervously.

I've never seen, he said, a more gormless group in my life.

You havent left the city much.

It's true I've lived in cities.

The meal and Tyrone's fee and the filling up of the gas tank made me aware of how quickly the road erodes money. And I wasnt prepared to embark on a cycle of theft. I tolerated paying for things, though I admired David's impatience and his decision at times to walk out of a store holding an item he couldnt be bothered to wait and pay for. When I was a boy my father brought home a second-hand pool table and the cues needed new tips. I went into a sports store and removed the tips from two cues in a rack. When my father noticed he asked where I got the cue tips. I told him. That's odd, he said. I looked all over town for cue tips, and you can't get them except if you buy the whole cue. No, I said. You can get them downtown. He thought about that. He said, Gabe we should get a couple more, for when these ones wear out. We should get them now because theyre hard to get. Let's take the car down now and get them.

I was in the porch, putting on my shoes, my father waiting at the open door. And I told him, I told him I'd stolen the cue tips. And he pushed the tops of his fingers into his front pockets. He knew I had. And there passed between us a sense of shame but also respect. He wasnt going to give me a lecture about this. He knew I'd learned something, a transference of moral conduct had occurred. And I have maintained that stance, often as a default mode, so that when I see someone like Dave in action, it shocks me, a bell rings in my spine.

I had built up a year's buffer of money, but now I was eating into it. I was down to nine months. That joyful feeling of a newly printed balance was now replaced with alarm. I didnt mention this to David, for David was made of money and he hardly spoke of it. Although it came to me that he'd mentioned he was on the verge of financial collapse. It's true that we can feel very rich and very poor at the same time.

We kept driving. We had averaged, on this our first day, about twenty miles an hour. We may as well have been travelling by horse. I shoved a flattened towel behind my back and hammered the gas. We passed a barn that was rusty red and beside it, a billboard the same size of bright red and yellow.

We could save money, David said, if we had a tent.

Since when have you needed to save money.

I've got money because I save money.

In Montreal we'll stay with Lars Pony.

David thought about that. I could see he wasnt sure if Lars was the type of person he wanted to spend time with. How about Sok Hoon and Allegra, he said.

Allegra.

David stated this without pleasure.

Who's Allegra.

She's a friend of my ex-wife's.

I was trying to put the name Allegra to something I knew, something about Montreal. And then I remembered. She isnt the Allegra, I said, from the radio. She isnt Allegra Campinghorst.

I didnt tell you about Allegra?

I'm with Lars, I said. Saying this made me feel pure. I was excited by
my early infatuation. It wasnt just David who had written her those
letters. I'd put myself into them.

Elsewhere, he said. In New Brunswick are we on our own.

My god are we ever going to get out of Ontario.

LEAVING THE PROVINCE made me think of how I'd come to it, how I'd
left Newfoundland rather hopeless, or, better, that possibilities in
Newfoundland had been rammed up against a wall and I should nudge
my craft around and try elsewhere. Sometimes a stock forms a head and
shoulders and is on the way down, and that's how my fortunes looked.
I'd spent time touring the storage facilities for natural gas and I had
grown tired of commercialism and energy and hoarding. It was the immi-
grant's impulse, and while I flew to Toronto and accepted the IKW windfall that managed to keep the wolf fed behind the Niagara Escarpment,
an ember blurred to life and I became happy again. I felt as if I were made
of kindling and some creature had bent down and blown life into my
wooden bones. If I had a proper Global Positioning System, and if I had
tagged Nell with a chip, I knew I'd find her in a rented car zooming
south. She would have gone to Richard Text, not Vegas. I had been mean
and she had thought to herself a safe thought. A safe haven. She was on
the phone to Richard saying that he understood her. And what I'd said to
her, the badness of it, would have made her want some consolation. Or
maybe she flew for it's a long way to New Mexico. She'd have driven to
Santa Fe from the airport in Albuquerque, passed fences with tires hung
on them. KEEP OUT brushed on in sloppy white paint. The hills dotted
with sage green bushes like the coat of a leopard. The road signs flared
up as she hit a rise, the sun behind her. She was driving like we were
driving. It is hard to imagine that for thousands of years we did not drive.

She ate in a café next to a Bail Bonds and ended up on a road that visits a corrections facility. The glass in her watch fell out on the plane, because of the altitude. At least that's what happened at her wedding. It's all there in the charred pages of her green journal. Nell ordered a rice milk drink with ice. A tuna taco. A sign near the jail: DO NOT PICK UP HITCHHIKERS, PRISONERS NEARBY.

I adjusted the stock-car mirror again. When Nell first moved to Santa Fe, she was startled when the rear view mirror fell off the windshield. Because of the heat. But it was commonplace, no one was surprised.

She had been in Santa Fe for five months and then a small wedding. They had to get married if she was to stay in the United States. They were clear on the fact that Richard was gay and that they would have an arrangement within that marriage. Nell spent the day before the wedding walking around Santa Fe, staring at roofs and walls and entering the foyers of museums. Then they drove out to Galisteo and over to Madrid for a lunch like this. A dirt road. They saw a tornado and a piece of tumbleweed smack up against a wire fence. Then to the wedding rehearsal. They stood under cottonwood trees. Richard's best man flew in from London. Algren Leonard. Algren doesnt use the tube, it says here in the diary. He wore a pale short-sleeved shirt and slacks and light socks and brown shoes. Sunglasses. Posh hand gestures. He sat down to talk to Nell. They have two houses, he and his wife. Where is she. She's the one with the broken arm. One house in Notting Hill, the other about twenty-five minutes southwest. Algren mentioned the latter first, and did not say southwest of what. His teeth were slightly long. He's aghast at the British cops acting like LA cops.

Nell's aunt out there in a floral top. Both her aunt and uncle were there. They stood at a wire fence trying to feed a llama some greens. Her aunt dyes her hair. Has laryngitis. It's the air, she said. Her aunt wanted the wedding in Burlington. She had brought dried silver dollars she'd picked from Nell's mother's garden. She had rung on the bell and asked the new owners if she could. The peeled silver dollars on the desk where they signed the register. When Nell had gone to take care of her parents' house she came home and a neighbour said he was so sorry. They knew something was wrong because no one had closed the curtains.

Nell said I do and then they heard an explosion. Richard drove them past the Los Alamos National Laboratory, written in a large globe on a tower. Streets named Bikini Atoll and Oppenheimer, where he worked. They drove northeast out of Santa Fe to Chimayo. Stopped into a church and dipped their hands wearing wedding rings into the dry grey dirt in a hole—said to have healing powers. Twenty-nine aluminum crutches and one wooden crutch hanging in the shrine. Three other aluminum crutches leaning on the wall. Pictures of Jesus done in thread, collage and paint.

I WAS TALKING about Nell's experiences before she knew me. That's how badly I missed her. I'd grown sick of remembering all our events. Now I was imagining the ones she'd told me about or had written in her diary. And it worked. I often felt like I'd lived in New Mexico. In a way, part of me was Richard Text.

We drove into Kingston and found a Canadian Tire, because David Twombly had shares in Canadian Tire. I asked him what made him invest in Crappy Tire.

I saw a woman, he said, who was helping a service person fix something. That's loyalty.

Let's get the three-man.

The two-man is on sale.

There's never enough room, I said, for two men in a two-man.

We passed a Value Village and realized with a tent you need two foamies and sleeping bags and a frying pan and four plates made by

Grindley with little sailing vessels as the maker's mark on the bottom. That was the nicest thing about the plates. They look better while youre washing them, upside down, in a stream. We bought a Coleman stove for nine dollars and a fishing rod. I got a gallon of white gas at the next Ultramar. There's a certain level of accoutrements you have to build up in order to camp.

Let's talk about money, he said. I'm going to say a little prayer here that everything will turn out all right. Or for the best. What are the right words.

That we won't be hurt.

That's negative, Gabe. How about that we'll accept what happens to us.

And he put a hand to his forehead and closed his eyes.

I didnt know you believed in God.

His eyes flashed open. I can't shake this hunch that there's a God, he said. Everything I've prayed for has come through. Though I've got rules about what I can pray for.

Sometimes vague rules.

That we'll be happy, he said, angrily. I'm telling you this now so you can judge for yourself if what I say about anything is influenced by the God-hunch.

TWO

A DOG WAS HITCHHIKING just after Kingston, or at least sauntering down the road and when we slowed down it hopped in through the open back window. It looked like it had learned it as a pup. It was brown and tan with a long stripe of silver down its back.

It's a girl, I said.

She just sat back there, open-faced, gamely sizing up the road ahead, as if to say keep her going.

We got out and looked around. Nobody and nothing anywhere. Hello, I yelled.

She looks like a free agent, Dave said.

She looks starved. She had found the chicken.

After three miles she was resting her cheek on the joints of her paws. She was asleep.

Trusting sort, I said.

Who could hurt that.

There are people who dont care for animals.

They arent the kind to slow down to allow one to jump in.

Well that one is living proof of your theory.

It isnt a theory, just reacting to your assumption.

What was it.

That she's trusting.

So instead she's ignorant.

She's experienced.

She's thirsty.

Youre thirsty.

Both our mouths were dry and we didnt want to talk. I dont like paying for water, and the places we passed all looked like they were stocked with bottled water in coca-cola coolers with narrow washrooms offering one tap that runs a mix of hot and cold, water probably infected with beaver fever and none of them with choice dog food.

We lost Lake Ontario behind our right shoulders, to the Thousand Islands, then the Gulf of St Lawrence narrowed into Gananoque. This is what we drove through in this part of Canada—the leftover froth of empire and the presidency of the New World.

Could I live here. David said he once wanted to buy an island but Sok Hoon wouldnt live on an island and now she was living in Montreal, which is technically an island. We passed a town famous for the platform scale. You can weigh anything from an ocean liner to a box of cherries. We crossed a brook and I stopped for that. The dog perked up. All three of us scrabbled down the highway gravel and sloped ourselves over rocks in the river and took gulps, even the dog. The bright dust we raised floated and sank over us and landed on the water.

Me: She's not a water dog.

She looks like if water touched the outside of her body she'd dissolve.

Do you think you could love a dog that didnt like water?

Dave: I love everything. That's my problem. I'm too easy with forgiveness.

No one mentioned absolving guilt. Youre such a not-a-good listener.

Okay I could love a dog that didnt like water.

We sat and stared at the bridge. How much money did it cost to cross this trickle of water. Who paid for it. That's the power of a federal government.

David found a piece of red rope in the woods and hauled it out for a temporary leash.

She needs a meal other than chicken.

We took a detour into Gananoque. We were close to the US border. We looked for a roof that suggested, we have dog food. But it was an Indian reserve. We asked someone, and he said, Follow me.

We followed him in the car as he walked down the street. And then down another street. Then he went into a house. The dog still with her head on her moist paws. If it was me, if I was that trusting, I'd flake right out on my back with my paws pointing to the roof.

You'd press your luck.

Did I say that out loud?

Youve been talking aloud, my friend, since we left.

I keep thinking I'm alone.

Strange how when we're alone we talk as if there's someone to answer.

What's strange is how often I'm quiet when I'm with people.

I assumed that would be understood as a corollary. Youre actually not much of a quiet one, Dave said.

I feel quiet.

We looked at the front screen door where the Gananoque reserve Indian had disappeared. Did he understand what I asked him? Had I offended him, called him dog food?

I could picture the strong elbow opening up the screen door, the shunt of a shotgun magazine and the double-barrelled blast straight through the windscreen, the hot weight in the chest.

Most people havent a clue what theyre like, David said. Sok Hoon kept complaining that I took over the conversation, interrupted her and wouldnt allow her to say anything. I believed her until my mother said that Sok Hoon must be a handful, she never shuts up and is always getting hammered with the babysitters.

How is your mother.

She's good. She's set up with that doctor. Dr Manamperi. She'll put him in the ground and then sell all the antique furniture and move back to Michigan. But Sok Hoon, my god.

You know I refinished that furniture.

What furniture.

Dr Manamperi's furniture. That was like my first summer job. He has great imported furniture.

Well my mother will auction it when he's gone. I'll let you know about the auction. But I'm trying to talk about Sok Hoon here.

I like Sok Hoon.

Yeah, David said. You used to share, what, a flirtatious sidecar of knowing glances with Sok Hoon.

Was he quoting someone? Some preface to a domestic novel?

What are you talking about, I said. And anyway who better to get hammered with than the babysitter.

Then the man returned with a yogurt container and passed it to David through the window. Here you go, he said.

It was pebbles of dry dog food.

We let the dog out and she lunged at the food. David poured it out on the grass and the three of us watched her eat it. The dog chewed at the grass like a goat.

We found her, I said, just outside Kingston.

I dont recognize the dog, the Indian said. That dog has a lot of faith in her.

And then we climbed into the car. Which way you headed, the Indian asked.

Montreal.

Could I get a lift to the highway.

And he got in with the dog and we drove him back to the Trans-Canada and he crossed the road and stood there, waiting for traffic to Toronto. There was something of the Indian in both of us. It's a male thing. In the end, if you stripped us down to a loincloth, we'd be okay. We'd get on. We'd find something to look at and to believe in. I guess it's love. Even without the love of a woman, a man can get by with the trees loving him, or a flat tract of water.

I was in terrible shape, Dave said, when Sok Hoon moved out. Everything I looked at in the house was full of Sok Hoon. She was putting chunks of furniture in the car. I saw half a bottle of Sumol on the front seat. Would I have ever tasted Sumol, he said, if not for Sok Hoon? And that morning, in the Land Rover when she strapped Owen into the back seat. They were headed for Montreal. Like us now. I saw the old man next door say to Sok Hoon, Your husband is waving. I was watching them from the window, Owen in his red kimono. I was in my underwear. I was waving through one of Owen's stuffed toys. A dog. I was trying to connect through the childish mode—you know all about that with your Toby act. The dog in my arms. Dog waving. And it's so silly, but that dog had a presence through us.

Dave I understand.

I made him sad, he said. I had him look puzzled at the thought of them leaving, I put his glass eyes under his paws.

The fact that he fessed up to this made me less angry about Toby. Perhaps it wasnt such an act of betrayal on Nell's part. Maybe most men have a channel to childish intimacy and men use it, when necessary, to lure a woman's heart. But this act did not retrieve Sok Hoon. She'd had enough. And by the time she was all set up in Montreal, David had cheered at his prospects. When you grab a tissue, he said, and the box lifts with the tissue then falls again. You know youve reached the end of your woes. When there arent enough tissues left to hold down a box, that's when you know youve been crying enough for one day.

He hadnt fully loved Sok Hoon. There were things about her. Something vulgar about her features that was arising with age.

Sok Hoon, I said, has to be the most beautiful woman youve ever been with.

He agreed that Sok Hoon was a gorgeous woman. These were small things you notice, he said, after being with someone for years. Sok Hoon has a good body and face and good feet and hands.

My god youre fit for no one.

Who is, he said. Who is.

And I had driven him into a deep despairing pocket of truth. That Sok Hoon was successful. She'd gone to Montreal after working with some fashion designers in Toronto, and now she was a partner in an eco-friendly fashion label. The brand had caught on with the people who wanted to save the world from warming up. The label was involved with a research lab that turned recycled oil into fabric. During a failure in the product the lab techs found they could stretch the oil so thin it could cover water like a blanket, which, in arid countries, means you can halt evaporation and prevent malaria. Sok Hoon designed a line of clothing that could prevent third world catastrophe. A first for fashion.

There was something true in David's account of my bond with Sok Hoon. We did connect. And when I first learned about David and Nell there ran a vein of retribution that made me wish Sok Hoon and I had driven over a state line. We were driving past Brockville as I thought this. The grey smooth eyeless factory. I was trying to make eye contact with this factory, find its eye, when something unusual rammed my hips and the dog was on top of me barking madly at the side window. And then behind us a car was veering away—it had cranged into the back passenger side. We were doing the speed limit.

David: Dont be angry.

Can you get this dog off me.

Be very pleasant and patient and remember we're going to make him pay.

It's obedient how we both signalled and slowed down to take a turnoff to a coffee shop gas station. The dog had an eyeline on the driver. I noticed the richness of his signal light, as if it was some internal pulse. David reached into the glove box for my wide-format camera. You keep him busy, he said.

The dog lunging for the door. We decided to lock her in.

She barked hard and muffled. Baring her varnished teeth.

He was a lanky man in a shorn fur coat. Perhaps fox. There was something wrong with his back. Oh my god, he said. If you hadnt been driving into me.

Sir, you swept into us.

There was a large impression above the wheel well. David kneeling to get a good angle.

It's so wide, David said, I'm getting the Brockville plant in every one.

So what do we do here.

The fox coat was too short in the sleeves. It looked like his mother's coat. The fact that he was driving a cranberry Lincoln made the coat into something precious.

David: We call the police, we share insurance numbers, your rates take a hike and we get our pursuit vehicle some original LAPD gear.

Okay okay we'll wait for a cop. I'm not sure this was absolutely my fault.

This will cost you thousands.

It's body work. On an old car.

The car was moving from the power of the dog's barking. We tried to ignore it.

I noticed the steering is affected, I said, from the accident.

I know my god dont I know it.

He was perspiring lightly and I thought he should take off the coat. But we stood there leaning against the damaged car and David took out his pebble to call the police. Faces getting gas turned to look at us. Men with trays of coffee passed by and pretended to be concentrating hard on keeping the coffee level. There's nine hundred acres of flat land facing this gas station. All that grew was billboards.

That's a nice coat, David said.

You want it.

I'm just admiring it. It looks South African.

It's not South African.

You know we dont need to go the insurance route.

The man was already coming around to it.

Five hundred would do it, David said.

Man: And there'll be no reporting.

Report what.

But answer me one thing. It wasnt entirely me.

He said this as if a greater truth had to be answered.

David: It was you.

He unbuttoned the one white button on the fox coat and reached back to his wallet. It was long and on a chain. Alligator leather. You dont often see money with no folds in it. All I have, he said, is eighty-five.

David: There's a cash machine.

Isnt eighty-five good enough. Look at what you did to my Lincoln.

It's five or nothing.

Where you guys from?

David told him Toronto.

Where exactly in Toronto.

David: We live on a barge near the Beaches. We're homosexuals. It's like a trailer park for gay barges.

He looked at me to see if this was true. I'm on my way, he said, to visit my family in Moosonee. I'm the successful son. I've got to look good and feel good and arrive good.

David: But youre not good.

I'm about as bad as you can get.

David: Have you killed anyone.

He pressed, with his thumbs, the capsules of leather in his wallet.

I've ordered killing.

He said it so succinctly that we believed him. A man who has organized murder. But maybe he was just matching the outlandishness of David's lies.

David: You married?

Married, he said. He shook his head. Like, who'd have him. It's just me and the car, he said, in this world.

Your Lincoln hardly felt it, Dave said. Can I sit in it?

The man let David sit in the driver's seat. The workplace of a murderer. There were no keys. We waited for David to enjoy himself. And David remembered who we were.

I'd ask to sit in your car, the man said, but that dog looks set to tear my throat out.

We can either do the money, Dave said, or we can trade cars.

The man thought about that, and I began wondering how the Lincoln handled. I wasnt averse to the idea, I just wasnt sure what a Lincoln would fetch for resale in Newfoundland. The man rubbed his neck and seemed disappointed with himself.

I'd do it, he said, but it's not technically my car.

It was then we understood this incident was stretching his mind. The implications. The car was a fixture in crime. The car had to maintain anonymity. But he was also thinking *Strangers on a Train*.

They walked over to the cash machine like men about to take a piss. I stroked down the dog and watched them talk. She licked me and I was moved. The man handed David the money from the crevice of the bank withdrawal and then the money from his long wallet. He took his receipt as if to remember what he'd done with the money. Perhaps he could use it on his taxes. Then he removed the fox coat. At one point they both laughed. He shoved the coat at David and David daintily draped it over his forearm. Then the man walked past me without seeing me. It was as if he'd forgotten he was dealing with two men and had driven the concern out of his mind. He was back to focusing on Moosonee and being the good son in the only thing he owned.

He had a three hundred daily withdrawal limit, David said. So we made it three eighty-five with the coat.

You look sad.

There was a woman in front of us, Dave said, did you see her? At the cash machine. I was staring at the crown of her dark hair. And I remember looking at Sok Hoon's straight hair.

Amen to that, I thought. What are you planning with the coat.

Doggy dog.

We waved as the Lincoln smoothly turned and departed like some foreign yacht.

David gave the dog the coat. Then he took a windshield squeegee from a container of washer fluid and opened the trunk and leaned inside. He jammed the squeegee at the dent and it popped out. The dog lifted up from her coat and barked. Her first friendly woof. You could hardly notice a mark.

A good wax job, he said. It saved the paint. You know he plans on putting that Lincoln on the train.

We caught up to the Lincoln and drove a little bit together. David wagged the undented rear quarter at him until he got the joke. The dog up on the back seat now happy. We kept a corner of that cranberry Lincoln in the stock-car mirror, just to make sure he wouldnt crang us again and drag our unconscious bodies into the ditch to wait for the slug from a hired killer. A malicious crang. Then he peeled off north while we crossed the border to a line of orange construction signs powered by solar panels. A row of fluorescent cones with heavy tire-rubber bases. Signs that read TRAVAUX. Welcome to Quebec, under construction.

THREE

IN THE DARK, gunning for Montreal. I leaned my head against the
passenger window and stared at a trapezoid of blue reflected light in the
base of the window, like a pilot fish tracking the car.

This is where the Greyhound stops for sandwiches, David said, and
pulled over. The customers were not the ones that you see on planes. I had
forgotten that cheaper forms of travel attract poorer people. One woman
with a chain of tickets—connections that would take her deep into northern Quebec. There were cases of emphysema, middle-aged men in worn
clothes, a woman carrying a toaster, students and no children.

David: You looking for someone.

There's always someone, I said, who stands in line with a pillow.

When we hit centre-ville, David said, I want to get some glasses. I'm
squinting.

Dont you need a prescription.

I have a prescription. I've had it for four months in my wallet. It's just
they dont make glasses I like.

And he widened his eyes again, trying to stretch the cornea.

Okay we'll get you glasses.

We veered into Montreal and took all those crazy ramped exits. There must be a billion dollars of concrete hovering in the air around Montreal. They remind me of the rings in the Olympic logo, and Montreal has that Olympic association. The word *Expo* too. When youre young you think a certain place has particular things, and when youre older you realize theyre all over the world.

We felt our way down to the centre of town, the way you approach stairs in the dark. We stopped into a Lenscrafters ten minutes before closing, but all their frames were too small. We asked for a boutique and there was one across the street. Apparently we were in the glasses district. Watching David point at frames in a cabinet lit with recessed light, the woman turning the sign in the window over, so it read OPEN to us inside. I hadnt known Dave to be so fussy. They need to be bigger, he said. I have a big face. The woman in the boutique helped him. She had a big chest and short arms and it was a challenge for her not to knock anything over.

These ones, she said, the frames have not been kiln-baked, or varnished.

You say that disparagingly, David said.

They've been rolled in cedar flakes for six months, she said.

And we both imagined a girl in Poland rolling a little box for six months, as though she's about to draw the winning lottery number painted on a pingpong ball.

Then he put on a silver pair. He stared at himself. Something happened to him. His shoulders stiffened and he backed away from the mirror. He almost careened into the kiosk of revolving frames. He pulled off the glasses and handed them to her. I dont ever want to see these again, he said.

He ordered the frames that had been rolled in cedar flakes. He gave her the prescription.

In the car I drove. David was laughing at himself now.

I put those silver ones on, he said, and a familiar feeling came over me, like a previous life. It was my father. Suddenly I looked just like my father.

IT WAS AFTER NINE and we drove to a pastry shop David knew. The women were wearing things like negligees over tops. What used to be below was now worn on top, and the same was happening with food. People were eating desserts and then they ordered rare beef on a bed of arugula. I called Lars Pony and David held his pebble and thought about Sok Hoon. He was just leaving a message, he said.

I said Lars sounded troubled.

David: Are we a hindrance? We can skip him.

It felt, I said, like I was talking to a wide-open sky.

There had been a movie shoot earlier in the day. They were still taking down props. While we ate near a pillar, a square of gold mirror unglued itself and fell on David's head. I watched it slice down like a guillotine and bounce off his skull, then his forehead bloomed one streak of red. A gusher. What was that, he said.

A panel of mirror fell on your head, I said.

A grip came over and picked up the mirror. Nothing happened here, he said in French. And handed David a fresh bar towel.

You should sue, a waitress said, also in French.

David stanched the flow and a woman passed by. She said something like, I'll get my boyfriend, he's a doctor.

She brought back a handsome man from across the street. Youthful, lightboned and Panamanian. He tilted David's head.

Oh you need stitches, he said, you need five.

A diagnosis in two seconds.

I'm glad, David said, there was a doctor.

He spoke quickly in Spanish to his girlfriend.

He's not a doctor, she said. He's a boxer.

The thing is, am I going to go bald.

Dave, youre bald.

I'm shaven, he said.

We took a vote, the woman, the boxer and me. A unanimous decision that David was bald and would continue to be bald.

I wasnt supposed to go bald, he said. This is news to me. I take after my mother's father, he said, and he had a thick head of hair.

There was something about David's mother's father that David connected with. He did not like his father, so he skipped a generation and took up his mother's father. And now this surprise uncoupling. Baldness was supposed to swing David to the idea of stitches. The vanity of a scar. But instead he said to the hovering waitress, We'll settle for a couple of free coffees and we're ready for our savoury.

BUT HE WENT THROUGH the bar towel and the bleeding would not stop. I drove him to a hospital and we waited in Emergency for two hours. The hospital made him think about his father, and so he phoned the hospital in Corner Brook. It was midnight in Corner Brook and he got an orderly who put him on to the nurse we knew, Maggie Pettipaw. His father was the same. There was no real need for David to come home. He could be this way for months. Then his pebble glowed and he had a message from his sister.

When's the last time you heard from her.

He called her back. All he did was hold the pebble and it called her.

She lives in New Hampshire. She wants to talk about my father. She says Richard Text's in town.

He would know where Nell was, I thought.

Me: Do we have a map?

We asked a nurse if there was a map and she came back with a revolving globe that must have come from a children's ward. It was the kind with a light bulb in the middle that you could plug in. In fact, it was sort of like how I thought the world really worked, from an inner glow.

Bethlehem, David said. Sasha's right here working in a lab. You cut through Vermont and cross the Connecticut River and youre in New Hampshire. We take the 91 and it's no more than what, two hundred miles.

I didnt care either way. I knew Sasha as a youngster and so she's remained a youngster.

What's Richard doing there.

A high-level government visit, he said.

Have you met him.

You havent?

And I told him that I'd met him once, briefly, early one morning but hadnt known it was him.

You never met him in Corner Brook?

I squeezed my forehead and knew I must have seen him there, but all that came to mind were the stories Nell had told me. Can you tell the nurse, I said, that there's a tightness in your chest.

Why would I say that.

It'll shave an hour off the wait.

But he wouldnt. David didnt fool with his own health. That was his only truth, never to pretend an injury, for that injury will seek you out and smite you. He did not possess morals over swiping craftily an alternator from a salvage yard, but he would not bend the truth about his own health. It was connected to his God-hunch and praying. So while we waited, every twenty minutes or so, I darted out to check on the dog. I gave her a walk to see if she needed to empty herself. Then a Haitian doctor suggested a needle and Dave's head was sewed up—the boxer was right, five stitches.

FOUR

IT WAS MIDNIGHT and Lars Pony was standing on his front step, waiting. His appearance made me wonder, made me slip into a Wyoming state. Lars did not look good, but he looked better than he had. His short black hair had gone grey. He was wearing brand-new white sneakers. He was looking like someone who was trying desperately for the part of Lars Pony, so much so that I left the dog in the car.

I've lost sixty-five pounds, he said, and shook hands with David Twombly. He remembered him from Corner Brook. What he didnt say was that we all gave his son, Lennox, a bit of a hard time. That's a nice wound, he said to David. Lars had his own wound, a wrapped hand he'd hurt in preparing a hose from the garage.

He did not show us in, for no woman lived here. We stood on the porch.

He'd been married in Toronto. He and his wife had loved each other. I've met her, she's attractive, a Newfoundlander. Lars is a tall man and his wife's eyes came just to his shoulder. Lars told me once that they ate in silence once a month at the Royal York. When the music began Lars snapped his fingers and the band played his song. They danced on an empty dance floor all night. He had his work clothes and then, during these evenings, his dress clothes. My Wyoming. They are lovers, the waiters said to new diners. And the waiters felt sorry for their children. They love each other so much, they did not have time for their children. The waiters saw the kids at a Sunday brunch. This was fifteen years ago.

His wife, Nora, was gone now and so were his children. He had two children, one in university and the other working in the tar sands of Alberta. Lennox. They did not write. Nora had left him for a woman, and they were living in Mexico. They swam at night in the sea while the tall hotels prepared bedrooms. A fortune teller in the park, strings clamped to her table, to hold the cards down. The Germans, shirts off, one tries to fetch up a carp. She sent postcards to their son.

LARS BREATHED IN SLOWLY and then exhaled, like he was drinking coffee. They said they'd be here for dinner but now it was midnight. It was the one thing he'd been waiting for. Last week he had come to the end of it. He had thought of a way with a hose through the back window. Shut the porch door with a towel under it and turn the car on, thirty minutes should do it. Then Gabriel English had called him and it cheered him. He had a friend. But they were late and there was nothing to do now, with a supper cooked and beds made for the men upstairs. He was on the porch with a beer and his breath had a shiver in it. He could bark like a dog he was that lonely and there was no reservoir left to muster a defence against loneliness. Then a car with the slowing sound of looking for an address.

Gabe had not heard about Lars Pony's wife. How men, absent from day-to-day scrutiny, can change on you. Gabriel had been his friend at *Auto Trader*. Lars had taught him how to take pictures, the simple questions you asked and how to get out of the clutches of some people who apparently sold their cars in order to have someone to talk to. Now I'm the one who has clutches, Lars thought.

They sat there outside on his step, and Lars was good for a couple of beers, and sometimes that's all you can ask of a wounded, older friend. Lars Pony had the base of his fingers wrapped in clean gauze, a gauze that seemed to be the exposed limit of a dressing that was keeping his frame together.

You want chicken.

We're good Lars.

Dave was sensitive to a trouble in the air but at the same time not impressed. He took out his pebble, I'm going to call Sok Hoon.

Gabe: Do you have email?

He had blurted it out and he knew it was selfish. Lars let Gabriel check his mail on his wife's computer. They were using him for his communication devices. When was the last time someone had called him. Well, it was Gabe, a week ago. There was energy in Gabriel's focus at the computer. Lars watched him as he looked to see if anyone cared if he was alive. There was desire to live in Gabe. He stared at the screen until it refreshed itself and the word *Ntark* leapt at him in the newness of its bold lettering, a new message for Gabriel. It was an attachment. It's Nell's typing, Gabriel said, all caps: SORRY FOR CHEWING YOU OUT LIKE A SLIPPER. Nell had drawn a dog and a moccasin (she had that kind of software). Chewed me out? The dog's tail was twitching. Twitch marks, who came up with those? Nell's illustrations looked like they were done by someone who's had brain damage.

David came in and Gabriel read it aloud. He realized he was the dog. Are you sorry for chewing me out like a slipper.

David: Does it say where she is.

I dont know how to look for that.

David keyed in some commands and came up with a server list that traced the email to Los Alamos.

That's where Richard lives, he said.

I EXTENDED MY WYOMING and thought of Los Alamos. Where they did not wear labcoats. They wore turtlenecks in winter, Nell said once, when we were tired of the Toronto winter. And now in the bloom of summer, short sleeves and golf pants and soft shoes with no laces. Nell had told me that. She often described what people wore in a given climate or country. They wore two ID tags, one on the shirt pocket and another on a retractable cord at the hip. The doors recorded when people entered and left. Richard Text was peeling off neoprene gloves when he got the call, and he swiped his hip card to accept the call. He had the pale skin of someone indoors. They want me when. For how long. For who. Okay he wants to make a tour of the plant or does he want to interact with the plant. That's the Bethlehem facility with the cold reactor, that's the one we're talking about? I can oversee that.

FIVE

So she's back with Richard.

David: And Richard's in New Hampshire with my sister.

Is that a common event?

Gabe no event is now uncommon.

We left the dog with Lars Pony. The dog had a pink neck from the temporary rope. Dye.

You boys have rooms upstairs you can use.

David: We have people waiting on us, Lars.

Do I have to keep her chained on.

You could bring her into the house.

Lars looked at her. No she dont even want to look at the house.

Dave's son is allergic to dogs, I said. That was our excuse for dropping in on Lars and our polite method of moving on. We'll call on you, Lars. Sok Hoon had said come on over she was having a party for the Prince of Wales.

What's his name, Lars said.

The Prince of Wales?

The dog's name.

She doesnt have a name.

David: The dog's name is Bucephalus.

So you'll come by.

We'll visit.

Bucephalus! It made me laugh but then I wondered if we were being bad. Was it wrong of us to drop off a dog and leave. But I could tell David wasnt curious about Lars, and during hours of exhaustion I cave to David's level of attention to the world, even though that attention is sometimes elitist.

The Prince of Wales. He was involved because of the fabric that covers water. He likes things like that. He was winding down a minor Canadian visit.

WE DROVE into NDG and ended up opposite a small private French school. We parked on the road. In Sok Hoon's driveway stood the black Land Rover. Beside it a security car with two armed men. A woman from the party was throwing rose petals onto their laps and the driver was pressing the button to wind up his window. It was about one in the morning, the front door wide open and music, as if music had opened the front door.

You sure this is it.

This, David said, is the exact address of my ex-wife.

He was admiring the moxie of Sok Hoon to create a new life.

Should we just leave everything in the car.

Let's risk it.

We had to talk to the men to get in. They were RCMP and they were impressed when David said the Land Rover was the same one Osama bin Laden uses. The men were wearing headsets and took a digital picture of us. They made a copy on a printer in the back of the security car and laid it on a stack in the back seat. Then they got out to look at us and we all walked over to the Land Rover. There was technology in the dash.

This used to be my Rover, Dave said to me. As though they were deaf or new speakers of English. There is something about the British speaking English that makes them sound now like it's a second language to them. I own this house, David said, with Sok Hoon. This Victorian with pressure-treated weave fence.

And he stared at it as if he did own it, but I knew that he probably didnt.

Enjoy yourselves, the RCMP said.

David looked at the front of the house.

Is the Prince of Wales actually present in the house?

The shorter man held up a piece of machinery and looked at it. He's thirty-two feet southeast of us, he said. Perhaps the Prince wears a chip, like a dog.

We ploughed through glamour, through tinsel and lights and flamboyant scooped numbers. We brushed our way out of the front hall and David found Sok Hoon on the lap of a woman in a green sleeveless gown. This was Allegra Campinghorst. Allegra, I said. And introduced myself. He was the one, David said, who helped write those letters.

Then you need a glass of whisky, Allegra said. And it was the voice. It was her radio voice.

She helped us find glasses above the breadbox and poured out some whisky. Her gown was ridiculous in the crush, but it was a gown made from insects, she said. It was a fabric woven of insects and wood. Well, cellulose.

Tiny desserts floated by. Several millionaires looked at their watches—they were visiting millionaires, as Montreal does not breed rich men. David kissed Sok Hoon and said goodbye to Allegra. Then he slapped the shoulders of a few men who greeted him, I thought, a little coldly. He knew these people, some of them, they were the successful graduates that Sok Hoon and David had gone to McGill with. Connections.

Ambiguity leads to richness, Sok Hoon said.

Be persuasive, I said. Cheers.

An expression, Sok Hoon said, has to be sandwiched by an impression.

Then, close to my chin she said, The only opportunity with David is to degrade him.

The Prince was standing in the next room. He was intently listening.

Look at his tie, Sok Hoon said. That's a regimental tie. And who else can get away with a double-breasted suit. Look at the flare of his shirt collar.

This made me touch the opening of my own shirt.

I plan, I said, to spend most of this summer drunk.

Sok Hoon: Thing is, when youre single, the best thing you can ask for is a fight.

I'm not single, I said. I've got Nell.

And Sok Hoon looked at me with a tenderness I thought might break her own heart.

We walked through the rooms past the Prince—I tiptoed—to the back deck.

Sok Hoon: Maybe I'm naive but I've never had casual sex. I was naive when I hooked up with David. And I've never not been present. Always present.

Me: You mean youve never fantasized?

That's not what I meant.

It was colder here, as if we had entered water. It was different air. We watched David and Allegra, beyond the Prince, move in on each other.

Me: She looks like she's hunting David down.

David, Sok Hoon said, likes to get in the middle of perverted things.

Sok Hoon was half Chinese and she grew up in Vancouver, or Hongcouver as she herself described it.

David came over. I'm just going to go in and look at my son.

Dont let him get up.

There's discipline, David said, and then there's quashing the human spirit.

Sok Hoon's parents had met as crew on a sailing vessel in the Pacific. They survived a rogue wave and that's where Sok Hoon was conceived, in the Indian Ocean. Perhaps her work at glazing over water is connected to a rogue wave conception. They were employed by tycoons who needed craft pushed from one group of archipelagos to another. They bought and sold fibreglass hulls out of Honolulu. So many marriages end in Hawaii, Sok Hoon had told me once, when she was still married and, I thought, happy. The year-long round-the-world voyage is fine out of San Francisco. But the monotony kicks in for one partner, usually the wife, by the time Honolulu rears out of the Pacific. Her mother is from Honolulu. Honolulu probably means Resentment. The marriage cracks, the boat is sold. It happened to her parents. So they sent Sok Hoon to private schools in Vancouver and then to McGill where she did a degree while hooking up with David and making a living in Toronto for three years organizing environmental credits for industrial polluters. They tried moving to New York but understood they could live a richer life in Toronto. They had Owen and then David fucked up, big time. Affair, she said. That affair was her Hawaii. She moved back to Montreal—her Chinese grandparents live here and offer support. Her work is in Asia now, the fashion industry is big there, and she also gets an unspecified amount from David, though often in the past year it is she who is making deposits in the joint account.

So how are things progressing in fashion.

Sok Hoon: It's not progress. Fashion is circular. Taste doesnt evolve, it revolves.

Me: That could be said for a lot of human ingenuity and wisdom.

She handed me a key from a nail under an old milk delivery chute. And then embraced a woman who had come up behind us. It was Allegra Campinghorst.

Sok Hoon: Are you getting outrageously drunk on white wine and club soda?

Allegra pinned her own corsage on me. She was a year older than me, we must have compared birthdates. There's something about women being just a touch older. Nell was a year older. Allegra's glasses were tortoiseshell and I realized up close she was tall and had some flesh on her. The green dress disappeared and it was just her skin you noticed. She was a bit like Nell when she talked and her voice, when I closed my eyes, it reminded me of those late nights in St John's, when Dave and I listened to her show, when she played music that mattered a lot to us. Her hair was cut like a boy's. I was getting a chill.

Let's go inside.

Two men grumbled around Sok Hoon's silent TV—playoff basketball. One said, What do you love the most. The other: The word *lucrative*. First guy: What do you hate the most. Second: When I'm wiping my ass and I get shit on my balls.

They made me nervous because they were wearing ties and they were cold to David and aloof to me. The bright hardwood on the TV made you realize how dark Sok Hoon's floors were. And then David returned and said, Allegra. He said it the way you'd say abracadabra.

David wasnt talking to the men. This was his graduation class, but there was a shunning going on. They had heard, or they disapproved or they did not want to be associated with the different angle David was now taking. It made us want to leave the room and so Allegra escorted us downstairs where I ended up on a leather couch holding hands with her. I asked Allegra for one outrageous fact. I watched her face search itself for a fact. Then she brightened and swivelled to me. She said there is a doll house that has a doll house in it. And everything in that doll's doll house is a replica, except for the champagne in the bottles. The bubbles of champagne are too big to pass through the neck of the bottles.

David's knees on the stairs. Then a moment when David casts an approving eye over me, an eye that feels like a too-big champagne bubble. He was considering me on the prowl when I wasnt at all, I was with Nell. I was happy and solid with her. I did not feel like a bachelor and I hated this eye of David considering it to be so. He made me feel like a shit disturber.

Allegra stared at me and wet her finger. Then she sculpted my eyebrow. She was a woman who ate three meals a day.

I have no idea where my bike is, Allegra said. Or where I am.

You came here on bike?

Then the Prince peered in with his bodyguards. He was looking for her. Are you Malaysian, he said to Allegra.

I've been to Japan, she said.

This made him comfortable. No one can read a park sign in Japan, the Prince said. Seventy percent of Japan is wooded.

Pardon?

It's forested.

He changed the word that might most be misheard. Nice shirt, he said of David's chest.

Does that mean I have to give it to you?

That's my mother, the Prince said.

And we raised our glasses in the basement of Sok Hoon's house.

Youre not to raise your glass, the Prince said.

His face, the friendly corrugated face, a famous face. We're so used to it in two dimensions. Soon, with the new hologram technology, we won't have awe. The Prince asked what I did.

I used to write gossip, I said.

Such as.

If there's anything interesting you hear tonight, let me know.

Gossip, he said, the story of my life.

A man with a headset waded in.

Allegra: Youre my father's age.

Then I'll act a little better, the Prince said as the headset directed him away, or you'll have a bad impression of your father's generation.

ALLEGRA'S YELLOW BIKE was on top of a Mini Cooper beside the French school. Someone had thrown it up there for devilment. Allegra dragged it off, the kickstand scratching through to grey factory primer. She unlocked the chain and we walked it home. I loosened and began to think about what I was doing. Allegra lived in one of those apartments with the wrought-iron stairs up to the second landing. Her ex-husband, she said, lives in Florida. I grew a little puzzled at my predicament. But I knew not what else to do and so I followed her. I am a good follower. I would follow someone to the edge of a cliff. In fact I have.

This is it, she said. And she lifted her bicycle up the stairs. She had probably chosen the bicycle for its weight. I held on to the small round of her hips. I just followed her to the landing like we were a train.

She locked her bike then bent and licked my arm.

You taste like cereal.

Me: Oh.

She found a hidden key and then said, Fuck David and Sok Hoon. They are the most fucked-up couple.

I must have asked her about David.

Do you or do you not, she said, have a wife.

We were in the hallway now. And then discovered a couch. All of her possessions seemed to be in boxes. I was very tired and drunk. She told me about her ex-husband, who works in securities. At first it was elevators and then, when the separatists got into power the second time, he moved to Florida. He lives in Indiatlantic, and I had to ask where that was.

He has to live by the sea, Allegra said.

She kept saying *he,* no name. She didnt want his name in the room, just his bio. He has a view of the shuttle launches, she said, and he was working on new security systems for condominiums and gated communities. How about you.

So I told her about Nell. How she left and she was with her ex now and I said her name, Nell. But telling this to Allegra made me heavy and I had to sit further into the couch. Allegra was balanced on an inflated yoga ball, almost a full year older, as though that little bit of wisdom was all I wanted to follow. We both seemed to say we were tired of young people.

Nell Tarkington, she said.

Did I say her last name.

I know Nell, she said. Nell is the one Dave's with.

When I'm under the influence I get loud or I get introspective. And here I became thoughtful. I was thinking woeful thoughts about love and career. How I'd given up writing because I was getting into trouble. I was writing too much about my own life and people who loved me were hurt. The Prince was right, story of my life. I wasnt successful enough to compensate for the surplus anguish. I'm not trying to get all modern on you, especially when I'm doing my best to be old-fashioned. What Allegra said had hurt and so my mind caromed off the hurt to another hurt.

Apparently, I said, she's with this guy Richard Text.

Oh I know Richard Text all to bits.

SIX

SHE PASSED a five-foot-tall gold hand grenade with a red pin and thought of Joe Hurley. Joe was dead now. Nell had heard through Richard. And now she was going to have lunch with a man who was there when Joe Hurley died. Nell pronounced *hand grenade* to herself. It sounded like a migraine. A migraine is a hand grenade in the mind.

She followed the sounds of cutlery, to breakfast. People left dollar bills as a tip. Then she drove out to the ranch where Georgia O'Keeffe had lived. She tried to become her. Then she drove back into town and parked near the restaurant where she'd had her wedding reception, on Canyon. El Farol. It was the oldest restaurant in Santa Fe. A long table out back through a twist of rooms, beams in the ceiling, a net over the bride and groom.

Hello Nell.

Nice to see you, Algren.

Algren Leonard had been the best man. He had flown in from London for the wedding. His face was like Gabriel's. He still lives in England half the year working at the Faslane nuclear submarine base, and what she remembers of Algren is that the first real swim he had was in the Suez

Canal. They ordered fried avocado rolled in pistachios; squid, halibut, chorizo and pork tenderloin. Algren suggested margaritas that were mainly triple sec, a splash of tequila, but Nell did not want a drink. When the food came they had a red wine from Argentina, a cooked romaine with goat's cheese. Algren was good at remembering food. Raw tuna red as watermelon. It was because of men like Algren Leonard and Richard Text that Joe Hurley was dead. They had encouraged him.

Richard's not here, he said.

I've just come for the box.

We can't authorize that. Even Richard can't authorize the box.

He told me he might be able to do something about that.

Well Richard's not here, he said again.

Had she fooled around with Algren? No they'd never had anything, she would remember those teeth. She'd gone through a bad spell but had left Algren alone. He was married, that was it.

Are you still married.

That was a long time ago, Algren said.

His wife had a broken arm. She'd gone around at the wedding with an ice pack in a sling. She was the only person in Santa Fe that summer to get frostbite. Nell did have a line. The line moved but that was the line while she was in Santa Fe.

Nell had driven to Santa Fe without her watch and now she couldnt read Algren's face well enough. It was as if the watch helped her eyesight. She couldnt tell if he was playing. She'd left the watch by the side of her plate that morning in the hotel in Las Vegas. She would have to call for it. Algren was wearing a New York Yankees cap. She could see him back at the hotel in the pool with that cap on. Margaritas were called silver coins.

Algren had known Joe Hurley in Afghanistan, two years ago. Algren and Joe had been logisticians. Joe wasnt meant to be travelling in a LAV.

He was fetching medical supplies, Algren said, when the left track hit an improvised exploding device. Joe Hurley made sure there were doors and windows, things like that. They blew up a man in charge of doors and windows.

He had been alive a long time. They carry tourniquets, Algren said. You stop the bleeding and stabilize fractures. You get them pronto to a hospital. But Joe had a hole in the bowel and it contaminated his chest.

Algren, for the other six months of the year, was in charge of a simulator in Landstuhl, Germany. That's where they brought Joe Hurley. He was given an ultrasound and digital imaging but it didnt catch the bowel. He was sent by Airbus back to Sunnybrook and that's where he died, of infections.

Now it was David's father, though Algren didnt know Arthur Twombly. Though it was probably because of Nell or because of Joe Hurley. A different scale, a different power contributing to this, but here she was, sitting here with Algren Leonard, trying hard to flirt, if flirting meant getting her hands on that box.

It was dark when she got back to the hotel, the swimming pool glowing emerald, with black silhouettes swimming. Did she miss Richard. He was not the same man since she left, Algren said. Algren knew that Richard was gay, but Richard was also protective. Richard had been concerned about her feelings for David. Though he allowed it. There was what, fourteen years between Nell and Richard, and their relationship made him almost a father to Nell. That's how she felt. She felt the word *grandfather* meant a man much older than your father. There should be a generation between father and grandfather, perhaps call it a goodfather. And Richard was her goodfather. He had got her into the country, employed her, but he wasnt convinced David was a good choice. No there had been nothing with Algren she was sure of it. Was that a mistake. Would he have given her the box if they'd had something.

Richard believed people could live together if they were the same age or some multiple of seven years. Seven years, it was like a time in office. Both of you at the inauguration.

Richard was not here. He had four days to make a president's visit smooth and inoffensive, Algren said. And no she couldnt have the box not even with his written authority. Richard's signature wasnt big enough. He had to be there in person for such a transaction. Even then it was iffy.

Nell had been to Bethlehem with Richard. She had met Kenneth Mosado and David's sister, Sasha. Sasha and Kenneth were married. Sasha knew who Nell was and yet not a word was spoken about Corner Brook. Nell thought she probably hated her. She had slept with Sasha's father. She had broken her parents up. But none of that could be said here. It was like a planet in another galaxy that breathed a different life force and they were never alone so it would be rude to speak of it in front of people who were not familiar with that galaxy.

Nell remembered sitting with Richard in a cafeteria when in walked Sasha's husband. Kenneth is going to sit with them. Then a commotion. A magpie inside the cafeteria, up in the rafters. The rafters are made from beams of wood sawed out of the local forest. The magpie stood up there, perplexed, studying the wall of windows. Kenneth Mosado sat himself down with a plate of cafeteria food. Magpie, he said. And they watched two waiters arrive with white tablecloths, but then Richard got up. He stood on a chair with a green dinner napkin. He caught the bird as it battered itself against the window. He carried it outside, the two waiters looking like men who accompany the matador.

I was thinking you were the magpie, Richard said to Nell. And that you should be outside, youre trapped inside.

SEVEN

WE ORDERED two smoked meat and coffees with a side of fries. Just
David Twombly and me with the rest of our lives strung out the open
door and down parallel sidewalks. I could tell he was not happy. When
David's unfriendly his jaw locks, his mouth ajar. Like he's chewing on his
cheek. It reminded me of my own swollen gum, how I was still favour-
ing the left side of my mouth. I had seen pictures of implants. If you dont
get an implant the cheek can collapse. A muscle under his cheekbone
flexed. We had it out over the coffee. Poaching, Dave said. He was
wearing those blue and yellow pants, and they gave him a military advantage I found unfair.

I take offence at that.

Youre enjoying, he said, a good-boy reputation out there.

Youre spreading bad things about me.

Allegra thinks you give mixed messages.

She licked my arm, Dave.

Let's take this outside.

We leaned against a rough wall outside Schwartz's. The daylight made
it hard to be serious. Dave in his caramel coat. The shoulder was getting

scuffed against the unpainted brick. He wasnt conscious of the scuffing and so I was worried, but then the bright unshadowed outdoors made our conflict feel trivial. Sunlight lit up his face and his face was unhealthy. Nature tends to diminish the grievances men contrive.

I'm getting upset, he said.

He pushed my chest with a finger. He suddenly looked a lot bigger. His mass increased and the folds in his face changed colour. He was like an octopus.

Well what about Nell.

It was as if all the internal meccano in his face and neck had collapsed.

I might have acted badly there.

What's badly.

He stared at the centre of my chest.

After you got together, Gabe. I wondered if I should say something to you.

You wondered.

I figured I'd leave that to Nell.

Youve had your cock in her mouth.

This blew air into his throat. He flared up, but it wasnt muscle, it was air. He was hard to get into new territory, to rip open the deep trestles he'd set and the easy yet nuanced version he'd created of his past. It was satisfying to him to relate his past in these entertaining chunks of anecdote. But it was blurred now, and false. I wanted to get him back on the knife edge of what had happened.

I said, Nell was evasive.

Dave: She made it sound like your connection with her wasnt one where she had to tell you those kinds of things.

You mean of your affair.

Youre upset, he said. He didnt mean to sound trite, but he was pissing me off.

I'm not about to give you the pleasure, I said, of my upsetness.

David looked around at the tops of buildings. Well youre here in my town poaching my women.

I received an arm lick.

You said a few things to Allegra.

And it's true, I may have said a few things. I'm a talker. I like to talk about being bad without being bad. I like to imagine badness and have someone enjoy our bad life.

I didnt mean, I said, to be putting a thing out there to make you look bad.

Fact is, you are acting in a way that can be considered outrageous.

I looked at David. He had changed in the year since Sok Hoon had left him. He had become hard. But I also knew he was on antidepressants. Allegra had meant more than what Dave was telling me. But I fought off this habit of mine to be conciliatory.

Youre mixing a trivial incident with a tough one, I said.

I could only bear to be ninety percent direct, so I crumbled the shoreline a bit, to get a firm anchor to the question.

I'm sorry, he said. And if it means anything it's over. She wants it over.

Wants. He said wants. Whereas, I said, you'd keep right on plugging.

I dont know what I'd do. I dont know what I am to do.

So it's an ongoing thing.

We've put a stop to it.

WE ENDED UP drinking all over Montreal and I let my crazy heart unravel. A round at the Ritz-Carlton. This lobby used to be filled with white Rhodesians, David said. And I thought he meant flowers. We racked it all up on Dave's black card that was soon to be taken and snipped in two by a judgmental stranger in a blue apron. After the seventh drink I got close to a truth: David was bad and he wanted me to be good. He was upset about Allegra because he didnt want me to have the same licence to be bad as him. And I've accepted this, over the years. I've let Dave get away with murder.

David: We were so private, me and Sok Hoon. We told each other the very private things.

Such as.

Childhood things. Weaknesses. We admitted them. Our heroism, he said, quoting another preface, does not entail withholding harmful information.

Me: You were not reserved.

We were careful. We didnt bash about. But it was good, cleansing, to speak of everything. We went to Holland for ten days and watched those performances. Three people on a white bed in a room with red walls. We stared at it and realized we were in the Canada room. They were doing Canadian things. There were snowshoes on the wall.

There were snowshoes?

It made us *think* there were snowshoes on the wall. Everything, it made you think everything, Gabe.

I'm not sure I know what everything is.

It's more than everything.

Nell.

He looked as though that were another topic entirely. That, he said, is a separate thing. That is hermetically sealed from—he searched for the word—noise.

How often did you see Nell.

He leaned back and looked over at a couple paying their tab. He realized that I had him on the everything front. It averaged about twice a year, he said.

So twice a year does it.

I thought we were through this.

David had an inward look. As if he was working on something inside. It gave him a reckless appearance. And it was attractive when your presence broke his inwardness. If he was attentive to you, you fell in love with him. Receiving his attention meant that you were important.

When I say everything I mean weakness. Admitting the wrong things that you feel.

In the washroom. We judged our faces in the mirror.

Shit, he said. Didnt we used to look hot?

That was fifteen years ago, David.

You know I could fly to Seoul and get a pair of glasses for less than what theyre going to cost me here. In South Korea theyre twenty dollars.

He was just going on with things. And if I pursued it I'd ruin something. I was exhausted and didnt have the reserves to push up the subject again.

So what is it, I said, with Sok Hoon.

It's port in a storm. Mother of Owen. I'm an optimist by nature.

Really. And how's that done for you.

Pretty shitty actually.

What's your ideal age.

David stared at his washed face. I could pass for thirty-two, he said. I often think I'm twenty and fifty at the same time.

Even that's not enough.

Gabe I'm glad youre not fucked up.

ON OUR WAY BACK to Sok Hoon's we passed a chalkboard with a quote from Wilde.

David: When that happens, it makes me want to look up the writer. It's a sign. But I've never liked Wilde. Once, Sok Hoon gave me a copy of *De Profundis* and I thought well that explains everything. She doesnt understand me. When she was leaving I threw it on the front lawn.

De Profundis, I said. Have you read it?

It's Wilde.

You think the title is satirical but it's not. Wilde wrote that—and I described the events that brought Wilde to his most serious work, his grappling with God.

Oh god, David said. And we walked, understanding that he'd fucked up royally with Sok Hoon. She understood Wilde the way he understood Mahalia Jackson. That Sok Hoon could have been the breakthrough event to a full life. I feel, he said, more isolated from the world of people.

Isnt that strange.

I always thought I'd have a house, he said, where people'd come in and pick up an instrument.

You mean like Sok Hoon has now.

We rounded the corner and saw the Matador. Something was different.

There's a pool beneath the pursuit vehicle.

It was a surprising pool that was not rainwater—you could tell from the surface tension of its edges that it was thicker than radiator fluid. There was an Esso, a man said, up on the main road. So we started up the Matador and drove down to the oval sign. We were not entirely sober. A man in a wheelchair wheeled himself around the car. He looked under it. He did a lot without getting out of the chair. In fact it looked more comfortable being a mechanic in that position. We can have that by Monday, he said, and it's five hours' work.

Five hours is a lot of units to pay. So we drove back to Sok Hoon's and David picked up the Land Rover and drove behind me. We went over to Lars Pony's. He was on the porch with our dog. I said Lars can you help me. The dog didnt seem to remember us. Very happy there with Lars. Lars looked at the engine. That's a recent alternator, he said.

I told him it was replaced in Whitby.

How much it cost you.

I dont know, I said. David paid for it.

David: I seem to recall it was very inexpensive.

I can fix this, Lars said. A hundred dollars. When you need it.

How about Sunday.

DAVID DROVE US HOME and we went straight to the kitchen and opened the refrigerator door and kept it open and drank all the beer the Prince had left. The fridge had food in it. I love to see bounty and I hate to see rot. Something about that made me think about Lars Pony. Perhaps it was that we were involved in disarray. We were supposed to have stayed with Lars. I realized that David liked the best of things and was soon put off by anything less than the best. And who was I to turn my back on a friend, was I worse because I wanted David to like me.

There was a water bottle on the dishrack and David remarked on it. Sok Hoon has things like that, he said. A sports bottle. That she reuses. I dont want to see Sok Hoon, he said, until she's drunk. She's nasty when she's sober.

David's son woke up and came down the stairs and closed the fridge door, as if it was the door that had woken him up. Owen, just seven years old. They called him Oven. Oven sat on a kitchen chair and waited for something to happen.

David: You want me to fix you a sandwich, Oven.

Naw I'm not hungry.

Me: You have Sok Hoon all wrong.

Youre basing Sok Hoon on the—and he thought about it—on the fifty times youve met her.

That made Sok Hoon come down. She was just like Owen, removing the two beers from our hands. They were both very reasonable and fixing fixable things.

Your sister called, she said.

Dave: My sister.

She was expecting you yesterday.

I'm trying to save my father.

Your father is not going anywhere. There's no rush on your father.

The pursuit vehicle, I said, is in the hospital.

Dave said he knew of a bar that we could have a last call in. Then he changed his mind.

You go, he said. You two. As if it was one of us who'd suggested it. I'm going to call my sister and tell this youngster a bedtime story. He pulled out his chrome pebble.

It's one in the morning, Sok Hoon said.

He was about to say something like, then I'll change what the time is. But realized even his pebble could not do that.

Okay, he said, then I want to stay here with my son. I'm going to have a conversation with the Oven.

Owen: I want a brother.

David: If we can get one cheap.

Owen, pointing to his privates: Sex is how you get them, right Mom?

Yes, Owen. But we dont have that any more, instead we have two houses.

THERE WAS A RED HEART in the window. The bar with a video hookup to other bars on the West Coast, bars that were just opening up for the night. You could compete in trivia with people you'd never met.

I know Dave drinks a lot, Sok Hoon said, but if he ever gets to that point where he has to sit down to sing karaoke—shove a bread knife in his throat.

Sok Hoon, rough and boisterous until she orders a drink at the bar, as if she's asking for a favour. A bourbon sour please?

It's sweet, I say.

They use Wild Turkey and bar mix. The guy mixes his own.

Were they made today?

Sok Hoon slurps on her straw.

They were made this afternoon.

I asked her flat out. I said, Sok Hoon you have to answer me this. About Dave and Nell.

His affair, she said.

You knew about Nell.

You know and you dont know, she said. When you have a kid and work and payments and a front porch to repair and ill parents and good friends then there's only four minutes in the day when you can let your mind wander into that kind of territory. And to be honest I wasnt all his either. So yes, I knew about her.

You knew it was Nell.

She looked me deep in the eye in a way that made me forgive her. What would I have done in her shoes.

I'm sorry Gabe.

Dave told her about Nell back in McGill. She thought it was over. Then Sok Hoon was getting their taxes together and found receipts. It was like a clock had fallen off the wall and the battery, she'd found the battery across the room.

Me: Nell and Dave.

Do you think that's fucked up.

I know I'm supposed to assume all that veneer of feeling betrayed.

Sok Hoon: You have complicated windows you look through.

It's damaging and deflating, I'm going to go through two years of feeling betrayed. I'm old enough to know that. But at the same time it's curious and arousing.

I think it's fucked up and brave.

Hurtful though.

It's unthoughtful, she said.

Though I'm sure a lot of thought goes into it.

I dont think, Sok Hoon said, she's seen him since you guys.

She has seen him since we guys. Now I wanted to hurl things. And then hurling gave way to the ridiculousness of hurling. I think, I said, in ways she's tried to tell me, but when youre older you become less careful. Less precious about it all.

She must love you, she said. I mean youre lovable.

We're all lovable.

She laughed at that. For a long time, she said, David would say things to me. Mean things. He's garrulous in both directions: loquacious in love, loquacious in hate. But hate is hard to forget. It sullies love. It made me feel leavable, when I want love to be supersonic. I asked my brother, I said does your wife like me? And he said Sok Hoon I'm not going to tell her you said that.

She'd be hurt if she knew you doubted it.

We talked until four and then we tried the corner depanneur for fresh rolls and cheese.

This is what I missed most when I lived in Basel, she said. Fresh *chausson aux pommes* at the dep.

I really wanted a piece of orange cheese. When I want something it appears above my eyes as a vivid photo. The sky was light blue, the streetlights still on. A couple of people about, people who've been up all night. Some traffic down on Sherbrooke, a cold wind. That time in the morning, it's as if the city has flushed itself out and anything still alive can own it, though all that's left is a creaky vessel low on power. We zipped up our jackets. I slipped a newspaper out of the middle of a bundle and left a dollar on the stack, under the plastic band around the waist of the bundle. Now the sun was shining directly along an alley.

On the front page: Four Murdered in Moosonee.

Are you far, I said.

We're far.

We waited for the light on the head of a taxi.

We met this man, I said.

Sok Hoon asked who.

This murderer.

I snapped the front of the newspaper.

You know a murderer.

He'd never murdered directly before. Maybe he ran out of money to hire someone else.

Sok Hoon said she feels she's exposed herself in public. That she didnt leave David really. That he fired himself from the job of husband. People have said how daring to leave David but in private they think to themselves, how embarrassing.

You should have talked to the Prince of Wales about that.

I did, she said.

EIGHT

I SLEPT FOR TWO HOURS and then got up. Often when I drink a lot I get up early in the morning. It feels like it's just me and the morning, the two of us. As if we're equals, this one human being and the universe. Instead of feeling small I feel as big as everything else combined. I thought about what I was killing and what I was cultivating. I was fixing myself a sandwich in the kitchen, burning up whatever reserves I had in my muscles. I turned around. Owen on the staircase.

You hungry.

He shook his head.

What are you doing.

I've been looking at you to see what you did on your own.

I heard you liked sandwiches, I said.

I made him a sandwich just like my own, I didnt make a kid-size sandwich. Yum or yuck, I said. And instead of ignoring it he kept up with me on the eating of it.

Owen: Can I have the car keys?

There's no car, I said. It's getting fixed.

I just want to open the trunk to the Land Rover, he said.

Then he put on a pair of socks. He put them on like he thought socks would make him appear more serious and therefore able to operate car keys and make the car materialize out on the road.

Me: It's the weekend right?

It's Saturday, Owen said.

Okay then tell me someplace I should see.

We left a note and took a bus. We get a transfer, Owen said, and we stand at that corner.

There was a panel of double mirrors near the wall of a bank. He'd noticed it one day and had wanted to try it out. You dim the light by narrowing your eyes, so your faces merge. Our noses, Owen said, theyre almost the same.

Then he did this thing with his biceps, a bodybuilding pose, and a distortion in the glass made him look powerful.

He was my son. I let myself be his father and a flurry of heat fizzed in the top of my neck. Owen opened his mouth to make a face. He was alive and I did not know what he would do. The tiresomeness of promises and commitment. The constant renewal of faith. Instead of just knowing. But then fathers leave all the time. Jesus, David Twombly.

Let's walk a few blocks, I said. Let's just follow our noses.

And I cheered at the thought that I was moved.

We walked around and I bought the Oven a comic book and I got an American newspaper and a couple of postcards. Three people were sitting in the grass at McGill, in a bowl of shade under a tree. This was David's alma mater. I hadnt thought to go to a school off the island. No one really told me I could.

We went to the café where I'd been with David when the mirror had fallen on him, and I ordered a coffee and Owen had a lemon soda. I told him to watch for people ordering sweet things and then meat. Let's write out these postcards, I said.

Who for.

Write one, I said, to your dad. We'll mail it to him in Newfoundland and when he gets back there he'll see the sneaky thing his son has done.

I handed him a pen, a good one, and he ruined the nib on it with his concentrated printing. I wrote to my parents. Coming home, I said. And then signed it with both my first and last names. Why had I done that? What other Gabriel would write them and say, Coming home?

We passed the McGill students in the grass. The shadow had moved on and the sun was glancing off their bent elbows now. It felt like the sun was their system of power, they controlled the sun and let it pour energy into their joints. They were refusing to let the sun shine into David.

We found a post office and stood behind a man who was short and balding. On his skull, at the boundary between scalp and hair, was the tattoo 666. Did he ever think those numbers would show up. What would his father think, or his son? Well, I guess Owen still can't see them. Maybe that's it. Maybe evil is not concealed from everyone, only the victims.

I bought two stamps and got Owen to lick his own. Then I found Helen Crofter's postal code in the book and wrote that in and gave the postcards to the clerk. He said to take it outside and use the box.

But I want to give it to you.

If you give it to us, I'll put it in this tray here where it'll sit all afternoon until one of us brings it outside to empty in that box.

We rounded a curatorial building and heard the rumble of bees. Cars over a distant bridge. We walked up Mount Royal and came upon a lookout point with a ramp to the sky. A man was receiving instructions at a hang glider. I thought that was something to watch with the Oven. The man and the guide were wearing puffy bags with tails. The man was barefoot and his wife carried his shoes. I pointed the shoes out to Owen. The men clipped into the kite on a running board over the cliff, two handlers holding the guy wires. Then off, and out and up, he waved back at us. He became a very small thing in the air. And his wife was still holding his shoes, the only thing left of him.

What about a museum, I said. Can you handle a museum.

Owen seemed easygoing and he knew where one was though he didnt know the name, the Musée des Beaux-Arts. I like free museums. Let's find one thing, I said, and concentrate on that. Part of the enjoyment is ignoring the rest, is saying to the piece, youre the reason I'm here. It's faithful.

Owen: What does that say.

It says archaeological.

What does that mean.

You dont touch anything.

I'm just going to sit on this bench, the Oven said, and look at everything.

I let my eye wander. And there, a crucifix. I pointed it out to Owen, but he was looking at his comic book. I walked up until my nose was an inch from it. I marry you, I said. I'd seen Nell once waiting for an elevator at IKW and she was so keen she was as close as I was now. In a hurry, I said, and she laughed. Thanks for laughing. Well, I feel like you now, I feel like I'm trying to make this crucifix open.

In a way, Christ is an elevator.

Dark weathered wood and traces of paint. His eyes looked closed but when I bent my knees the eyes were open. Theyre cast down. If they were closed he'd be suffering for my sins. But theyre open, so he is triumphant. Sneaky Christ!

Sometimes youre in a place because youve been kicked out of all the other places, I said to the Oven. Some days youre in the middle of the air without your shoes on.

And I realized I was sharing my Wyoming with a kid. I wasnt alone here, I was telling him everything.

We walked around the old city for the rest of the morning, and half the time I carried Owen. I put him on my shoulders with his legs around my ears. I caught us in a mirror and we looked like a pagan totem. The boy giving birth to the man. It made me feel vulnerable, but at least I had fifty-four dollars in my pocket. I bought another coffee and the Oven wanted fries but I said we had to wait until noon, you can't go eating fries before noon. It felt like I'd been up for days, and then I realized I had been. I thought about David and Nell. I saw them talking together and putting a hand where a hand should not go. I created whole films of them that were probably close to the films that exist someplace in space and will, soon, with the correct technology, be spooled back in and used to lay guilt on us all. Judgment day will come, I thought, and I wondered if there was any snap in that. All my life is devoted to thinking if there's snap to something, or if an event is empty.

I didnt see David that day. It was nice to have a break from him and it was good to hang out with a kid. Kids shake you up. I'd had it out with Dave and now this reprieve. But what kind of reprieve was it. This was David's son. Really I was hanging out with the ideas and acts of David, rather than the man himself. Here were his repercussions. For I had none. But then perhaps we are blind to our own repercussions. We are too short to see them on top of a man's balding head.

I went back to Sok Hoon's driveway and had Owen stare into the windows. I was shy, I said. And had never looked at my own home the way I was making him look at his. There was his mother, doing something, she was bent over to a task. It could have been rolling pastry or it may have been keeping herself balanced. I remember my father, building a new kitchen. He took my mother by the arm and had her stand by the window where the kitchen counters would be. He made a pencil mark on the wall next to her wrist. So the counters would be hers.

Okay Owen go in to your mother.

I let Owen enter on his own to her. They didnt need me barging in. And I turned and saluted the school across the street where Owen was beginning his education. Then I ended up on the Main and ate fish in a diner. The toilets were amazingly dirty.

But at around nine I called Sok Hoon. I was worried about you, she said. She was just running an iron over some clothes and could use the company. I thought, the Prince one night and ironing the next. Perhaps everyone irons.

There's a mattress for you in the guest room, she said. But when we looked David had returned, quietly sneaking in, and crashed on it. It was partly deflated. He was still in his clothes and his shoes were tightly on. He had probably seen Allegra.

Come on, Sok Hoon said. That's your cue.

She was emanating the thought that we could be closer.

Look, I said. Let's just have something small.

Right here by the bathroom.

And I kissed her. It was delicious, like eating apricots. It was a lip balm she was wearing. It made my shoulders relax. I pushed the skyline of her body against me. All I needed was to pull something towards me, something warm. And Sok Hoon, it was a conciliatory kiss. She was feeling sorry for me, that I was going through an anguish with Nell that she had already come out the other side of with Dave. It was a kiss that said it'll be okay, youre a good person, I like you.

I WOKE with David's arm around me, breathing his dead breath on my mouth. The mattress was flattened, he'd kicked off his shoes and one of them was under my chest.

Wake up, the Oven said. He was eating peanut butter and toast. The boy lived off things on bread.

Ahoy matey.

There is a shell of David, his eyes opening up, his lips a crease, barely alive.

Owen: Hi Dad. I saw you this morning with your boots still on.

David: You want to go see your aunt in New Hampshire?

Sok Hoon: I'm taking Owen across the street.

Dad you take care of yourself.

WE WATCHED SOK HOON and Owen cross the street and go to Sunday school, but as they crossed two police cruisers arrived and Sok Hoon was called over to one. A woman. They spoke and pointed at the school. There was a sign that said Early Intervention. I remember going to school and I know the type of boy the Oven is. He reminded me of Gerard Hurley. I knew Gerard Hurley when we were the age of Owen. We were the same age, with birthdays in March. When you share an astrological sign you can't help but like the person.

I recalled his red star in Grade Two, that moment of change for Gerard Hurley. He was what, seven. He was that boy there, the age of Oven. And now the policewoman was assisting them back across the street and then returning to the cruiser while two men from the other car walked down the school steps doing paperwork.

What's going on.

Sok Hoon: Theyre conducting an investigation.

Owen: I got the day off.

Me: Congratulations.

We went off to the kitchen and I heard Sok Hoon say, There's been a report of abuse.

DAVID WANTED TO SPEND THE AFTERNOON in Sok Hoon's bed, but I wouldnt let him. We have to pick up the car and dog, I said. It's Sunday.

He got the keys for the Land Rover. We drove to Lars Pony's and he hollered for the dog. She did this graceful leap in through the back window of the Land Rover. We were both proud of her. Dave drove away and Lars waved as if he always took care of out-of-town dogs.

That's a good dog, Lars said to me, that Bucephalus.

Me: What did you say?

The dog's name.

Me: What are you doing with that hose?

He was standing there with about eleven feet of green articulated hose and a roll of duct tape like a bracelet on his forearm.

Your car reminded me I got to check some things on my car, he said.

What kind of car.

A beauty, he said. The only thing I got in this life that's been faithful.

And when he said that he became the man in the fox coat. These men, thinking cars are faithful. Did I love our car. I opened the driver's door and started it up. Smooth. I put my hands on the wheel. Then I lifted them and looked at where my hands had been.

He was standing there delighted at himself. Lars had solved a puzzle.

You take care, he said. And waved. I saw him, as I went over the rise. He walked out into his street and kept waving. He waved like I was the last person on earth.

I ORDERED SOME PLAIN CROISSANTS and a bag of coffee and tested the car a bit before going back to Sok Hoon's. Then I drove up behind the Land Rover and got out and I looked under the chassis. Dry as a bone.

David and Sok Hoon were sitting at the kitchen table, just staring at each other. They looked like they needed to be programmed.

Some of the kids, Sok Hoon said, have been taped to chairs.

What about Owen.

He saw it. He said it never happened to him.

They looked like they had exhausted the subject but didnt know how to change it. David had dodged a bullet. The bullet had been marching him across the street and strangling a teacher. They were looking for me to change things so they didnt have to imagine any more the strangling and the charges and David incarcerated.

Duct tape, I said. And suddenly I knew what Lars Pony had in mind.

I drove back across town with David Twombly. I pointed there and turn right and no it's better this way. Finally we were lost because I was panicking and David looked up the universal number on his pebble and guided us there under the satellite for global positioning. We pulled up to the little house and I hoped the house would not be soon for sale.

The front door was locked. Try the gate. The house was joined to the next house by a wooden gate. It was pointy on top and I could not get over it. David did. Heavy but dexterous. I called to him. I said, Do you hear a car running.

Then I pressed my head up to the gate and I could hear it chugging in the garage in back. I couldnt see David because of the tall gate, just the edge of the garage door. But I heard him. I heard a window break and then a swear word. Now the car running louder and shutting off. But the garage door wasnt opening. So now he'd gone in the house.

The front door opened. A man's hand, bandaged. At first I thought it was Lars. I knew it was Lars. Then it's David with a cup towel around his fist. He had his pebble. He was calling for help.

NINE

WE NEED NEW SHIRTS, David said. If we're to go into the States we need new shirts. All the old adventurers wore good shirts.

Can't you, for a few minutes, think about what's just happened.

He was looking at the scale in kilometres. About the time. Refolding the Michelin map.

We take the 87 south and cross over to Sasha, he said.

Youre a cunt, you know that? All Lars wanted was a bit of company.

David took a moment to translate something in his head. Dont be responsible, he said, for any man's choices. That will lead you to ruin.

He counted off the days and where we'd be on the map. We had to stick around for Lennox Pony to show up. But then we'd hit the road south. If anything happens, he said, I take the next flight. If they dont let me on board I'll get Massimo to make me false papers. That anything, he added, could be here with Owen, or with my father.

There were big airports in Newark and New Brunswick and Nova Scotia. He would keep his pebble on alert.

David poisoned me. But he had a point. Or, he had a way of pushing through life which made him not feel bogged down by the badness. He had badness and badness affected him, but it seemed, every morning, he'd wake up to a new start.

We waited a day for Lennox Pony. We hadnt seen him since he was fourteen years old. And there he was, a big man. He didnt look anything like Lars. Except in his shoulders. His shoulders had the same hesitation, the deking move Lars had on the basketball court. In fact, shoulders can manipulate a lot of things. He had been an excellent goalie. He'd left Corner Brook and moved to Alberta and worked in the tar sands until a depression got him down. It was an illness and he was medicated so only his shoulders were alive. His eyes were dead. He'd lost his marriage. Something of the father had concentrated in the son, so it was an even stronger force, but also there was a more fierce tendency to live in Lennox. He wasnt going to kill himself. Everything in him was more powerful than the father, in both the positive and negative spectrum. He was like the nuclear era versus the dynamite era. Less total war.

I'm sorry for your loss, David said to him. And he meant it. I saw his eye and Lennox took him to be a sincere, thoughtful man. Which he was. But what residual feeling did Lennox have about being the young one, the black one, the second-last to be chosen, the one we all mauled a little, even me.

Lennox got off his chair and sat on the grass and lay back in the sun. He was flat in the grass, almost hidden. So I got up and did the same thing. It's good to let the sky take up most of your vision. It cleaves you from the world and you can think of it as a separate thing from you, like youve got your back up against the wall of the earth and now youre going to walk away from it. I peered up to see what David was doing and he too had come down to the ground. Three men flaked out in the grass, about to stroll away from the world. The grass is a big thing. Usually men are with smaller things, that's why we like women. Most men are uncomfortable with things larger than themselves, so it took some trust for us all to give in to the earth. Then Lennox spoke.

When I was a kid, he said, my dad bought an old diesel motor. It was the size of a Volkswagen. We built a shed for it out in the Lemon Yard. It had an exhaust pipe out the side. The motor was not used for anything, Lennox said. His father loved it for the sake of it working.

The ground in his back made his voice solid, like wood.

That was my first mechanical appreciation, he said. We'd go into the Lemon Yard, adjust the choke, turn the crank and have it sputter to life. It made power but it wasnt power harnessed to any use, just the marvel of power being made.

I tried to remember that motor, its little shed. I remember the Lemon Yard. There's a drug store built on there now. We used to play ball in the Lemon Yard.

Dave: Remember that movie we were in?

Lennox: We were never in a movie. We never made it into the movie.

Dave: We were in the movie.

What were they talking about. I searched out the sky above for some sense of it. And then, of course, I remembered. We were really young. People from Hollywood had come to make a movie. They used a house on Valley Road and they were shooting exteriors all around the town. It was a film about two friends who work at the pulp mill. One day we were playing baseball in the Lemon Yard. And Lars Pony came out to us and said he heard on the radio they were looking for extras. They want a whole bunch of extras down at the mill.

The actor starring in it, Gordon Pinsent, was a Newfoundlander, but he'd been in American films. In one movie he played the president of the United States—he was a sort of JFK dealing with the cold war. Then in *The Thomas Crown Affair* he introduces Steve McQueen to Faye Dunaway.

We left our gloves and picked up our hockey sticks and took an orange hockey ball down Valley Road to see what was going on at the mill. They couldnt get enough kids for this scene. They said the hockey sticks were good, pretend youre playing street hockey. And you, what's your name.

They were pointing at Zac Twombly.

You want a role in this movie?

Zac got a speaking part. He had to ask Gordon Pinsent if he'd seen his father in there. His line was, Hey Will. That was Gordon Pinsent's character's name. And we had to play behind the scenes, play some excellent street hockey, like we were also waiting for our fathers. It was pretty exciting. We'd never seen cameras and booms and the little caravan where you could get sandwiches and coca-cola. I must have drunk six cokes that afternoon. Then it was time for Zac's scene. We were proud of Zac. We'd heard him practising his line over and over. Hey Will, he said. Hey Will. And then Gordon Pinsent was cued to walk through the mill gates and Zac had to break away from us and go up to him. Hey Gordon, he said.

At that time, being six, we thought there'd be a film shot in Corner Brook every summer. We didnt know that would be the last one ever. It sort of spoiled us, expecting the big wide world to come to us as soon as school was over.

A year later the movie came out. We all went down to the Millbrook Mall to see it. There's a great scene where Gordon Pinsent spends his wedding night in the Holiday Inn on West Street. We were all waiting for the scene after that, when Gordon Pinsent's best friend is killed in a pulp vat, and Zac has to go up to Gordon Pinsent at the mill gates and say Hey Will. How they had to shoot that scene a couple of times because Zac was so nervous. But the next scene was the funeral and then Will getting bitter and losing his humour. The scene with the kids never got in there. Lennox was right, none of us are in it.

We said so long to Lennox and drove back to Sok Hoon and said our farewells to Owen. This wasnt planned, just something Lennox had done made David want to see Owen one last time. A grieving son and then a young son. I looked at David as we drove towards the border. Then he slowed down and pulled over.

My glasses.

We had to find an off-ramp and wheel around and drive back while Dave called on his pebble. This turning around and the phone call made Bucephalus nervous. It was as if she thought we might leave her, and so I stroked her down to get her to lie flat. We found the store and pulled over and quickly got out as if we were a pair of plainclothes policemen from a seventies drama. We walked in together. David had stitches in his head and a white bandage around his hand. You look like if you dont get glasses soon, the lady said, youre going to do yourself in. It was nice to spend a few last moments in a Canadian store. They had the glasses there behind the glass counter in a silver case. They seemed thicker framed now and as Dave drove he kept pushing them up on his nose, touching the lenses and frames until there were fingerprints and smudges all over the edges of the glasses. It was a new method of punctuation as he talked and there was something in their hue that accentuated the stitches on his skull. Then I noticed the fresh pavement to the south and the new striping was like white stitches on a charcoal suit. We'd head south then yank her east and hit New Hampshire and meet Dave's sister. Then it was Maine and carry on to Nova Scotia and push through to the ferry for Port aux Basques. That was the plan. When you have a plan you dont need to talk for an hour. Which Dave obeyed for about five minutes.

TEN

LET ME GET A WORD in edgewise, I said. I was driving now.

David: Have I been talking?

You havent stopped.

When does that word ever get used.

What word.

Edgewise.

It doesnt.

It doesnt get a chance to get edgewise into any other sentence.

It was the slippers, he continued. Then it was that she was wearing everything the same. I mean, she wore the same things. A pink sweater and pale beige corduroys. Her hair was up and Sok Hoon was telling him a story of a woman on the phone and Sok Hoon made that gesture of her hand being the phone.

She bored you.

I was bored.

Well you bore yourself. No one else is responsible for your being bored.

He flipped down his sun visor. He was amazed at how well he could see his face.

David: Have you ever squeezed your nose.

Pause.

There's a lot of oil in the nose. In every pore.

David scanned his nose. Then he looked at mine.

Youre not as bad, he said.

What are you talking about.

I'm going to start taking care of my nose. Allegra mentioned it to me. I was defensive but I can see what she meant.

Did Allegra mention it as a parting shot?

It doesnt matter, she said it.

Me: Men's noses are different from women's.

Yes but there's quite a variety in men too.

Youre not going to start plucking hair from your nipples are you?

Do you think I should?

We drove to the border like this. The closer we got to the States, the more maple leaf flags we saw. Then federal buildings with the Canada logo. Such a weak typeface for a national identity.

David finally gave in to a desire, he turned the mirror and squeezed his nose. Nozzles of white cream lifted up their heads. He sat back, satisfied.

Now you have a red nose, I said.

What will the border guard think of that.

What he thought was, here are two eligible candidates for smuggling (apparently an unlicensed dog, a newly acquired car, one man with a raw nose, that's what gets the console lit up).

The border guard was wearing a short-sleeved black shirt with stripes on the pocket and a blue crest for homeland security. There were gold pins on the flaps, and the rim of a tattoo from a previous life poked out of one sleeve. He asked if he could take a sample of the dust in David's suitcase.

You mean I can say no?

You can say whatever the hell you want.

And then what.

Do you have identification.

We flipped out our driver's licences. He saw my firearms possession and acquisition licence.

You got a gun with you.

No sir.

We have a Taser, David said.

A Taser, he said. You got it in the safe position and under lock and key.

We do, sir.

I need a citizenship card.

We looked at each other.

I lost mine, I said, when I was seventeen.

I dont think I ever became a Canadian, David said.

What are you.

American.

But you reside in Toronto.

I was born on a US army base.

Huzzah to the air force. And you?

I was three, I said, when we moved.

I dont care how old you were.

I was born in England, I said.

You sound like youre lying.

I dont remember England. I feel like I'm saying I'm from a country I have not experienced.

Well what's to stop you, he said, from coming in here and living illegally.

It wasnt a question he wanted answered. He asked me to put my left finger on a glass keypad. It lit up red.

Right, he said.

I reached for my driver's licence and was about to tramp the gas when he held on to the side of the window.

Your right finger is what I mean.

Then he hovered a webcam at us and took our pictures to be disseminated to every law enforcement jurisdiction in these here United States, including Hawaii, Alaska and Puerto Rico.

I'll just take a look at that Taser now.

And David got out and showed him what I did not know had been in the car. He unlocked it and the guard weighed the black gun in his hands and was not at all nervous about David possessing it. David had the papers and the cleared security. Technically he still worked for IKW and that type of work allows a lot of freedom.

You and your dog, he said, are free to rock 'n' roll. He did a little fishtail with the side of his hand.

Well then we're out of here.

He raised one finger. He had all the time in the world to tell it, this one. He was lording it over us.

Folks if you do happen to go—he picked his teeth with the corner of my driver's licence—I might have to arrest you.

Arrest.

And then I'd have to fill out the paperwork and apply for a search warrant. That could take one and a half business days.

He checked his watch and rubbed the face of my driver's licence. The entire manipulation of my licence was aggravating me. Wednesday morning, he said, then stared at the long line of hot summer traffic humming behind us. It really didnt bother him, this lineup. He waited for us to ask. So I asked. How do we get around that, officer.

That took a lot out of me, saying officer.

If you oblige us this sample.

He pointed to a raised windowless bungalow set off from the end of the bridge. It looked like the kind of building that houses hydroelectric circuits.

The lab is down the road yonder.

You want us to urinate?

With your permission these powders in your luggage will be examined.

Or we can go but youre saying you will arrest us.

My guess is I'm going to arrest you.

And that means.

A night in this complex whereas of your own volition we're talking forty minutes.

Dave clapped my hands. Let's do the forty, he said.

Me: Are we allowed to fish in that river?

It's a legal river, but as of now youre in the custody of US homeland security.

What if we promised to stay in eye contact.

I'm afraid I had to shoot the last man who lost eye contact.

But I'm saying we'll stay in eye contact.

You can only control your own eye, Mr English. Youre not thinking of me. What if I lose you. Then I come after you through that brush and shoot you cold and drag you back here and have an autopsy then I have to live with that, my wife has to live with that, my three daughters, well two—one doesnt give a damn what I do.

What's the matter with her?

Her parents are assholes.

You ever bring her out here, see what Dad does for a living?

You men dont look like you have daughters.

I just left my son in Montreal, David said.

You got a daughter?

A son, he's a seven-year-old.

He leaned in the window and licked the inside of his lip. It was as if sons didnt equate to daughters.

One day, he said, I'm gonna see the bad one in a car like this heading Canada way. Dont ever have three kids. Two is good, three you can never get enough seats in a restaurant.

Dave: That's what made her go bad.

Me: It's more likely she'll head Mexico way.

This here's a Matador, isnt it.

You might have driven one yourself.

He stood back to admire the flank of our old ghost car.

Before my time. Heard good things though.

Those were the days.

Yes sir those were the days.

Those were the days when you could have shot us on the spot.

Those days are back, he said.

WE WATCHED all the traffic that we had industriously passed smooth out along the border and zip off into New York like shorn sheep. We sat in two flexible plastic chairs, the maker of which Dave noted so as never to invest in, and I counted the triangles in a puzzle on the back of a kids' magazine. I was counting to give my mind something to do, but then the triangles turned into a firing range with men hurdling the triangles carrying Tasers. That he snuck that into the car and put me in that position. But the entire room was monitored and so I sat there and watched, through the window, our dog. The border guard was letting her sit with him in his booth, like a police dog. And then back to the kids' magazine. I was glad not to have kids. To have them stranded here at the border knowing dust was being inspected from Dad's bags. That sort of suspicion shouldnt be allowed to be born in children. It's like exotic foods.

I wouldnt feed a child extravagant things. Let them get old first and really enjoy the astonishment of their first mango. Let them think they were deprived. Being deprived is an excellent kick in the pants, to make a body want to search.

Then Bucephalus came back and David was rubbing her down. He used to have a dog. But it was like an arranged marriage, he said. They didnt hit it off.

That was Wolf, I said.

I had that dog for his entire life. I saw it being born. We respected each other, Gabe, but no deep love. I think for me to love something it has to be either half-broken or full of enthusiasm. This dog here. I could easily fall in love with this girl. Though she looks a little too full of the world now to be reined in. She's experienced and loves too many things to be loyal.

So a dog has to be a bit broken, or full of enthusiasm, but in either case he must not have too much experience in the world.

He can't be a slut before I get to him. But together he can do what he likes as long as he comes back to me.

THE DUST WAS NEGATIVE and away we peeled into New York. We drove on down Highway 87 to Plattsburgh. David wanted snacks so we pulled into Plattsburgh and found a grocery store. Trail mix is what he wanted. Nuts raisins and licorice. I said I was more in line for a sandwich.

I'll get you a sandwich, he said, you get me the trail mix.

I had to ask the guy at the deli counter, Where are the peanuts?

David: In the baking aisle.

Where are the chocolate bars.

In the aisle full of potato chips.

The deli guy looked at us. My friend here is looking for a job, I said.

Have you noticed, Dave said, the Americans stock the eggs right beside the bacon.

WE DROVE THROUGH PLATTSBURGH. We were in a new country and that seemed to call for a different attitude. It was like leaving a lover and realizing you could try to be less of an asshole. Youre too stubborn to admit youre one while youre in the old relationship. I was going to begin again with David. I was going to be honest and not persuaded.

David was rubbing his temples. I've lost half my brain, he said. Can't concentrate like I used to.

Then he blinked a number of times and searched the ground we were covering.

I look at the world, he said, pretending my eye is someone else's eye. Someone with integrity.

We switched the driving again and he was quiet while he drove. But once we got to the slow roads he wanted to talk. He said, I want you to know I'm in love with my son. I love him. I love nothing else. I'm not going to go on about it. I might not talk about him. I'm not that kind of boring dad. I take care of them financially. Sok Hoon doesnt have to worry. She pretty much takes care of herself as it is, sometimes in fact she sends money my way. But if there's a gap she knows how to fill it in. She doesnt need to ask me, there's an account. Anyway, Sok Hoon is possessive and she could have lived in Toronto. I can't live in Montreal, there's no work in Montreal. I could live in Montreal but I'd be broke. So she went to Montreal. Good. I love the Oven and that's the end of it.

We came to a river and David wanted to look at it. He parked the hot car up on the grassy bank and I unfolded the tent to air in the sun and Bucephalus took a bead on the river. We went down to the river with the fishing rod. Did we need a permit? There were no posted signs. All the rapids glinted in the bright afternoon. I strung up our rod and the dog watched me cast, up to her tail in water. The trout were hot and lazy. David stripped down and folded his new glasses and put them in their case. Then he waded into the pool I was fishing in.

Just to cool off, he said.

Well thanks.

You werent going to catch anything.

Then he tested the bank and got out and lay on the grass with the dog and both of them watched my fly, their bellies breathing in tandem.

David: Do you smell a burning.

Maybe theyre doing a controlled burn.

It's like a grass fire.

It smells close by.

We looked behind and the air around the car had that wobbly look to it. The Matador was on fire.

We ran up with the blankets and threw them over the car. It was weird, superficial burning. A man came out of the house and judged the car and asked what our plans were. David said we'd like to camp. You can do that, he said, but not where you were fishing. He said it as though we might catch the river on fire. He pointed to a flat spot amongst a copse of willows. That's a fair spot, he said. Then he looked under the car.

It was your catalytic converter, he said. That's what caught the grass on fire. You shouldnt park a hot vehicle on dead grass.

We slept on the banks of the Au Sable River and the moon turned the inside of the tent green and the green reminded me of Allegra Campinghorst and her iridescent costume. I thought about being inside the green dress, a tent of beetles, which felt like crawling into a radio. I became Allegra. I was trying to think of how she could speak so disparagingly of Sok Hoon, but I guess she liked David. I think it's good to know that you have a reserve. Out of David's ashes Sok Hoon had made a bigger life. It's both foolish and a relief, but we all rely on backup plans to our current predicament. Women especially. Most often, in the end, when it's over, the women win. They live for hundreds of years. But the world looks upon them as the support behind men's work. Even these days.

ELEVEN

Bucephalus climbed aboard us and wedged herself in and slept between us. In the morning I let her out. I watched her tail hover in the air. Then she was off towards the cows.

There's this theory about the butterfly wings, David said, waking up. Flap of a wing in Brazil causes a hurricane in Srebrenica. It's wrong. We thought it was right for maybe fifteen years. Do little things and the big changes will come. We powered a lot of technology on that wrong thought.

That's the power of a strong image, I said. It can overpower reason.

We had camped in the lee of a dairy farm. We had watched the owners feed the cows and sit under an awning with cheese sandwiches and a bottle of cold wine. Then slept. Now this morning.

David: Our computers at IKW told us you can flap all you want, no hurricane. So the truth is a little more refined. You have to get all the butterflies flapping. If you can encourage all this flapping, then you might rev up a hurricane.

David Twombly confessed he was working on a book but had been staring too much at the computer. Then he gets an email and bam.

Me: You have email on the computer that you work on?

He looked at me.

You have to get rid of that. You have to work on a machine that isnt alive.

More looking.

If you walked into a room and there was a dead dog in there. And say there's this happy dog wagging his tail as well.

And with that Bucephalus returned to the zipper of the tent.

Youre going to pat the happy dog.

We patted our happy dog. The pink valley of her tongue.

Youre going to roll around and play. There's nothing more distracting than an alive dog.

David: You have to work in a room with a dead dog.

Who can resist?

I THOUGHT of how close I was to Nell, but then, how much can you know of someone. How much of a relationship is dead-dog and how much alive-dog. The little assassins arrive and snip the connections or store information in little pockets and you end up looking at each other guessing and saying okay to the mystery but deciding that if there is an afterlife it must involve these secret compartments, which are more like sacs of fat stored around the body. And perhaps all David and Nell were doing was working to make an afterlife appear in this life. The next world, they were bringing the secrets of the afterlife into ordinary reality, and I wasnt ballsy enough to accept it. Nell and David were having an affair.

I felt like I'd chewed over the power of the feeling I'd been having and it was okay to leave this place. We bid adieu to a dairy farm, where an American artist I had written about had once lived. He had died here. We turned our backs on him and then we booted it towards the east, and although we were done with the man he sort of kept us company, as I knew he had taken this route ninety years before on his way to

Newfoundland, and perhaps not that much slower as we were only doing sixty kilometres an hour towards Bethlehem, New Hampshire. Just coasting easy, a canter. David Twombly was checking his stocks on his pebble. The pebble, he said, runs on the heat of his hand. There was a grip on it, and it matched his hand. It was like a mouth guard that you boil in water then set in your jaw to imprint your teeth. David is the sole operator for the pebble, his signature handgrip and his method of thought. He was invested now in ethical funds.

More was sure to come.

This thing called Sunleaf, Dave said. They tap into photosynthesis. It's a light leech and theyre buying thousands of acres of meadow. They will use trees as a solar panel.

When we stopped for gas he checked his whole portfolio using his eyes to scroll the screen.

A meadow, I said, implies treelessness.

Theyre growing the trees. In the meadow.

So what they havent even grown the raw material?

All our hydro, he said, is coal fired. The heart of the economy is still run by the nineteenth century.

I DOZED AGAIN while David drove. We were on our way to his sister's. Driving makes me sleepy. I set up a scenario where Nell is leaning on an elbow, reading. She's calm and well spoken, wearing smart wool pants and a blue top that gives her a thin waist, because she's tall. Then Richard arrives. They've been eating.

Nell: I ate so little with you. Once a day it averaged.

Richard: You can go a long way on beer and cigarettes.

I embraced her in the car. I moved Richard out of the way and held her. And I was holding David's shoulder. His eyes were on the road, blinking softly for he was tired too, and he'd grown very sad and loving.

I wanted to kiss him on the cheek but the seatbelt wouldnt allow it. He has a boy's face, until you kiss him. It's his unshaved chin. It's hard and sharp and old. And then the skin of chemicals and no-heat and inside-in-the-dark skin, awake with inside light.

That's enough now, he said. Which woke me up. It was still afternoon and I had that feeling you get when youve been in a bar in the daytime and you get drunk playing pool and leave and it's still not dark. A sodden feeling of unworthiness.

David: The thing I miss with this travelling is often I pull down the blinds at the office and take a nap. It's three in the afternoon, I've got the sports page, a glass of ginger ale, three fig newtons and the Argos on my portable radio.

Youve been let go, I said.

Let me just think it's the travelling.

WE DROVE HARD ALL DAY and arrived in Bethlehem by early evening. Sasha Twombly was at the university and we could see from monitors in hotel lobbies that the president was visiting the campus. We found a room and checked in, then David called Sasha and she said if we knew how to get to the college. The hotel had a map.

Sasha Twombly had married a man who studied economics and set up a wing of research at the college that studies nuclear power. In the seventies, when they let go of the gold standard, they tried to use power as a standard for money. How much power a thing had. The Bethlehem public school had a whirling atom for a logo.

Sasha was excited to see us, and then the excitement focused on its true cause: the president's visit. Her husband, Kenneth Mosado, had been in Washington sponsoring a lobby group to downgrade the latest environmental bill passing through congress. The opposite of progress? Congress. The president got wind of the college, the Middle East was tightening oil production, Iran was considering getting rid of the dollar and pegging the barrel to silver. Hydro was a hard issue with Canada and the Quebec separatists, and the high-grade unpolluting coal was vanishing from Virginia railways. Nuclear, the president had decided, was the fuel of the future, and Bethlehem, New Hampshire, was the birthplace of nuclear. He had arrived on Air Force One that very day to take a tour of the facilities, and David and I could go through the clearance wands and pat-downs and meet him.

Jesus, we just met the Prince of Wales.

Perhaps, David said, this is our time to visit heads of state. Remember when we played puddies?

And, while I had thought of those days, neither of us had mentioned them out loud.

Remember what our names were? You were the King and I was the President.

That's right, I said. Is the Prince the head of England?

David: He's the head of faith.

This stunned me, this blurting out of an intimate, childish time. We had to wait in a small room. This huge facility and they lock us down here. Kenneth Mosado brought in headsets for us to wear—we could take a little tour of the nuclear facility by blinking our eyes. Kenneth wore a white turtleneck and a suit jacket. He was amiable and I liked that he was to meet the president wearing his everyday clothes. This man had married Sasha Twombly, amazing. I put on the headset and looked for the president, but he was in a room that I could not enter, not even virtually.

David: This is bullshit, Gabe.

Me: How long have you waited for anything?

It was pissing me off, David's inability to wait his turn. I have patience. I dont expect the world to always turn its head and see me coming and open the door. But part of it for David was physical. He grew anxious when his body had to sit down and wait.

You know what I'm going to ask him, he said.

You think you'll get to ask him something.

I'm going to ask him about Goldman Sachs. I'm going to watch his face and see if he feels betrayed.

Goldman Sachs, I said, means nothing to me.

They reduced the gasoline component of its commodity index right into the November elections. I just want to see if he thinks it was politically motivated.

An hour passed. There was a whirring in the air. David's impatience was making my mind think that the box of a room we were in was being slowly cooked, or sterilized. Like every bacterium was being swept away.

It would have been nice of them, David said, to tell us it could be an hour.

And I agreed with him on that. It was a lark to see the president, but being next door to the president for an hour is tiresome.

Me: Should we go?

Let's tell Sasha we'll meet her at the campus bar.

And just as we got up the door opened and Richard Text came in. It was the man I'd seen in the penthouse off Bloor with the birthday cake and the two pianos. He was carrying a luminescent wand. He waved it over David's body and then mine. He left it a second too long, I thought, between my legs. You may view the president, he said.

Kenneth Mosado was showing the president the virtual room. The president had on eyewear and a glove and he was waving the gloved hand above his head. He looked like he was about to be shot by firing squad.

I could have brought the Taser, David said, and be done with him.

The president is short and I got that buzzing feel that comes when youre too close to something youve only ever seen in the media. It could be a pyramid or a painting or a president. Sasha arrived, her bright head, animated.

Sasha: You want to ask the president anything?

David asked him (he called him Mr President) if he thought the human animal and his emotions change much from age to age. He must change now, David said, or he faces absolute and complete destruction and maybe the insect age or an atmosphereless planet will succeed us.

It was a heavy line. It was a quote, David told me later, from some earlier president.

The president turned to David, the heavy eyewear distorting his face, and said, I care a lot about atmosphere and insects.

David, when he hates someone, usually invites them to join him for a drink. David had reached, I could tell, the outer limits of his generosity. I might meet up with you, the president said, though we both knew the president did not drink.

I drank with your father, David said.

The president took off the eyewear. Youve met my father.

Your father likes to fish in Labrador. I met him at a lodge in Pine River. He was shooting caribou from a helicopter and he had pizzas and beer choppered in.

That's my dad, the president said. Then realized what David had described might be illegal. He composed himself. He returned to the script that had been prepared. David, he said. About Goldman Sachs. I heard your question earlier. Youve got to think about the restructuring of Japan, the aging American population, water shortages, global outsourcing, the internet hub, emerging markets. Youve got to consider if the price collapse in oil will break the continuity of bullish thought on energy, dont you?

He knew what David's criticism and warning was. It was as if the eyewear had given him an insight—they were the x-ray specs David and I had ordered as kids. They were the fulfillment of that comic promise.

We walked to a campus bar with Sasha and Richard while Kenneth Mosado debriefed the president's attaché. When I heard this I realized where the words *briefcase* and *attaché case* come from. I bought a round.

He has small hands, I said.

Richard Text: A lot of fascists do.

Down the street was a ferris wheel. David noticed we were all a little uncomfortable with the static responsibility of drinks around a table. So when we were about to order more drinks he said, Let's drive to it. He meant the ferris wheel.

We took Sasha's car. It was a modified ferris wheel. You brought your car aboard it.

Sasha drove up to the gate and docked the car.

Kenneth's not going to find us up here.

Me: Tell us about Kenneth.

She looked at her watch. I said to Kenneth five years ago this week, If you want me you have to shape up. And he did.

Richard: What makes a successful marriage.

Sasha: Difference.

Yes, the two of you are very different, Richard said. Youre—

Sasha: Age difference.

And Richard and David laughed at that and looked at me. Richard knew who I was. That he'd had an age difference with Nell. It made him uncomfortable and so I got his life story. When Nell met him, he said, he was still in love with an impoverished duke, an Austro-Hungarian living in Germany.

Then he paused and Sasha said, Whatever happens in the ferris wheel stays in the ferris wheel.

We were slowly moving. The car was ascending. And we could look out over the roofs of Bethlehem.

The duke, Richard hasnt heard from him. Could be dead or married. His title is worth a precise amount, Richard said.

Sasha: Tell us who you first fell in love with.

There was a Spanish businessman. I was about twenty-two. He kept having boys over when I left town. Then a rich man in Santa Fe whose house was a museum. Candlesticks worth a hundred thousand, it was all garish, I had to leave.

But Richard's big love was a Bollywood actor who was on the way down and had trouble living with that. He had dyed his hair blond in India and was trying to write a screenplay. So Richard moved to London and worked at Canary Wharf. All this before his stint in Corner Brook. He's fifty-one now.

So Nell's with you, I said.

Richard: Nell called but I havent seen Nell.

I got an email from her that was sent from Los Alamos.

I think she's looking for a piece of equipment.

Do you miss her.

Youre her boyfriend.

I just learned about Dave and her.

Richard understood this. He was making calculations. Nell, he said, tried to adopt her son. We tried to get him. But it's a pretty fucked up bureaucratic nightmare to adopt a child youve given up for adoption, he said. I mean we're all crazy. But she's. I've said enough.

I let that sink in. David was asking Sasha if Virginia was the most northern southern place in the States.

The most important thing to govern where people live, Sasha said, is air conditioning. Power used to move east-west, but now, with air conditioning, it can move to the south.

That made me think of Nell's condition. She had moved south. She was of northern air. She had a lot to grapple with and, in the end, she managed to be lighthearted with me. Why didnt I try to get to this, why did I let her keep this depth of trouble over Anthony to herself. She was good, she didnt want it to weigh me down.

David: Do you feel like youre in a war?

Sasha: Me personally? Yes I do.

Richard: At war or in a war?

WE ENDED UP back at the bar but the president and Kenneth had not shown up. The bar closed its door but we continued to drink. Then the windows were shut with grey shutters and someone, perhaps David because he is the first to get antsy, said, Let's find something to eat.

We walked across the street to an upscale diner. It was dawn now and the regulars were having their first of the day. A man who looked like Elvis served us.

I'm alone, David said, chuckling.

Youre alone and enjoying it, Richard said.

We ate eggs with feta while six tons of rain slammed against the cars parked outside. I thought about Bucephalus alone in that car with a tinny roof. I didnt like to think of her worried. She was my responsibility in a world where I had little of it. I was next to Sasha in the booth and I retrieved her adult story while the men talked money. Sasha, after leaving Corner Brook, went out with a man for five years. Decided to get married. They were living a very conservative life. He mowed the grass every Saturday. This was in Winnipeg. She smoked pot behind his back. Three months before the wedding she called it off. They had a house she put her half into living in Asia for a year. Came back to Canada and made some money and headed again to Thailand. That's where she met her first husband, Carl Hoover. They drove their motorbikes to her parents' in Corner Brook. Then ran out of money, but Sasha's father really liked Carl. On the day of her wedding she ended up in a coffee shop with a guy she knew in school, in her red dress. She knew it wasnt right, but would prefer to get married and perhaps divorce a couple of years later than call off the wedding.

She looked at Richard and David. You never know how different people's histories can be from what they are now.

Do you know, David said, Itinerant Knowledge Workers made six hundred million last year.

You must have made some too, Richard said.

I was in line to get a fifth of one share.

Sasha: What's a share, brother.

She did not seem to mind that he was not listening. She had, you could see, an unwavering deep love for David.

A fifth, he said, of six hundred million.

So you made a fifth of a fifth of six hundred million dollars.

That's what I lost. I made a lot and lost a lot. I about broke even.

Me: What's a fifth of a fifth?

Gabe money is water.

And David put out his hands, his fingers stretched apart.

Me: Itinerant Knowledge Workers. Three guys with an idea.

No, good ideas. Lots of them.

Richard paid the bill and I left the tip. It's satisfying to peel off those American dollars, I hope they keep them. We stepped outside. Pale morning now. To our left was a shopping centre's movator, a man walking beside it, his wife on it. Above us a floating oval sign that read UNISEX. It was one of those words that made me uncomfortable as a kid. We were near some huge all-night supermarket. The man said, Where you going, Marge. Where you going, Marge.

Marge slowly got ahead of him. She was concentrating like she hoped that movator would take her way the hell away from him.

I can't help but notice, I said, that the two of you havent said a word about your father.

I didnt like growing up in Newfoundland, Sasha said.

Richard: Is something wrong with Arthur?

TWELVE

RICHARD DIDNT KNOW a thing about Arthur. He'd heard that Nell was in Los Alamos looking for a piece of hi-tech machinery. Richard's involved in the biggest secrets on the planet and yet he's not informed about the people that are deep in his life. The rain abated and Bucephalus did not seem perturbed so Dave and I drove and slept then kept on to Newport, where we watched a movie for nine dollars. David judged the screen was forty feet wide so we sat in a row forty feet deep. That's how you pick a seat, David said.

There was a fear, in one scene, of gum disease. When you have a sore jaw, all art looks like it's about gum disease. It's an honest selfishness, whereas David.

He said, When I saw the president, I wanted to shout out, The architects are here. You dont know what I'm talking about.

You were thinking about killing the president of the United States.

As you know I've had a quiet ambition to be president.

So if youre never to be one you can at least kill one.

In the old days the future king usually killed the old king.

There was something untruthful about this tapping into feeling.

Dont ever lie to me, I said.

David: Only lies of omission.

You didnt have to say that.

He was selfish. It's true he didnt talk much about his son. I mention his son because the old king is the father and the young king is the son. Once, when Owen was four months old, Sok Hoon said to Dave, Take him. And at eleven oclock Dave woke Sok Hoon up. Youre going to have to take him.

The more demands Sok Hoon made—after the separation—the more easygoing Dave got.

We skirted the Canadian border and then decided to head south to get clear of the dirty old weather, like a bum stock (Dave's words). We avoided low pressure fronts in newspapers. We pitched in a state park and cooked on our fireplace. We were delighted with ourselves: two whole tilapia, corn in their husks, tuna steak with onion and garlic, corn tortillas toasted right on the flat steel—the fish grilled on the bars. We ate in the dark with a flashlight balanced on top of a paper towel roll. Pancakes and bacon for the morning. The tent on hard ground and it wakes me up, the dog trying to sleep on top of me. Stars, bright Mars. A man came by to see how we lit our fire—his just smoke. He admired it with one of those big battery flashlights. Then the morning. It was hard to sleep in long, as the tent fabric allowed a lot of light and Bucephalus got anxious and her tail began to motor. The floor was thin. A clear sky last night, so no rain fly. The wind blowing through the nylon. I felt the wind and perked up and saw dark clouds from the west. I made coffee on the stove while David sat up on his blue foamy and watched the sun intensify on the green fabric. I just want to hang on, he said, to see if this will be one of those moments that change my life.

It wasnt.

So we collapsed the tent. All of our clothes smelled of smoke. That's when David came at me with his pebble in hand.

The hospital called me, he said. My father's not doing well. They need me there. They need to know my blood type. They want to look at my kidneys.

I took the wheel all day and then, after we crossed the border back into Canada, I put Bucephalus in the front seat which she loved and folded myself out in the back while Dave drove. I'd lean up sometimes to see what we were passing, the homes of the unemployed and then through the junctions to valleys where millionaires lived. Those little upside-down Vs in the pavement slipped by. What were they called. Every three weeks I remember the word. The same as stripes on a sergeant's sleeve. There was a noisy hay operation and then a town dedicated to selling you back your hubcaps. The surnames here would start to be solid and go back generations. The land felt older even though I know that's not true. We'd driven over the Canadian Shield and now it felt like we were heading back in time. Booth Tarkington's novel came to mind, his musings on automobiles, for *The Magnificent Ambersons* is nothing if not an examination of what the automobile has done to change civilization. With all their speed forward, Booth Tarkington wrote, they may be a step backward in civilization—that is, spiritual civilization. Booth Tarkington thought the car would alter both war and peace. And that our very minds would be changed because of the automobile. That's true of most things we feel apprehensive about—we know they will change us but we're not sure how.

The road smoothed out which meant a politician had a cottage in a pine thicket and then there was a field of school buses almost as if that was a retirement home for school buses, and then that thought of school buses growing old while children remain the same age. My eye opened to these fast-forward colour fields that David drove through at a constant speed and it felt as if the world were on a spool that reeled out rough edits devoted to panels of colour and it made me realize that we all do things that will be undone. You hammer a painting to a wall that, if left, will fall off before a hundred years pass. So on another scale, say a hundred years to the second, you stick something to the wall it will fall off the wall. It's a futile, temporary act that only seems permanent and then a neon sign rages across the slant of that thought, followed by the rough hills of abandoned rubber tires and a stinky teepee of a camouflaged smelter operation followed by the gradual buildup of a pulp mill's spruce farm making way again to pasture as we hit the sun's porch off the Nova Scotia causeway, the Scottish success and mowed gardens and well-painted fences and David yanks us up to a halt at a coffee shop and unclicks his seatbelt. Who knew at this juncture that we had hundreds of miles of windowless taverns and rain to get through yet.

Chevrons, Dave said.

This comment allowed wide associative leaps. Youre playing in a field, Dave, about which you know nothing.

Dave: Should I be hesitant to show my disapproval?

It's like youve got an army of disapproval lined up, but theyre in foxholes right now.

We drove on with the coffee all the way to the ferry lineup in North Sydney with the gas gauge warning us. It felt right to get on a ferry with an empty gas tank. The land seemed to pour away from us, like there was a drain to the west and it slurped down land. A couple ahead of us let out their dog and so we took Bucephalus out to greet them. You got your papers, he said. We forgot ours, we're going to sneak our dog back in.

I told him we had no papers. What papers, I said.

That she's had her shots, the man said. They won't let her in for rabies. I'm just going to bury the dog in the back and chance it.

Should we do the same?

You can put your dog in with ours. Wife, are you fine with that.

His wife thought that was acceptable.

So in went Bucephalus. The other dog was friendly enough and Bucephalus could sense some kind of favour was being done. Then the *Joseph and Clara Smallwood,* tall and stable, let down its backside and we got our tickets and drove deep into its belly like a pair of Jonahs. Ferries are like bridges, a huge investment that is nothing when it's only a dollar from each taxpayer. The government had just bought a squadron of helicopters and a fleet of cargo planes and the price tag was fifteen billion dollars. Which is five hundred dollars for every man, woman and child in the country.

We rushed up to the deck and watched the sun sink over the dreg of land and then ahead of us the sea shone before it darkened. The thing about the sea is not that it's the edge of land or that it delivers a boundary. It's a third way, a middle ground between land and air. If the sea could freeze it would lose its charm. We cannot stand on it, and yet it does not mix. It is a slave to gravity. The sea makes the world avoid the base choice between matter and spirit.

FOUR

ONE

WE SLEPT IN A CABIN. It was nice to have Joey Smallwood, in the form
of a ferry, bring us home to Newfoundland. Four bunks, with the
married couple in their sixties who were gentle, who had our dog. The
man had soft hand gestures, like a magician. They were from Daniel's
Harbour and had been in Nova Scotia. They'd darted down to Maine to
take advantage of some tax-free merchandise in a cross-border shopping
spree. We filled the truck too, he said. He meant with gas and I wondered
how much on earth he had saved on gas. Three dollars? He wore a baseball cap with a brim of five inches. It was worn with many fingerprints,
it looked good to garden in.

In the dark we started up the Matador in the belly of the ferry, shot up
our lights and rolled over the nippled metal surface of the drawbridge.
See you later, Joey. There were small lights that indicated a shoreline but
nothing of a town in the four A.M. darkness. There was nothing here, not
even road signs. We pulled over and collected our dog. Their dog was
nowhere in sight. Asleep, the man said. And we put Bucephalus in the
back seat and said farewell. We drove behind a transport truck with its
encouraging red lights and it seemed we were following a scout to some

destination, a bad one. Finally the white rectangle of a gas station sign, and the green panels of the building and we pulled off for a cup of coffee and a piece of lemon meringue pie that was surprisingly fresh. When we got back in the car I noticed the mouth of Bucephalus was red, it was as if the taillights had stained her fur red. She'd been wiping her mouth on the fox coat, streaks of blood.

David: Is she injured.

We checked her. I think she did the injuring, I said. There wasnt a mark on her. But we were both worried, was she a mad dog. The word *rabid* hung in our teeth.

We got to the Corner Brook exit signs by eight in the morning. Home.

We drove down the old way, avoiding the new off-ramps which I had presided over in my small part as an economic geographer ten years before, development that had destroyed the view of the bay. I judged Corner Brook the way people from St John's often judge it. I had become critical. Corner Brook was one of the little Canadas that had been seeded by Canadians and which St John's despised. English Canada had split its government and its economic heart between two cities, and so had the French. Nothing grand could happen, no flagrant tragedy, no dictator or revolution because the power was in Ottawa and Quebec City, while the business and culture were in Toronto and Montreal. But St John's possessed both, and St John's looked at Newfoundland as its country. So Corner Brook, a milltown, the largest pulp mill ever built in the world, made St John's vulnerable. It was wealth that was not controlled and so it was seen as uncouth and an upstart. If you were from Corner Brook, as we were, you were looked upon as a traitor, as the Canadianization of Newfoundland.

We took West Valley Road and then hooked up O'Connell Drive. The hill that had the new police station, the junior high and then the high school. On top of the hill, past the Arts and Culture Centre, was the university. It was on this hill I received my education. We were driving home the way we had driven home eighteen years before, when we lived together in St John's and were coming home for the summer, the summer David's parents split up. In a way, we had finally arrived home in Zac's car.

The regional hospital is in the centre of town, and you can see it from a mile away. There was a crane over the hospital, with a large object hanging there. Hospitals in Toronto are hidden in amongst other buildings. They have big signs near the top that are revealed when youve found the block. They surprise you in their suddenness. In small places like Corner Brook the hospital is seen from a distance, it stands, usually, amongst residential housing.

We tied Bucephalus to the bumper, her fur stained with dried blood, and went inside.

I'm a little nervous, David said. I might need to get something to eat.

I got him a bag of chips from a vending machine, then we found a nurse and she directed us to the proper wing. David asked her, Do you know Maggie Pettipaw.

She's a friend of mine, she said.

I'm a friend too.

We followed a yellow line down the hall then turned a corner to the wing that held David's father.

My mother might be here, he said. My parents. Did you know they still see each other? Dad can be sharp with her, and she can be right back at him. They seem to be momentarily curt and sick of each other, then they say some other thing and laugh and push each other around.

Me: I want to be pushed from a plane.

David looked around. What, when diagnosed with an incurable disease?

Or from a scandal so huge you can't recover.

My parents, he said. When there's nothing sexual you can have a deep friendship without the fights.

And then we saw the edge of David's father in bed. Mr Twombly. His skull stapled together. The hair had been split open and he had a moulded plate below one eye. He was alone here. His vulnerability made me think I did not have an invitation to see him this way. It was wrong of me. I took a breath and saw the machinery that was trying to save his life. Then the doctor came in. It was Dr Manamperi, David's stepfather of sorts.

We had to remove a piece of his skull, Dr Manamperi said, to relieve the pressure. Once it's gone down we'll put it back. He has another lump on the back of his head.

David: He's always had that.

It's a subcutaneous cyst and he should have it removed.

I remember as a kid, David said, asking him about that lump. He said it kept his hat on.

I hadnt seen Dr Manamperi since I was a teenager, refinishing his furniture. And here he was, the attending physician in charge of Arthur Twombly. He was living with Helen Crofter. He said they'd put David's father into a stable coma and that he could be kept this way indefinitely. But there was damage to his kidneys and he was bleeding internally. He's O negative, Dr Manamperi said. If David wouldnt mind giving some blood, for it was the rare type.

I thought, David said, O negative could donate to anyone.

Dr Manamperi: It's receiving that's the trouble.

There may come a time when a kidney might be needed. His father was being fed through a tube in his throat, and, while his breathing is erratic, a ventilator was placed in his nose.

Keep him that way, David said. I mean, keep him getting better.

He looked terrible. I knew he was in a coma with machines and a tracheotomy, but seeing it was worse. There were too many beige machines and not enough human being to garner the attention. It was as if Arthur Twombly was keeping the machines alive. He had no colour and he did not move. He could not even turn to look out his window.

I'm going to get them, David said. I'll get them.

If we could just get some blood, Dr Manamperi said.

I LEFT DAVID with his father and drove home to my own father. He was having breakfast and my mother was in the garden. We got your strange postcard, he said. And I could tell what he was thinking, that signing my last name was beyond him. He was beyond trying to figure me out.

My father used to be a schoolteacher, and he had taught David and me and the Hurley boys and Randy Jacobs. He'd even had Anthony just before he retired. My mother had a part-time job as a clerk at the Bank of Nova Scotia. I remember having to go in after school, to see her. And they'd call for her. And she'd come to the front desk, both pleased and a little distracted. She was wearing lipstick. There was a world going on here that I was breaking her away from. The next-door neighbour, Mrs Jacobs, also worked at the bank. It was as if they were pretending to be clerks and were getting away with it. Once, when I was four, I was left alone by my mother. I'm only across the street at Mrs Jacobs'. While she was gone the phone rang. Hello? And no one was there. Then the oven timer went off. My father's lunch cooking in the oven. I could feel it overcooking. So I put on my coat and boots and walked across the street and rang the doorbell. The two of them appeared to be sitting in large chairs in a dark room. There was not even a radio on. The chairs swallowed them.

They were happy to see the dog. They loved dogs, and their last one had been put down a year before. They werent ready for a new one, but enjoyed the company of visiting dogs. My father hooked the dog to the old lead out back and she made for the dog house, the old dog house that all my family dogs had used.

I told him what happened to Lars Pony. He had already heard. He had liked Lars. He had brought his car to Lars to fix and he respected people who were trying to begin anew, as he had done. But at the same time he could not agree with what Lars had done to himself. In the end, in my father's eyes, that was not just unfortunate and a sin, but weak and should have been forestalled.

I went to bed for an afternoon nap and I slept in the bedroom that I had grown up in. I dreamt that I was hunting with my father. The dog was with us. There was a bear sleeping on an island. And my father put a knife in his teeth and swam over to the island. He crept up on the bear and slipped the knife in his jaw. The dog and I watched. He was so quiet about it that the bear did not wake up. He skinned out the jawbone and the bear was killed with very little pain. Then I woke up and knew that my tooth was hurting and that meant I was tense. I looked around my old bedroom. I realized Nell doesnt have this, this return to parental life. She did not talk much about her parents, just the small time with her aunt and uncle in Burlington. My parents were not modern. They were old-fashioned parents who had gone through the war as children and the war would always affect them. They were careful with things. Anything wood in the house my father had made. All the food in the fridge was in the process of being turned into food you could eat. They were unlike David's parents. Who were modern, who embraced the modern ways. But I preferred my old-fashioned parents. I wanted to be the modern one, and yet appreciate the old ways of the previous generation. David was competing with his father's life, and this was best described by his relationship with Nell.

TWO

THERE HAD BEEN a previous incident, David said. He had just been talking to Randy Jacobs. His father, Randy said, had been driving on the arterial road when Gerard Hurley passed him. His father felt Gerard had come too close and when he passed, Gerard looked at him. It was the way he looked that upset Arthur Twombly. He wasnt about to live the rest of his life afraid of a look like that, Randy said. So he took Gerard Hurley to court. He told the judge all about his son, whom the Hurleys were raising. He said he felt there was extortion going on. He gave Loyola Hurley four hundred dollars a month. He thought that was a fine amount. He did not have to give the Hurleys anything. It was his own conscience that gave the money. But ever since day one the Hurleys have been trying to get more out of him. Actually Loyola Hurley wasnt the issue. It was Gerard Hurley. Gerard had it in for him ever since the Hurleys sold Arthur that land out in Rocky Harbour, land that wasnt theirs to sell, and eventually that debacle had gone to court and the Hurleys were told to pay Mr Twombly what they'd received. But by then they'd spent the money and a court order does nothing to make sure a verdict is followed through. So Arthur stopped sending Loyola the money. He stopped it for a year, he'd paid five thousand dollars for that land. A year went by and that's what solidified the bad blood between the Hurleys and Arthur Twombly. They felt they were owed something. The government had expropriated land for a national park and the pulp mill had prevented them from using land they'd been using forever. My ex-wife, Arthur said, she represents the pulp mill. The Hurleys look at her and me as the very cause of their misery. Though I dont see really what misery they happen to be wallowing in. Theyre just a family that likes to hold grudges.

The judge listened to this, Randy said. He was interested. He enjoyed gossip, but the evidence was not there. You have not established, he said to Arthur Twombly, that Mr Hurley here failed to operate his vehicle without reasonable consideration for others. The word *reasonable,* the judge said, does not contemplate perfection. And the word *consideration* does not include looking at someone in a manner they do not like.

WE WENT TO SEE David's mother. She's probably out back, Dr Manamperi had told David. We drove to the house David grew up in. We parked in the driveway and opened the door. Helen Crofter had kept the house and she was sharing it now with Dr Manamperi. He had moved in with his furniture about ten years ago and built a pool out back. We passed furniture that my father and I had refinished when I was a teenager. Who knew Helen Crofter would ever be living with it. It was holding up. So was Helen Crofter, she was in the pool, floating on an air mattress, smoking a cigarette and eating a fried ham sandwich. She looked like a dazzling otter.

Once, when we were kids, we'd seen David's mother in a parking lot looking for her car. We whistled for her. She ignored us. We whistled again. And then David called out to her, Mom. And she turned on us. Dont you ever whistle like that at a lady, she said.

It's true that David had nothing of his mother's frame. He was his father, thirty years younger. David possessed all of his mother's inner traits. He had the brain of his mother, and the heart.

Shall we swim out to you?

Let's have a congress alongside the swimming pool.

She paddled over a little, until she bumped into the tiles that read 1.15 M.

Gabriel, she said. How's your writing.

I'm at a crest, I said.

I must apologize if I was snoring.

No Mother we caught you eating. And smoking.

So how does he look to you.

He said his dad looked old. To see him with coloured wires taped to his temples. The adhesive had a brand name across it and David had made a note to look the company up. The frailty of a man who should be wearing glasses, his exposed face asleep in a hospital bed. David had never seen his father like this. He was vexed about the moose bar. He'd had a rift with his father, but he did not want to see his father die.

I want to make peace somehow, he said.

The last thing your father said to me was, You know yourself. You're who you are. Whereas I'm not.

David: Every relationship has a problem and it takes the entire life of the relationship to work it out.

He spoke of Sok Hoon being a drug user while in Asia. She fell in with men who had drugs. David discovered a folder with tissue wads in it— clots of her blood, which was news to me. Sok Hoon wanted to make an art project out of the blood. But we got over that, David said.

Speaking of Sok Hoon, she said. You got a postcard from your son. I didnt know you were calling him The Oven.

He wrote you a postcard and told you that.

He signed it, very deliberately, The Oven.

That was me, I said. That was my idea.

Thanks Gabe. Thanks for making me look like a goof. In front of my mother. Like I know how to raise a son.

Youre not raising him, she said.

Then Helen Crofter told us of Arthur's will. There's a provision for Anthony, she said. And an understanding between Loyola and Arthur over the raising of Anthony. That's gone on, Helen said, for eighteen years.

She relayed this without any sign of pain.

David: Do the other Hurleys know about this.

They think, Helen said, Arthur abandoned him.

THREE

I CALLED UP Maggie Pettipaw. I thought, I'm the bridge between David and the Hurleys. And Maggie is the other side of the bridge. We had fooled around together as teenagers and we had both been very moved. We had broken out of our youthful irony to know that we were human and vulnerable and cared. And yet she was never, for more than twenty minutes, in love with me, or I her. And we both knew it. We should all have people on this earth like this, people we deeply love and yet have hardly anything to do with, ever.

She was getting off work at the hospital, and I went up to see her. I drove her down to the Keg and Kandle. She knew the reason why I wanted to see her. She knew her side of the bridge-building. For she had gone out with Gerard Hurley. They had almost been married.

I've been breaking up with Gerard Hurley, Maggie said, for ten years.

She finally left him about two years ago. He was in bed with another woman. She found his jeans on the floor and stripped out his belt and stared at the two of them in her bed. Then she whipped them both with Gerard's belt. Then she left. Maggie Pettipaw has these flashes with her eyes. There's a muscle in her lower eyelid that flexes, and a white patch around her eye, which makes her blue eyes appear to be lying in snow. As if snow has fallen in the hollows of her face. Gerard Hurley has bright blue eyes too, and I thought if they ever had a kid, what eyes he'd have.

Maybe youre not over him, I said.

That might be true, but what's wrong with that? I still dont want to return to him.

Would he have you.

He refused my love with a various heart.

That sounds what. Like a psalm.

We didnt have chemistry.

Sounds like you did. At the start.

Maggie put her elbows on the table and sat her chin on one fist. That's not what I mean, she said.

Maybe compatibility.

That's it.

When Maggie started working at the hospital Gerard asked her to get cancer pills. At first it was just a bloated number purchased at wholesale, but then he got aggressive and she had to do some accounting. Gerard split the pills into their two active ingredients and sold them to nineteen-year-olds in the pool hall on West Street. I'd been in that pool hall once with Gerard. He was drinking white russians. He was small but he was a dirty fighter. He did dirty things like punch you in the armpit and shove his fingers in your eyes.

Gerard, she said, was driving that van.

We had a drink and then went outside. It had started to rain.

Maggie: Do you know what I like to do on a miserable day off?

She had scuba equipment. She had equipment for me if I wanted. All we had to do is rent air.

I'm supposed to meet David, I said.

David can spot, she said.

I took her home and we loaded up two buckets of gear and then drove over to David's and picked him up. We took the shore road to Bottle Cove and parked on the beach and checked our regulators and spat in our masks. I'd known Maggie in high school. In junior high she was a tomboy. And then, after the Grade Ten summer, she turned beautiful. When she was thirty-five she'd been on a talk show. They flew her to New York to do this show. And it was a surprise show, with Gerard Hurley and his new girlfriend. Chairs were thrown.

There was pity and humour in Maggie. Women are playful, she said, and men are all work. Even play is work.

At the hospital she worked with a lot of men. To David: When your father came in, he was looking around. He explained the origins of the word *chauvinism*. He said, It's the tendency to withhold things from the one you love, in case something better comes along. It's not male or female.

David: So my father was conscious when he first arrived.

Oh he wouldnt stop talking.

Did he say if Gerard Hurley was driving the van?

He didnt know what hit him. Literally.

She was telling me one thing and David another. In our wetsuits we held hands and walked backwards into the surf. Bucephalus walked in with us. The dog stood there up to her knees in the sea, tasting it, while we walked with our heels. I felt the water at the small of my back, then I slumped into the water and adjusted my buoyancy and found my regulator. I released myself to the sea. I sucked in the air, made the A-OK, and sank into soundlessness. There was a wild world down here, a turbot raced out of the murk and Maggie caught him by the tail then let him go. Goofy seaweed. It all happened in slow motion and slow motion makes things appear significant. The bad weather gone. I yawned to equalize the pressure and let the weight of water sink me and I remembered my

Wyoming over Nell in the desert. That scuba diver who repaired the Bellagio fountain. Maggie Pettipaw propelled herself into a deeper zone, past the anchor ropes of dories.

I followed her. The pantomime and the jungle. The water grew colder and darker, so I knew we were descending. I was trusting her. I yawned to equal the pressure in my ears. She turned to me and gave me a thumbs-up and I thumbed her back. I followed her legs and they kicked further down and now I was hers, she could kill me here if she wanted.

Something dark and large and dormant. A ship. An old ship. The stump of a mast in vaseline. There wasnt much time to see it as a whole thing. We were down near it, touching it, though we werent supposed to touch it. A lobster backed itself up in a doorway like a scorpion. He looked to be ten pounds, but as I put a finger near him he reduced in size. Refracted light.

Maggie Pettipaw slipped inside an open door. What the hell, I thought. And beat my way in.

A hallway and the small rooms of a galley. A table full of sea urchins. The deep release of air, bubbles now hitting the roof and trailing along it. We stood in what had been the cooking area, but no one had cooked here in two hundred years. Then Maggie came up to me, very close to me, the clank of her tank against a wall. She put her hands on me and the corners of her mouth around her regulator, she was enjoying herself. Then she became practical and checked her air. We wandered through a school of wheeling white jellyfish. The light shone through their bodies and they stroked me as they passed, indifferent and going somewhere. And then a final check of her air and Maggie giving me the sign to ascend.

DAVID WAS TALKING to someone, a woman. She had come down from a house in Bottle Cove. She'd recognized Maggie's truck.

You guys just sort of disappeared on us, she said.

You remember Gwen, David said.

I knew Gwen. And slowly I saw that David knew who she was too.

Youre Gwen Hurley, I said. I hadnt seen either of them since that last New Year's Eve, when we'd taken them up to Crow Hill in Zac's car.

I was waiting for David to tip over the table from all this bullshit. But instead he said, lugubriously, I committed to loving Sok Hoon before the love was there.

They were resuming a conversation. While we were undersea they had been talking. There was allegiance to family and then there was allegiance to romantic love, and they were picking apart the latter. Maggie leaned against her open tailgate. Help me off with these, will you.

And I worked on Maggie Pettipaw. I tugged at her neoprene leggings. My hands around her thigh, peeling.

Gwen: That's a powerful idea.

The love came after, Dave said.

But you'll never know, Gwen said, if love would have come without the commitment.

Gwen Hurley married out of it. She married a Nova Scotian cook, Jason Linegar, who is on a trawler now working out of Corner Brook. Gwen had us up to the house for coffee. The hard edge in Gwen, the storyteller, it's her voice, low and kind.

FOUR

I DONT KNOW what I am most of the time, David said. I came here to do damage to the Hurleys, and I end up flirting with one.

She's the good in Hurleys, I said. She's like Joe.

We were in my parents' basement. I used to tie flies down here, and make snowshoes and clean fish in the double sink of the laundry room. David was waiting for me to remember the combination to the gun cabinet. We'd decided to sight the Lee Enfield in.

We bought a box of Remington cartridges at Canadian Tire, then David steered past the pulp mill to the shore road. Bucephalus with her face out the open window, her eyes pursed. Hardly the face of a dog that can savage another dog, I thought, and wondered if this dog had rabies.

Perhaps, I said, we've brought rabies back to the island.

Rabies is making a comeback, David said, like Latin.

The gravel pit was the old Lundrigan's limestone quarry. It had closed down for the past three years. The old train was parked here and we both instinctively looked up to find that face in the rock that our fathers had both shown us when we were small. There he was, the Man in the Mountain in the hills over the Humber River, near Shelbert Island where I used to fish in the mornings with Loyola Hurley. We parked the car by the fence and Bucephalus leapt from the window. She ran furiously down the road and we saw it, a dog or a fox in the woods. Bucephalus grabbed the animal and tossed it in the air.

We ran after her and pinned her down and dragged her back to the car by the neck.

What'll we do with her.

Why can't she just be a patient hunting dog.

I wouldnt want her straying.

You afraid you might shoot her.

A ricochet.

Tie her on the bumper.

So I tied her to the trailer hitch and jumped the fence and found a cardboard box, emptied it, then tore it into two flat halves for targets. We used to drink beer at the cement plant and steal gravel from the fence of Lundrigan's. When they got a load it would spill out through the fence and, in our circles, what went through the fence was fair game. We'd load up the trailer with gravel and sand if we were making cement. Of course, it helped if you knew the truck driver off-loading stone. It helped just to reverse the tail-end a few feet more so the arc of the spill dragged itself through the fence. We knew men who bought dented cans from super-markets and resold them. It helped if you befriended a stock boy who could make sure enough cans were damaged. The thing is, as soon as you account for waste, and make waste a commodity, more good things will become waste.

Me: What's the meaning of life, Dave?

Kids.

I dont have kids.

But you have parents and you feel like a kid.

I promised I'd always be a kid.

Promised who.

It was a promise I made to the kid in me.

We marched off fifty yards and set up the targets.

We each get three shots then we run.

The shots would bring the police, as we were still within the city limits. David fired off three rounds in a standing position, then threw the rifle at my chest. I caught it. I was surprised though and had to wait to calm down. Risky fucker. I dropped to one knee. Then I shot and I knew I'd done better than David.

It's sighted, he said. Now let's get the hell out of here.

We left the targets and slung ourselves into the Matador. We were the old police making a getaway from the new police. We bombed back into town along the river highway, past coves and shoals I used to fish from, and only stopped on West Street when a body in a T-shirt jumped on the hood of the car and banged on the window and cried out, You cruel sick motherfuckers.

What's your problem sir.

Mainland assholes.

Hey he can read a licence plate.

But it struck me. An image of Bucephalus materialized in my forehead.

It's the dog, I said.

We'd forgotten the dog.

The speed we'd gone. And from the way this man was into us. But maybe it would be all right. I jumped out, my hands in my hair hoping not to see what we had to see. We'd forgotten Bucephalus. There was the red rope and a cruel side of her.

This.

It was far beyond any hope and the shock of it paralyzed the next step. But I became cold in the head and knew what to do. Open the trunk. Get the keys and open the trunk. Now just lift her in.

It's about the worst thing I've ever done.

We're useless, Dave.

We untied what was left of her. David had to turn her over so he could carry her without getting the rawness of her on him. I fished up the fox coat from the back seat. David held her. Then he put her in the trunk. Dave made a low groan that sounded like his organs were talking. The force of his emotion made me quiet, though I was in shock. We sat in the car a bit, then Dave drove around. I felt worthless and alive.

We drove up to Crow Hill and got out and looked down at the city. We were idiots. Or I was an idiot when I was with David. He's actually a bad guy, a disaster. I needed to love David less.

We need to bury her, he said.

We drove to my father's workshop. I knew where the key was and how the door is deadbolted with a bar from the inside. I flicked on the lights and the pipes shone in the rafters like veins of copper, like you could mine it. Excellent plumbing. Everything my father made was excellent, and everything I did was mediocre or half-assed.

David found a spade and a pick.

We drove out of the city past St Judes. Then through the new real estate David had purchased for IKW, to build condos for wealthy tourists. We drove past this and into the poorer region of the basin. Deep into Hurley territory. We took her out here because we wanted a place that was undisturbed but also a place where we wouldnt get caught. A road down near the bridge before the powerhouse in Deer Lake. We followed that in to the end where there's crown land and the watershed. We passed lengths of culvert being used to reroute water. We wrapped the dog in her fox coat, I could feel the shaved-down edges of bone. We dug a hole and buried her. We were both disgusted with ourselves, but relieved we could get away with such a horrendous act. We realized we werent going to mention it any more. It was like shipping your garbage to a foreign country.

WE CARRIED OUR JACKETS to a bar in the corner of the mall to meet Gwen Hurley. The jackets were a shell for the rain and they reminded us that Bucephalus was with her coat in the ground and we could very easily be buried in these jackets too. We let Gwen sit by the window. She wanted to talk of love. She'd been with Jason Linegar for five years. When they married he said he wanted to live in a town, population fifty.

I married him, she said, to get out of a town population fifty.

Now he's a cook on board a trawler. Population fifty.

Corner Brook, she said, was too big for Jason.

So it was more the type of life than the person.

He was the luckiest man I ever met, she said. He should have got behind a counter and sold me a lottery ticket.

Where'd you meet.

Right in this bar. I didnt notice for a long time that he was short. I just loved the colour of his skin. I always think I'm taller than I am. I can't go out with this guy because he's not six foot two. Is that silly? Small of me?

Gwen worked on building sites all through the Maritimes. She inspects their safety. Now moving into sites that blow up. She had all the gear in a truck with six wheels.

We passed it outside, I said.

You noticed it.

Gwen Hurley was on a site in Stephenville last week. And a guy fell sixty feet just a few yards from her. Blood coming out of his ears and mouth. On his back.

I held his hand, she said. Called 911. They have their own internal ambulance service on sites like this. Saw the guy wasnt breathing, put my fingers down his throat and up came clots of blood. Then did CPR on him. Still nothing. Ambulance hauled in and they used a hand pump, he came back. Next day a woman calls. It's the guy's wife. To tell me he's dead.

Gwen: I dont care about stereotypes. I'll be a stereotype if you want, I dont give a fuck.

David: Youre kind of lighthearted.

Been through a hard year. When Jason left I thought about killing myself.

She put her hand around David's and repeated, I thought about killing myself.

She knew by now what David was doing, that her brother Anthony was David's half brother. And that David was in town to talk to Gerard and Anthony about his own father. She laughed about the suicide thought, to make it into a joke. But David wanted to stand at the bar, his beer in a plastic cup. He removed himself from Gwen's arm and stood with crates of recycling on the floor beside him. The Hurleys were into recycling now and waste management. Then David made for the door. I'll be outside, he said. Behind him, as the door swung shut, one city bus, flashing by empty.

Gwen: You probably think I'm a little odd.

Me: Is there some expression I'm giving?

Gwen: I had long hair and a leather coat and people thought I was a freak. Jason didnt but people did. I roomed in a house with the toughest fucker in Halifax. I looked heavy metal but I was a punk rocker deep inside. I thought I could get any man.

You destroyed your wealth, I said. You let your emotions rule.

Gwen began talking as though she had never married, or that Jason Linegar was insignificant.

She asked if we wanted to go to Maggie's. She had to meet Maggie Pettipaw.

We took her behemoth truck. David was leaning up against it. The self is under attack, he said. There is a self but there may not always be a self. Right now the self is a mongrel.

We're a pack of mongrels, Gwen said. She had heard about Bucephalus.

The pressure, David said, is to make us all the same.

Me: Perhaps we are at risk of having the self lost to sameness.

Maggie's place was a tight little two-storey in behind the hospital, but Maggie wasnt home. Gwen called Maggie. She'd be right over.

My father is in there, David said. He pointed to the roof of the hospital where they were still hovering a heavy item a hundred feet in the air. He told Gwen the story of his father without mentioning names.

All my family are black sheep, Gwen said. I'm the fucking white sheep.

What about Joe.

Living white sheep.

Maggie arrived wearing a white leather coat she bought in England two years ago. It had one missing button that she carried in her pocket. She showed it to us.

Gwen: I would never let two years go by before I sewed back on a button.

David: You just have to, every couple of weeks, sew on your buttons.

That sounds like a motto.

On Maggie's fridge was a drinks recipe list. The last line was "add more tequila."

It began to rain. You could hear it on the roofs of cars parked out back. I love the rain, David said. Doesnt matter where I am or whose rain it is.

You laugh, Gwen said, even though you dont have a sense of humour.

How you doing.

I'm living a dream, mister.

Maggie: I've got a story to tell you but you wouldnt believe it.

Oh come on tell us.

No, you wouldnt believe it. Otherwise I'd tell you.

We'll believe it.

The reason I went out with Gerard was so I could hang out with Gwen.

Speaking of Gerard, David said. How do we get ahold of him.

FIVE

I DROVE DOWN to St Judes alone. I wanted to talk to Loyola Hurley the way that I talked to him when we were alone on the river. It was a compulsion to use youthful connections. If David was with me another type of conversation would happen. Gerard was staying at home with Loyola, Gwen said. Gerard worked for the plumbing business, that was his front.

I knew Mr Hurley from those early mornings on the Humber River. I called him Mr Hurley. Perhaps it was the time of day and the place where we met, but he seemed to be a person then. He tied his own flies, as I did, and if we met before sun-up he'd share his flask of black tea and unclasp his case of flies. I liked the cup on the top of the flask, it was tin, and I'd never had tea without milk before. My father liked the Hurleys. He taught them, and he knew of Mr Hurley in the woods. My father preferred these families, the ones who were directly from the bay, rather than the families who had moved to Corner Brook eighty years before, to exploit the paper mill. There is something different in the character, he said. There is something safe and conservative about the paper-mill workers, the shelter of a boring and cautious union. That caution helps build infrastructure, like regional hospitals. We are all born now in regional hospitals. We die in them too.

I slowed through St Judes, which is built along the highway. Once, someone had painted a crosswalk. For laughs. Then I saw the Hurley house, the new addition and the white van in front. I slowed down and parked on the grade. I didnt want to park on Hurley property, or get boxed in.

I stood there and looked at the Hurleys'. I looked at the white van. The dented moose bar on the grille. Behind the van was an open garage door and beside the house was a scarecrow in a field of potatoes, an early crop that was dying back already, others still dark and healthy. The scarecrow was sitting in a chair, as if the Hurleys were trying to make him comfortable. But then it wasnt a scarecrow. It was Loyola Hurley in a wheelchair.

I crossed the highway and walked into the yard and then up to the potato field.

I lost a foot, he said, to diabetes.

But he wasnt letting the wheelchair slow him down. He was getting around as good as ever.

They swiped two kitchen sinks off me, he said. So now I have Loyola Hurley written on the fridge in blue paint. With a phone number on the side.

I helped him into the kitchen where Gerard Hurley was sitting drinking a beer. He had a reciprocating saw on the table in front of him. He was taking it apart and staring at each part with his bright blue eyes. Cold. He looked less masculine. Something about less hair on his face, a weak chin. I opened the fridge. It had the scent of mould. It was warm inside.

Gerard: How much is a water pump, Dad? Sixty?

Loyola: Sixty? Try sixty and sixty and sixty and sixty and sixty.

Me: Why is your fridge not working.

I unplugged it, Loyola said. It was making too much noise.

Me: Didnt there used to be a basketball court out here?

That attracted every kid in St Judes, Loyola said. I didnt need to hear the language.

Then he knew I must have a nervous sense about me, with Gerard in the room. He said, I feel bad for David's father, for what happened to him. Accident as it was. I was hit last year by three teenagers on drugs.

With sticks, Gerard said.

Police asked me questions like, had I at all enticed the boys during the summer.

Well they paid for that, Gerard said.

Loyola wheeled over to the sink and put a net bag of potatoes in there to rinse. They had laid out the garden so he could get in there with his wheelchair. He found a cutworm. It had an orange shell. He smashed it in his hand and a yellow puss sluiced out. They attack the peas, Loyola said. Even though theyre in the potatoes.

My neighbour, Loyola said, he's a lawyer. His wife too. Two lawyers. He came over to me last month, said if I put that tree out City Hall would take it away. It was the Christmas tree from last year. It had blown up against the fence and I'd been meaning to cut it up and burn it. So fuck off, I said. Well the boys here got on a tear. And one night after I'd gone to bed Gerard hooked up lights and dressed up the tree right here in the yard. Next afternoon I was taking it all down and the neighbour comes home. He says Loyola, you know what you are? Youre like something out of *Pippi Longstocking*. What? I said. She would do that, have Christmas in July.

Then Loyola looked at me as if he wanted me to ask what I'd come to ask.

David just wants to talk to Gerard, I said.

Gerard has got his own life, he said.

I'll talk to Dave, Gerard said. I got a few things to ask him myself.

I PICKED UP DAVID and he wanted to get behind the wheel. He had been drinking.

You shouldnt drive, I said. Not that you can't, but if youre pulled over you won't pass.

David: I'm too drunk to walk.

So I drove and David tried his best to look sober, even though he wasnt driving. I think maybe he thought he was driving. He looked like he was concentrating on the road but then you saw that he was thinking hard about something else. If he thought about the road he would not stay on it. He had to let the animal part of him, the part not affected by alcohol, drive. Even though I was driving. I told him what happened out in St Judes. But he had something else on his mind. Gwen Hurley and Maggie Pettipaw.

You often, David said, talk about women the way women want men to talk about them.

We parked on Main Street. In a shop window men's suits were pinned to the wall at an angle, the ankles gathered together to points, as though suits were being shot from a can, like tennis balls. David was deciding what to do. He was both patient and anxious.

David: What time do you think it is.

You mean without looking at my watch.

David looked at my wrist and it was seven oclock. We were walking back to the parking lot behind Maggie's. Above us the hospital, with Arthur Twombly in it.

When I was a child, David said, they used to put up a string of Christmas lights in the bedroom. Zac called them sicky lights. Because when I was sick I got to stay home and stare at the lights.

We could see Gwen Hurley out on Maggie's patio, bent under a table to light a cigarette. Wind trouble. And the history of the Hurleys was in her very character. We said hello to Gwen Hurley and then kept walking, up to the hospital, to see Arthur Twombly. David's pebble went off. Sok Hoon, he said. And he listened. And the murmur of Sok Hoon sounded like she was saying she still loved David, and yet she agreed with David about grasping after beauty. They both believe, as I do, that you can allow beauty to walk beside you. She was telling him about Owen, about the school.

David said, I can't say in good faith that things are over between us.

I believed him tender and then, as he hung up, I heard him clear his voice. He cleared his throat and began putting more effort into walking up the hill.

They had the roof of the hospital open and that crane was lowering in a new generator. It was the only way to get it into the basement, was to sink it through the roof, and it reminded me of a riddle my father used to say when I was a child: You remind me of a man. What man. Man power. What power. Power of voodoo. Voodoo? You do. I do what. Remind me of a man.

And the voodoo brought back the Buddha I had watched get lifted into the new temple in Toronto. The Buddha and this generator, they were both doing the same job.

Did I ever tell you, I said to David, I once read in a hospital to patients who had half their blood outside their bodies?

David: Was that like a big magic trick?

ARTHUR TWOMBLY MUST HAVE heard some of this. Magic trick. It was echoing down a long corridor and into a room with high rafters. The sound of voices had no bass and the treble broke up—it was mainly vowels he heard. It sounded Spanish and so he went to Madrid. Arthur remembered a train that carried Richard Text and Joe Hurley. There was a magic trick. They drank in the bar, the low oval windows flashing scenes of dry fields. Sunflowers all turned to the sun. A man wore a coloured bead necklace and had a groove in his skull and a bump from the bullet of a .38. He was drinking clamato vodka with oysters and he stood up holding an oyster to do a trick. How to get a coin beneath a beer cap, inside the cap. The coin was very light. He ate the oyster then put his hand up to his forehead to concentrate. He stroked the groove in his skull. The beer cap moved off and the coin flipped into the cap. He must have been breathing out through his nose. I'm breathing through my nose, Arthur Twombly realized. There's a tube in my nose.

He knew we were there. Or a presence was near him, as you can feel the heat of hands that have been rubbed together and placed an inch away from your face. It is good to visit the unconscious.

SIX

SLOW IT, DAVE SAID. Okay put it in park. I'm going to give his door a knock.

He walked up the driveway past the white van worth about eleven hundred dollars. He pulled up his jeans. There was a child's pink skipping rope looped over the bars of a banana bike. He unharnessed the rope and tested it. It was rubberized plastic. He looked at the van, then he yanked off the rope handles. He leaned against the back of the van and peered through the rope tubing. He walked into the driveway and found a bucket in the garage. He nudged it with his toe. A galvanized pail. The garage door was slightly down now and on the door was spray-painted in red:

THE ONLY VEHICLE FOR PRISON REFORM IS A BULLDOZER

THERE IS NO JUSTICE ON STOLEN LAND

David walked back to the van and opened the driver's door. The pop of the lever for the gas lid. He shut the door. He opened the hinged lid and twirled off the gas cap.

I leaned out the passenger window and said, Dave.

Fuck off for one second.

He fed the skipping rope down into the tank. Then he knelt on one knee and sucked. He sucked hard on the end and looked right at me. It was a narrow hole through the rope and I thought perhaps it wouldnt work but then his cheeks were surprised with gasoline and he spat it out. He put his thumb over the rope end. He dragged over the pail and let a stream of gasoline spray into the pail. He knelt over, siphoning the gas in until Gerard Hurley came out of the screen door pulling on a white T-shirt and asked him what the hell he was doing.

I'm looking for you.

Everyone's looking for me.

David stood with the gasoline. He tapped the bottom of it. He looked over at me. Then he slewed it over Gerard Hurley. He decided to chuck the pail at his head too. It clanged off the door behind him as Gerard had crouched and jumped. They were sprawled now on the driveway. I got out of the car to assist. But David had used the force of falling and rolled Gerard over. He had him pinned, with a knee under his chin. Dave produced a lighter and merrily lit it.

I'm looking for the guy, he said, who put my father in hospital.

If youre all looking for him, Gerard said, then you havent found him.

Then Gerard gave a short punch into David's armpit and David reeled off him and Gerard pounced on him and put him in a headlock and squeezed until I heard a neckbone crack. Then he got off of David and let him up. You want Anthony you crazy motherfucker. It was Anthony who drove into your father. The cops dont know nothing.

SEVEN

I DROVE DAVID to his mother's house, he was shaking and laughing now. We each had a glass of whisky and then I drove home and went to bed early. I slept with the whisky on my teeth in the room that was my childhood room. The whisky numbed the broken molar. I remembered living in a house in Trepassey, south of St John's. This was when I first started to write. It was in winter. I wrote with my feet stuck in the oven of the woodstove. One day in May a polar bear was spotted off the coast. He was standing, perplexed, on a little sheet of ice. Heading south. Trepassey is the most southerly tip of Newfoundland and there is no land again until you hit Cuba. The polar bear realized this and was getting nervous. Late in the day he slipped off the ice. We saw him swimming for shore. We barred our doors. I woke up the next morning and put the stove in and noticed a change in the light in the room. In the window a shape, then the white fur, these big paws at the window.

They caught him that day, tranquilized by Wildlife. They phoned in a chopper. He was so beautiful and big and fast asleep. They wrapped him in a net but as they were loading him under the helicopter he fell out of the netting. He hit his head. His jaw. He's broken some teeth, a biologist said. We'll have to get that seen to.

They kept the bear sedated and brought him to the local dentist. The dentist put in a crown for the polar bear.

I woke early with my jaw hammering. It was five-thirty. My parents would be up in an hour. I made some coffee and two slices of toast with butter. I took a painkiller. This waking up early made me philosophical and introspective. It was also quiet. I could walk out to the car and sit in it and turn on the radio, which felt like a rich act. That's where I ate my toast, the slices of toast sitting on my lap. It was like living on another planet but being able to tune into home. The sounds of a radio are very much like a house. You can build a house in your mind around the soft atmosphere of a car radio. But often I wanted to deprive myself of that leash. I wanted to roam the mornings in the air of dawn cracking open the lid of the night, the hinges of the dark lid still clapped down on the western sky. I still wore a watch. I marked the passage of these impressions and then I realized I had opened up into my Wyoming and that I hadnt done that in a while. I took the keys out of my pocket, the keys of my old apartment mixed with the Matador's key and the key to my bike lock and one for the trigger lock of the Lee Enfield in the trunk. I knew what Owen meant about opening things. It was satisfying to open a lock.

The Matador has a soft rumble as gas explodes in the cylinders. They dont make engines like that any more. It was still summer but it was so early that it was chilly and I turned on the heater. Then I drove out onto the road and drove down to pick up David. He wanted us to drive out to Rocky Harbour for the day. He wanted to see a cemetery. The doctors were not happy with Arthur Twombly's condition. You might, Dr Manamperi had said to David, want to prepare yourselves.

So now we have to find Anthony, David said. Before I kill anyone I want to make sure I'm killing the right one.

But even as he said that I sensed he was excited, he was full of loathing and respect for the Hurleys. They were living a provincial life, a small life that he respected. His own worldliness he often despised.

The truth is, Gabe, just a little bit of roughhousing calms me down. I dont want to kill Gerard any more. Gerard is a waste of time. He's small. He's not worth the effort.

But it was Dave's neck that almost cracked off, it wasnt Gerard's. Though I was realizing that David had perhaps let Gerard roll him. Gerard was no longer that big a man. He had become dissipated, through bad food and drugs.

We drove around the Bay of Islands, along the Humber River. David wanted to see about a plot of land in Rocky Harbour. That's where his father wanted to be buried. We leaned down to look up at the Man in the Mountain. He looked like a man who would sweep your chimney or sharpen knives. One summer I was hired, with three others, to cross the river and climb that hill and find the Man in the Mountain and accentuate his face. Tourists couldnt pick him out. But when we got harnessed and rappelled up there and spiked ourselves into the rock, the face dissolved. We were too close to see anything.

We passed the Big Stop Irving in Deer Lake and drove north into Bonne Bay and then Gros Morne park. My father, David said, wants to be buried down there.

We steered into Rocky Harbour and the first person David saw he pulled over.

How do you go about buying a place in the graveyard?

That would be Father Mulcahy.

We found a parish house and knocked on the door and a woman answered. She said Father Mulcahy had overdosed on a pain medication, in an attempt to prove there was a vengeance against him. There wasnt any vengeance, he was just sick of Rocky Harbour and the rumour about him that involved a young girl.

It's a woman, Gladys Conway, who arranges the plots, she said.

We found Gladys Conway. She was a big woman, her husband was out back puttering around and he was half her size. Gladys said there was a simple form for that. She had one in a kitchen drawer. It had been photocopied over and over from the original so the text was fuzzy and bits of extra markings from the lid of the photocopier had been repeatedly copied onto fresh applications. It cost four hundred and nine dollars plus tax for a plot of land in Rocky Harbour. Can we go see it. She said it would be the plot nearest to a man named Thomas Guinchard.

We walked over and up into the meadow of the graveyard. There were no trees back here. If you lay down on the meadow you could still see the ocean, that's what Arthur Twombly wanted. There was a copse of pine trees near the bluff and a soft spot between some bedrock. David bought the plot next to Thomas Guinchard and signed an agreement that allowed a hundred and fifteen dollars to be withdrawn on his visa annually for maintenance and upkeep.

Guinchard, I said. Lars Pony's wife was a Guinchard.

We got in the car and stared back up the hill at the meadow where his father would be laid to rest.

Let's camp here tonight, Dave said.

We ate a fin and feather supper, then we set up the tent on his father's grave. Or what was to be his grave. No one had ever been buried in it. We stretched out and became corpses. Or at least that's how I felt. I slept as deep as I'd had since Nell left and the apartment blew up and we'd taken this return to home. It was important to have someone, and all I had was David. That seemed enough. I loved him. We'd wronged each other but when it comes to love these errors dont seem to affect a deep connection. I admired his breathing. I enjoyed whatever is the flare that is will and desire. Usually he was quick to sleep, whereas I took a half-hour and swore at the hardness of the foamy. What I loved was being alive and not being the only person alive. That would be lonely. This night I managed to get to sleep before him, and I knew it. I knew he was awake while I slept, I had left him alone in the world.

I woke up to a backhoe and the police. They were digging up a thirty-year-old grave. To get DNA evidence. I watched three men from forensics uncover teeth. They were in remarkable condition, the gums in fact were still on them. Then I saw they were dentures. There was nothing left in the damp ground. But then they found hair. A clump of it. There were hairclips in it. The plastic and hair was all that remained. I heard one of the men say he'd found a moustache once, attached to a skull.

EIGHT

We drove back into Corner Brook and took the arterial road that bypassed the city and led us into Benoit's Cove and Mount Moriah. It was the road David's father had used when he was hit by the Hurley van. We stopped at the turnoff and David looked up the road to where the van had come and you could still see the skid marks. So they had braked. The tire marks had been measured and the speed calculated and what had been in the police report was accurate.

We drove further down the shore, past the beaches where we caught caplin at night with dip nets, we drove into Bottle Cove and found Anthony Hurley in his girlfriend's back yard, fixing a white outboard motor beside a shed that had a schooner mural along one end. Anthony had the motor, a Johnson 6, clamped on the side of a woodhorse, with the propeller stuck in a five-gallon bucket of water. Every few minutes he'd pull it over and twist the throttle on the handle and froth and smoke spewed out of the bucket. We watched him from the car for about a half-hour. Anthony's dog in the back of a green truck, running from wheel well to corner, no tailgate on back. It made me think of Bucephalus, how good a dog she was and how goodness got her nowhere.

And then David made a move.

Anthony.

Hey boys.

He bolted. And Dave ran him down by the fence, twisted Anthony's arm behind and up, as if he was scratching his own back. He hauled him to the motor.

Bend your knees, Anthony.

Fuck off Twombly.

That's some scar.

I started the chainsaw up on my kneecap.

Didnt you get stitches.

I let the dog lick it for an hour.

Dave jammed Anthony's arm in the bucket.

Now you tell us what happened, Anthony. Or we're going to have to take this little Johnson for a spin.

Take the fucking arm. Take everything. You got everything already. What did I get. Take the arm. Go on you asshole. I want you to take the arm.

David let him go. So you were driving.

I hate your guts. I hate your friend's guts. I want you to give me a good going over. I want you to feel real proud of yourselves. Come on the two of you beat the snot out of me.

He looked just like Zac. I couldnt help but feel we were talking to David's older brother. Anthony was just eighteen and Zac was about that age when he drowned. It was hard not to feel sorry for him, and David was totally surprised. He was surprised at how quickly his feelings were changing.

Okay, David said. So you want to run me over too.

I'd love to crush your chest.

He was driving the van. It was Anthony, not Gerard. He'd meant to shake him up and the fact that it was more serious than that was an accident. I'm not into putting people in the hospital, Anthony said.

He was leaning up against the side of his girlfriend's overturned boat. He had been sanding it.

Your mother, David said. Youve fucked her up. Youve wrecked everything between you and her and your father.

And Anthony started to laugh. You dont understand, he said. I got no one. There's no one except me here. There is no mother and father.

Dave, I said. He's got a point. I mean he's got a point.

David looked around at what he had. The position he was in. He wanted to let off some arsenal inside himself and yet there was nothing to aim at. It was true. Look at him. Look at Anthony.

I just wanted to meet you and Gerard, David said, and make sure nothing was like a vendetta or anything. Because by rights you both belong in a furnace.

And then something else possessed them. Some brotherly formation crowded in and took them over. They were brothers for god's sakes. They were of the same blood. Or they were father and son. They both felt it. Can you take us on a little tour of the property, David said.

I was quite blown away by Dave's ability to become another energy. And Anthony walked us in past his girlfriend's house. He showed us the property that he personally had cut out of the woods. I need a culvert for here, he said. And David said he knew of a culvert. We could get you a culvert right now, he said. Or at least spot one for you and tuck it away for nightfall.

That sounds like a plan, Anthony said.

WE DROVE TOWARDS ST JUDES. And when we got there Anthony said, You know that Joe is dead.

Yes, David said, we know.

Joe had been killed in Afghanistan. David and I had known a lot of men
and some women in the army, men in the navy and a NATO petty officer
in Landstuhl and personnel stationed in Goose Bay and mostly guys we
went to school with who had to find a way to pay for an education and
now were in ground forces or were working for service industries
contracted out by Bechtel and Halliburton. Some of those men and
women were coming home dead. Joe Hurley had arrived in the belly of
a Hercules aircraft at Stephenville, and Anthony went to the funeral with
Gerard and his father. My own father had gone to the funeral. Joe Hurley
was the funniest brother, Anthony said, and he had been decorated in the
air cadets and his father had those decorations in a glass cabinet. An
aluminum coffin draped in a Canadian flag. It was like the flag they flew
over the baseball diamond when Anthony, as a kid, had marched around
the infield with troops of cadets that Joe directed. Joe had let him oil his
rifle and when it rained Joe let them march around the red line in a
Salvation Army gymnasium, where the marching echoed off the basketball nets. Anthony Hurley respected his older brother because Joe had
won several ribbons and one trophy in St John's at a shooting meet when
he was Anthony's age. Joe Hurley had become a captain in the army and
he knew how to carry himself over monkey bars, he could do chin-ups
until you were tired of counting them. He had bright black hair that was
shaved down to a crewcut which was unfair as it was beautiful hair.
Anthony had not known him with long hair. Imagine, he hadnt had long
hair since he was sixteen. He got his ears flicked on the school bus.
Anthony enjoyed the comic, but being funny was not an option. His
tongue might have been a little too big for his mouth, he had a lisp he
would grow out of. But he was popular and he managed to override the
lisp. No one made fun of him. He remembers Joe in training, when they
sent him into the woods for thirteen days with a canister of water. The
machines they learned and techniques for living. Joe told Anthony, when

he was posted to Afghanistan with a US-led force, that they werent peacekeepers any more. I just hope, Joe said, I get to use my training. All of it. Except I dont want to kill anybody.

Joe Hurley was dead now and his body was brought home for burial in St Judes. He was thirty-six. There was a colour photo of him on the coffin and he was wearing fatigues and a sun hat.

His father got up to say something. I talked to Joe every week, Loyola Hurley said. When he's up on the webcam it's just like youre sitting down talking to him.

In high school it was the Russians who were dying in Afghanistan. We played volleyball in the gym and twice a year there were drills to prepare for a nuclear war. We rolled the volleyballs into a corner then pressed our backs up against the cold wall of the gym. The Russians had a missile aimed at our high school and we had to know how to limber up before a practice and keep our body frames pressed against a load-bearing wall. We'd seen those Red Square parades in the snow, the columns of flatbed trucks carrying warheads. Even their hockey team was named after an army.

My father telling me we will live in the park. What will happen is Russian families will sleep in our beds. There will be perhaps ten or twelve people living with us or we will be sleeping in the park in tents. That's communism, he said. We'll have no money. You'll walk every-where. But it was sleeping in the park that did it. All of Corner Brook lying down together under the birch trees, hoping it doesnt rain.

WE DROVE ALONG THE HIGHWAY towards Deer Lake and Anthony did not look at David. David drove. I was stretched out in the back seat of the Matador. We were going to get a culvert and roll it across the road and hide it in the ditch. Then come back in the dark with Anthony's truck and haul it home. Somehow we'd come away from the idea of personal injury to personal gain. David was going to help Anthony out with a culvert for his girlfriend's driveway. I could tell Dave hadnt made up his mind about the accident. If it was an accident. I could tell though that he wanted to drive deep into enemy territory and stare at the landscape from their eyes.

We passed a motley herd of sheep outside of St Judes. They were Hurley sheep. They looked cold. No they won't freeze on you, Anthony said. They might starve on you if you got them barred up. But if theyre in the woods they won't starve. Won't freeze either.

They'd saved the sheep. They were skinny with not much fat. Yes theyre small but theyre sure-footed.

He was proud of their sheep. They got a barn but they prefer it outside. They get fed outside. They got water on every pasture, they got shelter. They got kelp from the ocean.

We drove down a side road where we'd buried the dog out near Deer Lake, but the culvert was gone now. It had been moved or used already. There's another one, David said. I saw it up by the power station.

This was news to me. So we turned around and drove further up to the power station. The turbines generate electricity that's then shipped by transmission lines to the pulp mill in Corner Brook. This transmission of power made Anthony want to communicate. He said Gerard was driving the van and that, yes, Gerard was upset with Arthur Twombly. At first it was his wife, Helen. Because she's the lawyer for the mill. She's got all those land claims for the pulp mill and also for the extension of the park. And then that transferred over to Arthur when they adopted me. They figured it out early on that I wasnt Joe's son, but they didnt care. Though they took Arthur's money. So when he stopped paying that, because of what happened with the land sold to him, well then that's when Gerard got upset. As far as I know it wasnt intentional to run into your father. But youre powerful in a van. Youre high up. Youve got the moose bar on the front. You can be aggressive. You can hurtle.

They meant to scare him, I said. He was turning when he shouldnt turn and Gerard didnt want to yield. He thought, fuck that. Fuck you old man. Then he lurched right into their lane. He couldnt swerve away.

They looked at me as though I had come close to the truth.

David: The cops said Gerard tried to swerve away.

Anthony: Between you and me because we're brothers, Gerard didnt do enough early on and I'm sorry for that. I'm sorry for your loss.

He was a youngster and he was tough but he still knew a tragedy.

Our father hasnt gone anywhere, David said.

He slowed as a blue minivan was on the side of the highway. A couple in sun hats kneeling with a camera. For some reason it made David want to pull over.

Let's see what theyre shooting.

They were Americans. The plates on their Winnebago said Michigan. My home state, David said to them.

Tourist: Youre from Michigan.

I could be President, David said. And this here man could be the King.

There's a moose in there, the man said. And he pointed to the woods. His wife showed us the camera, on it a male with a huge rack.

Youre handy with that camera.

We never thought we'd see something like that, the man said.

Arent you from Michigan.

Never seen a moose in Michigan.

We got back in the car. We were five minutes away from that culvert.

Boys what say we go moose hunting.

Anthony: We should at least go have a look for him.

Do we have a licence, I said.

Dont you have one, David said.

It's not for this area, I said.

Isnt this close enough?

It was obvious the moose had taken the transmission line and so we just darted into the next wood's road up ahead. It was Lady Slipper Road. David took it. As he sunk into potholes he reached across Anthony and pulled open the glove box.

Load up the Lee Enfield, he said.

Anthony: Youre going to have to get close with the outfit you got there.

He passed the box of bullets back to me, as there was more room in the back and it was my rifle.

Your old man like a piece of moose?

Anthony: Dad would find a spot to hang it.

I want to bring old Cake Hurley a gift.

It was disrespectful, that. That David would say Cake with Anthony there. It was like how he'd spoken to the president. He should have said Loyola. Anthony looked like he'd taken a lot of that kind of hardship.

Moose love cherry, Anthony said. Lots of it around here.

We drove in around a pulp log booth that wedged logs on the backs of paper-mill trucks. There was a fork where a big new pickup was parked. Two Micmac guys sat on the end of an open tailgate, they were quiet and cold, staring at some tremendous beams they'd cut, maybe six inches square and thirty feet long. Ends painted red. Anthony knew them but they did not even nod. The road was getting bad. David rolled down the window.

Can we get in any further?

There's a couple cabins in there, one said.

Can we get as far as the transmission line in this?

That'll get you halfway there.

We drove past their pickup. And in the bed was the product of their own poaching: eight quarters of caribou wrapped in gauze, a grey hoof pointing up from each sack. A discreet pink showed through the gauze, a wet pink of cured ham or feldspar, like a skinned knee. The hooves looking for their slippers. How a dog's hind leg will investigate the living room as he's asleep on his back.

We drove down a steep slope but halfway down Dave slammed on the brakes and we pulled tight against our seatbelts. There was the transmission line. And a moose shaking the woods off his antlers.

Pass up that rifle, Gabe.

I shovelled the gun in between the seats and Dave removed the rubber caps off the sight lenses. He got out and leaned across the roof, his elbows thumping on the roof. I could see the moose through the windshield, he was lifting his head high to scent us. Then swung his neck again, and up. He snorted. A swivelling of weight in his chest which caused his front legs to twist and turn in the marsh. He was beautiful. What'll those tourists think, I thought, when they hear this go off.

Dave's hips were hugging the hinges of the door. The moose stopping to turn and look, I guess, right at him. It seemed the car exploded, but it was the rifle firing and when youre inside a vehicle with the doors flung open that sound is very loud. Then something hard hit the roof and then scraped down the front window. Dave had dropped the rifle. The window smeared with blood.

Oh now that's not right.

David was kneeling at the driver's door staring at his hands. He was covered in blood. He was wiping away bits of tissue and hair from his fingers.

Something went wrong there Gabe, he said. His cheeks flecked with blood.

Are you fucking wounded.

Just take a look for me on the other side of the car, he said.

I checked for Anthony. He wasnt in the car. His door was swung open.

Then I saw the wet mess on the door window. Matter and hair. I pushed forward the passenger seat and climbed out.

Dave, I said.

Anthony was on the ground face first. He was stretching out with one hand and the other he had on the back of his neck. He had no head to speak of. Then a piece of his head on the hard mud.

David: I didnt see him.

Anthony must have been getting out.

The scope the fucking scope why do you have a gun with a fixed scope.

Yeah the scope is what killed him.

This is bad news, Dave said. This is the wrong thing altogether.

This is not good.

I've been doing not good things, he said, all my life.

He bent over his brother and looked at him and then he sat beside him and exhaled loudly and wiped his face with his sleeve. Then he put a hand on him and gave him a little wake-up pat. We should have rolled him over but he had no face and we did not want to see his absent face.

It was an accident, he said.

What do you mean.

It wasnt something I meant to do.

Dave you didnt see him.

I dont think I saw him. I'm just not sure any more what I'm doing.

Tell me you didnt see him.

I'm a little confused here, Gabe.

He shook his head and pushed his finger and thumb into the corner of his eyes. He stared at his brother.

So what do we do, he said.

Youre saying it like we have a choice.

Do we move him or do we leave him and get help or does one of us stay here.

We put him in the car, I said.

No we leave him right where he's to.

The moose was still there, watching us, very alive. I did not look at David or his brother any more. I just stood there and stared at the moose and breathed out a few times. I was disgusted with my part in this. It was a nice fall day, we should have been enjoying ourselves.

There was a culvert, I said. Right? You did see a culvert, like this was no fucking set-up.

I thought I saw one, he said.

What I want to know is you didnt plan this sort of outcome.

I dont know, he said. I might be a little bit out of my mind right now.

I'll go and get help, I said.

Call 911, Dave said.

We didnt feel rushed because there was no chance of him being saved and it felt like the respectful thing to do was to give the body a moment of peace. He was obliterated. You could hear cars on the highway in the distance. Those Micmac men slamming the doors of their truck.

Okay let's put him in the car, he said.

But I'd come around to the idea of not disturbing a crime scene. I'd remembered that. And when youre in a car and there's an accident youre supposed to stay with the car. Although the car was fine.

I'll just get some stuff out of the back seat, I said.

I opened the trunk and there was the shovel that we'd used to bury Bucephalus. We both saw the shovel, the dried mud on it. The moose walked off into the cherry trees and something in me imagined us burying Anthony.

Who saw us, Dave said.

Dave we're going to bring him back to the police station.

No one saw us pick him up, Dave said. Just listen to this, Gabe. I'm a dead man if we bring Anthony in like this. I may get off with manslaughter, I might be out on probation, but I'll wake up one night with a slit throat.

It made me think of David in a grotesque way, of the Hurleys gutting him and quartering him up. It felt, in some part of me, like the proper response. How it would be easy to transport a man like meat, for who would expect such a thing. A man in four quarters wrapped in gauze hanging from meat hooks in a shed in St Judes.

Then David's pebble went off. Hello, he said. Hey. It's good to hear you. We're good, I'm with him now, do you want to talk to him?

He passed over his pebble. It's Nell, he said.

Nell.

I'm in Santa Fe, she said. And I thought I'd give you a call.

David was silently saying No.

We're in Newfoundland, I said.

Of course you are, she said. She sounded distracted but trying to focus, as if there were many things going on very close to her face. I have to meet Richard and get a box, she said, and then I'll be on a flight to Deer Lake. I've got something to tell you.

She waited for me to say something, and what could I say.

It's a little fucked up right now, I said. I know this is crazy as I've wanted to talk with you for weeks. But I can't talk to you now.

Are you okay. Is everything okay with you and David. Did you have your talk? Is he like pointing a gun to your head?

We're good, I said. What flight are you going to be on.

It all depends on Richard. I have to get this box for Arthur.

A box.

I can't really describe it. I just heard about it and I thought it could help him. So I'll call you later about when I get in. Because I've got other things I want to talk about. I guess I'm praying it's okay between us.

Send me the details of your flight, I said.

I love you, she said.

I love you too.

And I did. I loved her and wanted to see her face. I closed up David's pebble and tossed it to him. We've just killed Nell's son, I said. Talking to her was the hardest thing I've done in my life.

Grab his hands, David said.

And I did what he asked. We put Anthony in the back seat. But we couldnt get the doors closed without bending him. Which felt very wrong. So we took him out again and laid him down nicely and then David called 911. We shouldnt have moved him, I said.

NINE

THE CAR WAS CONFISCATED and we were driven back to Corner Brook by Randy Jacobs and another police officer from Saskatchewan. Randy couldnt talk to us as buddies because of the guy from away. It was quiet in the car, a new police cruiser that felt more powerful than our Matador. You could smell the power. I looked at David and he was staring at the back of Randy's head. Randy Jacobs used to direct traffic at the base of Prescott Street in St John's. I remember him working one winter when a truck from Thomas Glass lost its footing on the hill, and slid sideways, horn blaring. Randy stopped traffic east and west then stepped aside as the truck slid through the intersection and down to Water Street. We were in shock now, I guess, much like that guy from Thomas Glass.

They drove us down through Margaret Bowater Park and up to the hill where we went to school. That's where the new police headquarters is, at the base of our education. Above us was the university, the campus where Nell had met Arthur Twombly; below us the hospital where Arthur Twombly now lay, where Nell had had a child, and now that child at the age of eighteen was being trucked back to that very hospital.

They walked us in and sat us down to a metal table in uncomfortable chairs.

Randy got us each a coffee, and then a new officer took us into a room and then I was asked to leave the room and follow a third man who was in plain clothes. He had a small folder with him and an expensive pen.

So you were hunting moose in Lady Slipper Road you won't deny that.

We were attempting to poach, I said.

And you blew Anthony Hurley's head off.

We were both questioned. We were questioned singly and then together. I was looked after by the officer from Saskatchewan and then a huge man from New Brunswick. Then Randy Jacobs came in and Randy told them that he'd known us since we were six.

They find it hard to believe, Gabe, that you guys drove down to Newfoundland and picked up a rifle at your parents', loaded it and blew the head off the kid who had put David's father in a coma. They find it hard to believe that was an accident.

Anthony Hurley wasnt driving, I said. It was Gerard who did the driving.

We didnt put that in the report. We didnt want any vengeance coming out of that report.

TEN

SHE WAS IN SANTA FE. She was with Richard. They were ordering something. Red turkeys darting in and out of a bramble. Behind a delivery window, some electric gadget tabulating the price of a meal. The sand over Los Alamos was falling away from the sky, allowing a new colour to slip in, a darkness that gave Nell and Richard a sense of their own short time, a bleeding off of the solid world that could be bought and sold, and a humbleness came over them both, a hunger too. They looked at their clinic menus. She had come for the box. As if in response to this need, warmth puffed out of the ground and while Nell had a chill to her shoulders, her legs felt like they were on a vent. All elements were inverted. Richard Text, as if to apologize for his distracted study of the landscape, turned to Nell and pressed the small of her back. His nails were long and he could not massage her. But she knew he was helpful and was not, in the bones, selfish. He was seeing a man from the research facility. A tank of lit goldfish in the clinic window resumed their fluid circle, and it was this movement that had indicated they had gone still.

But the warmth soon dissipated and Nell was cold. The red mountains lost their colour and dryness was overcome by the thought that sea fossils were in these rocks and they could argue for a long time and be right about the prevailing custom of the land. Nell and Richard too were changed. A scientist arrived with a black valise that carried a beaker of uranium in a nine-pound state-of-the-art machine and he left it on the chair beside Richard as though it too would pick up a menu and order. Someone had bought him the valise, and she wondered who had thought of him, if she could know that person.

So this box, Richard said, has instructions and you need a brain-injury specialist to attach it. You have your papers to transport nuclear material.

No, she said. She didnt have anything.

You won't get through security without papers, it's not hospital-grade uranium.

It would not survive the carry-on x-ray machine. It was too vulnerable for checked baggage.

We have a flight, Richard said, heading to Syria. It's going to refuel in St John's. This is next Tuesday. I can have the box on board that flight.

There's one last thing, she said. I might need to see a doctor.

NELL FLEW Albuquerque–Newark, Newark to Halifax and Halifax–St John's and realized, from the action of her jaw, that she was anxious. Across from her on the plane a musician had bought a seat for her cello, and the airlines have a canvas strap to bind a cello in. She rented a car at the airport and stayed at the Newfoundland Hotel, the same hotel she had stayed in eighteen years before, when Arthur wanted an abortion.

She waited until the flight time and drove back to the airport and parked at arrivals. She asked a guard and Nell said it was an air force flight. An American flight. You'll have to go to the silo out back just to the left of the doors. She walked out the doors that held artificial flowers and past the car rental lots and found a helicopter landing and three men in air force suits with white gloves holding their helmets on. They were waiting outside a security door. One of the men, a young one, maybe nineteen, took her inside and put a wand to her and she stepped through a metal detector and was told to see a man in a booth. The man was asleep. Hello, she said. And his mouth closed and his eyes opened. He was immediately alert. His arms flexed in a black short-sleeved shirt. She told him who she was. Youre for the American flight yes I have you here. It's running late. It will be fourteen hundred hours. Please take a seat.

She went out to the coffee shop and had a bagel. She read a magazine. She checked her emails on her laptop. Then she went back out to the silo.

The jet had landed and was turning on the tarmac. It was a grey unmarked plane and the high whine of its jet engines took a while to shut down. For a moment it looked like it had changed its mind and was to take off again. Then a set of stairs was wheeled out and hydraulically manoeuvred and clamped onto the base of the jet beneath the cockpit door. Then nothing happened. About eight minutes went by while the ground crew refuelled from a truck on the other side.

Then the man from the booth came out and said, Come with me.

They walked over the tarmac and up the stairs. The door was opened now on its thick white hinges. And she went in. There were two rows of seats facing each other, like seats on a train, with a group of armed men playing cards. In each of the middle seats of the three back rows sat a man wearing a black hood.

Can you recognize which one, the man from the booth said.

I'm sorry. Recognize.

He laughed. Oh yeah, hoods. You want the Canadian. Which one of you is the Canuck?

The supposed Canadian, said one of the card players.

A man was putting up his wrists. They were handcuffed.

I'm here for a box, Nell said.

Her escort opened his mouth and he softly blinked. He was shorter than her. You dont want to talk to the Canadian.

One of the men playing cards, without taking his eyes off his hand, said the box was strapped in a seat just behind him. He kind of pointed with his elbow.

The man got the box and lifted it out and took Nell's shoulder and led her back to the stairs. The three hooded men had their heads bowed.

She drove across the island, through the deep basin of the Humber Valley. She noted the cabins in Pasadena where, twenty years ago, she and Arthur had conducted their affair. She realized she was loyal. She hadnt known that. She'd been grateful to Arthur, that he took care of things. A deep side of her had missed her son. She should never have met Joe and had that little boy on the park bench. But again she would not trade that afternoon for anything. Yes she would. If she could not have to think about it. If she did not know she had traded it.

The windows were fogging up and the knobs to get the defogger on were confusing, so she wiped the windows with her sleeve. She remembered once, in the rain, when Arthur took her shopping. It was a day like this and she wiped the condensation off her passenger window. Dont do that, he said.

And she was shocked by his voice. It was a parental voice. That he cared about the Audi. He didnt want marks on the windows—the car's air-controlled unit took care of condensation. She realized then that he did not love her.

The self, she thought, is more vicious than God.

She passed the junction where you turn off to get to the cabins on Grand Lake. She drove along the river, the yellow tractors to her left that were widening the highway through the old railbed. She pulled into the Mamateek Motor Inn that overlooked the Bay of Islands, and as she stood at the check-in counter waiting for her credit card to be approved, she turned her back to the nineteen-year-old clerk and stared out the seven-foot-tall windows and she might have been looking into the canal of her own birth, remembering nothing. The insane smoke of the mill, the march of white bungalows up to Crow Hill, the dynamited side of mountain making a fresh scar for the new highway that was being built night and day by those yellow tractors mounted with revolving high beam lights behind their own German wipers. The motel was marooned in a phalanx of city-edge growth, no longer on the main road out of town but in a detour and catering to the auto repair shops and furniture upholsterers sprung up to avoid municipal taxes, and on the hill beyond the golf course the three wide, squat schools, sitting like ancient Egyptian foundations uncovered and about to be restored in a nineteenth-century manner. She could not see Arthur Twombly's house down in its wedge of green, but the hospital where he lay was smoking and, from its head, the shore road wound along the bay into Curling and Mount Moriah, wooded and undeveloped. She was going to see her son.

She phoned me and I was surprised at the sound of her voice. She was here. She was just a mile away. I was going to see her. We had a serious situation that was outside ourselves so we could be close.

How does he look, she said. Can you look at him.

Nell I love you, I said.

There was a pause and something digital that was shortening the pause on the phone. She said, Can I see you. There's something I have to tell you.

Those were the same words she'd used to tell me about David.

I DROVE UP THERE and I was nervous. When I saw her I realized I was relieved she was here and yet I had to tell her about Anthony. In the flesh. I thought perhaps she'd send a person kitted out in sensory devices, while she stayed safe in another country experiencing Corner Brook through a computer lashed to the waist of an employee.

I held her and we kissed. And something soft came over her. She took a piece of paper from her pocket, paper you associate with reproducing machines. A black-and-white blur of a solar system. It reminded me of the time I'd first met her, when she took my picture on a dot matrix machine. But this looked like the solar system humanity will one day end up in, once we've discarded this one. It was an ultrasound.

I'm pregnant, she said.

ELEVEN

I TOLD HER about Anthony. The whole works. The idiocy that went on in the woods. It was a split second, I said. It felt like the end of living. That everything was dead. That I was in the land of the dead. It was atrocious. Nell was pretty shocked. She had come ready to make an introduction to Anthony. She was open to whatever that might entail. It had taken her eighteen years to realize a side of her existed that she had suppressed and now I was telling her the window was shut. Her hands were gripping the collar of her blue coat. Too tightly. Nell, I said. She was really gone somewhere, she was numb but her eyes were wild, her lovely dark eyebrows, and her shoulders looked like they were inflating. There was something demonic in her, and who can blame her.

She had to get out of the hotel. Could I drive her someplace. I was in my father's car because they had impounded the Matador. There's the funeral, I said. It's actually going on right now.

She gave me a look, like, you asked for it. It was a bright warm day. My father said he'd come, I said. He'd known Anthony. He'd taught him in his last year teaching, before he retired. He liked Anthony. So we drove by the house and picked him up. But before he got in he tapped on Nell's window. Hello, he said. She rolled it down. And he leaned in and put his arms around her. He knew how much I loved her. And he knew about Anthony.

Thank you, she said.

I'll get in the back, he said.

I drove down Valley Road to take the shore road. It would be nice to have the water. Water's soothing. My father kept it quiet, and I was impressed that he would let my world unfold the way it had to unfold. Nell looked tired and I found her sexy in that tiredness. She was pregnant. That was something to tell my father. I was impressed with hard work. I admired drive and it did not matter that much what the drive was trying to attain. But now the drive would be focused on having a child. Nell would be good at that and I wanted to be close to her. I had no idea, really, what Nell would be, but I was interested in seeing it happen to her. And when she saw me she was soft and put her arms around me. She wasnt going to shut me out. We had been practising a quiet faith together and that was still between us.

We passed the mill, something you dont see up close often. The thousands of cords of wood became individual logs. And then the quiet in the car became unnerving and my father helped out. My father is a quiet man, he thinks a lot and only says necessary things. He doesnt ever point out obvious things. And so it was a bit of a strain for him, but I appreciated it. He was telling us about a trip we all took when I was small. He was telling it to Nell. It was the time we drove across Canada. We were looking for another place to live. Gabe, he said, must have been about six. And we drove a little green Valiant with a camper trailer. The kids, Nell, they made these maps. Treasure maps. And when it rained they rolled down the window and crumpled up the maps and then held them outside to get a bit of rain on them. To weather them. They looked authentic.

Nell: Did you ever find a place you liked?

Nothing as good as here. Though I liked Victoria, he said.

That got us to the funeral home. The parking meters were shrouded in maroon funeral bags.

The procession had taken the slow road underneath Crow Hill. And I realized that it might not be a good thing, our being here. Or me especially. Perhaps, I said, we should just stay in the car. And watch. I was nervous about the Hurleys.

Well I'm going to pay my respects, my father said.

My father, unafraid, crossed the road. He dug his hands in his pockets, and waited beside some raspberry bushes. Then he saw someone he knew.

He strolled towards them. A Hurley. My father had an in with the Hurleys. They had arrived with the varnished coffin. Sins travel down the line but not up. The sins of the son are not bestowed upon the father. The graveyard looked wet, as though the sun couldnt do work in there. We stayed in the front seats and wiped the window of condensation. Then Nell took my hand. We were new adults, Nell said, when I had Anthony. Now we have another chance to be adults.

That's what it means, I said, to be in your thirties.

We had the windows up and the doors locked and we were breathing in and out our own air.

I feel a lot of things, she said. And some of the things I feel are that I havent earned the right to feel the way I'm feeling. What was he like, she said.

Anthony. He was smart. He was handsome and game and he worked hard and he was generous.

I want to visit, Nell said, in a couple of days. Can we come back in a couple of days?

WE DROPPED MY FATHER OFF and then I drove Nell back to the Mamateek Motor Inn. She wept in the car, and then she got angry and then she calmed down. We had a soft drink in the windows that overlooked the city we had both, in different ways, grown up in. Her eyes dried and she would not look at me. She was depleted. She gave me the other side of herself, that side she only now was aware of, now that it was gone from her. I can't see David, she said. I can't believe it was an accident, I mean my various organs dont believe it.

I still loved her. My body hammered that message home. I did not want a complicated event to break us. That would be easy. I would never be in an uncomplicated relationship again. The truth is, if you dont marry and stay faithful to someone young, then the complications are bound to occur.

THE POLICE KEPT DAVID for nineteen hours and then his mother was allowed to come pick him up. Randy Jacobs told me the car was to be impounded for at least a week. The gun too. The gun I would never get back. There were tests.

David: I'm not that safe anywhere on this island.

Gerard Hurley had connections. Even if Dave could get a flight, the airport was easy. If they didnt get him on the way to the airport they'd have a man on the Queensway run his taxi off the road and then scurry down the grade and put a bullet in his head. It would be that man from Moosonee in a new fox coat and the man from Moosonee would love that. The ferry was obvious. He would try a private boat, he said. A Russian trawler. He'd been talking to Randy Jacobs. We both knew that Randy played the sides. He was a police officer but he was friendly with the brown shadows of the law. He had recently been embarrassed by police surveillance. It was a camera in a mall washroom. They were trying to catch men performing sex acts.

And on the tape in the trial Randy Jacobs, unaware of the sting operation, arrives to wash his hands. He looks around. He is alone. And he
stands back from the mirrors and draws his gun. He shoots the mirror
quietly. Then he puts his gun back in its holster. He postures himself
and draws again. Laughter in the courtroom.

Randy asked if I could drive David down.

I dont have a car, I said.

Borrow your father's car.

David was to sneak aboard and get off somewhere in the St Lawrence.
He had US dollars for when they found him. To leave illegally was the
safest way.

Who's the contact on board.

Jason Linegar, Randy said.

And I recalled that name. Gwen Hurley had been married to him.

Gwen is the good in Hurleys, Randy said. You can trust Jason Linegar.

I didnt know any more who I should be helping or who to trust.
Gwen, I would say, probably hated Dave's guts now. I half hated him
myself. But I drove him down that night. I used my father's car. We rolled
into a coffee shop for a doughnut and coffee and the cashier recognized
us. Where's the dog, the cashier said. She was reaching out with a nugget
for the dog.

The dog, I said, stays with the other car.

We pulled into the Curling marina. Randy Jacobs in a green hunting
jacket standing next to a waste disposal bin, a bin the Hurleys owned
the contract on for dumping. Randy had a life jacket and a set of
varnished oars in his hands. There's a Russian trawler quietly moored
in the bay.

We dragged the rowboat down to the wharf where the *Wayward Wind*
was tied up. The last letter was rubbed off and there seemed something
prophetic in the *Win* that was left. We settled into the dory. The seats

were from a pew. This dory is a sacred place, Randy said. Like a wigwam. Any place you pray in, they can't tear it down.

And then the three of us stopped what we were doing, and Randy said a little prayer. It was a private prayer that I can't write here. But it was touching and David was pleased that we could all be sincere. It was to wish him safe passage.

We rowed out to the trawler. It was in port trading Bulgarian shoes for barrels of herring. Hauling aboard fresh supplies.

Jason Linegar is aboard that, David said.

Randy: No, but this one will get you to that one.

The shoes were Italian knock-offs and Randy Jacobs was part of the system that allowed that trade. That's what I mean about brown shadows. It's not that terrible a crime. He peeled us close to the side and David threw a looped rope over the portside railing. He had a knapsack with him: water and sandwiches. I'll see you on the mainland, he said.

We rowed away and I held my eyes on David. Until he became a part of the bow. Even with the *Wayward Wind* and the prayer I had a bad feeling about his prospects. But David is affable and ruthless, he could rebound and survive. A large ship crossing the bay. There's the *Corner Brook,* Randy said. Leaving with a load of pulp. That doesnt come up, Randy said, where it's all wood.

Me: What do you mean it doesnt come up.

Randy: On the radar screen.

As we pulled into shore Randy began to cough. We didnt want to be noticed so I took over the oars to let Randy cover his cough. It's bronchial, he said. It's not the lungs, lungs are fine. It's the tubes.

The coughing, I said. Is how you'll go.

You never know, Randy said, what is going to carry you off.

TWELVE

THEY FOUND DAVID on the second day. He was thirsty and had been caught in the wash facility by a Canadian fisheries observer.

Youre not crew, he said.

I stowed away.

Youre Canadian.

I'm American.

He was reported to the captain and the captain was furious.

David: You can just let me off in Quebec.

They werent going to Quebec. They would be at sea another six weeks.

All the meat was either wieners or liver.

The captain didnt lay eyes on him for a week. That was when he ran out of vodka, and then he wanted to see the stowaway. He wanted to blame his troubles on that one. The captain was crooked for ten days, and the crew put up with him being crooked. By then they'd weaned the captain over to moonshine and he had gotten used to it.

The fisheries observer was named Rolly Junger. We hate the captain now, Rolly said, but when we get off this boat I'll cry to say goodbye to him.

He followed Rolly on his rounds. He tried to help him but there was not much an observer needed to do.

It's hard, Rolly said, to watch other people doing physical work when youre not. Observing is self-conscious work. So I often end up gutting fish instead.

They did gut fish and David got good at it. It was true what they say about sharp knives.

They caught fish no one had seen before. The crew gathered around Rolly Junger, who had a large book to identify fish. He photographed the fish and put it in the ledger. Then jumped into the hold on deck where they dumped the net, and poked with his knees through the catch looking for oddities. There was an angler fish that has an extension of its body that hangs out in front of its mouth. It's a kind of fishing lure, Rolly said. A lot of the fish from down that deep are all black.

They were on a large factory freezer trawler. David followed Rolly Junger along the winding path to the meal plant. At the end of all the paraphernalia was a man filling one bag after another with warm sweet meal.

After ten days the captain said they were to unite with a provision boat and be gone another six weeks. David was to transfer over. Some of the crew transferred over, and new crew came aboard. And then Jason Linegar came aboard and talked to the captain. That's how David transferred over to the provision boat operated by Russians. Jason Linegar was a cook aboard the boat. Youre to bunk with me, he said. They had been at sea for six months, Jason Linegar said. People had plants in their cabins. The captain had a radish garden on the roof of his cabin and tomatoes inside. There was a little dog. There was a chess tournament. Moonshine made in a corner cupboard. Back scrubbers were knotted and looped out of disassembled onion bags. People engaged in a lot of crafts and a game like backgammon. Lots of tea drinking. Tchai. You heard the word constantly. The only other word heard as often was fish. Ribka.

There were some musical instruments. David was in Jason Linegar's cabin. The crew piled in, drinking tea, and a guitar entered. It went around the room and it was only when it came to David that there was someone who couldnt produce a song on it.

They steamed north. The sound of loose ice hitting the bow, no one liked it. When are we going to go back to port, David said. Jason: We're off to the Grand Banks.

They were among a group of vessels that responded to a shrimp boat that sank from an ice puncture. When they arrived at the coordinates the crew had successfully been taken aboard another boat while three other shrimp boats floated there and watched a swirling mass of water where the sinking ship had been only moments before. Then odds and ends like life jackets started popping to the surface.

David woke to breakfast on the Russian boat. He began to forget there was a life on solid ground. He ate a kind of rye bread that was baked on board, the dough mixed in a huge industrial mixer that was probably working overtime. Bread on a Russian boat was the staple food, Jason Linegar said. Bread with butter. This is significant because butter was only served at breakfast and teatime. The crew used the butter like cheese. Cutting off thick slabs of it.

The longer I spend on Russian boats, Jason Linegar said, the more butter I put on my bread. Usually bread and butter and tea, that's it. There's no coffee served in the mess on Russian boats. Coffee is a scarce commodity.

David: If I'd known I'd have brought some.

Once in a while there's some sweet bread made as a treat.

THE LAST NORMAL THING David did was sit on his bunk and eat a can of peaches. He could taste the metal of the tin on the blade of his spoon. Then he read a book and fell asleep.

It was something about the hinges on the door. On the dark seam between door and wall. An animal was pulsing through the seam. It was moving too fast to catch. The pelt was full of blur. David strained his eyes for more light. Then the floor slanted up to meet the hinge and sank away again, as though the animal was a mink and the floor some kind of den mouth. There was the animal again. The floor was where the floor was, and then it lifted up to the arching animal. Or the surface lifted. It wasnt the floor it was a varnish lifting from the floor, some kind of transparent linoleum. A material was being pulled through the gap in the bottom of the door now like a magician and a sleeve.

David looked at the grey corner or was it blue. He put on his expensive glasses. An empty can floated in the air towards the blue. He recognized the can. It was the can of peaches. It was nudging itself in the corner. Then he saw the book he was reading, bloated and staggering about. He felt pulled towards the corner too. It was as if the metal of the walls had gone magnetic. Then the feeling hesitated and the can turned around and bumped into the novel and then floated over to the centre of the room. Its label was peeling off. There was a plastic bag with air in it, just there twirling about in the middle of the air, a well-used white bag. He heard a wind under his bunk. It felt like a cold wind for there was a sound to it. There was something weighty under the bed. The word *slosh* occurred to him. There was water in the room. A lot of water. Things on shelves were tiptoeing around the room. They were going for little swims. His blanket was heavy. It was sodden. The edges and now the bunk moved or lifted off a leg. They had yawed over. He could not shove himself from the side of the wall. Water crept up behind him and surprised his back. He tasted it. Sea water. Linegar's small globe of the earth buoyed past his chest. He saw South America.

He entered the water. He had to hold on to the bunk. He was up to his thighs and he was, technically, standing on the side of his bunk, such was his angle. Linegar was not in the room. So a side of the room was full of water. Maybe Linegar had turned into water. David made his way up to the door. But he could tell there was a lot of water on the other side of it. It was rushing quietly through the gap at the floor and now the one at the ceiling. The deadbolt was saving him. Then he heard a shout and a bullet of outrage zipped up his spine.

He fell into the cold water and was thrown up against the door. His head hurt and he cleared the water. Now the water was on him. The ship had righted. If I can get the door open. But now the water was behind him and on the door. The door had to open in. He realized he had his head against the door. He turned the lever and pulled. It was a heavy metal door. He tugged against the sucking. He jammed himself into the opening. Then he popped through and hit the wall across from the door. The hall was emptying down of water. The water was a bowling ball. Bulbs in cages were lit in a dirty glow on the ceiling. Then Linegar. He saw Jason Linegar halfway down the hall. Linegar was perched, jumping-jack fashion, in the doorframe of an open room.

David: What the fuck is going on.

Jason Linegar did not know what to do. At the end of the hall was a froth of water standing straight up to the ceiling. It was about to come back after him. Jason Linegar was going to run away from it, or close his door again.

I was paid, Jason Linegar said, five thousand dollars to take care of you. And now I won't get to spend it.

That was the last he saw of Jason Linegar.

The water carried David around three corners. It was lucky water. He caught nothing sharp. The water pushed him up a floor and he grabbed ahold of a mounting that used to carry a fire extinguisher. He held on as the dark water reflected back onto him. Then with the space empty he walked out onto the deck. Water was still slooshing out of his trousers.

His legs felt heavy. The ship was tilted in a swelling sea. The sea was less than an inch below the starboard side, breaking over. The ship was like a raft. The wind was raw and he realized he was freezing. A lifeboat had its keel broken on the trawler winch. A piece of fibreglass from the flydeck was hooked in the rigging. He pulled it out. A sheet of fibreglass eight feet long. The wind caught it out of his hands and it sliced his hands open. It made the sound of a drum. It pitched into the water and it floated. A panel of white streaming away from the stern. He fell into the sea and grabbed the panel and climbed aboard. It was enough to hold him. He curled his hurt hands into his body.

THIRTEEN

DAVID WAS HOLDING ON to a dead man. The dead man was wearing a yellow life jacket. Half his face was gone. A floating Russian had saved his life. He was under the wide hull of the coast guard vessel *Cape Roger*. Two container ships were parked on the horizon, and they were waiting for him. They were too big for search and rescue.

He had lost his pebble and his wallet and his shoes and trousers. Then he realized he was still wearing his glasses. The coast guard found him in just his shirt, and even the tails of his shirt and the sleeves of the shirt had been torn off. All the buttons. It must have been funny to see him like that, pretty much naked, but wearing his glasses.

It was a Norwegian-owned bulk carrier that spotted you, he heard a man say. A container ship did manage to rescue nine bodies from an over-turned life raft. Corporal Al Spratt of the Halifax search and rescue centre said *Cape Roger* picked up one body.

Was he the body. Perhaps a body doesnt mean dead.

What David can recall is thinking about himself and who he must be. He thought of his friends gathered around a picnic and the friends popped into place as he remembered them. He wanted chicken and a

glorious roasted chicken arrived but it was spackled with salt. He wanted
the chicken rinsed in fresh water, wet chicken. Something from a childhood book: gingham sandwiches.

Corporal Al Spratt was saying, We thought there could be survivors,
as your ship sank in the Gulf Stream.

Where was he. In some rescue vehicle. They had him folded into an
emergency sleeping bag and Al Spratt was in there with him. The sleeping bag was too bright to be used all the time. It would keep you awake.

Two planes and four civilian ships are still looking.

He thought, they can stop looking.

If you find a person in the sea that's a lucky person, Al Spratt said. You
find a body, that's a lucky family to have the body. The sea can hide you
in a lot of places.

It was obvious Al Spratt was not by nature a talkative man. He was
talking to keep David Twombly awake. He found he could not speak and
that the drawings in his head kept multiplying.

One man was pulled out of the water after eighteen hours, Al Spratt
said. Clinging to a dead crew member. Taken aboard the *Cape Roger*. They
tried to get your body temperature up. You were put into this here
warming bag, then John McCarthy, he's a good man, he got the first shift.
Body heat will warm you. You got John McCarthy pretty cold so I'm
taking over. John says you were in a lot of pain.

He was stabilized and confused. Fifteen bodies had been recovered
from his ship. Bodies meant they were dead. Filipinos, Lithuanians,
Romanians, Montenegrins. David suddenly added them to the picnic.
But he did not know them. He knew Linegar and where was he. And
what did Linegar mean. Was he there to take care of him or to get rid of
him. Was there a bounty on his head and maybe Jason Linegar had spread
the word. A ship on its way to Montreal with a load of grain spotted him.
It was Cypriot registered. Forty nautical miles off St Pierre. The wheel-

house blew off but the bow kept afloat by pockets of air. The only survivor this man here. The sea tore your clothes off. Were you the cook.

Yeah, David said, that's me. I'm Jason Linegar.

David recalled talking to a Russian technician, Petra. He said it was a safe ship, but didnt have enough ballast. It was unloaded and could handle rough water. The ship's agents won't be returning calls.

Al Spratt was passing his warmth over to him. Trawlers and bulk carriers at this age, Al Spratt said, they seem to have a habit of breaking up. We want to make sure there's compensation for your families.

It made him feel dead. David was at a picnic for the dead.

THEY ENJOYED HIM. There were too many men helping with the stretcher. Both feet in thick white bandages like some cartoon of injury. His hands bandaged to the elbow and his head wrapped in white. He held his hands up, look at these hands. These hands move. They hustled him from the ambulance through a bend in the drive to the automatic Emergency doors that were not yet open. They had all wanted to see him, the only survivor. The heavy doors slid open and he was transferred to a trolley parked against the plaster wall. The Canadian cook, Jason Linegar.

HE SPENT FOUR DAYS at the Grace Hospital in St John's recovering from frostbite and hypothermia. His true identity leaked out and he was now under police custody. They understood his situation but they could not pretend he was Jason Linegar. He hired a lawyer and was granted bail of fifty thousand dollars. David called me. He didnt have his passwords, he'd lost his pebble, he couldnt open his trading account and sell five thousand shares of Sunleaf. My father needs me, he said. He needs blood and he needs a kidney. My kidneys are a match.

You mean you have to return to Hurley territory.

If I want my father alive, he said.

This made me pause and he heard the pause.

You think, he said, this might be the end for me.

I dont think you should come back here.

You must help me to it, he said.

I walked down the road to the constabulary building and was led into the pound where the Matador had been cleaned and inspected and photographed. I checked the trunk and all of our gear was in there, even the box for the Taser. Toby was on the back shelf. They had kept the rifle, was all.

I showed Toby to Nell. She touched him. His shorn fur, the seams showing. He's heavy, she said.

It's the gold, I said. And I told her about the heat. David, I said, needs to be bailed out. I have to bring this gold to St John's.

Okay, she said. I'm with you.

We drove the Matador across the island. It felt strange. It was Zac's car. And now I was in it with Nell. I drove fast and we stopped in Badger and ordered pea soup and cheeseburgers and then Nell drove and she kept driving until the headlights lit up the rounded curb to the Health Sciences Centre. Six and a half hours. We found Dave not in bed but in a visiting room drinking coffee with a plainclothes police officer. David's feet and hands were sensitive. He was leaking from one of his feet.

You got that Taser, he said.

God youre relentless, I said.

He took us by the elbows. He said, You guys I love you guys.

We dealt with the cop. I showed him Toby. I said Toby is our Fort Knox.

We went down to the lockup in the basement of the old courthouse on Duckworth Street. I opened Toby up. Out clunked the little bar of gold. That's worth fifty thousand dollars, I said.

And then some, David said. Gold has gone up.

They took it. They weighed it and they checked the price of gold online and we filled out the paperwork as though bars of gold were exchanged for prisoners all the time. It was about ten oclock then and we drove to the Newfoundland Hotel and booked a room. The three of us in the room. David slept in the second bed. It felt like this was it now. The three of us were going to be together for a long time.

I woke up early and had a coffee and walked around St John's. I loved this city. I walked up to the Basilica and saw the new museum built right beside it. The Rooms. The secular competing with the religious for skyline. There were tourists, like me, staring at both. An old guy passed them and stopped to see what we were all looking at. That's the Basilica, he said, and that's the box it came in.

Someone opened the door to the Basilica so I went in. It's a good place to think in. The last time I was in there was when Joey Smallwood died. There was a procession past the casket and it was an open casket. He was in a suit. But the strange thing was, he was wearing his glasses. They had him laid out in those black-framed glasses. Like he slept with them on or something. I guess people like to have the dead look exactly as they do when theyre up and around.

We drove back to Corner Brook that day. We passed tractors embedding fibre optic cable and an underground storage facility where a red hose was pumping in a billion cubic feet of natural gas. The world was preparing for winter, though the world only ever had enough reserves for three weeks of deprivation. Nell turned on the radio and a dictator was shouting in court.

Saddam, David said. He was born the day after Guernica.

We drove past Grand Lake where Zac had drowned and David said how he'd like to someday get over to that island on an island in an island. He said he knew he wouldnt drown.

I'd made a promise a long time ago, he said, not to go the way Zac went. So I just pushed through it. When that trawler sank I refused it. I willed myself to find the Gulf Stream and stay alive. So what say we do this. I want us to take a boat across Grand Lake. We'll bring the tent. We'll put a little punt in the boat and drag it across the island and then row to that little pond on Glover Island. And then we'll camp there, in the middle of the planet.

I thought about my own middle of the planet, which is my childhood. I thought about the summer I fished on the Humber River. I tied flies in the basement. My father had taken me to the Arts and Culture Centre when Lee Wulff was in town. Lee Wulff was an American outdoorsman who loved Newfoundland. We tied flies that were named after him, the White Wulff and the Grey Wulff. So I was excited to see the man. I remember Dave came with us. He didnt fish, he just enjoyed theatre. Lee Wulff stood on one side of the stage and flicked a fly rod into the air. He was demonstrating proper casting techniques. At the end of his line he had fastened a red bow. And the tackle unspooled from his reel, floated over the audience, and the red bow landed like a feather on top of a man's head deep in the back. The audience exploded. They stood around us, clapping, and then my father got up and we got up too and madly applauded. To this day, theatre is connected, in some odd way, to fly fishing.

We stopped in Gander for dinner. The trout looked good, though Nell wanted something basic. She hadnt told David she was pregnant. You know who I'd have to dinner, David said. He was tearing open a package of vinegar to douse on his trout. The guy, he said, who invented x-ray specs. It was the same guy who made sea monkeys. Harold von Braunhut.

Nell: You know his name.

He also managed that Frenchman who dove forty feet into a children's wading pool, remember him?

We drove into town in the dark and up the hill to Western Memorial. I signed the paperwork for him while they treated David on a floor directly below his father, in intensive care. They had performed small grafts from David's thigh and lower back. They shaved coins of dead skin from the ball joints of his feet and hands. While they did this they took his blood. David was allowed up and he walked gingerly on his bad feet and he used a walker and the elevator to visit his father.

NELL WANTED TO TALK to David alone. I read a magazine article about a Canadian tortured in a foreign country. I figured she wanted to tell him about the pregnancy. I gave them twenty minutes and then I went back in and David looked at me with a sorry look. He was sorry. The two halves of him had caught up and they both had to appear in front of me. It's all right, I said. It's over with.

FOURTEEN

HIS FATHER WAS READY for the box. Dr Manamperi had practised how to position it and how to manage the power it required and they were just waiting for the family to sign a waiver. David was the family. Arthur would need the kidney, Dr Manamperi said. The machines could not cleanse his body after using the machine. So the operation was scheduled for a Tuesday morning and David spent the night beside his father, giving transfusions, and then he was allowed to go home. I drove him back to his mother's. He said, My mother wants to meet Nell.

Nell and I had been staying in the spare room at my parents'. I told her about Helen Crofter. Okay, Nell said. I'll call her up. I watched Nell's face on the phone. We had all, I guess, matured. Helen, she said. Can I call you Helen. It's Nell Tarkington.

So I drove her there and Helen answered the door. It must have been similar to how she had opened the door almost twenty years before, when she'd allowed Nell Tarkington into the house for that first dinner party. Come on in Nell, she said. It felt like it was all over, it was to be okay. In fact it felt wise that a drama from twenty years ago should not come to haunt us. Everything was calming down. There were bigger issues to manage. David saw this and opened the freezer door and grabbed a bottle of vodka by the neck. He poured himself a shot, straight from the freezer. You shouldnt be doing that, his mother said. Then he poured one for Nell and asked if I was in. I'm in, I said, and he poured another. This was something Nell did too, guzzle vodka straight from the freezer, and now I see she got it from David. It was a delight they both shared, a comfort that perhaps I could not offer. It depressed me. The fact that David had almost died exonerated him a little, or, the one-sided feeling had turned into a complicated mix that meant that if Nell tilted her head the right way, she could be warm to David. She was forcing herself to be kind.

But then I saw she did not drink it. She was pregnant. And David either did not know this or had forgotten. No, I could see—she hadnt told him. She looked at me, with this secret. She was with me more than she was with David. It made me rise on my toes. It made me notice things high up on the walls.

We sat down to eat and David took off his glasses. Everything was going to be okay. I didnt lose my glasses, he said. The one thing. I woke up in the sea with my glasses still on my face.

I remembered that Nell, in private, liked to remove her watch to eat. She'd lay it next to her fork, as if it were another utensil. But she'd lost her watch, she'd left it in Las Vegas or Santa Fe. The two of them, bare of the man-made objects that improved vision and time, and I saw them living together. But that was a history, rather than a future. David has a great resilience, I realized, though a coldness.

I've called the police, Helen said. Youre to check in tonight. If they dont hear from you in an hour then they'll be coming to get you.

And so we ate in the calm of this little time together. All you heard were soup spoons. Then we saw headlights flash through the living room window and a car door, a second, and then the front door opened. David stood to welcome the police—they were early, though police usually use doorbells. I could tell from the sound of the engine that it was not a police car. Then there was another car. David leaned out of the hallway but he could not see well as he had left his glasses on the table. He looked vulnerable. I saw who it was. It was Gerard Hurley. Then it was Randy Jacobs.

Randy: I'm sorry about this, Dave.

David said, calmly, The architects are here.

Gerard and Randy backed David up and were looking around for things. Gerard was holding a small crowbar called a cat's paw. Just move that chair, he said to Randy. It was as if he didnt want to harm the chair. Randy moved the chair aside. David reached into his pocket and tossed me the keys to the car.

I got up slowly and pushed Nell towards the patio doors. I opened them and we slipped out together. Helen was trying to intervene. She was holding up her dinner plate.

Get in the car, I said to Nell. Just get in the car.

I found the right key and popped the trunk. I could see through the open patio doors, Randy bending down to roll up an area rug. It looked like they had come to steal an area rug. They were careful about it. Then they approached the table with the rug and David could not get by the wall of rug. He was still lame in the feet. Helen threw her dish at Gerard and then picked up another one. She said, David get out the door. I looked for the Taser box in amongst the camping gear. I found the key on the ring that opened the box. A crash. David's mother was throwing soup plates off the buffet and the men had run through the plates as they clattered and rimmed on the hardwood floor. Now there was screaming. Helen was screaming and Nell got back out of the car. They rushed David and threw the rug over him. The rug was heavy, the canvas backing, and David fell against a chair. Then they tipped over the chair and knelt on the rug over the chair and David. They were being deliberate and guessing. They rolled the rug around the chair a little, just to box him in I guess, and the chair was cracking. Helen had reached into the buffet and was throwing all the china at Randy Jacobs.

I unclasped the two snecks and opened the box to its plush green felt and picked up the Taser, which weighed about six pounds, and smacked it into my left hand. I ran inside while looking at the red trigger mechanism and a power switch. The switch was like an old stereo button.

Hey! I yelled.

Gerard put down the cat's paw and reached for his belt and unsheathed a filleting knife. He pointed it at me and I squeezed the trigger to obliterate him but nothing happened. Then he shoved the knife into the carpet and jiggled it until the carpet ripped. He pulled it out.

Randy: That's enough now.

Gerard punched it through the back of the carpet. This time blood pulsed out the first hole and a low groan. Then he grabbed the cat's paw and swung it at the carpet and tore into the side of the chair and then he hit out again and this time it was softer.

Jesus, Gerard said, it's like opening a can of tomato juice.

Randy: That's enough!

Gerard held down the carpet with his knees and the carpet flexed and then went slack.

Gerard: That's for Anthony.

That's what unfroze me, the mention of Anthony. I flicked buttons until a whirring sound filled my fist with a powerful heat. I aimed the Taser at Randy and nailed him with the current and then I swung my aim over to Gerard and I kept nailing him, for he was the one with the crowbar and he had continued laying it into the rug and somehow a crowbar felt worse than a knife, even though a knife does the damage. I drilled them with juice until Nell was saying okay okay and I found the little switch because

I'd jammed the current on. I ended up zapping the curtains and a scorch line across a piece of furniture I had refinished when I was a teenager. The jolt travelled up my arm and into my shoulder and then my ear. It was rattling the jawbone, the one with the split tooth, as if it was trying to fuse it back together again. Helen was on her son, but she wasnt screaming now, though there was still a ringing—it was the little glass panels vibrating in the light shades.

FIFTEEN

BREATHE IN, she said. Take a deep breath.

It was a nurse. I calmed down. Then the tooth was pried out and I had a gauze pad in my mouth, a hole between my teeth. I paid at the counter and Nell held my waist and directed me out of the glass doors. We walked along Main Street. I felt old, and asymmetrical. We were heading up to the hospital. I felt sad and realized that the height of my own strength had just passed me. It was my old dentist, he was seventy-three now and still practising. He did not seem to mind being seventy-three. He took x-rays with film that I held in my sad jaws, and he looked at the film and said the molar was cracked clean through. The Taser jolt had split a filling as well, a filling he had put in when I was eleven. That made me think of myself as a boy, in this chair, with this man. Getting that filling put in. And now I had lost it, one of the first artificial parts of my body.

We walked up to the hospital and met with Dr Manamperi. I did not want to drive, I wanted to lean up against Nell's shoulder while I got used to not being my full self. I wanted to see David's body after having walked. Then I heard what Dr Manamperi was saying. David's come back, he said. He's going to make it. Can you believe it.

There was a real youth in Dr Manamperi and he enjoyed the miraculous. It seemed David could survive anything. We had driven him to the hospital and they had tried to resuscitate him and they had used paddles but the blood transfusions had weakened him and they could not tear him back to life though they kept working on him another thirty minutes. This is what Maggie Pettipaw had told me. Then Dr Manamperi arrived and wheeled him into the transplant unit and they fished out his one good kidney—Gerard had ruined the left one with his filleting knife. They scooped this out and brought Arthur into the theatre and performed the transplant. They did this roughly, as they were sure David was dead. Then they began the neglect of his body in order to save his father. But there was one machine still attached to him and a bright blip appeared on a screen. Someone saw it, for they had the volume down. Hey look at that. They turned to the body and they pored over him. They wheeled more machinery around the body and tried to coax a larger flame out of it. They found a pulse. He had come back from some deep distance all on his own. He's going to pull through, Dr Manamperi said. He'll have to go on dialysis, but what a miracle.

WHEN I CAME OUT Randy Jacobs was in the waiting room. I have to take you in, he said.

Get someone else to take me in.

Look I was only there to make sure Gerard didnt go berserk.

Good job.

Gerard's saying self-defence.

You fucking asshole. He voluntarily came in with a filleting knife.

He wants to report the Taser. He's looking to press charges against you.

And I realized what was going on here. The way that Randy and Gerard were swinging it. You think, I said, youre going to be clear of this?

I was just following a suspect, Gabe, and breaking up a possible homicide.

They had come in two cars, not one. Randy, a little after Gerard.

I filled out a report in the new RCMP building at the bottom of the hill. I wrote down everything as it happened, and I wrote down my involvement in David's boarding a trawler. I had lost the gold. The bail gold was gone now. I didnt care. It was windfall gold. It was gold from David's company. It belonged to him, or at least it didnt belong to me.

The policeman from Saskatchewan asked me about Randy.

Randy says he saw Gerard driving up to Helen Crofter's, the cop said. Randy knew Gerard doesnt have a reason for going up there. He said when he entered the house you went a little gonzo with a Taser.

Me: Gerard knifed David first and then I opened up.

Youre sure now about that sequence of events.

They would need material to lay a charge, my father said. It was shaping up to be about whose word can you believe. Were there any witnesses, my father said, not related to David.

They let me walk, for the moment. I had other things on my mind. Nell was pregnant. Nell wanted to finish her business with Arthur. I pushed through the grief and exhaustion. It was exhilarating in a strange way to be pushed so hard. It made everything clear. I went to see Dr Manamperi. He had heard of the box at a conference in California and he needed clearance to use it from his medical board and this would take another three weeks so he was going to use it without permission. It was a ninety-million-dollar piece of technology designed for high-altitude pilots and deep-sea divers and for several divisions of the US Army, but now being used on coma patients. There was a green button and one dial with a red mark for maximum. It looked a bit comical, Nell said. She felt like if she had unscrewed the housing there'd be nothing inside. They had built it so an astronaut could use it.

Dr Manamperi had studied the software. Nell and I sat and took in Arthur Twombly, slack yet there was presence. Arthur had never remarried, and yet the doctor working on him was living with his ex-wife. Arthur was concentrating. The mouth and neck and eyes of Arthur Twombly as Dr Manamperi set up the box. Nell's father was a doctor. She told me of her first memory, when she was three. Her father hauling chairs out into the back yard. Then he carried out the television and fed out yards of orange extension cord. It was summer and it was past her bedtime. It was dark and there were people up and down the street pointing to the moon. Her father switched on the TV and there were astronauts, the interior of a module. Then Neil Armstrong testing the ladder. Her father watching the television without sitting down. He was standing on the picnic table, rolling on the balls of his feet. He would have liked to have been on his roof. He wanted to be as close as he could to the moon. He looked up there often and then back to the television, as if you could see the men up there, leaping in that slow motion way, a slow motion that implied significance.

Nell looked at me and I knew that we could do it. Next twenty years, I said.

Nell: Plant it there, babe.

And we shook hands, like basketball players. Then we kissed and I held her waist, where our little one was. Somehow all the complications that we had gone through would secure us. There was an electric current to her kiss, a kiss I loved for it often felt like we had never kissed before. We were not wedded, we were welded.

She wanted to drive down to visit Loyola Hurley. She had called and asked and Loyola had said yes. So I took her. He was in the yard in his wheelchair. Gerard now gone to the lockup. His foster son Anthony, dead. And Joe Hurley, the good son, killed in Afghanistan. He'd wanted to bury Anthony in the back yard but they wouldnt allow him to bury on private land. You can burn him, Loyola said to us, and scatter his ashes. Apparently that is allowed.

From his wheelchair he was spreading a wheelbarrow full of kelp and caplin, to prepare the ground for winter. I just wanted to thank you, Nell said. For raising my son.

Loyola: We're all emperors over our own lives.

I WAS SLEEPING in the spare room with Nell when they took him that night. I was safe in my childhood home. They walked into the hospital— they dont know who yet—about four of them, and unhooked the machines and wheeled him into the elevator and towed him to the back of the hospital where the new generator was. They hot-wired the ghost car and opened up the front doors and propped David in there, between the driver and the passenger seats. They drove him down to Bottle Cove in the Matador, two others in a car behind. They veered down off the breakwater onto the beach. They stopped there for a bit, then revved the motor. Their tires ruining the clam beds, their breathing holes under the moon. Then they drove that car deep into the sea. They plunged into five-foot waves. They got about thirty feet in and then someone turned on the dome light. A witness saw water up to the dash. They punched him in the car and they beat him up, half of their punches were underwater. Then they pushed David's head down and they continued to punch into the water. There was a lot of splashing. They drowned him in that car. They opened the doors and walked up out of the sea.

SIXTEEN

DAVID WAS AS BIG as Goliath, I said.

Perhaps we're all Goliaths, Nell said. Struggling to break free of our inner, delicate Davids.

SASHA ARRIVED and I picked her up in Deer Lake. I drove my father's car to the airport. It's hard to love my father, she said. I dont want to meet Nell if I can help it. But I loved my brother. He was like the sister I never had.

She went with Helen, and Nell and I followed the hearse as it drove out to Rocky Harbour. I let my head shake back and forth, a bit like a Parkinson's patient, something like Muhammad Ali would do, because in the end it's Muhammad Ali I'd have to dinner, not some guy who invented x-ray specs.

We used the plot meant for David's father. I had slept on this ground in Rocky Harbour with David and now he was being laid into the ground reserved for his father. Goodbye David. You are the biggest man I've known, a strong big man, funny man. Generous guy you are. Fucking asshole too but what can you do with appetites. In fact you were restrained. You could have been worse, but you tried hard to be good. For some people it's hard to be good. The coffin lowered down on three ropes. I held a rope. I held it wearing white gloves. Marks on the gloves. Then we dropped the gloves on the coffin.

My own father came and he looked around the graveyard and thought Rocky Harbour had not improved since we'd been there to buy fish thirty years before. I love my father but he did not much approve of David Twombly.

WE SAT IN VIGIL. We were going to pull him out of the medically induced coma. We'll see if he reacts to pain and to light. Some of the machines were shut down, and they applied feeling and they operated a laser and then Nell's machine was taped to his temples. His eyes moved. Then, one moment, his eyes clapped open. He stared at Nell, then at Sasha and then at me. I could tell it confused him, then he realized where he was, that a lot of time had passed. Gabe had travelled with Dave, and Nell was here for Anthony. But Sasha. Did Sasha forgive him? His lips opened and Nell opened a bottle of water and moistened a pad of gauze and leaned over to wet his lips. He took in a tremendous breath of air. Nell. His tongue on his teeth and his eyes widened. But he could not speak. He worked his hand, his thumb moving like a mouth, and he looked at his hand. I thought of those hand puppets Dave and I made up as kids. Puddies. Am I crazy? He didnt know anything about those. He was making a writing gesture with his hand.

I took out my notebook and pen. I bent the notebook open for him. And he wrote with a blue tube coming out of the front of his hand, as if it was his own blood the note was written with.

Where are my sons.

SEVENTEEN

WE FLEW TO CUBA. We spent a week there, on a beach near Havana. We needed this, Nell said. The sun sort of burnt everything away. Bright blue jellyfish, the water spilling up over the bank of sand and surprising us. It soaked our towels and shoes. A man emptied his boots and socks. A boy of fifteen, they were Mexican, was sharing a white earphone with his grandmother. He leaned over so the wires reached.

This was before Castro died. Kids were flying kites beside the underpass. Small white kites. It was a Saturday. Kids playing baseball, using a square piece of varnished furniture for a bat. We were both looking a lot at children.

We bought tickets for the Museo de la Revolución. It was full of pyjamas shot through with blood, ponchos that fought in Spain, and letters. The boat Castro beached in a modern glass garage in behind Batista's house. Nell was impressed with the embroidered 26 July badges. And how much of the museum is devoted to others, not Fidel. It must be the only museum in the world that has nothing made of gold, Nell said. There's a slumped, shrunken spacesuit of the first Cuban cosmonaut.

Birds in the rafters of the airport. I bought a box of cigars and gave my suit and sneakers to a young man who saw us on our mopeds. He was wearing a white undershirt. He loved the jacket. He had probably never worn a suit jacket before. He looked beautiful.

We slept on the plane and I woke up as we made our descent over Newfoundland. The island is drenched with lakes. It looks like it's sinking. As a kid, I thought they had towed the island across the sea when we joined Canada. People did that with houses, why not islands. If only they had anchored us a little further out in the Gulf Stream, we'd have weather like Cuba.

Nell woke up. She was moving a hand over her belly.

I thought I felt something, she said.

ACKNOWLEDGMENTS

Readers: Larry Mathews, Lisa Moore, Christine Pountney, Claire Wilkshire.
Editor: Nicole Winstanley.
Agent: Anne McDermid, with Martha Magor and Jane Warren.
Funding: Canada Council, Ontario Arts Council.

Words appearing in the novel without an apostrophe: arent, couldnt, didnt, doesnt, dont, hadnt, hasnt, havent, isnt, oclock, shouldnt, theyre, wasnt, werent, wouldnt, youre, youve. This is intentional by the author. Please dont send letters to the copy editor, Shaun Oakey.

To the seventy-one people like Shima Aoki who helped make this book, I thank you.